Road Kill

A Novel

Paul Paré

Published by Piscataqua Press
An imprint of RiverRun Bookstore, Inc.
142 Fleet Street | Portsmouth, NH | 03801
www.riverrunbookstore.com
www.piscataquapress.com

Printed in the United States of America

ISBN: 978-1-939739-79-7

I

Amusement Parks

Everybody said Claude was a good boy. His parents, his teachers, the neighbors, the parish priest – all of them agreed. He was quiet. He listened well. He managed to stay out of trouble. He had one teacher, however, who said he had a habit of staring, and it made her uncomfortable. Examining people and watching them was a way of learning, he argued. Claude was smart enough to know that staring could make people think he was a strange little boy. A good boy, yes, but not strange. So, he tried very hard not to stare at people. He settled on trees, having discovered that trees were much like people: they came in all shapes and sizes, they changed with the seasons, they grew old.

In 1980, on his way to school during the final week of sixth grade, Claude stopped in front of the Sinclair house which harbored some of his favorite trees. He had been watching the batch of apple trees on the rear corner of the lot and he was pleased that they were in full bloom of white and pink. In front, close to the sidewalk stood what Claude referred to as an abandoned tree, with gnarled black limbs and branches, naked and scraping the springtime sky. Next to it was a younger tree full of new leaves, delicate oval shapes the color of peanut butter.

Standing on the sidewalk in front of the house, Claude positioned his feet a comfortable distance apart and carefully placed his lunch box between them. Only after a while did he

1

notice Phil sitting on the steps leading up to the side porch. Phil was crying.

Philip Sinclair lived with his mom. Everybody knew Philip as Phil. No one knew how old he was. He could have been 30 or 16; his body was small, and he walked like an old man, hesitant and bent over, yet nervous and awkward like a teenager. Everybody in Williams, Connecticut, thought Phil was simple. Claude wasn't sure. All he knew was that Phil had no job except for mowing lawns and shoveling walkways. He didn't have any brothers or sisters, or friends. Claude didn't know where Phil's father had gone to. Once, Phil's mother had appeared at a window.

Claude had never seen Phil cry, but there was no doubt about it that morning: Phil was wiping his eyes with a large blue handkerchief and he kept lifting his shoulders and dropping them with little yaps, like a puppy.

After a while, Phil saw the boy staring at him from the street. Phil swabbed his eyes and started to get up. Then, Mrs. Sinclair appeared at the back end of the porch. She took a step forward, and Phil cowered.

Mrs. Sinclair appeared to be wearing a mask. Claude stretched forward for a closer look. It was a Halloween mask, it was large and it covered her entire head. It looked like a devil mask. Phil's mother moved closer. She was looking beyond her boy crouched below her. She had found a new target: Claude. The woman's eyes were on fire. Claude nearly lost his balance as he scooped up his lunch box. He ran all the way to school.

In class, Claude couldn't concentrate. Outwardly, he was the same good boy, listening and seeming to pay attention, while inside, he was terrified. He tried to convince himself he had imagined the mask. He had a good imagination; everyone told him so. After all, he didn't know what Mrs. Sinclair looked like. He had never seen her up close.

While his teacher kept on with the day's math problems, Claude's mind was stuck on the prospect that he might have seen the devil. What had he done wrong? Was he being punished? The devil doesn't appear to good boys. He should talk to Father Carey after Mass on Sunday. But how? What should he say? Oh, Father, guess who I saw the other morning. Father would think he's crazy. Or worse, he'd think he was evil himself. A kid who sees the devil! Father would certainly take him off the altar boy roster.

Claude reviewed the episode. His mind went from the crazy mother with the face of evil to the son with the face of despair. Why was Phil crying? Claude hated himself for stopping and watching the house. If he had minded his own business, he wouldn't have seen anything. Now, he was convinced he'd have nightmares.

During lunch recess, Claude sat at his usual spot all by himself and opened the latest issue of *The Avengers*. The more he read about his usual characters, the more convinced he became that he had imagined the episode on his way to school. Maybe his mother was right: he read too many comic books.

He saw no villains in the lunch room, just other students, all of them classmates at Lincoln Elementary, the hot lunch kids on one side, the box lunch kids on the other. A pair of boys started teasing a group of girls from the fifth grade. The girls moved to another table where they were welcomed by the giggles of friends. All perfectly normal. No devils here.

Afternoon classes flew by, and suddenly it was time to go home. Claude hated to walk by the Sinclair house. What if Phil was still out on the porch? What if Mrs. Sinclair was still fuming and looking like the devil? There was a longer route home, and Claude told himself that was the way he should take. Curiosity outplayed trepidation, however, and he took the usual way.

Approaching the house, he spotted cars and a cluster of people, and he knew that something very bad had happened. His path was barred by police tape stretched between orange cones with the words *Williams PWD* stenciled in black up their sides. Two police cars blocked the driveway. A State Police cruiser completed the blockade. Officers herded Claude across the street where everyone was watching. He caught a glimpse of a couple of vans from the Hartford television station and he asked the ladies standing next to him what was going on. They explained that Mrs. Sinclair had been taken away in a police cruiser. Claude wondered if she had removed her devil mask. He wanted to stay longer to watch the goings-on, but a policeman crossed the street and told everyone to go home. He looked directly at Claude. "Hey, you! You're Gene Simard's kid aren't you? Now, be a good boy, son. Go on home," the cop said.

That evening after supper, Claude and his parents did something they rarely did: they watched the evening news. Along with everybody else in Williams, the Simards learned that Philip Sinclair, age 18, was found dead on the porch of his house shortly after 9 a.m. The reporter quoted the police chief as stating it was a gruesome scene. The newscaster added that Mrs. Estelle Sinclair, mother of the deceased, was taken into custody, and arraignment was expected the next morning at Putman District Court. As to the exact charge, there was no official word.

"It's going to be murder," said Claude's father, adding that his buddies at the police station told him the old lady just went crazy and started hacking away at her son with a butcher knife. "The cops found Phil's hands in the garden on the side of the house".

"Gene, please," Claude's mother said. "There's some tender ears here." She threw a worried glance at her son.

"He'll find out anyway. Everybody in town knows the gory details. Believe me, hon, that's all they'll be talking about at school tomorrow."

"That poor lad," his mother said. "He was a nice person. Wouldn't hurt a soul."

Claude's father was right: the Sinclair murder was the only topic the next day. Everyone had a theory. Everyone knew the old lady was crazy and her son was simple but harmless. The severed hands attracted the most speculation. The girls said Phil was caught stealing from his mom; the boys said he was caught jerking off. Claude didn't place much faith in either explanation. He was convinced it was the work of the devil.

The patterns of summer vacation soon swallowed up the Sinclair murder, and by the time the August heat wave of 1980 hit, everyone had found other preoccupations.

The Sinclair house was boarded up, the grass grown tall and wild. Most people passed by without noticing. Claude Simard, however, made an almost daily pilgrimage to the scene. He would sit in the shade of a wide maple across the street and stare at the wind playing with the leaves of his favorite tree. Those leaves had lost their creamy luster and like everything else had turned dry and leathery.

Claude wondered about the lives of the mother and her son and about Phil's final moments. He still read his comic books, but the adventures of his favorite heroes and villains paled in comparison to the horrendous act he had nearly witnessed.

The murder scene was the first thing he would share with his new friend Tony Diangelo.

A new family had just moved into the house behind Claude's. Mrs. Simard couldn't stop talking about the new people with a strange name – Italian maybe – and all those cars in the driveway overflowing into the street. The worst offenses seemed to be that the new neighbors would have their meals late at night and they were loud.

Claude had noticed them too. It was a large family with a boy around his age who kept to himself. Claude did what he did best: he watched. From his second story bedroom window, he had a perfect view of the neighbor's yard. The new kid spent all his afternoons in the shade, reading. Books. Real books, not comics. Claude had never met someone his age who read books. Teachers read books, not kids. Claude was intrigued. One day, Claude's curiosity took over and he ventured into the neighbor's backyard to talk to Mr. Diangelo. The next afternoon, Claude cooled off in their brand new pool from Sears. The Diangelo kid joined him, introduced himself as Tony and told Claude all about the book he was reading. It was a detective novel.

A few days later, Claude escorted Tony to the abandoned Sinclair house. He told him the place was haunted because of the murder. Claude recounted how he saw the victim just before his mother killed him. He said he got a good look at the mother and he thought she was going to come after him, and that's when he ran away. Claude didn't divulge that Mrs. Sinclair looked like the devil. He didn't know what words to use.

For many months – well into the next spring – Claude would lie awake at night wondering what happened at the Sinclair house. He convinced himself he saw a devil. Gradually, he came to believe that he had received a gift. He remembered traveling each year to the county fair in Putnam and going on the scary rides. Somehow, that morning on his way to school he was given a free pass to one of the fun houses. The House of Horrors, or something like that. Maybe it was a lifelong pass.

He would fall asleep both wishing an encounter with evil would happen again and afraid that it would.

5

"Hey, Claude. Come here."

The command rolled out the open window of a station wagon parked across the street. The man who spoke it looked as worn as his vehicle. The words pushed their way against the first winter winds sweeping Main Street and hit their target: the half dozen antiwar protesters fighting the cold and the apathy of the good people of Williams.

The picketers all heard the command, but only one paid it any attention. He stared at the parked Pontiac until he recognized its occupant. Realizing the words were meant for him, Claude stopped in his tracks. The others walked around him. He handed his sign to a fellow picketer who laid it to rest on the dead grass and placed a brick on it to keep it from being blown away.

"Claude Simard. Yes, you. Come here!" the old man repeated, louder this time, his arm extended through the open window, his hand gesturing with a flick of the wrist.

Claude broke away from the group and started to cross the street. The traffic was lighter than usual for a Saturday morning in the square that defined the downtown. Few motorists paid attention to the group of protesters walking back and forth in front of the post office. The antiwar demonstration had become a fixture, not unlike the Civil War monument or the gazebo in the park across the street. The protest was too small and quiet, as mundane as the daily news from Baghdad.

"Get in," the man said.

"Morning, Mister O'Regan," Claude said in a low voice.

"Get in. I got to talk to you, son."

Claude slipped into the car, melding his frame with the worn upholstery.

"Gee, Claude, you stink." The driver stuck his head out the window.

"Well, the water wasn't running this morning at the Ritz."

"Sorry, son. I should know better." The wind picked up an

armful of dead leaves and sent then crashing into the windshield. "Claude, I've known you since you were a kid. Why, your mother'd roll over in her grave if she saw you. And, your poor dad, what would he say?"

"It's tough on me too, you know." Claude couldn't look at the man. He glanced at the protesters to check to see if anybody had picked up his sign. "You know, it's not just me. This mess isn't just my fault."

"I understand. Believe me, son. I'm on your side. My job is to help. That's why I came looking for you. We have to talk." His tone had changed; he was now using his official voice: that of Terence Hugh O'Regan, Welfare Director for the town of Williams. "Let's get out of here." He started the Pontiac and put it in gear.

"Wait! I want to get my sign," Claude said.

"You won't need it." O'Regan pulled out of the parking spot and headed north. Claude sensed it was better not to object.

As they drove away, Claude turned and stole a glimpse at the sign bearers. They kept on walking their little course, back and forth, ignoring the few folks passing by who ignored them in return. O'Regan drove down Main Street, turning onto Church Street at the end of the square. "I don't know why they bother," he said. "No one approves of the war any more, but it doesn't matter. It's got too much steam behind it." Claude wanted to counter that someone had to speak out, that history would demand it, that witnessing against the war was crucial, not because it was failing, but because it was wrong, immoral, illegal. He knew the slogans, but he remained silent.

Claude's eyes fell on Mr. and Mrs. Washburn, the organizers. He admired their sincerity and commitment. He was grateful for their acceptance, knowing that some of the protesters would rather not have him around. Mrs. Washburn gave him a heavy sweatshirt, and he wore it every time, even on the warm summer days. It made him look neater, he figured, and, since he wore it only on Saturday mornings, the sweatshirt had a sweeter smell, with none of the week's accumulations. He also liked the garment because it had a hood which he could quickly slip over his head when someone he knew walked by. Not that he expected anyone to talk to him. His old friends and former co-workers had found several ways of ignoring him. The hood simply granted him a layer of dignity. The gathering afforded him a rare contact with other human beings, and he was thankful that, at the conclusion of each session when everyone created a circle and, arm in arm, observed a moment of silence, no one recoiled from him. He didn't mind the lack of an invitation to join them for lunch at The Puritan Restaurant, and he greatly appreciated the few times when Mrs. Washburn brought cookies and made sure he got some.

The welfare director and his charge passed the small downtown and headed down Water Street. Claude realized O'Regan was taking him to the mill yard.

"What you doing? What's going on?" Claude became agitated. He felt a desperate rush for whiskey.

"Listen, son. You can't stay here," the old man said as he stopped the car in front of the cotton warehouse. "The roof's fallen in. There's no water. Winter's coming, and you'll freeze to death."

"I told you it wasn't the Ritz." There was no sarcasm in his voice; he recognized the truth in O'Regan's words.

"Listen. I'll make this short and sweet. You've got to get out of town. You can't stay here this winter." He paused, looking directly at Claude, trying to determine if his words were sinking in. "It's for your own good. You're new at this. You're not seasoned like Tom or that other guy he hangs around with; they know how to cope with cold weather. You're a softy. I tell you, Claude, you'll freeze to death." He stopped, waiting for a reaction. None came. Claude stared away, examining the abandoned warehouse as if trying to figure a way to make it more hospitable. "Are you listening to me, son?" he said, reaching out to place a heavy hand on his shoulder.

"Yeah." It was a one-word answer and it came slowly, painfully. He opened his window and took a deep breath of chilly air. "So, what you want me to do?"

"I tried getting you in the shelter in Putnam, but it's full."

"You could have me committed. My wife's been saying all along that I'm crazy. So does half the town."

"Claude, I know what your wife thinks, and I don't care about half the town. I know you're not crazy. Don't even think that way. You're just going through a tough period. You'll get out of it. But for the moment, we've got to make sure you survive the winter."

"What do you suggest?"

"Well… I've got some discretionary funds. Not much, mind you, but I'm going to use some to buy you a bus ticket south, as far south as possible."

"You really want me to get out of town!" Claude was surprised. "You really mean it." He wanted that whiskey now, more than ever. "You're going to put me on a bus, aren't you? This is what this is all about."

"Yup. And we're going to do it right now. There's one leaving at two o'clock. You've got just enough time to get your stuff."

"You can't do this. You can't just throw me out of town. This isn't the Wild West, and you're not the sheriff. It doesn't work that way." Suddenly, he wanted to laugh.

"Go. Go get your stuff." He pushed Claude gently on the shoulder. "And, don't pack too much. You're traveling light. And, besides, it's going to be warm in Florida."

Something – some kind of energy he thought had bypassed him forever – took over. The word Florida didn't register. The destination made no difference; the going was all that mattered. Claude got out of the car, and walked briskly into the old brick warehouse that had been his shelter for the past six months.

The welfare director stayed in his station wagon. In his 28 years on the job, he'd seen some pretty sad cases. Claude Simard's case wasn't just sad, it was downright weird, and scary. O'Regan knew that the kid had always been an oddball, a loner, with just one friend, that Diangelo boy. Claude never got into trouble; he just happened to be around whenever it occurred. Like the fatal accident the night of the prom. O'Regan remembered Claude acting like a zombie for weeks after. And this past summer, Claude had been throwing accusations all over town, scaring lots of people.

Ten minutes went by, and the old man grew impatient. The thought crossed his mind that Claude might have slipped away. Although much of the Chicopee Mill had been torn down, there was still a lot of it left, and he assumed that Claude knew it well. O'Regan felt foolish and not slightly pissed off. "He could be on the other side of Mill Street by now." He quickly climbed out of his Pontiac and puffed his way towards the warehouse.

The musty odor of multiple floodings and rotting timbers greeted him. He walked into a tower that had once contained a set of stairs, and then into a chamber littered with chunks of brick and

9

mortar from a wall that had caved in. "Claude, you'd better be in here," he yelled out, scaring off dozens of pigeons. He allowed the echo of their wings to die down and was about to shout out another warning when he heard Claude's voice.

"Up here, Mister O'Regan."

The old man struggled up the concrete steps in the back of the room and stopped in front of a heavy metal door left half open. His jaw dropped in amazement as he stood on the threshold of a vast room flooded with light from a gallery of still-intact windows several yards above the floor. The wall facing him was covered – every inch of it – by painted figures and large words in careful script. O'Regan shook his head.

"What the hell is this?"

"Mister O'Regan, it's just…"

"Wait, don't tell me. You did this?"

"Well, I had nothing else to do." Claude was clearly embarrassed. He hadn't shared his work with anyone except two homeless guys who, on occasion, haunted the warehouse, and were too drunk or depressed to pay attention.

"I didn't know you were an artist." The old man spoke with reverence. He tried to catch the entire scope of the mural all at once: children, flowers, kites and birds and bright spheres that looked like beach balls, odd shaped animals, all cartoonlike, in soft pastel colors, floating on blue and pink clouds, clusters of trees, odd-shaped with brown leaves, uprooted, about to float away.

Claude observed his visitor, a shrinking man who, against all evidence, still believed in his panache. His official, purposeful gait concealed a man bent by work and life. Yet, he beheld the mural and examined it like a child seeing a starlit sky for the first time.

Single words or phrases in black or blue fancy lettering accented the mural. O'Regan ambled back and forth in front of the rendering, reading the words out loud: *Wailing…Nothingness…Quit… Heaven's Angels…Dancing into Doom.* He turned to face the young homeless man, failing to notice at the far end of the mural drawings of human beings with deformed and grotesque faces.

"You did all this?" He made no attempt to disguise his awe.

"Yeah. As I said, got plenty of time. The ladders were already here. Wally from the hardware store – he's the only friend I've got left – brought me the paint and some brushes and stuff."

"Where do you get these ideas? What do all these words mean?"

"The library. Told you, got nothing else to do. I go there a lot, and they leave me alone. You ever hear of Chagall? I like his paintings. They make me feel like a kid again. And I read lots of Kerouac and Ginsberg." Claude thought he was explaining too much.

O'Regan shrugged. "Anyways, I'm quite impressed."

"Thanks."

"Too bad you couldn't turn this talent into something. Maybe something profitable."

"Keeps me from going crazy...crazier, that is."

O'Regan interrupted him: "Ok. Let's get going. Where's your stuff?" Claude pointed to an oversized gym bag. It was far from full and lay limp at his feet. They both looked at the bag for a moment.

"That's it?"

"Don't have much," Claude replied.

The two men walked silently out of the building. Claude dropped his bag into the back of the station wagon. He didn't wait for O'Regan to close the hatch, he pushed it down himself. "Can we swing by the house? Maybe I could see Mikey."

"Not a good idea. I wish we could, son. I really do. But the restraining order is still in effect. You can't step anywhere near your house or your wife or your boy, no matter what."

"Shit."

There was nothing else to say. Claude reclaimed his seat in the front of the car. He felt angry, and the taste of the previous night's whiskey rose from his stomach.

The duo did, however, make a detour. O'Regan drove out on South Street about a mile, to the new CITGO station, and while he gassed up, Claude used the bathroom. He cleaned himself up as best he could. He washed his hair and tied it up in a ponytail. He examined his scraggly beard, thinking that it made him look older and wiser.

Back in town, O'Regan parked next to Gallant's Pharmacy, the town's bus depot.

"Listen, here's how we'll work it. I can't buy the ticket for you, so I'm going to give you the money. You buy the ticket from the driver, but only after your bag is in the baggage hold, mind you. I'll be watching. I can't have you keep the money and not get on the bus and use the money for something else." The old man was talking rapidly. "I'll be right here watching everything. And once you're on the bus, I'm going to follow it for a while to make sure you stay on it."

"Gee, talk about trust."

"You know, I'm doing this for your own good."

"Yeah, whatever!" Suddenly, Claude saw his son's face. That had become his phrase lately.

With a puff of steam and a metallic moan, the Peter Pan Bus stopped in front of the drugstore. O'Regan placed an envelope in Claude's hands. "There's $165 here. That'll buy a ticket to Daytona Beach. I wish I could send you all the way to Miami, but I don't have enough. Besides, Miami's too big and too tough. And there's an extra $20 in there. For some food."

"I suppose I should thank you," Claude said.

"No need. Just take care of yourself. Don't do anything foolish. Don't want to read about you in the newspapers."

"Do me a favor and keep an eye on Mikey?"

"Absolutely. He's a tough kid and he'll survive. I'll keep an eye on him. Now, go," he said, pushing Claude out of the car.

Claude walked to the bus and placed his bag on the ground next to the baggage hatch. The driver went inside the pharmacy, holding the door open for a frail old woman who was emerging from the drugstore. Claude recognized his great-aunt Yvette, who, thanks to encroaching Alzheimer's, was the only one in the family who still talked to him.

"Allo, Claude, mon p'tit chou," she said in her Canuck French. She referred to all her grand-nieces and grand-nephews as little cabbages and she pronounced his name as *Clowed* instead of *Clawed*. "How are you doing?" she asked. "You being a good boy?"

"Yes, *ma tante*." Claude spoke loudly, keeping his distance from the old lady. He didn't want her to catch his smell.

"You need some money? Here," she said, reaching into her purse and pulling out a wrinkled five dollar bill. "You go in Gallant's and buy something nice for your *maman*."

"Thank you, *ma tante*."

She smiled and waved. Claude watched her take tiny steps down the sidewalk. "I love you *ma tante*," he said. Once he was certain she was beyond hearing, he added, "Tell Mikey I love him."

The bus driver returned to the sidewalk. "Guess you're it today." He picked up his sole passenger's bag and gave it a rough shove into the baggage hold. O'Regan stood in front of his Pontiac watching the exchange of money for a ticket. His eyes followed Claude as he climbed onto the bus.

Claude was relieved that the bus was nearly empty. He brushed his way down the aisle to the last row of seats. He wanted to be alone and he suspected he'd find comfort in the murmur of the engine back there. The driver took his seat and started writing in his log book. Claude scanned the sidewalk for a final look at his home town.

The driver yanked on the clutch, and the bus lurched towards a cautious acceleration. Surprisingly, Claude found himself thankful for the ride out of town. He sank deeper in his seat, covering his head with the hood of his sweatshirt. He closed his eyes tightly and pressed his temples connecting his tired body with the soothing purr of the bus as it found the highway.

Father Tony gazed at the postcard on top of the day's mail: a vintage photograph of Williams High School. He didn't have to read the granite lintel over the front doors or the tiny script at the bottom of the card, he recognized the building.

"Dear Mother of Jesus," he muttered. "Where did this come from?" Tony knew the answer: it was from Claude, Claude Simard. His old childhood buddy had come back to life a couple of weeks before with a letter. Now a postcard. The priest inspected the postmark: Oct. 18 '07 – Williams, CT.

His eyes jumped through the neatly-controlled script and landed on the signature: Simmy. He smiled, remembering how Claude had adopted the odd nickname and had proudly explained that it came from Simard but sounded Italian and sort of rhymed with Tony. Tony and Simmy, they would call each other.

Tony returned the postcard to the stack of mail and pushed himself away from the desk. A full day's accumulation of paperwork waited, but his heart wasn't into it. His third floor office was all windows. Protruding from the plain brick turn-of-the-century rectory of Saint Petronilla's Parish, it could have had a prior life as a sun parlor, a private sunny space adjoining a sick room, perhaps. Tony loved the room. It was at tree level, and the deep browns and ambers of the oaks vibrated in the crisp afternoon sun and showered everything inside with what Tony regarded as the light of absolution.

If anyone needed forgiveness, it was him, Father Tony. The postcard from Simmy carried with it a heavy mantle of guilt. He had yet to answer Claude's surprise letter and felt terrible about it.

He heard the phone ring in the parish office below him. He waited to see if his secretary, Nicolette, would shout to him in her Haitian accent. He listened, hoping the call was for him: something to rescue him from the postcard and letter and from Simmy and from Connecticut. But there was no summons. No postponement.

Tony Diangelo hadn't given much thought to Claude Simard recently. Parish work in his rundown neighborhood of Philadelphia overwhelmed him. He had no time for anything else; no time for daydreaming about growing up next to the Simards, no time to reminisce about his high school days. "You move on," he said to the empty office. "Everybody moves on. Things change. You can't go back." The recitation wasn't sufficiently convincing, so he rolled his chair back to the desk. "Ok. It's not going to go away, so...I might as well read it."

The letters, small and tight, but perfectly formed, filled the back of the card. No upper case and almost no punctuation. Urgently telegraphic.

"Dear friend Tony, hope you received my letter which if you did you should know that I truly need to hear from you...told you all about my troubles and how I keep thinking about you and how you were the only one I could ever talk to...if you did answer maybe it got lost... I told you I don't have an address but if you send it to Mrs Jane Washburn at 24 Pine Hill in Williams I'm sure I'll get it... hope you're ok your best friend Simmy."

The priest read the message slowly, unsure of a few words written in the tiniest of script. The words crossed the boundary between the message section and the address part, wandering over the top and the bottom, covering the small type that said where and by whom the card was printed. "Boy, Simmy, you sound like you're still in high school." Tony tossed the card back onto the desk and moved to the windows. He looked past the aging trees to the surrounding rooftops and he felt a profound sadness. He told himself he had no reason to feel this way. What could he do for his friend?

The last time Tony had seen Claude was when Tony served as best man almost 20 years before. He stood next to Claude who was marrying this poor girl who was visibly pregnant under all that white taffeta, and had swallowed hard, unsure if he was grieving the loss of their friendship or fearful of his own future. It was late in August during his first summer home, and he was leaving the next day for the Franciscan Seminary in upstate New York. During subsequent vacations, all so very brief, Claude had been busy at his job or at home with Margie and the baby. A few phone calls and the promise to get together, and it was time to head back to the seminary. Then there were no more vacations; just summer projects in the inner-city, courses at the university, and that endless year in the novitiate.

Simmy didn't even show up at the funeral for Tony's dad, sending instead a plain sympathy card a month later. Then, nothing. Not a word for all those years.

A siren sang sadly in the distance. Father Tony looked at his watch: 4:30. The sun was setting quickly. Monday night, his favorite night of the week. Nothing scheduled; no meetings, no study groups, no training sessions. He thought he might go downtown, walk around a bit, sit at his table in his favorite restaurant, sip a glass of the best wine the place had to offer – always a gratuity of the house, Adolfo insisted – and spend the evening surrounded by people enjoying their lives. Not the poor, not the needy, not the desperate.

His old pal Simmy had apparently joined the ranks of the helpless. Tony knew from the letter that Claude had lost everything and was now homeless, living in the old cotton warehouse where they had played haunted house as kids. This he knew, yet what he suspected from the tone of the letter was that Simmy was also unstable.

The priest left his office and walked down the hall to his bedroom. Without the benefit of many windows, the room was already dark. He sat on his bed, turned on the lamp, opened the top drawer of the night stand, and delicately removed the envelope with Simmy's letter. He turned the envelope over and slid it under the shade of his lamp and read the words:

> *For no Church told me…No Guru holds*
> *me…No advice…Just stone*
> *– Bowery Blues*, Jack Kerouac.

"Dear Mother of Jesus, Simmy, when the hell did you ever read Kerouac?" Tony said, returning the letter to the drawer. "I thought all you read were comic books." He dropped his frame onto the bed. He closed his eyes.

Moving to Williams from Massachusetts when he was ten,

Tony was the scared skinny kid who told his parents he'd never leave their new house and he wouldn't talk to anyone because all the people in this hick town were stupid. Weeks later, he had expanded the boundaries of his world to include his backyard and the parish church and the public library.

The summer of 1980 had been one of the hottest, stickiest summers ever, and Tony's father had come home one night with a shallow plastic swimming pool. He set it up in their back yard and, after supper, filled it. Tony was watching from his upstairs bedroom window and that's when he first saw his neighbor.

"You guys sure are lucky," the kid next door said to his father, through the nearly dried-out hedge that separated their backyards.

"It was on sale. And, it's been so hot."

"That's really gonna be nice," said the kid.

"You know, you – what's your name, son?"

"Claude."

"Well, Claude, you can come over and use it, you know. Whenever you see one of us in it, come on over."

And that's how it all began.

Claude was amazed by the suddenness and the power of his dislocation; in just a few minutes his life had turned dramatically. He was equally surprised by his calm acceptance. As he listened to the heavy monotonous hum of wheel upon pavement, Claude acknowledged that he had fallen into deep shit: constantly fighting with his wife – abusing her, the cops said, – losing his job, being kept away from his son by a court order, walking the streets with everyone in town staring at him, his clothes and his skin stinking, street punks running after him, yelling and calling him names, the cops telling him to keep moving. Now, he sat on a bus with money in his pocket. Claude started laughing, the nervous vocal jumping tinged with mistrust that had become his trademark. He laughed as he reached into the pocket of his worn camouflage pants and fingered the wad of cash, warm and clammy, yet solid and secure. He didn't have to count it. The one-way ticket to Philadelphia had cost $48; the rest of Mister O'Regan's money and the $5 from his great-aunt came up to $142. Claude whispered to the empty seats around him: "One hundred-forty-two dollars and zero cents." He laughed. "I'm rich, I'm rich. I'm rich," he sang under his breath.

17

Phi-la-del-phi-ah. He rolled each syllable in his mind. Never thought you'd be going there, did you. O'Regan just had to run you out of town; least you could do was choose your own destination. And pocket some money. Phi-la-del-phi-ah, PEE-AYH. Tony, your pal Simmy's coming. On a bus. Rolling towards you, bud.

The driver announced they would be in New London in 30 minutes where they would transfer to a Greyhound bound for New York and points south. None of the dozen or so passengers seemed to pay attention, not the quiet old men sharing the seats in the center, not the teenage couple so happily in love, not the Black lady and her sleeping toddler, not the family in the front chatting in Spanish. Claude heard the announcement and pushed his seat back. He hummed a non-tune, trying to match the pitch of the motor vibrating beneath his seat.

"You can go to Philadelphia. I'm going to Kansas City," Claude said. He and Tony argued during and after each of the 1980 World Series games. They argued about who had the best team, who would finally win the series, which player would be voted Most Valuable.

"We watching it at your house or mine tonight?"

"My mom's got her shows tonight."

"Ok, you come to my place. I can talk my dad into it."

"He may watch the game too."

"Doubt that. He'll probably wind up at the American Legion with his buddies."

The boys planned their evenings while walking from school. The world stopped for the World Series between the Philadelphia Phillies and the Kansas City Royals that October. Everyone everywhere was glued to television sets for an entire week.

Neighbors first and then classmates, both scrawny and shy, Claude and Tony had become each other's best friend. The Simards and the Diangelos occupied two nearly identical track homes built in the mid-'60s on streets christened with girls' names, a neighborhood of aluminum siding pastels and colonial front doors. The two families, however, were constructed of vastly different materials. And the boys quickly became enamored of each other's household.

Claude was an only child. His dad worked at the textile mill. When it closed, he got a job at the post office. His mother worked in an assembly plant. Tony was the youngest of six, all the others being girls. Mrs. Diangelo sold Avon products out of their house, and Mr. Diangelo worked as a roofer for a local contractor.

The Simards were barely Catholic because old Mrs. Simard had insisted that Claude's mom, a purebred Yankee, convert to marry her son. Their wedding was the last time Annie Simard née Stover set foot in church. The Diangelos, on the other hand, were Catholic to the core; there was always at least one member either at church, doing something for the church or talking about church. Meals in each household followed the devotional patterns: simple, bland, and quick Betty Crocker crock pot at the Simards; ample, communal, spicy, and never-ending at the Diangelos. Tony's house seemed to be in an eternal state of chaos. Two of the older girls traveled back and forth from community college, leaving three sisters at home, popular girls with lots of friends and suitors. Mom's Avon products filled the garage and customers were always stopping by. At least three cars clogged the driveway. By contrast, Claude lived a monastic life, surrounded by the silence of a mother too tired from work and a father often out with his buddies.

"Wish I could live at your house."

"My sisters would drive you crazy. I'd much rather live at your house."

"You'd starve to death."

The World Series went into six tight games, the final one on a Tuesday night at Philadelphia's Veterans' Stadium. The boys turned it into a sleepover at Claude's house and they made quite an event of it, with Cheese Doodles and Nutter Butters and Pepsies.

Claude's mother wasn't too charmed by her son's infatuation with both baseball and the neighbor boy. She kept her feelings to herself, though, since Mister Simard highly approved. "He needs friends, you know. And baseball is the national sport. It's good for Claude to like the game. I'm glad he's finally interested in sports. It'll make a man out of him," Mister Simard told his wife.

The final game dragged on until 11:30 when Tug McGraw struck out Willie Wilson of the Kansas team, giving Philadelphia its first World Series win in history.

19

Claude's parents had gone to bed at 11 o'clock, warning the
boys to keep the noise down and to get to sleep right after the
game. Of course the boys couldn't hold back their cheers for their
favorite players. When the Phillies won, Tony yelled out and
Claude had to hold his hand over his buddy's mouth to smother
the sound. Mrs. Simard came to the door and sternly ordered the
boys to keep quiet and go to sleep. But they replayed the game
over and over again in excited whispers, teasing each other, and
finally dozing off in sleeping bags spread out on the living room
floor.

The Phillies' win further cemented Tony's desire to visit
Philadelphia – for all the history. "You know, all that stuff about
the Revolutionary War we're studying in school."

Although the Royals had lost, Claude was still interested in the
comic-book-cowboy world that Kansas City embodied.

"Yup, Philadelphia, here I come," Claude said to an imaginary
seatmate at the rear of the bus. He wanted to yell out and to laugh.
He thought it was hysterical that in a matter of hours he had left
the stench and cold of his warehouse and would soon be having
coffee with his best friend. Gone was the craving for that next
whiskey, replaced by the urgency of a friend to talk to, a shoulder
to lean on. Yet, Claude wondered about Tony. How would he
react to having a bum knock on his door? They hadn't seen each
other for so many years. His mood shifted into doubt and back
again. Claude forced himself to reconnect with the power of the
moment. He watched the sun skirt the horizon as the Peter Pan
Bus threaded into the increasing commercialism and the salt air
of Southern Connecticut. He felt hungry. The Dunkin' Donuts
someone had brought to the antiwar protest at the post office had
long since left room for more. He would get something to eat in
New London. He had money in his pocket. He might even buy
some clothes, a shirt maybe, definitely some new pants.

"You never answered my letter."

"How in God's name did you ever find me?"

'You're looking great. A bit fatter, but still…"

"Wish I could say the same thing about you. Geez, Claude,

you don't look good at all. How *did* you find me?"

"I never thought I'd make it to Philadelphia. Remember that World Series game when we were kids?"

The conversation flowed across the conference room table at the rectory as it always had. Staccato. Non sequiturs. Hands in the air. Eyes wide. Two friends who knew each other's question before it was uttered and who really didn't care about the answer. Except this time, Father Tony was amazed that Simmy had located him.

"You have to tell me how you found me."

"You've heard of Google. You *have* heard about the Internet, haven't you?"

"Yes, of course."

"Mrs. Washburn with the antiwar group googled you; she even printed out directions."

"What group?"

"I told you in my letter."

"Oh. Forgot about that."

Father Tony stood up. Judging that his friend must be hungry, he said, "Let's order pizza. And we can talk." He didn't wait for confirmation; the priest walked into the darkened kitchen and headed for the wall phone. He turned the lights on and studied the list of phone numbers on the refrigerator. "Well, no time for my quiet table at Adolfo's. Not tonight."

He refilled his cup with the last of the coffee Nicolette had brewed before going home that afternoon. Father Tony needed time to think. "What's Simmy doing here? What am I going do with him? God, he looks like hell!" he uttered in the same tone he would use to dispense a penance in the confessional.

The heat was getting to him. Waiting for the bell to ring, Claude could feel the sweat swelling around his balls and he wanted to stand up, move around, shake one of his legs, but he couldn't. Mr. Bass already had it in for him; he didn't need any more ammunition. Finally, the bell sounded, and the mad rush started, with Mr. Bass yelling something about a test scheduled the next day. The hallways at Williams High School at the end of a school day were riotous. Claude Simard made his way through the crowd as fast as he could, pushing like everyone else down the stairs flowing into the terrazzo lobby with the crest of his high school – soon to be his alma mater – emblazoned into the floor. An early warm spell, highly unusual for June, had suddenly blanketed the area. No one was ready for it, no one dressed for it, everyone got grouchy. Freed from another day of classroom minutiae, the students poured out onto the sun-filled and apple-blossomed apron between the school building and Washington Street.

Claude stopped in his tracks, creating a small logjam. He had spotted his new girlfriend, Margie Pelczar. She was talking to Kevin Rideout, so Claude gave her a quick wink and kept on going.

He was looking for Tony. They didn't walk home together as often, but Tony had said he'd be there. Claude stood patiently by the curb watching the traffic: buses swallowing their usual crews, rich kids showing off their cars, others like him waiting for someone to walk home with, others just hanging out, no after-school jobs to go to, no welcoming homes to rush to.

Claude had stopped his habit of staring. He wasn't a kid anymore, and he knew it made people uncomfortable. However, he had found ways of observing, of taking in a scene, of watching how people acted. He had learned to be subtle, non-threatening. Watching without staring had become his passion. It made him feel invisible, beyond and above everyone. Powerful, even.

He saw Tony walking towards him, leaving behind a few of the smart kids he had started hanging around with. In their final year of high school, the two best friends had grown apart, Tony gravitating to a group of brighter students, leaving Claude dangling, not fitting with either the smart kids or the jocks. Claude resented Tony's new crowd. He didn't know them, but he disliked them for being smart. For going on to college. For talking about things that didn't matter. He tried to fit in with the jocks, but he was not athletic. He managed to get by in gym class; did what he had to do, no more. Not like that Rideout kid, the star of the school's basketball team. Claude glanced back at Margie and Kevin and studied them, trying to figure out what they were talking about. He thought Margie looked especially pretty in green; he thought Kevin was freakishly tall.

"Hi there, Simmy boy!"

"Don't call me that, Tony. Shit, we're not in grade school anymore."

"I told you not to say *shit*. You don't listen to me either," said Tony, giving his pal a friendly shove of the shoulder.

Claude ignored the comment. He rubbed his crotch. "It was so hot in there today. Shit, I'm going to get jock itch. Just sitting there in those stupid classes. Jock itch... and I don't even play sports."

"Speaking of sports, was that our state champion basketball star talking to your Margie over there?"

"Yeah, I saw them."

"Wonder what they were talking about?"

"Geez, Tony. What's it to you? She's not your girlfriend. She's not going to the prom with you. Why should you care if she talks to her old boyfriend?"

There was no reply. Tony had noticed his buddy becoming more irritable. He knew it was the prospect of graduation and what lay beyond. Everyone was being affected, especially the kids who had no plans.

The river of high school kids had thinned out, and the two friends had the sidewalk to themselves, Tony walking on the street side, Claude swinging his backpack, nearly dragging it on the ground. The mid afternoon sun was strong, and the breeze flowing down the Naugatuck hills carried the smell of new vegetation. Tony thought spring was the most beautiful season; Claude didn't seem to notice. They stopped on a corner.

"I think I'm going to the library," Tony said. "I still have that paper to finish."

Claude said, "I told my great-aunt I'd turn over the dirt in her flower bed. I'm already sweaty; I might as well go over now."

"Well. Ok. Maybe I'll see you later. Tonight?"

"Yeah."

Tony was about to step out into the intersection when a bright red compact screeched to a halt, the front wheels eating up the fragile turf between the sidewalk and the street. Three girls known only by their first names spilled out of the car.

"Did you see that?"

"Yelling and screaming."

"Oh. My God! She kicked him in the shins."

"The principal said he was calling the cops."

"Claude, she was crying," said the tall one.

The girls were stumbling over each other with their excited reports. Claude couldn't tell if they were thrilled or scared.

"What *are* you talking about?" Tony told the girls to speak one at a time.

Claude knew what they were talking about. "Margie and Kevin?" he asked.

"You should have seen it. It was hysterical," said one of the girls, clapping her hands like a kindergartener.

"Ok, ok. Calm down and tell us what happened." It was Tony again, taking charge.

Claude felt a rush of resentment, but he kept quiet.

Appointing herself as spokeswoman, one of the girls described the episode: Margie and Kevin talking, gesturing all of a sudden, screaming at each other, Margie trying to get away, Kevin grabbing her, Margie kicking him and running down the street.

"And do you know what he said?" asked one of the other girls.

"Who?" asked Tony.

"Kevin, of course."

"What *did* he say?" asked Claude.

"He's gonna get you." The trio told him in a conspiratorial unison.

"He's gonna make Margie regret dumping him and he's gonna make you suffer. Those are his exact words," reported the leader, the other two nodding in agreement.

Tony shot a worried glance at Claude. "What did he mean?" he asked the girls.

"Shit, Tony. What do you mean what did he mean? What do you think? He's going to get even with me for stealing his girl. That's what he thinks: I stole his girl. Margie was ready to dump him anyway. Shit, she told me Kevin has a mean temper." Claude was pacing up and down the sidewalk, his arms all over the place looking for a target.

"Calm down, Claude. It's just talk. It'll blow over."

"Yeah, easy for you to say, Tony."

The girls backed away. "Thought you should know, that's all," said the ringleader as she herded her friends back into the car.

"Dizzy bitches!" Claude sent his condemnation down Washington Street after them, no emotion in his voice. The two friends stood alone on the sidewalk watching the car disappear into the hazy sunlight. Neither of them spoke. The calm that replaced the girls' outburst of frenzy was almost visible. The boys seemed trapped, standing next to each other. Claude came to life first. "Oh. I nearly forgot. We're supposed to talk about the prom, aren't we? You going to come or not?"

"Listen Claude. I can't. Really, think about it. I'm going to the seminary in a few months; why would I go to a prom?"

"Well, it's not a date. It doesn't have to be."

"I know, but…"

Claude said, "I thought what's-her-name had agreed to go with you. Not as a date. Just a friend, you know."

"You mean Roberta? Roberta Robichaud? That's not a good idea." Tony hesitated. He stopped walking and looked at his friend. "Anyway, she's backed down. Everybody knows I'm going to the seminary, and when word got out that Roberta and I would be going to the prom, people started making jokes about it. They asked her if she was going dressed as a nun and stuff like that."

"Oh."

"Right."

The boys were silent again. Tony knew Claude felt hurt. For years they had planned on going to the prom as a team. They had even picked their prospective dates as early as the eighth grade. It was going to be a rite of passage, an end to their school years together.

"Well, I should get going."

"Yeah. My great-aunt's probably wondering where I am."

25

"Ok."
"Yeah, see you."

The corned beef with potatoes and carrots and cabbage tasted better than usual. Claude wondered if his mother had tried a new recipe, but he didn't ask. Cooking had taken up the slack in his mom's life since being laid off from work. Annie Simard viewed cooking for her husband and son as her new vocation. Some kind of semi-redemption for all those years of quick-and-easy-two-step dinners; some kind of Yankee yearning for forgiveness for not pulling her own weight as a wage earner. Her meals, though, were still basic, if not bland. But this Sunday dinner surpassed the others. Boiled dinner was still boiled dinner, but there were hot Pillsbury rolls fresh from the oven. It all gave Claude a measure of courage because on this second Sunday of June, he was going to bring up the subject of using his dad's car for the prom.

The dinner ritual itself was something new at the Simard house. For as long as Claude could remember, Sunday had been a cereal, then sandwich, then maybe pizza kind of day. You ate when you wanted to and what you could find. The menu matched the laziness of the day's unfolding. You didn't dress special, you didn't go anywhere, nobody came to visit. It was a cipher sort of day. Except for Claude, who alone went to Mass. For years, Claude, the altar boy at the 9:30 Mass at Saint Patrick's, salvaged the Sabbath on behalf of the Simard household. He brought structure to the day; he rescued the Day of the Lord from the drudgery of their weekly schedule. But even that changed during his junior year. He maintained he was getting too old to be an altar boy, and that had a ring of truth to it since he did tower above the other servers. But the real reason for abandoning the altar steps was the new priest. Father Morin, young and eager, kept hinting to Claude that his parents should be recruited. As fallen away Catholics, his mom and dad ran the risk of eternal damnation, and did he really want that on his conscience? Serving Mass was fine and worthy, but witnessing – the priest's favorite preacher word – was even better. Claude decided that quitting his job as altar boy was easier.

His father's thought-you'd-never-ask answer floored him. The Buick was a prized possession, wiped down and polished at regular intervals, taken out and parked at the edge of the driveway whenever his dad needed a morale boost. Claude learned at a young age to venerate the current model, and, with time, he was able to read his father's moods depending on how often he'd take the car out for a quick spin. If he took it to one of his outings at the American Legion to show it off, that meant he was really depressed.

His mom's disbelief matched his, emerging as she did from the kitchen, a dish cloth in hand, her mouth wide open. Was he truly going to let his son use the Buick? The father explained that having a vehicle worth showing off was an important part of the prom, a once-in-a-lifetime event in a boy's life. The car had to measure up. But permission came with a price: a list of what to avoid and a recitation about the dangers of what his dad called the after-prom shenanigans. Mr. Simard chose that moment to announce that he would be there to help out. As a volunteer special deputy, he would be patrolling alongside the local constabulary on prom night. "So, "I'll be watching you, young man," were his final words. Claude wanted to respond by saying he'd really be watching his Buick, but he let it pass.

A special request from Margie, the song seemed to go on forever, and the MoonDawgs were squeezing every drop of sappiness out of it.

> *"I've never seen so many men ask you*
> *if you wanted to daaance.*
> *They're looking for a little romaaaance,*
> *given half a chaaaance."*

Claude shrank from the spotlight following him and Margie as they swayed in the center of the crepe-papered gymnasium. His date had obviously orchestrated the moment as her time to shine. Everyone, look at me in my expensive red dress, and look at me with my new boyfriend. The song concluded and was seamlessly replaced by another from that year's hit list. Dancing couples took over the entire floor, and the special moment was again everyone's: the class of '87 at its senior prom. The popular and the not-so-popular blending into a swirling mass of misty eyes and

27

banal music.

Kevin Rideout literally stood above everyone else. He maneuvered himself and his date – a last-minute trashy showoff from Putnam High School – in Claude's and Margie's direction until the two couples were next to each other. None of the surrounding dancers gave an outward hint that something was afoot, but you could smell the tension under all the satin bodices and starched collars.

The soundless words could have had the weight of a thunderclap: *I – will – kill – you*. They came from Kevin's angry lips, the words taking exaggerated shape, attended by the glare of his expanding black eyes.

Claude looked away, sweeping the large space, searching for an escape, knowing there was none. The words and their anger were meant for him, for him exclusively. None of the seniors dancing to the MoonDawgs broke away from their dreamy ceremonial. Not even Margie, with her back inches from her old boyfriend and her head cradled in the shoulder of her new one. Needing confirmation, Claude returned his gaze to the couple next to him. The fill-in girlfriend was hanging like an ornament from the neck of her date, her feet sweeping the floor in abandon. The super-tall basketball star ex-boyfriend stood erect, aiming his face straight down at Claude. He mouthed the words again: *I – will – kill – you – Claude – Simard*, and this time a foul-smelling steam enveloped the incantation. Claude saw the smoky substance, smelled the odor that defied any human match, watched the eyes turn fiery and the skin stretch into the grotesque.

Then it was over. A new song from the band; a new mix of dancers. Claude told Margie he needed to get some fresh air. She said she had to go to the little girls' room.

Walking in circles outside the gymnasium, Claude surveyed his memory and came up with the hideous face of Mrs. Sinclair, the face that many years ago should have been a warning.

Making out at Mount Blue overlook, an integral part of prom night, had been a disappointment. Margie was always super cuddly and she knew the right moves, and Claude was certainly willing, but his head was elsewhere. Finally, her whatsa-matters didn't matter anymore, and both of them acknowledged that the night had been too long. Parading her new boyfriend around the dance floor under Kevin Rideout's nose had given her plenty of satisfaction. There would be other times for some serious making out.

As he drove down Logging Road, Claude struggled to force Kevin out of his head. His hands firmly wrapped around the leather-covered steering wheel, his foot exerting just the right pressure on the brake pedal, he made the Buick respond perfectly. Claude smiled despite himself. It wasn't the most recent model, but the vehicle was in such highly polished intactness that he felt some of that perfection rub off on him. He had recognized the stares of admiration from his classmates. Envy, even. Yeah, these guys had been jealous. Really sexy wheels! At that moment, Claude knew the depth of the gratitude he would always owe to his father.

Out of nowhere came the thud and the jerky movement. Margie turned around and shrieked as she recognized Kevin's car. Bang! Another metallic shove from behind. Another one, this one stronger. Claude struggled to keep control of the car on the downhill road. Margie yelled a combination of useless instructions to Claude and hateful curses to Kevin. Panic grew tangible in Claude's brain as he grasped the possibility that Kevin might just run them off the road.

The next moment, Kevin's car was speeding alongside the Buick on a straight stretch of roadway. The ex-boyfriend slowed down and the two vehicles rolled on side by side. Kevin glowered at Claude. The look was unmistakable. Claude saw clearly the face of the devil, the same devil he had seen in old catechisms, in comic books and in his nightmares about Mrs. Sinclair: the maniacal eyes, the menacing snarl, the sharp red tongue slurping at its victim. And, the protruding horns: erect, angry little penises. Claude knew this wasn't just a bad dream. This was real. Kevin had become, not a devil, but *the* devil, and, at that moment, the two of them were dueling. With a blast of exhaust fumes and burning tire, Kevin pushed his car forward and speeded out of sight. Claude slowed down, Margie still screaming. He resisted the urge to check for damage to the rear bumper, deciding the priority was to get back into town. He managed his breathing and ignored the sweat filling his rented tuxedo and brought both the Buick and Margie under control.

They were now on Cemetery Road, and the street lights of Williams were visible in the distance. Claude convinced himself they were out of danger. Kevin had given up. Kevin was out in the middle of the woods getting drunk.

A flash of metal up ahead on his left, and Claude understood that Kevin was back. Rocketing out of a hidden roadway, Kevin's car was headed for a perfect collision with the driver's side of the Buick. Claude's foot reacted and slammed on the brakes. His vehicle skidded out of control and out of reach. Kevin's car had such momentum that it crossed Cemetery Road in front of Claude and shot into the pasture across the roadway, straight into the gnarled pine tree waiting there. Twenty seconds is all it took. The duel was over. Claude had won. Prom Night 1987 had found its tragedy.

Officer Cavanaugh of the Williams Police Department and his sidekick for the night, Eugene Simard, were first on the scene. They found Claude wailing like a baby and Margie staring at him, unable to speak. Eugene examined his car; Officer Cavanaugh needlessly advised the teenagers to stay put.

Within minutes, another cruiser had arrived, and then another, and then an ambulance. Through the rotating red glare of the police lights, Claude watched the men gather at the wreck, peer inside and back away, forming a ring of helplessness around the old pine tree and its victim. Claude desperately wanted to join them, to look at Kevin's face. Instead, he closed his eyes and imagined it. Bloodied, empty and white, the face of an angry jilted teenager. Nothing more.

"So this is where you hide out," said Father Tony. He made his way around the park bench and stopped in front of his friend. "Mind if I join you?"

"I'm not hiding out." Claude said, sliding his body over and widening the empty space on the bench. He kept his eyes focused ahead of him, looking at nothing in particular, barely aware of the half-dozen kids on the playground swings. Tony sat down and unbuttoned his jacket. Both men avoided looking at each other.

A nearby bench was occupied by a Black woman watching her daughters play. Claude had been in Philadelphia a few days only, yet he had adopted a routine which included spending time at the playground attached to the former Saint Petronilla's School. It was an in-between kind of place, connected to the big city around him, but at the same time, a haven that was quiet and let him be, not unlike the empty warehouse back home. Seated on a bench across the gravelly area was an elderly couple. They were also there every day, and like everyone else in the playground, their lives ran parallel to Claude's for a few hours each afternoon.

"I know you're not hiding. I didn't mean anything by that."

"That's Ok."

To any onlooker, the men would have appeared as strangers. Two guys who just happened to be sitting on the same bench. No apparent reason to be there, just coincidence, with nothing to say to each other. Claude felt more the outsider; Tony simply felt powerless.

The night Claude arrived in Philadelphia, they had spent hours catching up over pizza, managing to keep the memories distant and safe. The lazy afternoons spent in the backyard pool that hot summer; how they watched the Sinclair house, convinced that it was haunted. They laughed about the time they built a fort in Sampson's Field with bits of lumber they assumed were discarded but weren't, the lecture from the police captain, the dismantling of the fort which turned out to be as much fun as building it. They relived the summer when they went to the drive-in with Tony's sister Tina and her boyfriend, and how the two pals kept one eye on the screen and the other on the pair making out in the back seat. The long-time buddies wrapped up their first meeting with generalities. News about Tony's mom since his father died, about his sisters, their husbands, and their dozen or so kids. An update on Claude's father who had moved into a retirement village and about the problems with his feet which kept him from driving. They joked about Mister Simard and Mrs. Diangelo bumping into each other at the Senior Citizens' bingo night and how they would start dating.

Like a mine field, the two avoided the content of Claude's recent letter and postcard.

Claude was given a bedroom on the second floor of the rectory; neither broached the subject of a time limit. Claude appreciated the hospitality, especially the showers, the clean clothes and a safe place to sleep. He also felt guilty. So did Father Tony who, for the first time as a priest, felt incapable of healing.

They sat on their bench, the sixth day into Claude's surprise visit, and listened to the street traffic as it competed with the shouts of the children in the playground. Claude studied his old friend. The more handsome of the two, Father Tony had become softer and heavier. And a lot sadder, Claude thought.

A still strong November sun bounced off the looming brick walls of the empty school that surrounded the play area on three sides. A group of boys, around five or six years old, kept running around the place. No apparent pattern, no rules, no object to the game. Just running around 'til they dropped, laughing and panting. Claude watched them intently. Running around, going nowhere, out of breath. The youngsters seemed to know Father Tony. One of them waved and the priest waved back. Another one, red-cheeked and poorly dressed, ran towards the bench and crashed into Father Tony. The laughing and the running stopped abruptly, all eyes on the bench. The priest gave a quick hug and held the boy solidly in front of him at arm's length. With a smile, Tony gently pushed the boy back towards his waiting playmates.

With his eyes, Claude watched the scene unfold; with his mind, however, he revisited that corner of his being that ached for his son Mikey. He felt the heat of his young boy's body in his arms when he hugged him the last time. Claude tried to remember his son's voice whenever daddy would chase him around the yard. Mikey had turned five in October. Claude wondered if his mom let him have the dollar-store birthday card he sent in violation of the restraining order. No contact whatsoever, personal or written, the judge had decreed. But a simple little birthday card, what's the harm in that? It's just a card. He's just five years old, for Christ's sake. A son needs to know his father loves him. The power and the joy that had filled Claude on that crystal blue October day when Mikey was born never left him. Even during the recent months of dark despair groveling for sustenance and dignity, the only ounce of self-worth he could cling to was having given life to Michael Eugene Simard. Mikey was his second born, but he was the first to confirm fatherhood. With the first child, Claude easily acknowledged, he had been too young and too angry to understand or care.

Claude listened to the heavy-breathing little boy – a stranger in a slum neighborhood in a strange city – and he watched him leave Father Tony to run back to his friends. At that moment, Claude felt his badge of fatherhood turn into an open wound, a portal that allowed the pain of separation to come and go.

"I have to go," he said. He jolted from his end of the bench.

'Where to?" asked Tony.

Claude stood motionless. "Eh…not sure. Back to the rectory, I guess."

"I'll walk with you."

The two men walked side by side on the cracked asphalt, making their way slowly to the side door of the rectory, not unlike two monks returning to their cells, their backs bent from a day's work in the fields.

Claude stared at the cans of paint lined up on the worn carpet inside the vestibule. He was reminded of a line of altar boys in the same formation back home. Since he was the tallest, he was always placed at the head of the procession, and here, the paint cans happened to be lined up according to size, the largest at one end, as if it were the leader. The project was Father Tony's idea: to keep Claude busy, and out of the way. That was obvious, and Claude didn't mind. He welcomed the opportunity to be useful.

The doors were ancient, as old as the church itself which, from the inscription on the cornerstone, was built in 1896. Father Tony thought the last time the main doors were painted was in the '50s. The priest had included paint on a list of needed items that he distributed to local businesses, and one day a truck pulled up to the rectory and discharged a dozen odd-sized cans of Cathay Red.

For the last day or two, Claude had been uncharacteristically nostalgic. He felt uprooted. Ironic for a homeless man, he thought. He found himself drifting into another place, another time, viewing scenes that he believed had been purged from his memory, looking for answers to questions that had become murky.

As he spread the drop cloth and opened the cans of paint, Claude was reminded of his first Christmas season at Pelczar's Hardware. He was 19, working part-time, and his first task was to move painting equipment into storage to make room for tree decorations. A newlywed high school dropout with a wife who was expecting any day, working at a mercy job in his father-in-law's hardware store. Margie's pregnancy had been a difficult one and she shared her discomfort with everyone. She was due in mid-December, but it dragged on until Christmas Eve when Margie screamed her first-born out of her womb. Mrs. Pelczar scolded her daughter for not holding on a bit longer, to cash in on all the gifts that accompanied a New Year's Baby.

The two families became locked in a battle over the newborn's name. Each grandfather had entertained the idea that the first grandson should bear his name: Eugene on the Simard side and Stanislaus for the Pelczar lineage. The parents weren't thrilled with the prospect of either one, even in the abbreviated forms of Gene and Stan. Claude's great-aunt Yvette came up with the idea that the boy should be christened Noel, the French word for Christmas. Out of the blue, Claude's mom, who scarcely offered an opinion, suggested Nick – like Jolly Old Saint Nick. That became the compromise.

Neither Claude nor Margie knew what to do with little Nicholas. The involvement of the grandparents was limited to a Sunday dinner with frayed nerves and nagging advice on the menu. Otherwise, the young family was left to itself, Margie buried in diapers and formula, Claude trudging to his dead-end job.

The old church doors wound up needing more work than

anticipated. The exterior was severely weather-beaten and demanded to be scraped and sanded. Claude told Father Tony they would need to be primed. There was no money for primer, and Tony said he'd have to go begging again. Claude suggested starting the project on the interior.

Properly launched each morning with Nicolette's strong coffee, Claude went to the church. He was grateful for the routine and the sanctuary. At first, Claude thought the red paint was hideous, garish, not very church-like. He shrugged and told himself he had no choice, and had there been a choice, it wouldn't have been his to make. He threw himself into the task and, in the stillness of the vestibule, he forgot who he was and where he was. The red paint with the exotic name carried him back and moved him forward, skipping the unpleasant present. In a few days, the project moved outdoors. As he stripped away decades of old paint, Claude became fascinated by the intricacies of the ridges the years had left. He ran his hand over crevices and veins and his imagination wandered, and he began to see his own life peel away, being bared and exposed.

The pale sunlight cast a shadow of a man on the bare wood, and Claude recognized the scared teenager hitchhiking the week after prom night. He remembered feeling like a sleep walker, running away from the worst of nightmares. The police chief's questions, his father's complaints about the Buick, his classmates' accusatory looks, all were more than he could stand. He wanted to escape. He moved into the shed behind his great-aunt Yvette's house, but soon he realized that wasn't far enough. Three successful hitches later, he found himself in Providence, Rhode Island, wandering in awe around the ornate downtown and the tony college neighborhood and the office buildings surrounding the white-domed capitol. This was the largest city he had ever seen, and he allowed himself to be swallowed up by the activity and the congestion. He spent his days listening to the street musicians in the Arcade, and his nights watching the bar patrons carousing though the maze of downtown alleys.

Clambering countless times up his ladder on the front steps of the church, Claude found release in the physical stimulus of his painting job. At the end of each day, he relished the ache of his back muscles and, flexing his arms, he was reminded of the body he had as a teenager. His imagination returned to the days he spent scrambling over the dunes on the beaches south of Narragansett. Providence had lost its sheen: noisy crowded streets with nothing but unfriendly faces. Claude decided to explore the seashore, something else he had never seen. He walked the seemingly endless miles of beach, back and forth, bracing himself against the ocean gusts, feeling the burn of the sun on his skin. He stared at the sunbathers and wondered if their faces would turn hostile and evil-looking. He spent his nights sheltered by dwarf pines and tall grasses, counting the stars, listening to the constant waves and the sounds of small animals whose territory he had invaded. Each morning, he found himself half buried by shifting sands, and each day, his mind came closer to finally cleansing itself of the faces of Mrs. Sinclair and Kevin Rideout.

As he walked down his street back home, he scratched his hair and beard grown to the point of disguise. He felt like Marco Polo returning home. Claude braced himself, however, for the inquisition he knew awaited him. His father was the worst. "You nearly killed your mother with worry." Claude tried to ignore the questions and accusations. He had missed the last few weeks of his senior year, yet he was satisfied with the tradeoff. He had put his mind at rest; he had wiped the slate clean. At separate times, Margie and Tony greeted him in the same fashion. "Welcome home." Nothing else. And Claude never loved anyone more than he did at each of those moments.

Finally, the shiny red doors were completed, and Claude stood back to admire his handiwork. Numerous times during the project, he had wished for a full palette. The high and wide doors begged for portraits of angels with wings spread wide, visages of smiling cherubs, perhaps the flames of hell at the base, definitely some holy words here and there in handsome Gothic letters. Left with only the fierceness of his red paint, Claude still found satisfaction in the nuances created by the light and shadows as they played on the old wooden planes, and he tucked away his ideas for a future mural in an unknown space. He then cleared away his implements and swept up any debris at the base of the doors.

Claude's eyes glazed with pride as he inspected the finished product. He knelt down and scratched his initials, C.E.S., on the bottom left-hand corner of the doors – on the inside, to preserve them from the elements.

Mister O'Regan walked out of his office after an unusually hectic day and spotted the young girl sitting in the reception area. "Damn, Margie Simard, what's she doing here?" he whispered.

Margie got up and went directly to the welfare director. "Mister O'Regan, you probably don't know me. I'm Margie Simard..."

"Yes, I know who you are. And, how's your little boy?"

"Ah, Mikey? Oh, he's fine. So full of energy," she replied, surprised by Mister O'Regan's concern about her son. The two stood in the reception area while town hall employees filed past them on their way home. There was an awkward silence.

Margie spoke first. "Well, there is something I'd like to talk to you about."

"Yes, of course. What's on your mind?"

"Well." Margie hesitated. "It's about my husband, Claude Simard." She said his name as if she were asking a question.

"I know Claude. It's my job to know lots of people. What about him?"

"Well. Where is he? Do you know where he is?"

"Ah... I'm not sure. Why do you think I would know?"

She explained that her husband's friend at work, Wally, told her he saw Claude and Mister O'Regan a couple of weeks before outside the old mill where Claude was living. Wally said that the two were talking, and that Claude got into Mister O'Regan's car.

"No one's seen Claude since. His great-aunt Yvette told me she saw him a while back, but she doesn't remember where. I'm getting worried." Margie was agitated. "I was going to go to the police, but my dad told me not to, you know, since it was my idea to get the restraining order. At least that's what my dad says."

The town welfare director donned his official tone: "There's not much I can tell you except that he's gone out of town for a while."

"Out of town? Where?"

Paul Paré

A phone rang in Mister O'Regan's office. He welcomed the opportunity to avoid Margie's question. "Excuse me, I have to take this. Don't go away, I'll be right back."

"Don't worry, Mister O'Regan, I'm not leaving."

What a little bitch. No wonder she and Claude broke up, the welfare director thought as he returned to his office, closing the door behind him.

Margie sat down and watched a janitor maneuver his equipment into the waiting area. She couldn't figure why she was so concerned about Claude. All summer she was glad to be rid of him. But now, why was she worried? The question floated above her, and it made her think about her married life, the nearly 20 years of her prime spent with this guy and how she loved him but never really loved him, not like she wished she had. Why worry about him now? She doubted if he was worrying about her. She persuaded herself she needed to know where Claude was for Mikey's sake. Besides, those 20 years, they weren't all that bad. She remembered how much she missed him those weeks right after the prom and how she was so glad to see him when he came back and how she never asked where he had vanished to and he never offered to tell her and that was all right as long as he stayed in her arms at night. She didn't want him in her arms anymore. That time had passed. She just needed to know where he was.

Finally, Mister O'Regan decided he had no choice. The girl wasn't going to leave. He came out of his office.

"Now, where were we?" he said, as he took a seat next to hers.

"Claude has gone out of town for a while..." She used his exact words. "I want to know where and for how long. I have a right. I'm still his wife."

"Yes, and yes," he replied as if filling out a questionnaire. "Listen, Margie. I'm sure you'll agree that winter in Connecticut is no time to be living in an abandoned mill with no heat, no water, and with most of the windows blown out."

"Well...yes."

"Good. So, we agree that Claude had to move someplace safer. And, that's what I did. I found him some accommodations in a warmer climate and that's where he went to."

"What warmer climate?"

"Eh. Florida." Mister O'Regan had hesitated. He wasn't used to being on the receiving end of an interrogation. "Listen, you

38

have to trust me. This is for his own good. For the good of everyone involved."

"But I want to know where."

"But I can't tell you. Well not exactly. Not yet." He was growing impatient.

"What do you mean?" Margie wasn't about to give up.

"Ok. Claude took the bus to Florida. He had enough money to get to Daytona Beach. I told him that once he got there, he should send me a postcard with his address. But he hasn't yet."

"Money for the bus fare? Where did Claude get money to go to Florida?"

"What difference does that make? He got the money. And now he's in Florida. That's it."

"So, when's he coming back?"

"I don't know, Margie. I've told you everything I know. As I said, it was for his own good. You've got to believe me."

"But, what if I wanted him back? And what about Mikey? What am I going to tell him?" At that moment, she felt a stabbing guilt cloud her words, remembering that she hadn't given Mikey the birthday card from his father.

"Well, you should know that the last thing Claude said to me was: 'Tell Mikey I love him.'"

"Oh. And when were you going to tell him? Tell Mikey, I mean." She was losing patience. She felt she was being lied to.

"I'm sorry. I planned on going to see you but, you know, I've been so busy with work and things got pushed to the back burner and…"

She interrupted him. "I'm sorry, Mister O'Regan. As I said, I have a right to know."

"You are one hundred percent correct. Listen, as soon as I have any news from Claude, I will let you know immediately. Trust me."

He moved closer and placed his hands over hers.

"I'm glad we had this conversation," Mister O'Regan said with a final pat on her hands. He was out the door in less than a minute, leaving Margie with the janitor.

The voices bounced through the hallway and greeted Tony as he came down the stairs. The tone was elevated and spirited, the female voice all over the place in singsong, the male voice responding with overlapping vigor. Father Tony halted on the final tread. In his two years at Saint Petronilla's he had never heard such gaiety in his rectory. He stopped again, hesitating in the doorway of the kitchen.

Nicolette was making coffee. To her it wasn't simply making coffee, it was a solemn ritual, and a private one, which was why she usually wouldn't allow anyone in the kitchen. Claude was sitting at the table. Tony thought his old friend looked a bit healthier. He watched them interact, talking about odds and ends and nothings, and enjoying it all, punctuating their comments with laughter. He had never seen this jovial side of Nicolette, and he wondered what quality of Claude's had drawn it out of her. The lady remained sort of a mystery to him. Nicolette came with the parish, and, two years later, Father Tony knew very little about his parish secretary. Half of his parishioners were Haitian, and it seemed that Nicolette knew all of them, and for that reason she proved valuable. He had grown to trust her, and he didn't mind her incessant chattering on the phone in Creole. She was the first to remind Father Tony that without the Haitians, Saint Petronilla's would have been shut down. She was also eager to remind him that she was not a housekeeper but the parish secretary, and that making coffee was the extent of her kitchen work, although she did keep it well stocked with snacks, soft drinks and fruit.

Unsure, Tony stayed in the doorway. He didn't want to interrupt the jovial domesticity. He felt like a voyeur, witnessing a scene that excluded him, the priest who had no right to expect a fertile home life.

"Ah! Good morning, Father Tony," she said with a musical lilt. "Coffee is ready."

"Good and strong, too," chimed in Claude, lifting his cup in a mock toast.

The priest absorbed the welcoming words and took a step into the kitchen. "My, my. Everybody seems so cheerful this morning."

"Madame Nicolette here has been telling me about her two little boys and the trouble they get into."

"You have two little boys?" asked the priest, unable to conceal his surprise. "I had no idea."

"But, Father, I am sure I have mentioned it before. Jean-Jacques and Jean-Yves, you must remember...I have brought them to church many times."

"Of course. Nicolette."

"And, you, Monsieur Claude, do you have any children?" she said, turning her attention to her guest at the kitchen table.

Father Tony noted that they had pet names for each other, a combination of formal and endearing titles. She was Madame Nicolette and he was Monsieur Claude, his name pronounced in the French manner. He wondered when that had started.

"Two boys, just like you, except they're not close in age."

"And, they have names these two boys?"

"Yes. Nicholas is my oldest. He's 19 and in the Marines. He was shipped to Iraq this summer. Mikey is the other. He's only five and sweet and beautiful and smart."

"Ages 19 and five. And...what happened in between? Did you forget how to make babies?" she countered with a heavy laugh.

"Don't answer that, Claude," Father Tony threw in. "And, you Nicolette, that question is very inappropriate." The priest stepped to the counter and poured himself a cup of coffee.

"Oooh! Oooh! Oh!" Nicolette swayed out of his way. "*Mon Dieu, Mon Dieu*," she mocked in French. "...how inappropriate."

Claude ignored the badinage. He looked at Nicolette. "The first time was an accident... then it just took us a long time to get it right," he said. His tone was somber and it was met with silence in the small kitchen.

The temper of the room had changed; gone was the conviviality. The trio remained still, each one feeling uneasy. Nicolette was first to recover. Her body tensed and, checking her watch, she cloaked herself in the routine security of her job. "I must begin my work. There is much to do today." She glared at Father Tony, and he knew she meant for him to clean up after himself. They could sit and have their coffee but they had better leave her kitchen spotless and in order.

She was on her way out of the room when she stopped in the doorway. "How long will you be staying with us?" She directed the question to both men. Her voice was surprisingly delicate, but her words were strong, their meaning was clear. Claude looked at Tony. The priest reciprocated with wide eyes.

"I am asking the question because I will be buying coffee and some supplies today. I need to know the quantity."

Both Tony and Claude were taken by surprise. Their expressions not only conveyed their resistance to deal with the question but with the suddenness of Nicolette's mood change. Tony wondered what he said to make her angry. His notion that she would forever remain a mystery was reinforced. Nicolette stared at the two. "You will let me know?" she said before walking out of the room.

The priest warmed his coffee. He presented the urn to his school pal who nodded that more would be welcome. Tony poured and sat down at the small kitchen table. The sound of his chair scraping against the old tiles took flight and filled the entire first floor of the rectory. The kitchen was small. It had been a pantry in the first years, when there were a large dining room for the priests and a small eating area for the hired help. All of that, plus the parlors and sitting rooms, had been stripped and converted to meeting spaces and conference rooms years before. Cozy and hospitable, the kitchen was where Tony felt the most at home. The simple cabinetry, with layer upon layer of ivory paint and shellac, reflected the soft light that made its way to the back of the building, even in winter. The sturdy hand-wrought pulls and handles, the gently worn wainscoting and the plain black and white tile floor, they all accepted and welcomed Tony's moods. The room was his mother.

"That Nicolette. She certainly can cut through the bullshit," Claude said.

"Well, I still think that comment about knowing how to make babies was inappropriate," Tony added.

"No. *That* was funny. I mean her question about how long I'm going to hang around."

The priest studied his long-time buddy, searching for what he suspected was still there: Simmy, the noisy skinny kid who splashed madly in the backyard pool, and not even as much as a *sorry* or an *excuse me* when he stomped through his mom's favorite bed of impatiens, all the while laughing and talking like he'd always belonged to the Diangelo clan. Tony examined the current version of Simmy. He was so thin. He had always been thin and a bit sickly looking, but this was *thin*, his tanned and scarred hands revealing every vein like the road map he might have followed to Philadelphia, his neck muscles stretched and his jaw bone defined. His sunken eyes were not as red and teary as when he had first landed at his rectory's door, but they were the eyes of an old man.

"We need to get you a haircut," Tony said suddenly. The idea surprised him as much as it did Claude. His friend's hair, wild and thick when he arrived, was now washed and neatly tied; it should have been the last thing on his mind. The priest pushed himself away from the table and walked to the counter. He played with the apples, a colorful display that Nicolette had carefully polished. Suddenly they linked him to the comfortable autumns of his adolescence in Connecticut and of his seminary years in the apple country of Northern New York. "You want an apple? They're real good."

"I know I need a haircut." Claude ignored the offer of a Macintosh. "I know I look terrible. I can't stand to look in the mirror."

'Listen. Let me take you to Gerry's. That's where I go. He's just a few blocks from here. We can go this afternoon. It'll be my treat."

"I've got money. I can pay for it." Claude spoke low, his words muddied. He suddenly felt depressed and he didn't know why. Through his jeans, he scratched the inside of his left thigh which harbored the ghost of a mysterious rash.

"It doesn't matter who pays. You can pay if you want. Gerry always gives me the clergy discount, and I'm sure he'll do the same for you. He only charges me ten dollars."

"If you insist."

"It'll make you feel better." Tony placed his hand on his friend's shoulder. He wanted to pull it back quickly. His friend's bones were so present, nearly at the point of piercing skin, but, he left his hand there, a gesture of warmth and support. What a priest should do – and a best friend. Standing behind Claude, Tony was swept back to those October days of the Philadelphia-Kansas City

43

World Series when the two of them had shared so much, their laughs and teasing, sleeping together the night of the final game. Tony realized that was the single time in his life when he had touched the emotions of love.

The phone rang upstairs in the parish office and Nicolette's voice cascaded down the back stairs. "Father Tony. It is for you. The Monsignor wants to talk to you."

"I'll be right there," the priest answered. Before removing his hand from Claude's shoulder, he gave it a cautious squeeze. "We're still on for that haircut. This afternoon, ok?"

"Right. It's not like I got anything else to do." Claude was smiling with an expression that was both subtle and raucous, one that Tony recognized immediately.

That's my Simmy, sarcastic as ever, Father Tony thought as he climbed the stairs. He entered the office and saw Nicolette sitting at her desk, and he marveled at how he and his friend had thoroughly avoided dealing with the lady's brazen question about the length of stay.

Left by himself in the kitchen, Claude stared at the two-toned liquid coating the bottom of his coffee cup. His hand stroked his ponytail and he identified the cause of his melancholy. He had become attached to his hair, his long hair, clean or dirty, tied or untied. The symbol of his new existence. Nothing else so clearly identified him as both an outcast and a prophet. He would miss it.

On his way out, he grabbed a Granny Smith, and briefly gave a thought to painting the kitchen ceiling, covering it with apples and sunflowers and gourds and smiling children.

Nicolette shivered. Could she have heard wrong? No. She was sure. She had clearly heard one end of the conversation: a new priest, a Haitian priest, would be arriving this weekend to be permanently assigned to the parish. What she had not heard so clearly was his name. Nicolette decided not to ask Father. She wasn't sure why. She just knew she was afraid to know. She would wait until he left his desk and she would examine the notepad because she had seen Father Tony writing the name after his conversation with the Monsignor. But, why not a simple question, matter-of-factly? Just a question and the priest would answer. He would say the name she was so afraid to hear.

Darkness and screams blanketed her reticence. There were so many names affiliated with those dreadful days in Cap-Haïtien. But there was one – Julien Mondésir – that filled the young girl's head with fear, the name that still populated her nightmares 20 years later. She was too young to understand the reason for the terror that saturated the lives of her family. There was so much chaos and violence, and her mother did what she could to shelter her brood from the world outside, yet nine-year old Nicolette Saintolien heard the mobs every night. She listened to the screams and she smelled the fires. She heard her father, the local headmaster, whisper the name to her mother. She felt her mother tremble as she repeated the name. She still heard it even though her mother placed tired hands over both her daughter's ears, to protect her child from the horror of that name: Julien Mondésir. Julien Mondésir.

Her father happened to be on the wrong side of the latest power grab and, as an educator, he presented a threat. Her father was shot down one night along with her older brother who tried to protect him. Nicolette had no confirmation of this until days later when she arrived in Miami with her mother and her four sisters and a handful of hastily-gathered belongings. The name Julien Mondésir was never again pronounced by her mother, and it slipped into the nebulous memory that the young girl carried of her unfortunate homeland.

The name, pronounced that morning in the rectory, pierced through the tranquility and the comfort she had achieved as a new wife and mother and parish assistant. Removed by space, time and willpower from the strife of her young years in Cap-Haïtien, Nicolette had managed, like so many of her compatriots, to banish the old rivalries and create a bubble wherein they could build a life out of the commonalities of dialect, religion and color. Her new family, her neighborhood, her church had been safe havens. Until now.

Nicolette excused herself and left her desk. Father Tony failed to notice her agitation. His gaze was fixed on his computer monitor, waiting for the e-mail from the Chancery containing the new priest's credentials. She went downstairs to the kitchen and, finding it empty, picked up the phone and called home. When her maman answered, she quickly asked to speak to her little boys. She needed to hear their voices.

It had been raining for two days, gently but steadily, in one of those summer storms that cling to the low hills of southern New England. Claude had been forced to stay inside his deserted warehouse, alone with his thoughts, deep in somber reflection.

> *angelheaded hipsters burning for the*
> *ancient heavenly*
> *connection to the starry dynamo in the*
> *machinery of night...*

He liked the sound of his voice, how it engulfed the large space, how it vibrated with each word. It was the middle of the night, and Claude was sitting on his dirty mattress, cross-legged, a small book cradled in his lap. He had arranged a circle of candles around him, their points of light reflected on the metal lids covering the cans of paint and the glass jars holding the brushes assembled at the base of his wall – his canvas. The soft candlelight respected the mystery of the shapes and colors of the mural, still young and fresh, and Claude's gaze swept reverently over his work. His eyes climbed to the emptiness of the high wall, to the virgin spaces far above waiting to be covered with his fantasies. The humidity of August had made itself at home inside the cavernous Chicopee Mill and the silence was broken only by the drone of the night's rain and the discrete cooing of the sparrows in the lofty arches. Claude bowed back into his book.

> *who poverty and tatters and hollow-*
> *eyed and high sat*
> *up smoking in the supernatural*
> *darkness of*
> *cold-water flats floating across the tops*
> *of cities contemplating jazz...*

Claude screamed the last few words, halting to hear his echo flow in and out of the rotting alcoves where just a generation ago bales of cotton had been stored to feed the mill that gave his town its lifeblood. He stood up, stretched out his arms, like on a cross, pushed his head backwards, and, with his mouth wide open, tried to swallow his echo, attempting to make his again the words of the poet. Suddenly, he laughed. A rich belly laugh, thunderous like an organ fugue filling a cathedral, drowning out the words of the priests. "I'm not even drunk," he said, interrupting his own laughter. It had been exactly two weeks since his last whiskey. There was pride in his words, and this was the celebration he arranged for himself. Just him and Ginsberg, the poet and true friend. Claude reached for his book and examined the cover: *Howl and Other Poems*. He turned it over and spoke to the photograph of the poet who looked like a rabbi: "Hello, my dear Allen. I guess it's just you and me again."

Of all the transformations that had leapfrogged through his life in the past six months, his love of poetry was the most startling. Claude would have been the first to identify himself as a mediocre student, a high school dropout, a TV addict, a poker nut who wouldn't have picked up a book if his life depended on it. And, now, his life did depend on a book, this one and the others he managed to sneak out of the public library.

What would Margie say? What would she think of his new pal, the crazy Beat homosexual Ginsberg? What would she say if she saw his living conditions, how he spent his days and his nights? What happened to his pretty little Margie? Why had she turned against him? He hated these questions. He avoided them most of the time. It was the abstinence talking. Claude sat down again and, in the moist murkiness of his warehouse, stopped his recitation. He listened to the rain. He remembered.

He heard his father-in-law announce that Mrs. Chassé was retiring and that he had named a new bookkeeper who would also become the general manager of the business. Then he introduced his son Frank. Everybody looked at each other quizzically. Frank? Frank who? Most people had never heard of old man Pelczar's son. Claude was among the few who knew him. Frankie was about ten years older than Margie, and she worshipped her big brother. Claude thought Frankie was a big showoff and he mostly tried to stay out of his way, both at Margie's house and at the hardware store where the two of them worked briefly. At the wedding reception, Frank insisted on giving his own toast and made some nasty remark about having forgotten his shotgun at home. Claude's memory of his immediate reaction was hazy. He was reminded afterwards how he darted across the dining room and gave his new brother-in-law a punch on the jaw. Claude did remember Margie bursting into tears, however, screaming at her new husband, saying he was drunk and he should be ashamed of himself for starting a brawl at their wedding.

Margie started changing after the wedding. It was as if her streak of independence had been assaulted, as if she finally realized she wasn't queen of the prom anymore, but a pregnant nearly twenty-year old, forced to marry a bore who seemed resigned to work a mercy job at her father's store.

Margie had managed to keep her father and the family business at arm's length. As a teen, she allowed herself to be coerced into helping out once in a while at the cash register, but as soon as she graduated, she landed an office job at Casey's Insurance and Real Estate. She acknowledged being ambitious. She barely hid her disdain: hardware was dirty, insurance was clean. Margie did well at Casey's. The owner took her under his wing, promoted her, and offered a decent maternity package when she had to leave. Nicholas was barely four months old when Margie returned to work, her mother having been pressed into service as the babysitter. Soon, Margie became office manager. She thrived at her job, giving it more and more of her time and attention. Years later, the death of Mr. Casey and the birth of Mikey, occurring within months, brought about the end of her career. The business was sold to a competitor, her maternal impulses kicked in, and Margie decided to stay home.

Frank Pelczar had returned after an absence of 15 years, and now, this prodigal son was going to take on a top position with the family business. And Claude was supposed to applaud? He didn't. Instead, he went up to Frank in front of the assembled employees and said: "Hello. When d'you get out of jail, Frank?" Both brother-in-law and father-in-law were not happy. And, that night, Claude had a lot of explaining to do before Margie let him into the house, let alone into the bedroom. Of course, no one knew if Frank had really been in jail. No one knew where he was all that time. Not even Margie. The official Pelczar explanation was that he worked overseas. In the Middle East somewhere, on some top-secret oil exploration projects involving some high level government agencies and influential financial backers. Bullshit, thought Claude.

Margie still worshiped her older brother and she was thrilled to have him back. She had him over for supper two or three nights a week. She placed him on a pedestal for her son Mikey who started calling him Unkie Frankie. Claude would leave early, preferring to spend the night playing cards with his buddies. Margie exerted a positive influence on Frank. The braggart bully of a brother mellowed; he even came to forgive Claude for his jail remark. An unspoken truce seemed to develop between the brothers-in-law. For his part, Frank gave the appearance of total commitment to his new position with the family business. He spent much more time in the office than seemed necessary, staying late, encouraging his father to take the time off that was well deserved but postponed. Claude remained the skeptic, but he kept his thoughts to himself.

It only took one confrontation to cause all hell to break loose. One night in April, Claude was driving home after a poker game at Wally's place – an increasingly common event – when his eye caught a reflection and some movement in the alley next to the hardware store. He parked his vehicle and walked to the side where he spotted a U-Haul truck at the loading dock. Two men, short with dark, full beards, were carrying items out of the store. Claude moved closer and saw his brother-in-law standing on the dock. "Hurry up. Hurry. We don't have all night," Frank said to the men. Then, he realized Claude was observing the scene. "Get out of here. Now!" Frank screamed at the two strangers who jumped inside the truck.

"What's going on?" Claude said.

"Nothing." Frank approached his brother-in-law and, placing his arm around his shoulders, pulled him aside. They were the same height, but Frank was by far the huskier of the two. "Nothing's going on."

Claude heard the U-Haul pull away. "Doesn't look like nothing to me."

"It's just an emergency construction project. One of our good customers, they called late and said they ran out of things. That's all."

"Which customer? In a U-Haul? This looks fishy to me, Frankie."

"Listen, brother-in-law. I don't have to explain anything to you. Just mind your fucking business."

"I...I don't like this."

"I don't give a shit what you like and don't like. You're still the snotty moron who got my sister pregnant, and what *you* think doesn't matter. So, get the fuck out of here."

Claude took a step away from Frank. "Still an asshole," he said under his breath. The resentment he harbored all those years surfaced, and from an unknown place came the urge to strike back. Claude formed a fist and was about to throw a punch.

"Go ahead, Simard. Give me an excuse. You wanna die? You wanna die?" Frank said the words slowly, savoring each syllable.

The two stared at each other and Frank's face began to change. Deep inside his memory, Claude found the freaky image stored there of Kevin Rideout the night of the prom. The same ferocious eyes, the same hideous skin color, the violence, the hatred, the evil pouring out of his mouth with the words: *I will kill you.*

Frank grabbed his brother-in-law's forearm and Claude felt the fire. He jumped away.

The look on Kevin Rideout's face on that back road years before was identical to what Claude saw on Frank's face at that moment. And, as he did that prom night, Claude tasted the danger. He started to run as fast as he could, and only after he'd reached his car did he dare look back. Frank was walking towards him, slowly, each step heavy and deliberate, his whole body larger than life, his head pulsing and fuming. Claude jumped into his sedan, put it in gear and peeled off just as Frank caught up to it. With his hand, Frank tried to grab the rear of the vehicle, but the car pulled away, carrying scratches in the blue paint like the claw marks of a beast.

"He wanted to kill me. He was going to kill me." Claude kept repeating to himself as he raced down the quiet streets of Williams.

At home, he looked in on his little boy to make sure he was safe. Claude was still shaking as he climbed into bed. Margie stirred and, without turning, asked him if he'd been out playing cards again. "You're brother's up to no good," was his only reply.

Alone in the warehouse, clutching his Ginsberg book, Claude's memory of the days that followed the incident with Frank took the shape of a long, incoherent elegy. Revelations of inventory discrepancies and missing money, accusations all around, confrontation with Pelczar the father when Claude pointed the finger at Pelczar the son, confrontation with Margie when the mess at work was reported to her, more frequent poker games, more nights getting drunk at Wally's, arguments at home getting nastier and nastier – in front of little Mikey who got scared and cried all night, the ultimatum from Margie: *shape up or ship out,* the smack across the side of her head and the cries that sliced through the darkness, the flashing blue lights on the police cruiser, the night spent *cooling down* at the lock-up, his day in court, the judge reading sternly from the restraining order and then signing it.

The final and most painful vision: Margie ushering little Mikey out the back door into the security of her mother's arms, and returning into the house to make sure that Claude didn't take anything with him except the duffle bag she had packed, all within sight of that stiff bitch from Child and Family, and with Sgt. Rourke, his dad's old buddy, waiting for him in a police cruiser parked on the street for the whole neighborhood to see.

> *who cowered in unshaven rooms in*
> *underwear, burning their money in*
> *wastebaskets and listening to the*
> *Terror through the wall...*

Claude screamed out the words in the gloom. No need to read them from his text; he had learned the language of the Beat prophet by heart. He wailed, rocking his bony frame back and forth.

Claude looked into the highest reaches of his warehouse haven and saw the darkness. No sound. The sparrows had fallen into sleep; the summer rain outside had died. The place was his, his alone. His life was his, his alone. He started singing, nonsense resonances meaning nothing. He bowed, reaching into the shadows, finding a jar filled with wet paintbrushes, picking it up and letting it fall onto the bare floor at his feet, studying the pattern of the splintering glass, choosing one of the sharpest points, gently and reverently carving one large cross on the skin inside each of his forearms. He watched the blood form tiny blossoms and he marveled at their warmth.

"So, are you happy here?" The phrase cascaded out of Claude's mouth the same way the creek bordering his and Tony's yards would overflow following a spring thunderstorm. To Father Tony, however, the words were more like giant boulders from an avalanche. The *here* in the question was obvious: It was his kitchen, it was his rectory, it was his parish, it was Philadelphia.

"That's irrelevant," the priest replied slowly "I don't have to be happy, I'm here to serve. And, you're one to ask. Look at you, Claude."

"What's that supposed to mean?"

"Well, you don't strike me as the picture of rosy contentment. You know… with this predicament you're in."

"There are moments. Good ones and bad ones. Anyways, I asked first."

"There you go. Back to the old days in junior high." The priest grimaced and threw the words at him in a sing-song: "I asked fe-a-a-a-st."

"Well I did. I don't know many happy people. I just wish you're among them."

The two fell silent. They sipped their coffees – a weaker-than-usual brew that Tony had made himself. The room was cold despite the ray of December sun that sliced through the kitchen. Claude examined his mug, trying to decide if he should refill it. The priest looked at his watch impatiently. The soundless moment stretched beyond the pause that sometimes connects and turned instead into a defiant wall.

Mercifully, the phone rang. Father Tony jumped to answer it. Claude kept his seat at the small table and adopted the most disinterested look he could muster. It was a brief conversation. The priest simply said "yes" a couple of times and concluded with a "hope they feel better".

"That was Nicolette. She's not coming in. Her little boys are sick."

"I see," said Claude. He didn't know what else to say, or if he ought to say anything at all. It was none of his business.

The priest felt a bit of relief. The phone call explained why Nicolette was late, why there was no coffee waiting, and why the heat in the downstairs rooms had not been turned on.

Claude swirled the creamy liquid filling half of his cup. "I miss her coffee. Madame Nicolette makes good coffee." He smiled.

The priest nodded in agreement. "I'll be in my office."

Claude's only acknowledgment was a hand sign that oddly looked like a blessing. His eye caught a dark cloud just as it was about to obscure the fragment of sky pictured in the tall narrow window. The room temperature dropped a few degrees, and Claude felt grateful that O'Regan had thrown him out of town. He dumped the rest of his cold coffee into the porcelain sink and started washing out the coffee maker. Tony had run out of projects, and Claude hadn't had much to do in the last few days. He figured he could at least keep the place clean.

"Do you have a driver's license?" Father Tony asked as he seemed to appear out of nowhere.

Claude was confused. "I think so. Yeah, I still have my license."

"I mean, do you have it with you?

Claude responded with lingering puzzlement. "Why?"

"And, you still know how to drive don't you?"

"Of course. Tony. What do you mean?" The questioning irritated him. "It wasn't that long ago that I was a productive member of society, you know. Yes. I have my license and yes, I still know how to drive." Claude saw himself holding his license for a moment, inspecting it, checking the expiration date, just before dropping it into his gym bag at the Chicopee Mill, with O'Regan watching.

Tony stepped further into the kitchen and was all businesslike. "My problem is that with Nicolette taking care of her sick boys, I shouldn't leave the rectory, and the new Haitian priest is flying in today." Claude looked at him and shrugged indifferently. "I need someone to drive to the airport and pick him up."

"Oh. I see." It started to make sense to Claude, who, in a spark of brightness, saw himself behind the wheel heading south on the interstate, not even close to the airport. "You sure you can trust me?" he said with more than a bit of mischief in his voice.

Tony didn't notice. He placed the car keys ceremoniously on the kitchen table. "He'll be on Delta, from Miami, at 11:30. His name is Mondésir. Julien Mondésir."

"Sure."

"I appreciate it."

"You know how to get to the airport?"

"Not really. But, I'm sure you'll tell me." Claude immediately regretted the sarcasm, which Tony either ignored or didn't note.

A couple of minutes later Tony was back in the kitchen with a hand-drawn map. He was alive with a good agitation; the business details of his job lifted his spirits. "And, how will you know each other?" he asked himself. "Wait, I'll make a sign with his name. And, here, take my card and present it to him with my excuses for not being there."

"Ok," Claude replied.

"Ok," Father Tony repeated. I'll be right back. And, dress warmly. It's cold out there. Wear one of my coats. And, here's my cell. In case you get lost. You can call me here at the rectory."

"Oh. Tony, stop, will ya? You sound like my mother."

"Sorry. I'm just nervous about this new guy. I've been the only priest as long as I've been here. I just don't want anything to go wrong."

"Don't worry. I'll get it right. Don't worry."

"I'll go make the sign."

As much as Claude hated airports – he had never been on a plane – the ride to Philadelphia International Airport turned into just the right escape. It was easy to find, with plenty of signage all along I-95, and although Claude kept toying with the idea of driving much further, on a real escape, to Florida perhaps, where it was warm and where there was less guilt than in the Philadelphia parish of his best friend, he cruised into the parking garage and quickly found the right terminal.

His fear of flying was – like all his fears – perfectly logical. He was a man of the soil, of simple peasant stock, one who needed his feet firmly grounded, one who respected the time it took to get from one place to the next, the natural way. The best way to travel was on foot, the next best was on horseback, and in final place was travel by car, or by train or by bus. One might sacrifice time to some extent, but these forms of transportation still kept the traveler close to the earth, unlike getting on a plane.

Travel to Claude had less to do with destination than the trip itself. The landscape, the people, their cities, everything to be experienced between points A and B, all made the pilgrimage worthwhile. The best trip was a really a voyage. Although Claude had forgotten much of the French language of his father's family, he sensed that the word *voyage* was magical, that it included the word *voire* which meant *to see*. You couldn't do that on a plane. It was too fast, and so far up, you couldn't see anything. His new friends, Kerouac and Ginsberg, understood that. All artists understood that. Claude would never step onto an airplane.

Claude Simard sat quietly thinking about his crusade against air travel, surrounded by fathers and mothers and girlfriends and bosses who were grateful for the speed of the instrument that would soon deliver whomever they were waiting for. To Claude, Miami was about as far as you could go in this country without falling off, and he had no imaginings of what it would be like to be from there. He would go someday and find out, and he would do it like Kerouac and his buddies who crossed America, slowly and indirectly. And, reverently, he thought. Like pilgrims...on a quest for the best and the purest that this land has to offer.

Then, a gate opened and the people of Miami flowed into the waiting area. Claude stood in expectation, boldly holding up his sign.

He nearly drove the parish car into the side of the garage. He ran into the rectory, leaving his passenger to struggle by himself with his luggage, and, once inside, he threw the car keys onto the kitchen table as if they were the source of some contagion. He took the stairs two and three at a time. He stormed down the hallway and into his room, slamming the door behind him. Father Tony was startled by the noise. Leaving his desk, he got up to catch a glimpse of Claude running by.

"Claude," he yelled. "What's going on? Anything happen?" he said as he followed him to his room. He knocked on the door. There was no answer. "Claude. Claude, say something."

The priest remembered the errand he had assigned and went downstairs to greet his guest, his new collaborator, *le Révérend*

Julien Mondésir, and to apologize. He reached the back door just in time to open it for the Haitian priest, who, loaded with bags, was breathing heavily.

"Here, let me help you, Father. Welcome to Saint Petronilla's Parish." He didn't know what else to say. He had no idea what had gone on, what had caused Claude to run like a madman, abandoning his charge.

The visitor stood just inside the door, catching his breath, his luggage at his feet. The two priests appraised each other. Father Mondésir spoke first, "There is no problem, Father. I assure you." His voice, a very deep baritone, rushed through the first floor of the rectory, crashing through decades of controlled Irish and polite Polish with an accent that couldn't have been more musically tropical. Father Tony was amazed and enchanted. He immediately saw the potential of such a voice. "The trip was most uneventful," the new priest said. Father Tony accepted his outstretched hand and was surprised by its heat and thickness.

"Well, in any event. Please, make yourself comfortable, Father Mondésir."

"Call me Julien, *s'il-vous-plaît*. And I may call you…"

"Tony. Of course."

"Well, Tony, I am sure we will get along beautifully. It will be a privilege to perform God's work here with you."

Father Tony smiled broadly. He was charmed.

The next morning, the sky threatened with the first snow of the season, a series of brief dustings that warned of more to come. Father Tony counted the worshipers, mostly women, at this Wednesday Mass of the first week of Advent. They couldn't have filled an entire pew even if they had been forced to sit together instead of scattering themselves all around the small chapel. All nine of them presented themselves for Communion, and the priest knew them all, uttering their names with each *Body of Christ*. The Mass concluded, the communicants simply buttoned up and filed out of the chapel A few minutes later, having straightened out and battened down, the priest braced himself against the wind and walked out of the side door into the courtyard. Cloistered in a corner, their backs turned away from the priest, Claude and Nicolette were linked in intense conversation.

"What are you two doing outside? It's cold out here," Father Tony said to them. The duo dropped their conversation and stared at the priest as if he had caught them committing a sinful act. Tony suddenly felt the ineptness of the moment. "Is there coffee inside?" Nicolette nodded. The priest walked away. Nicolette and Claude exchanged worried glances.

"Here, Monsieur Claude, is my telephone number," she said, as she wrote on a small piece of paper. "If anything happens, you call me. My husband and my two brothers will be here in a minute." They gave each other a supportive pat on the shoulder and headed into the rectory.

The priest struggled with his curiosity. What were they doing out there? What *were* they talking about? Were they hiding? From what? It didn't dawn on him that they could be hiding from someone instead of something. The warmth of the kitchen soothed his inquiry, and he headed directly to the coffee maker. Turning with a full mug in his hand, he faced his parish secretary and his childhood friend.

"What's the matter with you two? Please close the door." Tony rushed behind them to push the door they had left open.

"I'm sorry, Father," Nicolette said.

"Goodness, Claude! You look like you've just seen the devil," Tony said to his friend. "Are you sick?"

Claude didn't reply; he dropped into a chair. Nicolette was braver. She decided someone had to tell Father Tony what was on their minds. She removed her heavy coat.

"Sit down, Father," she started, and he obeyed. "We have to tell you that we – both of us – are very worried."

"About what?" the priest interrupted.

"Father, please listen." Nicolette glanced at Claude and took a deep breath. "It is about Father Mondésir. We are concerned. He is not what you think. I know him from my years in Haiti. There is bad history there, some bad blood. He is not a good person."

"But he's a priest. What *are* you talking about?"

"I know he is a priest. But in Haiti that means all kinds of things, some of them bad. Listen to me, Father Tony. I know this man. I know his name. I know what he has done. And Claude agrees with me."

"Claude? When were you in Haiti?" Agitated, the priest glared at his friend. Claude didn't reply. He continued to stare, apparently unable to focus on anything, unable to contribute.

"Tell him, Monsieur Claude. Tell him what you told me," Nicolette pleaded.

"Tell me what…" Tony nearly yelled.

A dull silence fell upon the trio, Claude seated at the table, Nicolette and Tony tall before him, waiting. Claude stared vacantly at the floor tiles. Nicolette gestured with her hands and hunched forward towards Claude, an expectant look in her fierce eyes. She turned to face the priest.

"What I can tell you, Father Tony, is that this man Julien Mondésir – and that *is* his real name – is well known to me." Her tone was ominously calm. "As a child in Haiti, more than 20 years ago, this man terrorized my family and many others in Cap-Haïtien. He is responsible for my father's assassination. He is a priest, I know. He was a priest then too. And, in Haiti being a priest only means that he is a man with power. Julien Mondésir used that power against his own people. He used it for evil, not for good." She stopped abruptly. She wiped her eyes dry. "He may have been a priest, but his followers were hoodlums and murderers." Nicolette Saintolien straightened up, took a deep breath, and walked out of the room with a dignity Father Tony had rarely witnessed.

Another spell of silence greeted her departure. Tony took a step towards the door of the kitchen and examined the empty hallway.

"I don't understand. I don't get any of this," Tony said, shaking his head and pacing the small room. "This doesn't make sense. Father Julien has all the proper credentials. She must be mistaken." The priest looked at his friend. "Claude, what do you know?"

Claude pulled the hood of his sweatshirt over his head. He placed his hands over the hood and patted himself consolingly. "No, no. Not again."

"What do you mean, Claude? Not again?" the priest asked impatiently.

Looking down at the Formica kitchen table, he said in a cautious voice, "Tony, I'll tell you. But, you've got to promise to listen quietly and not to interrupt and not to argue with me."

Tony nodded. He sat across the table and listened.

"You promise? Say you promise…"

"All right, I promise," Tony said.

What Claude had to say was even more incredible than what Nicolette had just spilled. Claude told him about the faces he had seen during his life – the faces of evil, he called them. "I never told you about Mrs. Sinclair. Remember that house where the murder took place? I saw Phil's mother the morning she killed him, just before she cut him to pieces. She had the face of a devil. It was so ugly. It was hideous. I was scared to death. I didn't know how to tell you." Tony closed his eyes. He searched for any hints that his friend Simmy had been going crazy that long ago. Claude continued with Kevin Rideout and what happened at the prom of 1987. He told him about his brother-in-law, Franck Pelczar, who had tried to kill him just a few months before. He described as best he could how terrifying those faces were.

"That's the same face I saw when I met Mondésir at the airport," Claude said in a low voice. "But this time, blood was dripping from his eyes."

"I saw his eyes. There was no blood…"

Claude interrupted, "You and me, we don't see the same way." Claude pleaded with his friend to believe him, to do something before it was too late. "Tony, please listen to me. This man will only bring you trouble. He is evil."

Tony wanted to scream, to shake Claude, to tell him he was out of his mind, but some force instilled in him during years of seminary training took over and he became the priest, the healer. He closed his eyes and took two deep breaths. "Claude, I think you may be possessed," he offered soothingly.

"Possessed? I'm possessed? Shit, Tony! That's all you can come up with?"

"I'm sorry, but with that kind of talk, what else can I think."

"That's the same kind of mumbo-jumbo voodoo shit your new priest would come up with. Tony, please. Don't…" Claude didn't finish his sentence. He clamped his fists to his temples and wailed: "No. No, not again. Please, not again. Please"

Father Tony stood hastily. He was about to leave the room, then he stopped, faced Claude and issued a warning. "I don't want to hear another word about any of this. Keep this crazy stuff, these faces of evil, to yourself. And I don't want you influencing Nicolette in any way. You understand?"

Claude watched his old friend wave his finger at him like an angry mother, and like a stubborn little boy he refused to back down. "Tony. Tony Diangelo," were his only words, like a plea, like the last words of a condemned man.

The priest stormed out of the room. Claude withdrew deeper into his hood and in that darkness he understood that he would have to leave Saint Petronilla's. That very day, he would be on a bus out of Philadelphia.

The Sinclair house was the oldest in the neighborhood. The New England cape served as a farmhouse at one time, and, when Williams was still rural, it might have stood proudly on its granite berth surrounded by well-kept orchards and fields. Perhaps a noble elm tree shaded it. But, the Sinclair house had seen its domain shrink as the hamlet became a mill town and the acreage gave way to a medley of modest Victorians and false Colonials. When, in the late '60s, a new school filled the last stretch of open space, the street gained importance, and what vacant lots were left came to accommodate neat bungalows and ranch houses.

The notoriety of the house lay in its occupants: the reclusive woman and her mentally-challenged son. Kids walking to and from school didn't notice it, except at Halloween, when the Mrs. Sinclair and her son Phil fed a young imagination's need for ghouls and goblins. No one dared stop at the house for trick or treat, but every year saw some mild vandalism such as smashed pumpkins and toilet paper draped on trees. Mrs. Sinclair would clean it up, cursing under her breath. She never called the cops; she didn't like the cops poking around.

But, as Phil grew older, the police responded on occasion to complaints: harmless acting out, like yelling at the girls who walked by, once grabbing his crotch. The cops would talk to him and his mother and that would be the end of it.

Terence Hugh O'Regan, the town's new assistant welfare director, gradually took an interest in the boy and the police started calling upon him to intervene. Soon, Mister O'Regan was spending a good amount of time at the Sinclair house. He easily exerted his authority and proved a calming influence on the 17-year old Phil.

Mrs. Sinclair was grateful. "Phil is turning into quite a handful. He doesn't know his own strength and he's getting hard to control. You have a way with the boy; he listens to you, Mister O'Regan."

"Please, call me Terence."

"Of course, and you can call me Estelle."

The two were having dessert; Phil was watching TV in the next room. New and alone in town, Mister O'Regan had started accepting Mrs. Sinclair's increasingly frequent invitations to supper. He learned she had a penchant for sherry which he was pleased to satisfy.

"I don't mean to pry, Estelle, but what happened to Phil's father?" Terence asked.

"Well, he blamed me for everything. He said he couldn't stand to see his son turn into the village idiot. He left us, oh…about ten years ago."

"Does he help? With the expenses, I mean?"

Estelle hesitated.

"I'm sorry. It's really none of my business," Terence said.

"It's not that. I just don't think about Phil's dad anymore. He does send money. Every other month or so, he sends a check – always made out to Phil and addressed to Phil."

"So, you can tell where he is. I mean, by the postmark…"

"I don't care to know where he is. He could be in hell for all I care."

"I see. And, I don't blame you, Estelle. He sounds like a real scoundrel," Terence stated. He leaned forward and patted the back of her hand. She smiled, keeping her eyes down.

The suppers became a Monday night routine. Each week the event became a bit fancier: special appetizers, linen napkins from the cedar chest, prized glassware. Terence contributed the sherry each time. He paid special attention to Phil, trying to engage him in conversation.

Estelle learned that Terence was from New London and that he served a stint in the Air Force and attended a community college. Being assistant welfare director in Williams was his first job. He had no family: his parents had died, he had no siblings.

For Thanksgiving of 1979, Estelle suggested that they change their Monday night supper to Thursday. "That is, if you don't have any plans…" she said.

"Excellent idea. I have to be in New London that morning, but I should be back in time," he replied.

Estelle's curiosity was aroused by the mention of New London, yet she said nothing.

Thanksgiving evening, Estelle wore her best dress and her most expensive perfume. She was in a cheerful mood and opened a bottle of sherry earlier than usual. Terence wore a white shirt and tie. The supper's formality rubbed off on Phil who seemed more sedate than usual. Estelle suggested that everyone move to the living room for dessert: home baked pumpkin pie with whipped cream. Before long, Phil was spread out on the sofa and soundly asleep.

The conversation flowed easily and it gradually turned to the Sinclair house. "It's a grand old house," Estelle said. "My great grandfather built it in 1817. Doesn't look like much outside, but the rooms are all large and the ceilings are high. Did you know there's a working fireplace in each of the bedrooms upstairs? These floors are all pumpkin pine, the very best at the time. I've always thought the place would make such a fine house of ill repute," she gushed. "Oh, did I say that? Oh. Terence, don't listen to me. I've had too much sherry." She laughed and added, "Oh. I'm being so silly."

"And you'd make a grand madam," Terence said. He laughed as well.

Estelle giggled like a schoolgirl. "I think we need some coffee. Let me get you some coffee."

"No. No, thanks. Sit down, Estelle. Just relax."

Terence turned serious. "You know, I'm new in town and I don't know many folks and it gets lonely at times."

"I don't doubt that," Estelle said.

"You're one of the few people in Williams I can talk to. And..." he hesitated. "I'm glad you brought up the subject of the house, your house. It just happens that I'm looking for a place to..."

"Oh, Terence. I'm flattered but that arrangement wouldn't work. People would talk. You know what I mean."

"No. No. Not for me. I don't mean I'd move here." Terence interrupted her. "I'm talking about someone else."

"Who?" Estelle, annoyed and embarrassed, yelled out.

At that moment Phil stirred in his sleep and groaned a series of incomprehensible words. Estelle went to him. "Let's get you to bed, my boy. It's getting late." Phil put up a struggle and kept saying he didn't want to go to sleep, yet he followed his mother's orders and the two left for Phil's bedroom.

"Phil is angry at me. He wants to watch TV. I said no and he said I'm mean to him." Estelle sat in her recliner. "Sometimes, I think I might have to put him in an institution."

"You want me to intervene?" Terence asked.

"You mean find a place for him? Have him committed? I really couldn't do that."

"No, not at all. I mean now...talk to him, calm him down."

"Thank you, but I think he's settling in. I'll check on him in a few minutes." Estelle turned to face her guest. "I'm sorry. Just now, what I said...I shouldn't have assumed you wanted to move in."

"Don't worry about it. It was a natural thing to conclude. I should have explained it better."

"Explained what?" Estelle was balancing curiosity with irritation. "Did you mean you know someone who could stay here and help me take care of Phil? Is that what you meant? Of course, that would solve some problems, but you understand, I don't have any money for that person."

Terence saw his opportunity. "Well, it so happens, that I...know someone who might...from New London, a girl, she could move in and help you...help both of us, as a matter of fact. And, I could pay you to keep her here."

"A young girl? I would need someone older and stronger. You have no idea how strong Phil can be...and how stubborn."

"Of course. You're right Estelle. Let's forget what I said." Terence looked at his watch and announced it was late and should be heading to his motel room.

"Well, we can talk about it some more, at another time," Estelle said as she picked up the dessert dishes.

The young welfare director thanked his hostess, accepted his coat and walked out. On the sidewalk, he stopped to look back and remembered Estelle's giggles when she talked about her house making a good house of ill repute. "In due time, all in due time," Terence said.

The change in speed, subtle but certain, was first to penetrate his sleep. Then, the sway to accommodate the exit ramp threw Claude slightly off center and his head reacted by snapping back. He startled himself into awareness. Where the hell am I? At that instant, as if his question had been heard, a sign proclaimed in white over green: Smithfield. Claude understood he had reached his drop-off point. Freed from the snarl and speed of the interstate, the Greyhound was now the king of the road and, as it slowed into the modest downtown of Smithfield, North Carolina, vehicles of all sorts gave way.

Claude examined his surroundings and found them neither familiar nor unfamiliar, except for the billboard proclaiming Smithfield the home of the Ava Gardner Museum. The name carried a vague recognition and he often heard his father utter it with considerable reverence. Claude asked the passenger next to him, a man in his sixties, who Ava Gardner was. The fellow grunted something unintelligible. Claude didn't pursue the matter; he had other things on his mind. He leaned across the aisle and ventured a question to his other neighbor, a Black guy in military uniform. "You know what time it is?"

"Just before ten," the Marine replied.

"Thanks. Guess this is where I get off," Claude said.

"Guess…You're not sure?"

"Yeah, I'm sure. This is where I have to get off."

"This is my stop too. Switching to another bus that's taking us back to base."

"You guys all headed to the same place?"

"Yes, sir. Camp Lejeune."

The Marine had been on the bus since Philadelphia, taking one of the few empty seats in the front. Later, after a stopover in Washington, two other military guys joined him, and the trio had spent the night talking and laughing, keeping their neighbors awake and annoyed. Only since a recent stop, had the Philly boy moved to the back of the bus.

"You live around here?" the soldier asked.

"No. I'm from Connecticut. I'm heading south for the winter, probably Florida. Where you from?"

"Philadelphia."

"Oh. I just spent some time there…visiting a friend."

"I hate it. Nothing there for me anymore. The Marine Corps' my home."

"Oh." Claude didn't know what to say. The idea of the military providing a home had never occurred to him.

"Two more weeks, and we're being shipped out to Iraq. All three of us."

"Oh," Claude repeated, still at a loss for words. He felt he should say something patriotic. He thought about it for a moment. He could say that his son Nicholas was in Iraq, but Claude didn't know where. He could talk about his days with the anti-war protesters at the post office back home. He got an urge to talk him out of going to Iraq, to convince the eager Marine to go AWOL, to join the quest, to become a partner in Claude's escapade. He decided to keep his mouth shut.

It dawned on Claude that during his time in Philadelphia, he hadn't thought much about the war. He had seen protesters the one time he had ventured downtown, at Independence Mall, and that group of picketers – young college students mostly – had seemed foreign to him, unlike the folks back home. Claude continued his reflection about his time in the City of Brotherly Love. He regretted not having done much of anything. The city of his – and Tony's – childhood dreams during the World Series had escaped him. It wasn't even baseball season, as Father Tony was quick to remind him. "And, there's a new stadium now. There's not much left of the World Series of our youth," Tony said. Instead of running up the stairs at the Museum of Art like Rocky Balboa or gazing with reverence upon the Liberty Bell, Claude roamed the neighborhood around Saint Petronilla's. The maze of narrow littered streets crowded with brick houses of a better time held a certain fascination. Off the beaten path, the quarter had many layers – of history, of hope and despair, of interminglings. Claude felt like an explorer with his own slice of America to discover.

The Greyhound slowed for a red light, and Claude watched

the languid small-town traffic cross the intersection. The bus headed south beyond the downtown, and, moments later, pulled into a large parking lot and abruptly braked to a stop, punctuating, for Claude, the finality of the trip. Claude braced himself. He wasn't ready. Don't move, he told himself, just sit still. All of a sudden, Claude wanted to ride further. Smithfield had never been his destination; it just happened to be what he could afford. He really wanted to go as far as Florida. Somewhere in Florida. Didn't know why. Didn't know where. O'Regan had put the idea in his head, and that's where he wanted to be.

"What the hell am I going to do here?" he said louder than he expected to.

"What?" asked the old man who shared his seat.

"Oh... Nothin."

At that moment, the bus driver stood up, his schedule in hand, and looked straight at Claude.

"Ok. Gotta go," Claude acknowledged.

"Right behind you, sir." The Marine saluted him.

Stepping off the bus into the mid-morning sunshine, Claude shielded his eyes and stretched to ease the tightness in his neck and back. His soreness reminded him of the pampering of the past few weeks: a warm soft bed, clean clothes, plenty to eat. He felt waves of gratitude and guilt as he remembered the generosity of his friend Tony.

The driver dragged Claude's gym bag out of the hold and let it fall harshly on the asphalt. He pointed to a combination general store and filling station. "Smithfield Market, that's the terminal...if you need directions or something."

Claude didn't thank him. The driver pulled himself back onto the bus, noisily closed the door, and yanked the hand brake. Just then, Claude remembered leaving his coat on the seat, and in a mild panic, banged on the door.

"What?" yelled the driver.

"Forgot my coat."

"Stay there. I'll get it for you."

It all took less than a minute, and the bus was on its way back to I-95. Claude was left standing road-side like an immigrant just thrown onto shore with his meager belongings at his feet.

Through the cloud of dust shrouding the departing Greyhound, Claude saw Father Tony present the coat, the same one he had loaned him to fetch Father Mondésir. "Here, you'll need this," the priest said.

"Really? It'll be warm in Florida."

"I know, but...God knows where you'll be between here and there, and you can sleep on it," the priest added and immediately regretted saying it. "I mean..."

"I know what you mean," Claude replied. "And, thanks. I appreciate it. I appreciate everything you've done for me, Tony. Really, I do."

The two friends stood facing each other as the crowd flooded the main concourse of the Philadelphia bus terminal. They hadn't spoken since leaving the rectory, not since Claude announced that it would be best for him to leave Philadelphia and continue on his journey, and not since Tony said he'd give him a ride downtown. The priest was first to break the silence as he offered the winter coat. A ritual of passage, a sort of investiture.

"Bless, you. Be good." Tony held his arms outstretched, and Claude fit himself between them. Tony patted his childhood friend on the shoulders. An errant child. A lost soul. Suspended in an aborted embrace, each one thought the other looked so terribly sad.

Claude hadn't told his friend he didn't have enough money to get all the way to Florida. He didn't tell him he had purchased a ticket that would take him only as far as some God-forsaken place in North Carolina. He didn't tell him how scared he was.

Tony repeated his blessing, leaving unspoken his dread about the emptiness he knew would greet him back at the rectory. He let pass the urge to hug his friend tightly and to hold him.

"And, you be good, too," Claude said.

The three soldiers, smoking, laughing, and joking, had bivouacked in a corner of the parking lot of Smithfield Market, their gear surrounding them like a fortification. Pick-up trucks weaved around them as they pulled into the market to fill up on gas and on sundry groceries.

Pushing his hand in his pocket, Claude felt the few ten-dollar bills he had left and decided he could afford a couple of donuts and a coffee. He waved to the friendly Marine as he walked by.

"Just get off the bus?" the store clerk said in her southern accent as she handed Claude his change.

"Yes, ma'am."

"Well. Welcome to Smithfield. It's a fine little town we've got here."

"Just passing through." Claude didn't feel like starting a conversation.

"So where you'all headed?"

Claude realized that this middle-aged lady with her hair piled high above her head and her neon lipstick wasn't about to let him go. "Florida," he replied.

"Shoulda stayed on the bus, then."

"I know, but...you know..." Claude wasn't about to reveal any more. "Not in any rush."

"Ah. The scenic route," she said with a chuckle. "Listen, young fella, you gotta talk to Cal over there. He's been around an awful lot and he knows all the byways, if you know what I mean." She pointed to a man sitting on a stool in a corner reading a newspaper. "Hey, Cal. Help this stranger out, will ya? He could use some directin'."

Claude was astounded by the rapidity of his induction into the circle of old buddies at Smithfield Market.

Cal looked up. "Where's he headed for?" he asked the store clerk.

"He says Florida," she replied and, looking at Claude, nodded towards Cal. "You go talk to 'im." Another customer inched his way to the counter, and Claude, coffee and Krispy Kremes in hand, took a few steps forward. Suddenly, he paused and looked back at his bag and coat on the floor near the door. "Don't you worry about your things, honey. They're safe there," the clerk said.

Cal had the wrinkles and the leathery skin of a well-travelled man. He shook Claude's hand like it was some kind of lifeline. He squinted, looking up at the newcomer that Elsie had suddenly taken a shine to. He quickly sized up his protégé. He knew where this young man was going because he had been there. His advice, if he was going to hitch, was to stick to Route 701. Cal didn't speak in full sentences. And, he jumped from one subject to the next. Grammar and narrative were other men's rules.

"State Route 701, all the way. Lots of locals. Lots of small towns. Nice folk. Safest way to go. People like to pick up hitch-hikers. Somebody to talk to."

Claude listened studiously as he devoured his donuts.

"Route 701. That's what I'd take. I know the map like the back of my eyelids. Connects with Route 17 later on. Stay on 17 all the way: Charleston, Savannah, Jacksonville. Stay away from truck stops. Except for the food. Good and cheap. The truckers, can't trust 'em."

The other Marines entered the store. One of them asked where the restrooms were; the other one bought a pack of cigarettes. The young ladies in Smithfield Market admired the uniforms and giggled after the soldiers walked out. Elsie hushed them and said something about God and Country.

"Soldier boys. Good lads. Feel sorry for 'em, though," Cal said. "And, the cops on the road, never look at 'em straight in the eyes. If they stop you, just say you're going to the next town. They're real mean in Georgia for some reason. Tell 'em you're going to see your mama."

Claude asked Cal where he would recommend going to in Florida.

"Jacksonville's as far as I got. Don't trust the rest. State's full of crooks and crocs." Cal found his description amusing and chuckled.

"Well, thanks for all the info," Claude said, concluding that his tour guide had said his final words.

"Good luck. Five miles south on this road here. You'll pick up 701. Can't miss the sign."

Claude nodded his appreciation and, and scooping up his belongings, made his way quickly out the door.

The main highway leading south from Smithfield, with its small businesses and mom and pop enterprises in drab one-story concrete structures, reminded Claude of his hometown. The trees and shrubs that survived the asphalt and the motor vehicle fumes were not unlike those in New England. Claude was surprised to find he was homesick. He plodded along the gravelly shoulder and thought of his job back in Connecticut. Of all things to miss, he thought, that stupid job at Pelczar's. He saw his father-in-law's face, always red from high blood pressure, and the smiling face of Mrs. Chassé, the bookkeeper, behind her desk. His mind stumbled upon his brother-in-law standing inches away from him, his face full of ugliness and danger. *You wanna die? You wanna die? You wanna die?* These months later, the threat could still fill his head if he let it.

71

Claude picked up his pace and took a deep breath of warm Dixie air and started singing his brother-in-law's words as loud as he could, giving them a rock beat, diffusing the menace, trivializing the intent. *You wanna die? You wanna die? You wanna die?* Gradually the rock song turned into a ballad. He kept at it, knowing that if he uttered the words long enough, they'd turn into meaningless banter, the ravings of a fool.

None of the cars and trucks whizzing by slowed down. None of the drivers heard his song. Claude's instinct told him this was not the place to hitchhike. Too much traffic, constantly turning in and out of driveways and parking lots. Everyone with nearby destinations and short attention spans. He hoped Cal was right and that Route 701 would be more hospitable.

He kept walking, trying not to think, trying not to remember. The day grew warmer, and the flat farming country regained its hold on the landscape, the fields brown and empty, groves of trees shrouded in mist. Claude stopped to inspect these new surroundings. An occasional heavy truck disrupted his contemplation, but they grew scarce, and after each one, the silence was heavier. His fears and uncertainties faded, and for the first time in months, Claude felt free. He scanned the ground before him and started to feel that connectedness to the road. "No other way to travel," he said. He repeated the phrase, this time yelling, shattering the rural quiet. "No. Other. Way. To. Travel." As he resumed walking, he tested his new slogan. He said it again and again, giving it a military-like cadence that matched his stride. His arms swinging, the duffle bag at the end of one, and the rolled-up winter coat in the other, his steps grew longer and surer. Claude had found his marching orders.

During the first months of 1980, Connecticut suffered through one of the harshest winters on record with bitter cold and several inches of new snow almost every other day. Mister O'Regan's visits to the Sinclair house increased with the severity of the weather: helping to repair the old furnace in the basement, buying a new jacket for Phil, encouraging him to take his work shoveling snow seriously. Phil enjoyed the task. He was strong and indefatigable. The heavy and frequent snowfalls meant that he was busier than ever. He and Mister O'Regan arranged a schedule and a route whereby he would give Phil a ride in the morning to his farthest shoveling job and the lad would clear his driveways and sidewalks until he wound up close to home at the end of his day. The best part, as far as Phil was concerned, was the money. For the first time, the 17-year old was earning money.

Mrs. Sinclair was also very pleased and quite grateful.

By the time March rolled in, Terence felt confident enough to bring up his suggestion that someone might move in with the Sinclairs. Since Thanksgiving, neither he nor Estelle had broached the idea.

"You know, Estelle, now that the worst of winter is over, your Phil might feel lost without the shoveling jobs," Terence stated during one of his visits.

Estelle agreed.

"Perhaps, a new person in his life would distract him. Remember when I told you I could find someone to live here and help out. I also said it could also be a source of revenue."

Estelle said she remembered.

Not entirely assured but not totally dissuaded, Terence went on. "Estelle, I don't know how to say this, but I'm in a predicament."

"Oh, Terence, what's the matter?"

Her tone was just enough encouragement. Terence stated that the motel where he was staying had a strict policy about visitors not being allowed. He slowly explained how one day last fall, he had met a girl – a very sweet but lonely girl – at the bus station in New London and they had taken a motel room and spent the night together.

"I hope you're not shocked, Estelle, but I have no family and I get so lonely."

Estelle replied softly, "Not really, you're a very nice person. And, I've read a few books and seen a few movies and I know about life and I don't shock easily and I can…"

Terence interrupted her. "Then you'll understand that it wasn't a one-time affair. I still see the girl – two or three times a week – in New London, which is quite a distance as you well know. This is beginning to wear on me. It's not only the time traveling, but the extra expense for gas and for the motel in New London where I keep her."

"*Keep* her? That's a strange expression. She's a kept girl, *your* kept girl? That sounds rather bizarre – right out of a horror movie," Estelle said very loudly.

"Well, she agrees to it. She's the one who first used the term."

"Oh. It's becoming clear to me. You want to *keep* her here, in my house."

"Well, Estelle, you're the one who mentioned that this house would make a great house of ill repute. Remember, last Thanksgiving? I know you meant it lightheartedly, but your comment got me to thinking."

"Oh, I'd forgotten. Yes, I did say that, and now that you mention it, I do remember you saying something about my being a good madam. Oh my, oh my. You're serious, aren't you? You want your own private whore house. And, you want me to run it! Oh my. I need some sherry."

Estelle took her time in the pantry and in the kitchen and walked slowly back to the living room, all the while mulling over the proposition.

Terence decided to elaborate. "She would be the only one, and I would be her only customer – or, if you prefer, visitor. The house is large, there's plenty of room. And, of course, I would pay for her upkeep. Besides, the girl would be a distraction for Phil, he would have a friend. A friend only, however, if you understand my meaning."

Estelle took a hefty gulp of sherry. "I need time. I have to think this over."

"Of course. I understand. Take all the time you need."

Estelle took a week to weigh the pros and cons. She acknowledged that any bit of romantic interest in Terence on her part had long before vanished. That was not the problem. Part of her was pleased that Terence found himself a girlfriend. At first she had labeled him a mama's boy and briefly wondered what the root of his interest in Phil was. It was perfectly normal for a man like Terence to find someone. She admitted though that keeping a girl as his sex slave – she hated to even think of those words – was far from normal. "Oh! What is normal?" she asked out loud to the empty kitchen one morning as she waited for the toast to pop out of the toaster.

Terence stayed away for the entire week. He waited for an invitation; he wondered if he had overstepped some bounds. In a few dark moments, he feared that Estelle would report him to the police.

Phil could sense that something had happened. He kept asking his mother when Mister O'Regan would visit. He said he missed him. He started acting up, refusing to go to one of his shoveling jobs, throwing snowballs at kids passing by on their way to and from school. Phil's behavior became the excuse his mother was looking for.

Estelle sat at the kitchen table and made a list of pros and cons. There were two columns and they were nearly even. At the bottom, she jotted down some conditions: establish a schedule for Terence's visits, the girl would have to live in the cellar, she couldn't have the run of the house, Terence would have to pay at least $50 a week. She ended with a question: What do we tell Phil? She underlined the words several times. Finally, she wrote a note inviting Terence over for Sunday dinner.

The girl moved in Monday morning. Terence was late for work when he dropped her off. There was barely time for brief introductions. "You'll see, Estelle, things will work out real well," were his parting words as he ran out to his car.

Her belongings were all in a grocery bag, and despite the sharp March winds, all she wore was a thin sweater over a t-shirt and jeans. Estelle asked if she had breakfast. The girl signaled *no* with her head. Estelle made her toast with apple butter and poured her a cup of coffee. The girl ate without talking. "Better not get used to this. In the future, if you want breakfast, you'll have to follow our schedule," Estelle told her sternly.

Estelle took the girl to her room in the cellar. "Here you go. There's the bathroom, and there are board games and old books and magazines on those shelves. Home sweet home!" Back in her kitchen, Estelle thought about her new boarder. Probably in her mid-20s, can't tell if she's bright or stupid, looks sad, not threatening. What kind of a girl would lead such a life? What does Terence see in her?

She didn't ask herself what kind of a woman would play the madam.

Freed from the hassle of having to ride to New London, Terence saw his girl twice a week, according to a pre-arranged schedule. He'd park his car in back of the house where once had stood the barn. The visits were brief – 30 to 60 minutes – and there was no chitchat either before or after. Terence kept the socializing for the weekly dinner with Estelle and Phil. He never would go down cellar that night. Every Friday evening, he would pay Estelle the negotiated amount of $70 cash.

Terence asked why she kept the girl in the cellar.

"It's more appropriate, considering what's going on. Besides, the upstairs bedroom isn't private, and we'd have to share the bathroom," Estelle replied curtly.

The girl was maintained at a minimal level of subsistence. She would be fed just enough to ward off any illness, just enough to maintain the strength required to service Terence. She would be let out only at night when Estelle walked her in the back of the house on a leash. Just enough exercise and fresh air. The only heat in the cellar was residual from the noisy furnace whose function was to heat the upstairs. There was only one room, with thin wooden flooring over the dirt floor, the granite foundation exposed, the one window covered with pink insulation. The bathroom had merely a toilet. Once a week, Estelle allowed the girl to use the upstairs bathroom to take a bath. A twin bed with a mattress that sagged, a folding card table and two garden chairs, and an old steamer trunk were the only furnishings. Estelle kept it all clean and tidy.

Phillip did pose a problem, however. He had been made to understand that the cellar girl was a secret. She was his friend. He could play checkers – his favorite game – with her, and he could feed her. But he couldn't tell anyone. Phil was very happy with his friend in the cellar and he yearned to tell someone, if only there had been someone to tell.

The captors were pleased with the arrangement, the girl didn't complain, and it probably would have continued much longer had it not been for the night when Phil nearly let the girl escape.

It was a mild night in June of 1980. Estelle was watching her favorite, *Three's Company,* when she heard her boy in the kitchen. She recognized the sound of pantry doors being opened. "Phil. What are you doing?" She waited for a reply. There was none. She heard footsteps heading down the cellar stairs. She tiptoed to the door and, bending her body nearly in half, looked down at her son and the cellar girl.

Phil had both hands on the girl's exposed breasts. There was a bottle of sherry on the table along with two teacups from the kitchen.

"Phil, you stupid boy. What do you think you are doing with that girl?" She didn't yell, but the menace conveyed by her voice was clear. Her son recoiled. The girl quickly covered herself up. The boy started whimpering like a cornered animal. The girl laughed provocatively.

The mother nearly lost her footing as she stormed down the narrow stairs. She went to the girl and slapped her fiercely. Then, she turned to Phil and pulled him up by one of his ears. "You, go kneel in that corner while I decide what I'm going to do with you."

Estelle sat on one of the lawn chairs. "I told you, Phillip, you cannot do those things to that girl."

"Well, well... Mister O'Regan does."

"You are not Mister O'Regan. And, she is not your girl." Estelle slapped her son on the side of the head. The girl winced.

"But, but, mama...she's pretty. And, I was sad."

"Shut up. Just shut the hell up. You stupid boy. You don't know anything. Just shut up, so I can think of what do to about this."

Phil started crying, sobbing loudly, tears melding with drool and dribbling to the bare floor. The girl folded herself deeply into her soft mattress and looked away.

Estelle understood what she had to do. She walked over to the old wooden trunk and pulled out a chain and a padlock and some rope. She grabbed her son and pulled him over to a large sewer pipe that dropped from the ceiling. She wrapped the chain around her son's waist and around his two hands and around the pipe and secured it all with the padlock. She placed the rusty key into the pocket of her smock and looked down at her son. "If I ever catch you playing with that girl's titties again, I will cut your hands off. You understand me, boy? I will cut them off." Phil nodded but kept on whining.

Estelle walked over to the girl and tore off the front of her dress. In a quick powerful movement, she twisted the girl's arms behind her and tied each hand to the bed frame. "You want to show him your titties, go ahead."

Triumphant, Estelle stood in the middle of the room, scowling first at her boy and then at the girl and back again. "This is how you two are going to spend the night."

Phil was still crying. "Mama. Please. Please," he pleaded.

At the head of the stairs, Estelle stopped and sent down to the cellar her final words: "Sweet dreams, children." She slammed the door and returned to her television program.

Estelle Sinclair thought she was dreaming, yet her son's voice sounded sure and clear. Phil was actually speaking to someone; it wasn't a dream. She shot up out of bed as if stung by a scorpion. Through her bedroom window she heard her boy. She heard the girl's pleading. She looked out and, through the breaking dawn, she saw the two of them sprawled out on the grass in the back yard.

"Your mother's a mean person. She's very mean," the girl kept saying. "I have to run away. You come with me."

"No. No. She'll find us. We have to go back," Phil said. "I promise I won't make her angry anymore."

"No. Please, let me go. Now! Before she wakes up."

"Too late, children," said Estelle, emerging from the shadows behind the house.

She was holding a spade across her shoulder. With a single forceful sweep, she whacked the girl on the head, the spade nearly severing it from her body. She turned to her son. She reversed the spade, using the handle to hit him repeatedly on his back and shoulders. He withdrew and she followed, hitting him again and again on the legs and stomach. The boy finally stopped, breathless and nearly lifeless.

Estelle went to the girl and saw that she was dead. She ran down to the cellar and emerged with the rope that had failed to keep the girl tied to the bed. She pulled her son across the grass and dragged him all the way to the base of an apple tree where she tied him. She thought the boy had fainted, but she tied him up anyway.

With the spade, she dug a hole inches away from the girl's body. The soil was sandy and rocky. It was hard work, but Mrs. Sinclair was no longer working with just her strength. There was new energy. It had to be done. It took time, but when the hole was deep enough, she shoved her prisoner into it and covered her up. She fetched her garden tools and raked the pebbles and stones away and spread them in the tall weeds on the edge of the yard. She evened out the bare soil to camouflage the fresh grave. In the end, she sprinkled branches and grass clippings – anything she could find – all over the yard. To make everything blend together.

She went inside, washed her hands in the kitchen sink. She did a load of laundry. She decided to take a bath and then to make coffee and toast. She went into her living room, sat down in her lounge chair and watched *The Today Show* like she did every morning.

Just before 9 o'clock, when Jane Pauley was switching over to a commercial, Estelle heard footsteps on the side porch. Looking out the window she saw her boy Phillip sitting there, and she went crazy.

"I tell you, Terence, that new manager's going to drive me crazy. He thinks this is Hartford. I tell you, he's already trying to impose his big city ideas. You should see all the paperwork …" Mister O'Regan had stopped listening to Chief White. He was concentrating on what looked like a bit of eggshell lodged in his pancake, picking at it with his fork. The police chief went on complaining about the new town manager. Larry Castonguay, the real estate agent, nodded in simulated empathy. Joining the three was Jimmy Martin, the owner of Martin's Restaurant.

"Hey, Jimmy. Don't your people in the kitchen know how to break an egg? Look at this." O'Regan pushed his plate over to the restaurateur, pointing at the eggshell.

"Oh! Thank God you found it instead of the health inspector," Jimmy replied. The remark prompted chuckles from the group – all but the police chief whose foul mood was firmly in control.

The four men met every Thursday morning for breakfast. Jimmy Martin kept a table open at the rear of the popular establishment just for them. Once in a while, someone else would join them, like Joe Gallant, the owner of the pharmacy, or Hal Gammon, the commander of the American Legion post. The men would plow through their country-style breakfasts and spend an hour or so hashing out the problems of their little town. The coffee was free as was the flow of conversation.

Chief White was still on the war path against the town manager. O'Regan felt a need to change the subject: "Hey, you guys see that new movie at the Empire, *The Shining*? Real creepy." Jimmy said he and his wife were planning to see it the next weekend. "Well, don't take the kids. It's from a Stephen King book, and Jack Nicholson plays this guy who becomes completely…" O'Regan was interrupted. The front door of the restaurant opened to let in a patrolman who cautiously made his way to the group and waited for the police chief to spot him.

"Damn. You guys know I'm off for an hour," the chief

growled.

"Sorry, sir…"

The chief joined the cop, and the two retreated to the side, and everyone in the restaurant watched and listened. In very little time, it became clear that something unusual was going on. The chief slapped his forehead like a character in an old-time movie. He backed away from the cop, paced the floor for a couple of minutes, went back to the policeman for more information, and finally tapped the cop on the shoulder and sent him on his way.

"Trouble?" asked the real estate broker as the chief returned to the breakfast group.

"Quite." Chief White grabbed his hat and stood erect. "Gentlemen, I have to leave you. I have a homicide to attend to."

"What?" said the men in unison.

"Seems like old lady Sinclair killed her retarded boy. Mutilated him, it appears."

O'Regan's jaw dropped. He swallowed some of the stale air of the eatery along with a chunk of pancake, choking on the latter. Red-faced and teary-eyed, O'Regan's mind was transported to the scene of the crime. He heard the sirens and the tires screech to a halt at the home of Estelle Sinclair. He heard the cops' voices as they stormed into her kitchen; he heard the heavy boots on the stairs to her cellar.

"Is there anybody else?"

"What do you mean?" asked the police chief.

"I mean, is there someone else involved?" O'Regan tried to erase any emotion from his voice. He faked another bout of choking. "Damn it, Jimmy, there's some more eggshells in here."

"Lemme see." The restaurant owner grabbed the plate.

O'Regan stood up. Looking at the chief, he said, "I just thought there might have been some neighbors or passers-by, or something. You know how crazy that woman can be."

"Don't know about anybody else. Officer Johnson just mentioned the boy, Phil."

"Can I go with you?"

"Sorry. This is a police matter. And, I've said too much already. There's going to be an investigation."

The three remaining members of the breakfast circle finished their food, and over the final sips of coffee speculated about the murder and its motive. "You know that kid, don't you, Terence?"

said one of them.

"He's simple and gets into trouble. I've kept an eye on him. Part of my job, you know." O'Regan wished his voice had betrayed less irritation. He pushed his chair back. "I have to go."

It took nearly two months before Mister O'Regan ventured out to the murder site. By that time the furor over the incident had died down. There had been no public funeral for Phillip Sinclair, just a simple burial in the pauper's section of the town cemetery. The trial had been brief with Estelle Sinclair pleading innocent by reason of insanity. The judge ordered her committed, and the townsfolk of Williams soon forgot about the whole thing.

Just before Labor Day, on a steamy Saturday morning, Terence Hugh O'Regan visited the grave of his cellar girl. He assumed she was buried on the property; he felt a need to pay his respects.

He had made numerous but discreet inquiries about the case, usually over breakfast with the police chief, who, with time, spoke freely about it, describing in detail how the Sinclair boy had been beaten and both his hands hacked off and tossed into the garden. O'Regan felt certain there was no evidence of his cellar girl.

O'Regan parked his car a prudent distance from the house. He walked around the boarded-up cottage slowly, examining the stone foundation, avoiding the soft soil lest it acquire his footprint. He saw nothing but abandonment. He ventured into the yard at the rear and into the garden plot on the side. The grass had grown tall in spots; elsewhere the rocky soil exposed the roots of ancient trees. Dead branches and a variety of debris littered the place. He hadn't expected a grave marker, but somehow, he had hoped for a clue. He found none. He stood silently in the stale late summer air, surrounded by decay, and wished he had seen his cellar girl one more time. To say goodbye. O'Regan convinced himself that the girl deserved a moment of respect. His eyes washed over the property, absorbing its desolation, remembering its gratification.

On his way back to the car, he noticed two lads watching him. They were seated on the curb across the street. O'Regan thought he recognized one of the boys: the Simard kid. "That kid's creepy. Wonder if he saw anything."

Without a map or a watch, Claude found it difficult to measure time or distance. He knew he was on the right highway, the North Carolina Department of Transportation having been kind enough to place Route 701 markers at regular intervals. He had no idea, however, how far his two rides of the afternoon had taken him. The last driver, a nervous tattooed guy with a pickup truck, had left Claude at a major intersection. Highway signs announced places that had no meaning. He ignored them and continued south on 701, stopping at a general store and gas station that occupied a strategic corner – a strong duplicate of Smithfield Market. He studied the refrigerator cases for the longest time, comparing prices. Orange juice was too expensive. He avoided soft drinks. He settled on a quart of milk. At the cash register, he succumbed to a banana and a Reese's. "Peanut butter's good for the traveler," he mumbled.

Outside, over the doorway, an old clock told him it was almost 6:30. Enough walking for one day. Nobody's going to pick you up anyway; nobody trusts strangers at dusk.

He left the general store and soon found himself walking along a welcoming stand of tall thin pine trees. A historical marker commemorating a Civil War battle served as a sentinel to a small rest area. Claude wandered in and selected a picnic table far into the thicket. He remembered Cal's advice: "Don't sleep on the ground. Slimy things. Critters'll lick your face." He spread his thick coat on top of a picnic table, and, using his duffle bag for a pillow, quickly fell asleep.

Hours later, his sleep was disturbed by voices. Close by, a group of men had camped out to drink and to party. Claude identified the voices as young and Southern. There was boasting about the night's conquests. A bottle was being passed around. The male voices filled the space with recklessness. Torn between his sudden thirst for alcohol and his distrust of strangers, Claude lay quietly in indecision and struggled with a wave of loneliness.

He scanned the sky and found it without stars. He fought back the urge to join the campers, allowing their voices to eventually die down. Only then did he return to sleep.

The next morning, he watched long lumber trucks pull out of the parking lot of the general store. Each one belched dark fumes as it groaned onto the roadway, turning onto the other road, the one that, according to Claude's calculations, headed east. None of them took the southerly direction on Route 701. That route – his route – was quiet, with the exception of the wind slicing the tops of the pine trees. Claude wondered how tough it would be to hitch a ride on his second day.

In a moment he would later qualify as enlightened, he decided to start a journal. A record of his perambulations, like the great explorers. He argued there would probably be no more bare walls or ceilings that cried for his paintings on this trip or at its destination, so he might attempt to express himself by writing. If Ginsberg and Kerouac could do it, why can't you give it a try? Start with a travel journal and maybe it'll turn into some poems, a novel, who knows? He returned to the rest stop and settled on the closest picnic table. He pulled from his gym bag a yellow ruled notepad Father Tony had given him along with a ballpoint pen that advertised Pelczar's Hardware.

His first lines were simple, the quick retelling of his first two rides as a hitchhiker. The middle-aged couple in the big Chrysler who didn't speak except to inform him that they had reached their destination and that he would be on his own from that point on and that they would pray for him. The young punk with tattoos all over his arms and neck with the pickup that smelled of vomit who asked him first hand if he was a pervert and for the rest of the ride couldn't stop talking about this hot girl he was on his way to fuck. Claude re-read his entry, and added:

First morning, December 7, 2007, cloudy, mild, wind high in the trees, mosquitoes at ground level.

Armed with the pride of accomplishment, even a minor one, Claude resumed his walk. His step was full of energy. This puzzled him. All that time in Philadelphia, he had felt tired and lazy, and the night on the bus had made him edgy. Here he was facing his first full day at the mercy of the road, yet he felt confident, free, audacious.

It was an hour or so later that he started noticing the roadkill.

The pavement had narrowed, and a foul-smelling swamp sandwiched the road on both sides. Claude didn't attempt to identify the first victims, but as they increased in quantity, he became curious. He braved a swarm of busy flies to kick one of the carcasses. It was unlike anything he had ever seen: too large for a beaver, perhaps a possum. He stopped poking at the dead animal and looked further up the road and saw dozens more. He wondered if the swamp was to blame, with its abundance of wildlife. He wondered if the clean-up crews were on strike, or if the prison wardens had found another way to keep the inmates busy. His mind played with the idea of an epic battle between all the varmints of the South and the highwaymen in their orange jump suits. He speculated about chain gangs. Claude had never seen one; only in the movies with Paul Newman in some prison. No chain gangs in New England, no roadkill either, not like this.

Just then a fierce memory assaulted him, and he saw himself walking along a highway in a hilly section of Rhode Island on one of the hottest days of a summer long ago. Claude was hitchhiking back home after his escape to Providence and the beaches of Narragansett. Although lean and hungry, and despite the heat his step was bouncy. He felt he had exorcized the face of Kevin Rideout. The evil of prom night was behind him, and he was going home. On a lonely segment of highway, he had spotted the dead animal and had been attracted to it. A doe, obviously struck by a motorist, was sprawled on the edge of the asphalt, its neck twisted and its haunch bloodied. Claude jumped, feeling the chill of recognition. Standing there in the July sun, he saw what he might have looked like if Kevin Rideout had succeeded. Claude's mind created the scenario: the cars crashing into each other, his body thrown out of his father's Buick, bouncing off a tree and landing with a thud on the side of Logging Road, the local cops later staring down at his broken neck and his bloodied torso.

On the edge of North Carolina Route 701, Claude yelled out to the silent swamp. "Go away, Rideout, you're the dead one, you're the roadkill, not me." Claude screamed away the bad memories of prom night and of the dead doe that had briefly brought it all back.

His eyes were now focused on one of the dead possums. He kicked it again, releasing a swarm of confused maggots. The smell of rot exploded. He felt a weakness in his limbs and a stab to his midsection. Claude vomited. Dry heaves and more dry heaves. He wiped the tears from his eyes and the sweat off his forehead.

Claude scanned the roadway and, to his relief, saw no one. For several more miles through the steamy swamp he continued on his way, switching from side to side of the highway to avoid whatever roadkill he could identify through the humid haze.

Turning to her three kids in the back seat, she told them to hush. She just might pick up that young man and give him a ride. "You kids better behave." She slowed down to get a better look and decided this one was safe. With some disbelief, Claude squeezed his gear between suitcases and grocery bags in the back of the station wagon and folded himself into the seat next to the youngsters. He was surprised to note that his new friends were Black; he had supposed that in the South, even in 2007, Black people didn't pick up white hitchhikers and vice-versa.

Ruby introduced herself and her teenage son in the front seat and her three kids in the back. She said she was on her way to Savannah to look after her sick mother and that she needed some adult conversation and she didn't care if he was white and they were Black since on the road, the Good Lord made no such distinctions.

The mother kept on talking, the son catnapping next to her, and the young'uns in the back seat staring at the passenger. There was no air conditioning in the old-model Dodge, and Claude sensed that the odors of his night in the picnic area and of the more recent vomit might be telling. Suddenly, Ruby turned to the back of the vehicle and screamed out, "Tamara, you poop again?" Looking in dismay at Claude, she added, "Hope you don't mind. I'll change her as soon as there's a good place to stop."

"No problem," Claude replied.

They talked non-stop, Ruby spilling out her entire life's story and Claude reciprocating cautiously with bits of general information. Finally, he acknowledged that he had "family issues" back home and that he was taking a break and had decided to spend the winter on the road, with Florida his ultimate destination. Ruby offered that each person has dignity, no matter what their circumstances. "The Good Lord takes care of *all* his children," she proclaimed.

She shared her philosophy of the road. Never had any problems with hitchhikers, although her mother tended to worry a lot when she was on the road, especially with the kids. "But now that I've got myself a cell phone, my mom feels better about it. As long as I check in every hour or so. Whoever invented those things…they're just wonderful, although there can be abuses, you know," she said, throwing a glance at her teenage son napping next to her. She went on to say that she avoids the interstate. "People just go too fast, they're crazy. All in a hurry, in a rush to get into an accident." She added that she actually feared the big trucks and that she got into a bad accident once because of an eighteen-wheeler. "Never got into an accident because of a hitchhiker, though."

By the time they crossed the Savannah River, Ruby and Claude had become friends. She asked him where she should drop him off and he admitted to having no special place in mind.

On the steps of Bethany Goodwill Church of Christ, Ruby's youngest children gave Claude Simard a hug. "Just avoid the drugs and the drink, and you'll be all right," were Ruby' parting words.

Claude watched her drive away before taking in this new place. "Savannah, Savannah," he sang under his breath. The word was perfect, like a breeze, like a flower. Whispered or hollered, made for song, made for poetry. He looked down the street where Ruby had left him and saw groups of people strolling and, in the distance, a leafy enclave of a park. It was near dark and the atmosphere was heavy and pungent.

II

God Rest Ye
Merry Gentlemen

The little girls ran into the den screaming with one voice: *"Pépére, pépére, pépére."* Raymond Champagne turned away from his television set where some analyst for NBC was bestowing frontrunner status on Barack Obama.

"Look at me. Look at me," said one of the girls.

"No, *pépére*, look at *me*," said the other, pushing her sister out of the way.

The granddaughters nudged each other as they invaded the sanctuary that Raymond had created in a new wing nestled between the dining room and the garage. Their shrieks drowned out the voice of the man on television.

"Now, now, girls, leave your grandfather alone," said their mother as she caught up to them. "I'm sorry, Dad," she offered. "I know you want to watch the news in peace."

"Don't worry," he interrupted. "Nobody knows who's going to win; it's just October. There's a whole year to go. Anything can happen." With that, Raymond clicked the remote, and the television screen went blank. He pulled himself out of the cradling comfort of his wingback.

"Now, what can I do for you young ladies?" The teacher in Raymond took over, and within seconds, he had calmed the youngsters. Taking the oldest by the arms, he pulled her gently to him. "Well, who are you dressed up as tonight?" he said with exaggeration.

"A pirate, *pépére*, can't you tell?"

"Of course. A pirate," he said, casting a quizzical look at the girl's mother.

"Don't look at me. It was her idea. And you know when this one gets an idea into her head, there's no way around it." The mother was tempted to add a comment about stubbornness being a trait that skips generations.

"And you?" he said, turning his attention to the younger granddaughter. "Don't tell me, don't tell me. Why, you're Tinkerbelle aren't you?"

"Yes, *pépére*." The little girl glowed, and her grandfather pulled her into him for a big hug.

"Did you go trick-or-treating when you were a little boy, *pépére*?" the older girl asked, refusing to be left out.

"Of course, your grandfather went trick-or-treating."

"Who did *you* dress like when you were a little boy?" one of the girls asked.

Equally surprised by the question and the swiftness of his recollection, he started telling them about his sixth grade Halloween experience. "That year, the nuns in my school wanted us to dress like saints, and I decided to go as St. Louis of France, the Crusader King."

"Who's that?" the girls cried out in unison.

"Oh. You're too young to know him. But he was a very important man in the old days."

"Older than you, *pépére*?"

Raymond laughed heavily. "I'm only going to be 60 my next birthday. St. Louis lived hundreds of years before me."

The mother stepped in. "Come on, girls, time to go. It's just about to get dark. And, we don't want to stay out too late, do we?" She scooped up the two little ones and ushered them out of the den.

"Bye, bye, *pépére*. Happy Halloween," the girls yelled.

Raymond could hear them all the way down the hallway and beyond, deep into the kitchen, and finally out into the dusk. He slid himself into the familiar folds of his chair and took pleasure in the returning solitude. He turned off his reading lamp and lazed in the setting that he had created over the years. Through a wide bay window, a streetlight cast a warm glow on walls covered with gentle landscapes alternating with diplomas and framed theater posters. His antique mahogany desk occupied nearly half of the room. Its top betrayed his obsession with neatness and organization: a few choice books between windjammer bookends, a desk set displaying his favorite Montblanc pens, one solitary file folder positioned in the exact center of the leather inlaid surface, closed and waiting for the scholar to review its contents. The décor replicated perfectly the mood, the tastes, the propensities, the life of Raymond Champagne, lover of the theater, connoisseur of fine art, principal of Packers Falls Junior High School, husband, father, grandfather.

Sister Rose cleared her throat and used the voice of authority she nurtured during her 35 years as a nun: "Next week is All Saints Day. Does everyone understand what that means?" Her eyes ran up and down her classroom, stopping just long enough on each student to make sure they were paying attention. "And what are Catholic boys and girls supposed to do?" she asked. "They do not go running around the streets dressed up as monsters and devils." As she answered her own question, Sister Rose inspected the faces of her students and gave herself permission to record a moment of pleasure. She liked to see confusion in the eyes of her pupils. It was a trick of hers: you sow doubt and you erase it. "Of course, I am referring to Halloween," she announced. "The first day of November is All Saints Day and the day before is Halloween. The former is a Christian holy day and the latter is a pagan feast." She was fully launched into her lesson. She enjoyed using the *former* and the *latter* juxtaposition. Because this was religion class didn't mean she couldn't teach proper English at the same time. Standing in front of the chalk board, she turned away from the students to write two words: *good* and *holy*.

"Now, students, we all know why we have such a day as All Saints Day, do we not?" Sister Rose searched for some nods of recognition and found very few. She went on, "The Church teaches that we must revere the saints, and since there are so many, there are saints who do not have their own day, so the Church has given us a day to venerate them all: All Saints Day." She pronounced the last three words as if reading from an invisible proclamation, giving a strong emphasis to each one. "All Saints Day," she repeated. She scanned her classroom. She sensed that her pupils were about to cross that boundary between acceptance and boredom. She picked up the chalk and wrote two more words on the blackboard: *pagan* and *evil*.

Walking to the front of her desk, she explained. "Halloween

comes from ancient pagan practices. Ignorant peasants, fearing the approach of the cold and darkness of winter, would build bonfires and throw in the bones of slaughtered livestock and would dance around wearing hideous masks to scare away the evil spirits." She gave her account as much drama as she could. She knew she had captivated the wandering minds of her students. They liked scary stories.

The sixth graders at Notre Dame School in Packers Falls, New Hampshire, had never heard that account of the Halloween story. They were much more familiar with the 1959 version of Trick or Treat. Most of them had already carved their pumpkin, their moms had stocked up on extra candy from the A&P, and some had started talking about whom they'd be trick-or-treating with and where they'd go. Hardly anyone had thought about costumes: that was always a last minute rush to Woolworths, and a frantic rummaging through closets and attics back home to find whatever was funny or scary.

"Now, students, have we not gone beyond that kind of ignorance and witchery? Are we not more enlightened? And, as good Catholics, should we not avoid all form of superstition?" Sister Rose's questions were unanimously greeted with nods. Most of the students figured out where she was headed. A few of them had their curiosity piqued just enough to be irked; they wanted to hear more about the pagans and their rituals, not about what good Catholics should do. Many in the class started slipping into a cozy reverie, maintaining for Sister Rose just enough of a facade to keep her happy.

Suzanne went into a daydream about getting a Barbie Doll for her birthday, realizing she was too old for dolls but unable to avoid the frenzy around the new toy that was so adult and so glamorous. Marcel, the altar boy, was thinking of the upcoming trip to Manchester to see the movie Ben-Hur, a reward Father Couture had promised the Mass servers. Jimmy's eyes looked beyond the long dark dress and stiff headgear of the woman at her desk and instead recreated the pictures of Earth that Explorer VI was transmitting from space. Jimmy wanted to be an astronaut and he wanted to tell Sister Rose that good Catholics should all want to go into space because that's where God is.

The nun suspected she might be losing her audience. "So, I repeat. Catholic boys and girls do not run around the streets dressed up like monsters and devils." On the blackboard, she circled her first set of words, *good* and *holy*, and she traced a large X in broad strokes over the words *pagan* and *evil*. Proud of her exposition and its accompanying visual aids, she took a deep breath and stood silently for a moment allowing the strength of her thesis to sink in.

Finally, she leaned back towards her desk and picked up a stack of mimeographed papers. She then started passing out a few sheets to the first person in each row with a gesture of her hand that was clearly an instruction to keep one copy and to pass on the rest. Like a wave in reverse, Sister Rose's mimeographed sheets flowed to the back of the room as she explained that she had prepared a list of saints – suggestions for boys and suggestions for girls – saints who could inspire costumes for Halloween.

As she read from her list, the nun held up an illustration for each saint, painstakingly collected from a variety of sources. She had started her catalog with the more famous saints: St. Patrick, St. Francis of Assisi, St. Joan of Arc. There were more modern saints as well: the Mohawk maiden Kateri Tekakwitha, and the models of piety and purity, St. Maria Goretti for the girls and St. Dominic Savio for the boys, among many others. "Now, students, I will give you time to review the list and choose your saint. You can come to me if you have any questions." Sister Rose spent a moment basking in self-appointed authority. She absentmindedly patted the silver crucifix suspended from a chain around her neck, drawing comfort from its familiarity and its proximity to her bosom.

The kids' reactions to the list of saints ranged from bewilderment to disinterest.

Suzanne still thought of her Barbie Doll, Marcel couldn't wait to see Ben-Hur, and Jimmy remained fascinated by space travel. No one paid attention to Cathy who was staring out the window at the naked tree limbs, or to Tommy who decided it was time to tie his shoe. Coughing and shuffling broke the silence that greeted Sister Rose's invitation to select a saint. The classroom took on the sepia tone of suspension in which movement slowed, the air languished, and everyone waited for something and for nothing. The teacher hadn't expected anyone to jump at her suggestion of saints' names. She knew how to plant a seed. She had been teaching long enough to recognize that a response from students could be late in coming. That's why she had brought it up more than a week before October 31ˢᵗ. She would wait a day or two. She would bring it up again and she knew there would be some takers. The work of the Lord took patience.

The bell rang through the corridors and sixteen nuns and their students waited for the shrill metallic echoes to subside before simultaneously reciting the Our Father and the customary supplications to Our Lady and the Sacred Heart. The school day had come to a close.

Sister Rose arranged her books and papers as her classroom emptied. When she looked up, there was only one student left, the smartest lad in the class, and also the most quiet and reserved. Raymond Champagne stood rigidly in front of her, and in his characteristically low voice, said: "I've chosen my saint, *ma soeur*. I will be *Saint Louis de France*. I will be the Crusader King."

"Oh!" Sister Rose was caught off guard. "That is a very interesting choice, Raymond." She hesitated; she hadn't expected anyone to follow her instructions so quickly. Nor would she have thought of the saintly king of France. She felt a bit of annoyance at that, and at the student's showy use of French. "You will be certain to let me know if I can be of any assistance, young man," she added in a tone that carried a heavy measure of formality.

"That won't be necessary, *ma soeur*. But thank you anyway. I can manage nicely," he said to her. They gave each other a polite smile, the kind of tribute that individuals give when they understand that a certain level of parity has been attained.

Raymond was well ahead of Sister Rose. He had already decided that for the Halloween of 1959, he would assume the identity of St. Louis. It had nothing to do with his sainthood or what good Catholic boys should be doing. It was all about being different, being heroic and spectacular. It was in the sixth grade that Raymond discovered his love of the theater, and he decided his Halloween persona would be his stage debut. The costume was elaborate, and it took several afternoons and weekends to work on it, his mother a befuddled accomplice, his father an amused spectator. Mr. Champagne would have preferred that his son spend more time with gadgets and inventions. His first choice would have been for his son to become an engineer like himself;

an architect was his second choice. As he realized that his son's talents were more artistic, and that the stage was where – even at the age of 12 – he was determined to make his mark, the elder Champagne convinced himself that set design and stage lighting required some of the manly technical skills he so admired. He hoped fervently, however, that his son would veer away from acting. Mrs. Champagne had no opinion. She loved her little Raymond and she knew he was smart and that he would do only good and great things with his life.

Raymond emptied all the trunks and storage boxes in the attic, and when that didn't prove promising, he invaded the closets. There he found a glittery sweater dress his mother had purchased for a New Year Eve's bash some years before. It was silver lamé and could easily pass for a knight's mail coat. A white sheet, cut and stitched, with a red cross carefully painted on the front and rear panels, turned the knight into a crusader. A tall shield made of silver-painted pieces cut out of packaging materials from his father's factory, and a dime store crown completed the outfit. Raymond would have liked a sword at his waist but in the end, he decided there was no time to make one. Besides, he didn't want his St. Louis to look menacing as much as edifying.

Before leaving the house, Raymond stood in full costume in front of the floor-to-ceiling mirror in the foyer. Both parents, silent acolytes for the final inspection, stood to one side. His older brother, aloof and snooty, was watching television in the living room. At fifteen, he was too old for Halloween, a fact he made abundantly clear. Mr. Champagne enlisted his services, dragging him from the living room and placing the family Brownie in his hands and instructing him on its use.

"Stand still, Raymond. Look at your brother and smile," said his father. Flanked by both father and mother, the young King Louis refused to smile for the camera. If the moment was to be memorialized, he wanted his King Louis to look serious.

"Raymond, what are you going to put your candy in?" his mother asked in a voice that carried too much drama for the occasion.

"Good question," chimed in his dad. "You need something. And, I suppose the plastic pumpkin you used last year wouldn't work with this," he added, waving his hand up and down next to his son as he said the word *this*.

Raymond agreed with them, but he had no solution. A trace of doubt crossed the forehead of the Crusader King. His mother left the room and returned a minute later with a large leather pouch. "Here, use this," she said, handing him one of her old handbags. Raymond inspected the item: it was plain brown leather and had a long strap. He draped it over his shoulder behind his shield.

"That should work," said his father. "Ok. Looks to me like we're ready to go."

Mr. Champagne drove his son a few blocks to a quiet, respectable neighborhood, and Raymond started his Halloween night under the safety of Victorian street lamps and leafy elm overhangs about to turn golden. The night was mild for the end of October, and the atmosphere was heavy with the odor of burnt leaves. Raymond couldn't have asked for a better stage. He marched from house to house, ringing doorbells and knocking gently, smiling at the polite greetings, and graciously accepting compliments and treats.

He was oblivious to the other boys and girls scampering about. He didn't hear the snickers of the three boys dressed as cowboys who had stopped across the street to face him. "Hey, you. Who are you? Prince Valiant?" yelled one of them. Raymond looked at the cowboys and noticed that the tallest was in a Lone Ranger costume – dashing black mask and tight silver pants – and Raymond directed his answer at him.

"Ah, masked bandit, I am St. Louis, King of France, leader of the Seventh and the Eighth Crusades," he said in the most regal voice he could muster. "At your service," he added as he bowed and bent his knee. From across the street the cowboys laughed loudly, then, distracted by a band of kids dressed as Indians, started running after them, hollering into the night.

Unaware that he might have been spared, Raymond decided to continue on course. He attempted to get off his knee and in so doing lost his balance and, using his makeshift shield for support, broke it in half before falling to the ground. Sitting on the sidewalk, he felt grateful for the lack of an audience. Some of his treats had spilled from the leather hand bag that to Raymond now looked exactly what it was: a purse. He quickly picked himself up and decided to draw the curtain on his Halloween. His father was waiting in the car exactly where they had agreed to rendezvous. Wordlessly, they drove home.

The father manned the grill with the same fervor he would have used to design a machine gun. Arthur Champagne faced it squarely, his legs apart, his eyes focused. Just enough charcoal in just the right formation, with forks and tongs and spatulas lined up like tools, the cooler ready and waiting with the hamburger patties, the hot dogs, the American cheese slices, the rolls and buns. The grill was brand new, as was the flagstone covered patio, and the house itself, a spacious ranch on an oversized lot, purchased two months before in the best and newest neighborhood in town. While waiting for the coals to fire up, father and son were catching up.

"So that's the girl you're going to marry," Arthur said to his son.

"Yes, in one week we're going to embark on the path to holy wedlock."

"Finally. Thirty years old and just about to tie the knot."

"Well, you know, it's going to be a lifetime, so what's the rush?" the son said, barely hiding his annoyance.

"Then we should have our father-son talk. I mean, about your wedding night..." The older man poked his son in the ribs and laughed.

"Arthur, you don't have to worry. I've read the manual."

Raymond Champagne started addressing his father by his Christian name when he turned 14. The same with his mother who ceased to be *ma* and became Ruth. The parents were confused at first but they came to accept it as one more sign of their son's independence and uniqueness.

The year 1977 was turning out to be a year of firsts for the Champagne family: a promotion for Arthur at the ammunitions factory, the brand new house, and Raymond's wedding.

Arthur told his son to watch the coals while he went into the house for a beer. He didn't offer one to his son. Raymond didn't drink. The younger Champagne had no idea what he was supposed to be watching for. His older brother was playing catch with his two little boys. His sister-in-law, his mother, and his bride to be were sitting in a tight circle at the edge of the flower garden. Picture perfect! A Rockwellian moment framed by the young trees in the background swaying gently in the New Hampshire summer breeze.

He focused on his pretty fiancée. A few months older than him, Jane Tracy was also a teacher at Lake Street Elementary. For seven years they had known each other. Raymond squinted as the sun split two menacing clouds and banished them from the scene. He switched the characters in the tableau and saw himself and Jane some thirty years later at their back yard barbecue with their children and grandchildren gathered around for their own pretty moment.

"What weighs on your mind?" asked the elder Champagne, beer in hand.

"Oh. Nothing. Just admiring the place."

"Go ahead. Admire it. You'll never be able to afford something like this on your teacher's salary."

Raymond made believe he didn't hear. He took a few steps off the patio and hesitated. Where to go? He didn't care to play catch with his brother and nephews and he couldn't see himself joining the ladies' circle. So he sat on one of the Adirondacks and mulled over his fathers' last comment. It was always about money: the lack of it for so long, and finally its abundance and what it could buy. He didn't blame his father. He worked hard all those years, commuting through winters, never complaining, and finally being promoted head of the engineering department. He earned the right to show off.

The coals had reached the desired heat and the hot dogs and hamburgers were grilling to perfection. Arthur called to his wife to set the picnic table and announced that in five minutes everyone could eat.

Long after the meal was over and several beers later, father and son were left to themselves facing each other at the picnic table.

"Jane reminds me of your mother."

"Really, in what way?"

"Pretty. Quite pretty... and she knows how to use it."

"I never saw Ruth as pretty."

"You're not supposed to."

"And, what do you mean: she knows how to use it?"

"Not sure exactly. But, I can see it… and you'll find out."

The two men picked at their slices of blueberry pie, a contribution to the meal from Jane.

"She makes a good pie," said Arthur.

"She bought it."

"Hum, looks home made." The father took a long swig of his Bud. "That's what I mean," he added, wiping his lips with the back of his hand. "Looks are deceiving. That's how it is with women."

"What in the world are you talking about, Arthur? I've never heard you talk like this before."

"Well, maybe it's about time. You need to know these things. Women, as a species, are dangerous. I've always said that the world would be better off without them. Of course – and here I'm speaking as an engineer –we need them to procreate. But there again, I can think of more efficient ways of having babies."

"What?" Raymond was both offended and fascinated.

"It's just that women are messy. In every way. Their bodies are just messy, and so's their thinking. They're just messy. You'll see."

"This is absurd."

"You'll see," he repeated, stretching the *ee* in the last word. "I've always believed that the world would be better off without 'em." He finished his beer. "I prefer men."

Raymond pushed himself back from the picnic table in sheer shock. "Arthur, do you know what you're saying? You *prefer* men?"

"Oh. That doesn't sound right does it? I mean I'd rather work with men. I'm more comfortable around a bunch of guys. Women bore me. Some of them irritate me."

"Are you talking about my mother?"

"No. All women. But her too. And, your little angel of a bride. You'll see."

"Arthur, you've had too much beer, or it's the fumes from the charcoal, or something. Just stop talking foolishness."

"Talking foolishness, the exact words your mother uses." Arthur took a deep breath. "You'll see."

Raymond stood up abruptly and started gathering the paper plates and used plastic. He refused to continue the conversation, so he kept busy cleaning up. Raymond's brother and sister-in-law were packing up their kids and gear and braced themselves for hugs and goodbyes. His mother and his fiancée, arm over arm, walked up to the house and announced they were going to review wedding plans. Raymond felt a flood of panic. He tried to decide which scared him the most: his upcoming wedding or being left alone with his father.

The glare of headlights invaded the den. Raymond turned on the lamp and the television, settling on *Wheel of Fortune*. It was his wife's favorite show; his was *Jeopardy* that immediately followed. A good compromise, he thought.

Jane was home. The snug harbor of his den had vanished, replaced by the week-night routine: cocktails and tidbits in the living room, a light supper in the kitchen, reading and paper work, the late news, and finally, Jay Leno who usually had both Mr. and Mrs. Champagne nodding in their respective chairs. That had become the theater that referenced Raymond's life as he approached his sixtieth birthday.

Whatever had become of the life he had promised himself as a youngster? His devotion to making magic on the stage, not as an actor, but as one who designed the sets, who framed the décor, and arranged the lighting, everything so that actors and musicians could effectively enchant their audiences, where had it all gone?

That was the life he enjoyed during his high school and college years. The best years of his life, he freely admitted. But necessity reared its proverbially ugly head, and he settled on a teaching career. He returned to New Hampshire for graduate school and quickly landed a teaching job in his home town. He told himself countless times that he abandoned the stage because of his obligations to family and community. On occasion, however, usually in a dark moment heavy with monotony, he acknowledged he left the theater because the large venues, the competitive cities, the desperate cast of characters had become frightening. There was boredom in Packers Falls, but there was also ease and safety.

"You missed the girls in their costumes," Raymond said to his wife between bites of leftover pot roast.

"I know. I'm sorry. I couldn't leave work. We were so busy, and my replacement was late." Jane sounded tired. It had been a long day at the new Walgreen's. Every kid in town and their mothers needed some last minute something for Halloween.

"Our oldest granddaughter was dressed like a pirate, would you believe?"

"Really?"

Raymond wasn't sure if Jane was interested. "The little one was Tinkerbelle."

"I'm sure they were both adorable. Too bad I wasn't here."

Jane picked up the empty plates and went to the sink.

"Here. Let me do that. Let me clean up. You look tired. Go. Go sit down."

Jane walked to the living room. "Thanks," she said.

Jane the math teacher, not exceptional, but well-liked by faculty and students, had retired that spring and, after her "summer of insouciance" as Raymond called it, went to work as a part-time cashier at the drug store. She complained about the job, especially about being on her feet so much, but she seemed to thrive. Raymond concluded that Jane was better with customers than with students, especially unruly ninth and tenth graders. And, her evenings were now free. What happened at work stayed at work; she brought none of it home. Raymond envied her for that.

While Jay Leno was interviewing Russell Crowe about his latest film, Raymond watched his wife yield to a catnap. He examined the woman in the matching chair just a few feet from him. Jane was still pretty. Flashes from the television screen reflected in her eyeglasses resting on the bridge of her nose. A book was on her lap, open in the middle, the cover displayed upside down. Raymond leaned over to read the title, *The DaVinci Code,* and he smiled the smile of condescension. Jane loved a good page turner, especially a mystery, one that flirted with historical personages.

It was a subject of amazement how deeply his wife could fall asleep. He listened for the snoring that normally should accompany that kind of sleep, but heard none. His wife was aging more gracefully than him: still trim with a healthy complexion, her hair always cut short in a way that made her look younger. He, to the contrary, looked all of his soon-to-be 60 years. Just enough excess weight around the midsection, not enough of his graying hair left on top of his head, and much too much worrying about growing old leaving tell-tale trails all over his face and neck.

Raymond decided to abandon his nightly rendezvous with self-pity and, moving closer to his wife, carefully removed the book from her lap. "Let's go to bed, honey," he whispered to her.

Jane stirred, stretched a hand that had become numb, pulled herself up to the front of her chair, and looked at Raymond. He saw the query fill her eyes and then quickly vanish. He smiled at her, and she nodded.

One hour later, Jane was sleeping soundly in their bed with her husband inches away lying on his back, his eyes wide open, his mind speculating on what other turns his life could have taken.

The rest area looked empty. Ray was relieved; he liked it that way. He drove in slowly, his eyes scouring the landscape. It was a very pleasant spot, the terrain typical of the foothills of northern New England: strong granite outcrops, tall blue spruces, shorter green pines, slender white birches. In autumn, leaves blanketed the vistas in red and gold, and during the warm days of spring and summer, a profusion of wild flowers grew in the sunlight on the edge of a stream that flowed pure and ample. An assortment of birds and small foragers made it their habitat.

It had been his father's favorite place, the elder Champagne droning about the juxtaposition of order and haphazardness in nature. Ray had enjoyed countless afternoons there with his parents and brother picnicking and wading in the cool stream, playing pirate games, impersonating explorers and discoverers. Ray had no idea where the spot was located; his father did the driving, and the lad paid no attention to the roadways. It had an official name – Rest Area N-44 – that figured on some map at the Department of Transportation in Concord. Despite the name, there was no sign at the entrance, and the majority of motorists on rural Route 16 zipped by without noticing it.

He had started visiting the spot early that summer after an absence of several decades. On an excursion one day with no specific purpose or destination in mind, Ray found himself on Route 16 and noticed a roadway to the side which brought immediate recognition. As he drove into the rest area, all the memories of the happy picnics came to the surface. Finding it had been a surprise, a welcome benchmark during a season of disquiet and moroseness. Somehow, man had done very little to harm the place over the years. Gone were the picnic tables and benches, but the spot was well maintained, with metal trash containers here and there, and new grass on the banks of the stream.

During an early visit, while walking near the water, Ray saw another vehicle drive in and was surprised by his resentment of the intrusion. The driver slowed his car as he passed by and gave Ray a wave. He watched the vehicle climb to an overlook and stop next to another car. Ray continued his tour of inspection, going down to the edge of the stream and recognizing the ledge from which he and his brother dove into the cold water. Returning to his Subaru Outback, he noticed that the other two visitors, both of them men, were standing next to each other seemingly having a conversation. Moments later, the two cars left the rest area, one following the other closely.

On his way back home, Raymond Champagne realized that his rest area might have become a magnet for something he would rather not think about. Two weeks later, Ray was back at Rest Area N-44. After a few more visits, he had no doubt that gay men were using the place to rendezvous. At first, Ray simply observed. He started recognizing the same vehicles and the same faces. Many of the men never left their cars. They talked to each other through open windows. Then one would drive off, and another would leave right behind him. Sometimes, after an initial conversation, one of the men would join another in his car. At other times, someone would wander off into the adjoining woods. Each time Ray drove into the rest area, his first thought was that perhaps this time he would have the place all to himself, and that he could enjoy the peacefulness of the spot, a shrine to happier innocent days. His second thought was that perhaps this time he would have the courage to participate in whatever presented itself.

On the first Saturday of December in 2007, Ray drove his car to the highest level, a flat expanse of ground covered with crushed stone that offered a glimpse of the White Mountains to the north. The trees were naked, and Ray maneuvered his car so he could take advantage of the view. In that position, he could also spot anyone who might drive into the rest area. The day was remarkably warm for December. The sky over the distant mountains carried just enough pink and amber to turn it mysterious, and the low angle of the sun created shapes and shadows that Ray had never seen before. He rolled down the windows, allowing the mountain air to flow through. He glanced at his watch. Only eleven-thirty, plenty of time before he had to return home. He had brought a book, but he decided not to read. Instead, he filled his lungs with fresh air and listened to the wind as it rustled through piles of dead leaves. His eyes followed the naked lines of the branches up into the sky and he thought of the set he designed back in college for Becket's *Waiting for Godot*.

The rumbling sound of a heavy vehicle interrupted his reverie. He spotted a pickup truck below and reacted with a mixture of irritation and panic as he realized the vehicle was climbing to his level. Ray watched out of the corner of his eye as the driver positioned the pick-up next to his car, no more than four feet away. What's the idea? A dozen parking spaces and this guy has to snuggle up to me? The driver of the pickup truck gave his accelerator a final push, and the engine crashed through the silence with a roar that stated: *Here I am*. Ray avoided looking in the direction of his new neighbor, a battle raging inside him between curiosity and self-preservation. He heard the door of the pickup open and then slam shut with a bang that made him jump. He heard footsteps, heavy and deliberate. Finally he looked. His body temperature rose a degree and his heart leaped. The driver appeared to be in his early 40s, tall with wide shoulders.

"Quite the view up here." The man's voice, loud and authoritative, commanded Ray to respond. He resisted and watched his neighbor lean back against the pickup truck. The man stretched his arms up and, forming a *V* with them, placed his hands behind his neck and arched his back. Ray was sure he could hear the man's bones creak and his muscles moan. The neighbor walked towards Ray and stopped halfway between the two vehicles. "Love that view. I could live up here and never get bored."

Ray wasn't sure what that was supposed to mean and he didn't care. The theatrical component of his brain was taking over, and Ray allowed himself to admire the truck driver's outfit: red plaid shirt, rolled up sleeves, dungarees just tight enough, sturdy work boots. The perfect stage lumberjack. Right out of *Seven Brides for Seven Brothers* or maybe the missing member of *The Village People*.

"It *is* a great view. That's for sure," Ray said, hating once again the weakness of his timbre.

"Nice day to be here. Record breaking highs for this time of year."

"Right. I don't remember it this warm in December."

The conversation had started. The lumberjack look-alike turned to face the Subaru, looking straight at its lone occupant.

Even with the windows down, Ray was sweating.

The lumberjack – Paul is what Ray named him in his mind, after Paul Bunyan – stepped to the edge of the parking lot. "Nice and quiet up here. Just you and me," the lumberjack yelled back to Ray. He walked towards Ray's car and stopped next to the open window. He leaned downward and extended his right hand. "Name's Paul, by the way," he said, clearly expecting a handshake in return.

"No kidding," Ray's words gushed out. "I'm sorry. Of course, you're not kidding," he said as he grabbed the extended hand.

"Why would I kid? That's my name," Paul responded.

"Of course not. I didn't mean anything."

Paul pulled his hand away. Ray couldn't take his eyes off the width of the hand and how it blended perfectly into his muscular forearm.

"And your name is…"

"Ah… Mike," replied Ray.

Paul nodded and, pulling back slightly, stood erect, his feet firmly planted on the crushed stones of the parking lot, his legs spread apart just enough. He rocked himself back and forth in a deliberately slow cadence.

"So, Mike, you come up here a lot?"

Ray didn't hear the question. He was captivated by the man's posture and movements. He saw beyond the brusqueness of the lumberjack and contemplated the muscular athlete, the Olympian, the dancer. Ray's breathing was laborious. His mouth was dry, yet he was wet all over with perspiration. He could hear the thumping of his heart like the timpani of a major orchestra.

"It's a great place. Can get pretty active, though," Paul said.

Ray had no idea what to say next. What's he talking about? Does he mean what I think he means? Damn it, how come I've never seen him before? He scoped the parking area, knowing full well it was empty, but needing confirmation. Does he want to have sex? Is that it? No, no. I can't do this, damn it. Ray avoided looking at Paul. I really can't do this.

"Sorry, I have to go." Ray wasn't sure what he was saying but he welcomed the release of his words. He pulled out of his parking spot and headed for the exit. Picking up speed, the car sent up a burst of dry gravel as it rejoined Route 16.

He raced south towards Packers Falls, his eyes focused on the road but his mind wandering at high speeds and in unchartered territory. You really can't do this. You don't want to do this, damn it. Maybe I do. No. No. Damn it, you're almost 60 years old, the principal of a junior high 20 miles down the road. You're married; you have a daughter, granddaughters. It's foolish. It's dangerous. It'll destroy you. What exactly is *it*. We're just talking. It's a public place. Why can't two men talk to each other in a rest area on a fine day? What's wrong with that?

Moments later, Ray was heading back to the rest area. He forced himself to focus on the positive thoughts. Nothing wrong with two guys having a conversation. As he drove in, part of him hoped Paul would be gone and when he spotted the pick-up truck he started sweating again. You're just going to talk. That's all.

Paul smiled broadly and stepped out of his vehicle. "Forget something?" he asked.

"Thanks for coming to my rescue".

"Well, that's what the Lone Ranger does," Jimmy replied.

Raymond didn't laugh, but he appreciated his friend's humor. The two – Raymond Champagne and Jimmy Cavanaugh, Attorney James Cavanaugh – were driving back to Rest Area N-44. It was getting late. The booking at the Sheriff's Office in Rochester had taken more than two hours.

"I didn't know who else to call."

"That's ok. I was just watching a game at home. Not really doing anything."

Silence filled the lawyer's SUV for most of the ride back to the rest area. Neither of the two had found a way of conversing. Catching up or chatting about nothing would have been too artificial; talking about what just happened would have been too awkward. Having turned the radio on, Jimmy made believe he was interested in the UNH football game that Raymond's phone call had interrupted. The December afternoon had remained unseasonably warm, and even though the sun was failing quickly, the two friends were still in shirtsleeves, and the SUV windows were partially down.

Jimmy and Raymond knew each other since grammar school. Jimmy had recognized the kid wearing the crusader outfit. During lunch break, Jimmy had gone over and introduced himself as the

Lone Ranger, the kid who was trick-or-treating on the same street Halloween night. They kept in touch throughout high school, calling each other Lone Ranger and King Louis. Over the years, in a variety of social and business situations in Packers Falls, the two often bumped into each other.

"Where's your car?"

"Up there." Raymond pointed in the direction of the winding roadway leading to the upper lot.

There were four cars in the picnic area; two of them near the stream, and two up where the State Trooper had forced Raymond to leave his car. "That's the one, the blue Subaru Outback." Jimmy nodded, parked his vehicle next to it and turned off the engine. The two friends sat quietly, watching the sky over the White Mountains turn dark purple. Suddenly, they concluded – at about the same time and with the same start – that sitting there was not the best thing to do.

"Well thanks again, Jimmy," Raymond said as he opened the car door.

"Listen, Raymond. You can fight this, you know."

"I wouldn't know how."

"These sting operations are very controversial. Lots of people think they're wrong. They can have tragic consequences, like in Vermont last year when police arrested a bunch of men in a rest area and one of them turned out to be the fire chief and the arrest was so devastating that he wound up hanging himself." Jimmy immediately regretted sharing the information.

"Look. I know you won't do anything that foolish. This isn't the end. I strongly suggest that you make a record. When you get home, make some notes. Write down everything."

Raymond's mind quickly reviewed his afternoon. Closeted gay man goes to rest area, meets handsome seducer, opens his pants up for seducer who turns into a cop and arrests closeted gay man. "I got one" is what he heard the cop say in his cell phone calling in a patrol car to assist. Raymond kept repeating the three words to himself: I got one...I got one...like the stalker, the hunter. I got one.

Jimmy continued, "I mean it. You have to document every little detail about the event. What he did, what you did..."

"I know what I did, Jimmy," Raymond replied testily. "I know what I did," he repeated. "And, tomorrow morning or the day after, everybody in town will know what I did. Look, Jimmy. It's a small town, everybody knows everybody. And, I'm the principal of the junior high, damn it. This isn't going to go away."

"Ok. You may be right. But you can still fight it. There's some redemption in that. You shouldn't just roll over and play dead."

"Why not? My life *is* over."

Jimmy had nothing left to say. He watched his friend get out of the car and head towards his own vehicle. He could see the finality, the gloom in his step.

"Don't do anything foolish. Try to stay calm. Just stay put for the rest of the weekend. We'll talk Monday. I know a lawyer who has experience with this. He can help. You and I will talk before the arraignment, Ok?"

Raymond unlocked his car door.

"Ok? Raymond... Ok?"

"Yes, Jimmy. Ok."

Raymond started the Outback. He didn't pull away. He opened his door and, sticking his head out, started yelling at the occupants of the other cars in the rest area. "You guys better get out of here. This is a trap. You never know who's in the car next to you."

The driver of one of the vehicles turned on his headlights. Two of the cars down below rolled out of the rest area. Stretching his torso out of his open door, Raymond shaded his eyes from the glare of the headlights. Defiantly, he faced the unknown driver and held up his middle finger, a gesture he realized at that moment he had never used his entire life.

Twenty miles later, Raymond stood inside his garage on the quiet street where he lived peacefully for so many years. He inspected the space, noting how clean and unencumbered it was. None of those manly things like tools or fishing poles or baseball bats.

His wife's car was there, but the house was dark. Probably at a neighbor's, or out for a walk. He didn't care. On the return trip to Packers Falls, Raymond Champagne reached a decision. Jane would have no say in his decision. Her absence would only make it easier. He was leaving. He wasn't staying. He wasn't waiting to see the looks of pity and mockery. He wouldn't be there for the recriminations. "If this is to be a final curtain call, I won't be here to see it," he had yelled out on the ride home.

Raymond acted swiftly. He showered, he put on warm clothes, he filled a suitcase, he took all the cash he knew was in the house, he left his keys to home and school on the kitchen counter, and returned to his car.

Downtown, he stopped at two ATMs and withdrew the maximums. Ten minutes later, he turned onto the southbound ramp of I-95. It was 6:45 p.m. on Saturday, December 8th, 2007, and Raymond Champagne said goodbye to Packers Falls, New Hampshire, for good.

Sandra chose her table cautiously. She liked sitting in a booth, the tall upholstered back giving her a feeling of security, but on this rainy Saturday night, they were all taken. Umbrellas and raingear were scattered all over Lucky's Diner, giving the eatery's already heavy air an extra layer of humidity. Sandra scanned the oversized menu, then dismissively returned it to its metal holder. She decided to order her usual, grilled cheese sandwich with a tall ice tea, and she would linger over it. She would sip her drink and avoid Lucky's glare. Reigning over his Formica domain from behind the counter with the cash register and the extra menus, Lucky knew what she was up to, and, on a busy Saturday night, his already low level of tolerance could evaporate easily.

"Your usual, deary?" asked Amy, a veteran waitress of 20 years. Amy had a strong back and a strong memory. She knew her customers' likes and dislikes. She remembered their family stories, their tragedies and their conquests, which left little room for people's names. To Amy, everybody was *deary*. She'd known for a long time that Sandra was a hooker. She didn't dislike her because of it. She more or less pitied her, yet part of her was envious. "So, how's business?" she asked, looking at her pad, pen in hand, not really expecting an answer.

"Get me the usual," Sandra replied. "And, do me a favor, will you? Tell the kitchen to slow it down. I could be here quite a while tonight."

"Don't worry, deary. I won't put your order in right away."

"Thanks, Amy. You're a doll."

"Yeah, right."

As she left the table, Amy passed Lucky behind his cash register. He gazed at her with enlarged eyes and whispered "Make it fast with that one."

"Sure. I'll do what I can."

Sandra had a good view of the place. There was one guy seated at the counter who captured her attention. He was handsome in a

113

way, but his body seemed stretched and about to snap. His movements were jerky and unfocused, his eyes constantly scanning the dining area and darting toward the door whenever someone entered. This guy intrigued her. Sandra guessed late 50s, probably well-off, married, maybe kids in college, bored and lonely. Out on a rainy Saturday night in a cheap diner near the interstate, probably a man in town for a convention, maybe looking for some entertainment, some action. He wouldn't be the first one she'd picked up on a very similar Saturday night. Lucky's was often patronized by what she called in-between men.

Sandra found herself hoping that the guy at the counter would settle on her during one of his visual sweeps, but each time he looked in her direction his gaze never stopped. She began to worry. Am I losing it? Maybe he really isn't looking. Maybe, just nervous. The more he seemed to ignore her, the more she became interested.

She thought of leaving her table and walking the long way to the ladies' room, slowing down at the counter and maybe saying something to him. Hell, what is this? A trashy romance novel? Or a B-movie? An old-fashioned western; a madam in a gritty saloon – howdy stranger. She closed her eyes and envisioned Lucky retrieving his rifle and aiming it at her. Back off, evil woman. Sandra chuckled.

Up until the rain slowed him down, Raymond Champagne had been sailing smoothly, his automatic pilot set at 68, a speed he knew from experience would not stir police radars. The radio was turned to the public radio station from the University of Massachusetts, and a trio of experts was discussing the early chances of the primary candidates, lingering on the prospects of former Massachusetts Governor Mitt Romney. Raymond had a penchant for politics and appreciated the drama inherent in the candidacy of a somewhat right-wing Mormon ex-governor of the most liberal state in the Union. After a while, he tired of the debate, and found another station, this one playing classical music. He recognized the *Ride of the Valkyries* from Wagner's opera and concluded that it was a most appropriate accompaniment to his own ride into the unknown.

It started raining a few miles after he turned onto I-290 heading for Worcester. The warmth of the day had culminated in a series of violent rainstorms. With windshield wipers failing to keep up and the roadway promising to be slick, Raymond joined other drivers in slowing down on the sharp inclines leading into downtown Worcester. He had been on the road for almost two hours, fueled by numbness and desperation and a strong sense of victimization. He decided to stop, to take a break, to catch his breath. The next exit led to a rundown section of warehouses and empty factories. Ray drove down a wide and heavily pot-holed street until the glitter and neon of Lucky's Diner, reflected in the fresh puddles, caught his attention. He was surprised to find the parking lot nearly full, until he remembered that it was Saturday night. He also remembered that he hadn't eaten since his late breakfast of French toast with Jane's home-made apple butter.

Running towards the diner through the downpour, he hoped the coffee would be strong enough to fuel him for the next leg of this trip. Once inside, he shook the rain off his shoulders. He looked around. The steamy smells of plain food and plain people oddly comforted him. He selected a seat at the counter.

Almost every table was occupied as were most of the counter seats. Older couples on a modest dining budget, young families with crying children, a few teenagers on a cheap date, a couple of single fellows. Folks just like those of Packers Falls, New Hampshire. Except for this one girl all by herself who seemed as nervous and apprehensive as he did. She was pretty, and better dressed than the others, although in a slightly garish way. She was looking into a compact, inspecting her makeup. When she glanced up, Raymond veered his eyes away from her.

He ordered the meatloaf special. He ate it quickly. He left the bland coffee practically untouched. He was scanning the dessert menu when the door opened and a customer walked in and took the only seat available, at the end of the L-shaped counter, facing Raymond. The newcomer appeared to know the place; he ordered without looking at a menu.

Raymond couldn't take his eyes off the man: handsome, in a white open-necked shirt, his generous dark hair a bit too long. The party of four seated next to Raymond paid for their meal and left, offering a full view of the newcomer who looked up at Raymond, nodded and said "Hey." In an abrupt flash, Raymond saw the smile of the lumberjack state trooper, a smile built to beguile and

115

entrap.

Raymond closed his eyes tightly and reviewed the events of the day. What in God's name are you doing? Go back. Go back home. Clean up the mess. No. No. The mess will suck me in. I'll never get out of it. It'll kill me. You made your bed, you lie in it. But it'll be my death bed. The dispute raged on in his head.

Sandra got up and headed towards the counter. She took her time, arranging her skirt, shaking her hair, looking straight at Raymond. She walked slowly and stopped to leave her check and payment on the counter, waiting for Lucky to pick it up. Raymond's eyes lifted from the dessert menu and the two shared a smile, hers friendly and enticing, his fleeting and passive.

"Terrible night to be out," she said.

Raymond nodded.

"You're not from around here, are you? I know most of the handsome men in town and I've never seen you before. My name's Sandra."

Raymond decided to pass on dessert and asked for his check. He tried to ignore the girl next to him.

"Did I say my name is Sandra? What's yours?"

"Ah...Paul. Well, no. Listen, I've got to get back on the road. Have a long ride ahead of me."

"Well, I just thought that if you're all tense from driving in this rain, you might need to relax a bit..."

Lucky stepped up to the counter and grabbed the slips and cash, all the while giving Sandra an unmistakable look that screamed *lay off, whore.*

"Keep the change," Raymond said.

As he stepped out into the Worcester night, Raymond shivered from the cold. A New England shift. No more rain from the south, just winds from the north. Strong. Quick. Arresting. He zipped up his jacket and hurried to his car.

Sandra stood under the plastic canopy over the door of the diner and watched her prey escape. As he unlocked his car door, Raymond heard his cell phone. He frantically grabbed his phone and flipped it open. Looking down, he read the caller's name: Jane. His hand opened, and the cell phone fell to the pavement. Raymond stared down at it and in a swift movement jumped into his vehicle and pulled out of the parking space. Sandra watched as the car backed up, crushing the cell phone under a rear tire.

"The worst demons are those that reside in you. They make themselves so familiar that you learn to live with them and eventually you forget them." Raymond Champagne remembered Sister Rose's words and smiled. His teacher always maintained a vivid fascination with the devil. "Be wary, most of all, of those devils that no longer tempt you; they are truly dangerous." Those were her concluding words as she sent Raymond and his fellow eighth graders, if not into the world, at least to secondary school.

Raymond hadn't given much thought to his eighth-grade graduation or to Sister Rose for several years, but on this windy night driving through New York and Pennsylvania, it all seemed like yesterday – and most appropriate. That was a major benchmark in my young life. This is a major benchmark in my adult life. What? Running away from home is an adult thing? That's what kids do. When they can't face the music. When they can't deal with the results of their actions. The solitary overnight drive through unknown territory was feeding Raymond's mind with all sorts of phantasms. A concoction of old and new, good and bad. He decided to dwell on the happy days; he was 13 years old, the smartest kid in his class, compliments and honors everywhere, the pride and joy of his parents.

Reception on the car radio was weak and the only classical radio station at this time of night kept fading whenever he coasted down into the valleys of eastern Pennsylvania. Irritated, Raymond turned off the radio.

With the gentle modulations of his Subaru as background, Raymond recalled the gangling youngster with the ill-fitting burgundy graduation gown and cap, walking into his parish church on a hot Sunday in June of 1961. Father Blanchette invited Sister Rose – the newly-appointed school principal – to the pulpit to speak to the graduates. Sister Rose couldn't resist noting that it was the first time a nun had been invited to address the students at their graduation Mass – a welcome change in the Catholic

117

Paul Paré

Church. She didn't fail to note that also for the first time, a Roman Catholic was president of the United States. She then turned her attention to the graduates, exhorting them to measure up to the demands of the challenging times without ever losing sight of all they had learned during their eight years at Notre Dame Parochial School. Then, she went to the devil, her favorite subject.

How have my devils fared all these years? Raymond's thoughts skipped four decades, and he saw the face of the husky lumberjack as he emerged from his pickup truck and tossed him a warm and inviting smile. No need to wonder which of his devils had been unleashed by the handsome tempter. Raymond braked as the highway dipped steeply into another valley. He tried to focus on the road but his mind was captivated by the demons of his life, especially the one that had become so familiar, the one that Raymond thought he had under control and, for so many years, had stayed in the background and had kept quiet. Was it the same devil who was compelling him west on this interstate? Scranton, Wilkes-Barre. Signs on a near-empty highway. Flashes in his mind from history lessons, geography lessons. Names of places never seen, never experienced. "So, my devilish friend, what shall I do with you?" Raymond said out loud. "Now that you've come out of hiding, what am I to do with you?" He started to see the dramatic potential. He saw himself as the tragic character embarking on a quest with his faithful companion, the queer and sinister fiend.

Raymond decided to clear his head. He stopped, and on the shoulder of the westbound lanes of I-81, he paced back and forth, filling his lungs with crisp air. He stretched his arms to encompass the valley below with its chaplet of towns blinking in the night. He gazed upwards to a sky full of stars and he inhaled the smell of fires burning in the hearths below. The wind had fallen, and it felt like December should feel like in the hills. Raymond zipped his jacket as he absorbed the night. How could any demon create such a thing? So peaceful and perfect. Decidedly, the devils had gone to sleep, along with the good country folk living in this valley.

It occurred to him that he hadn't slept in a long time. He calculated it had been close to 20 hours since leaving his warm bed. His body was running out of fuel. He continued along the highway until an exit announced a decent choice of motels. To the desk clerk awakened from a nap, Raymond felt a need to explain. "Been driving all night. Have to be at a funeral tomorrow." The clerk gave him an automatic smile, processed his VISA, and handed over a magnetic key card.

"Continental breakfast runs from seven to nine. You'll probably miss it, though."

"Probably."

In his run-of-the-mill non-smoking room in Grantville, Pennsylvania, Raymond greeted his exhaustion and collapsed into a devil-free sleep.

The next day, his body rejuvenated, he managed a marathon ride, following interstates in a generally westerly direction. As he emerged from the western suburbs of Indianapolis, he asked himself where he was going. His hasty departure from Packers Falls and his breakneck pace had given him little opportunity to plan. Earlier, while crossing from Connecticut into New York, he toyed with the idea of heading to New York City and taking in a few Broadway plays. But he suspected that New York was full of demons. Dancers, actors, free spirits. At a later point in his escape, he conjured up scenes of buff blonde surfer boys at the beach in Malibu. He thought of cowboys on the open range. He saw himself in communion with the open skies and mesas of the Painted Desert. Mojave. Hopi. Sonoma. San Xavier. Santa Clara. Surely places where devils can't survive. All destinations were eventually put on hold or dismissed outright, and Raymond just pushed forward, heading vaguely west. Got to build distance. Have to keep moving. Go west, young man. Sage advice. But I'm not that young man. Not anymore.

As he approached Terre Haute, he stopped for gas and purchased a road atlas, his first concession to the nagging question of destination. That night, in another quick and easy motel, he studied his maps. He was both surprised by the distances he had accumulated and how much still lay ahead. Should he continue on his western course, or should he head south? He couldn't decide and he blamed one of his devils – the one named Hesitation – the one he thought he had exorcised years ago when he forced himself to make the tough decisions: going back to his home town, accepting the school principal's job, getting married. He took the atlas to bed with him and lazily scanned state after state, reading brief descriptions designed to entice the traveler. He turned on the television set to the Weather Channel and was informed that the first winter storm was heading his way. Amused and unafraid, Raymond slowly fell asleep, no decision having been reached.

He kept hearing bells. School bells, church bells, the ringtone of his cell phone shattering the stillness of a wet parking lot outside a diner in Massachusetts. He saw his hand let go of the cell phone and he watched it fall to the ground in slow motion and he could still hear the ringing and he could detect his wife's voice, asking for him, shrilly repeating his name. Ray. Ray. Ray? The bells grew and invaded his head. Alarms. Bank alarms tripped by masked robbers. Warning bells with red lights commanding motorists to stop for trains. Sister Rose and her hand bell putting a stop to recess fun and games. Raymond awoke to the sound of someone pounding on his motel door. "This isn't a test. Everyone must leave the hotel. This is not a test."

Standing in the cold in the early morning hours at the far end of the parking lot, watching the firemen go in and out of his motel, Raymond, wrapped in a spongy hotel blanket, felt homesick for the first time. He saw the glow of his fireplace and the gentle play of shadows over the familiar and soothing possessions that decorated his life in Packers Falls. The warm tones of his home office, the smell of a roast in the oven, Jane's voice on the phone gurgling baby talk to their granddaughters. A haven. An imprisonment. A stage set, perfectly arranged for his own private drama.

Having found no fire, the lieutenant declared there had been an electrical malfunction. The news was greeted by snowflakes and a Nordic wind. Raymond and his fellow guests filed silently into their hotel decorated with Christmas lights. Inside, the alarm was still ringing. Someone kept walking up and down the hallways, assuring the guests that electricians were working on the problem. Raymond wished the alarm to stop, but it persisted. It competed in his head with the tinny bell that rang at the start of the school day and again between classes.

The fire alarm refused to acquiesce to the machinations of the electricians. Raymond decided to pack his bags: no more sleep tonight, might as well hit the road. Before leaving he decided to put another devil to rest. In the night stand drawer next to the Gideon Bible, he found some hotel stationery and wrote a brief message in a shaky hand.

Sorry for the confusion. Rest easy. I am well. Have always loved you.

He was about to sign it *your husband* when he decided to simply affix his name. The pen, poised and lifeless, hesitated. Ray. Raymond. Deceiver. Coward. Devil. Are you doing the right thing? Does your life's drama really require this final act? He had no answer. He addressed the envelope, writing the number of his neat Cape on the shady New Hampshire street he knew he'd never see again. Raymond finished packing. Checking out, he had to yell at the desk clerk to overcome the sound of the alarm. He asked for a stamp and dropped two quarters on the counter. He laid the envelope on the hotel counter and slowly pushed it towards the clerk. "You'll mail this for me? Please?"

Raymond Champagne drove away from Terre Haute and, smiling, realized what the name of the city meant in French. He *had* taken the high road: he owed Jane some kind of sign. He felt comforted. He turned on his radio to the early morning traffic report and the sound of bells faded and vanished.

Nearly alone at an all-night coffee shop a dozen miles down the highway, Raymond sat facing the window and observed the snow falling to the ground. The storm was making its intentions quite clear. This would be a stubborn one. His road atlas spread out on the plastic table top, Raymond studied and thought of changing his course. Just over the Illinois state line, I-57 headed south. With his finger he traced its progress and how it branched out. The land of Dixie. Peaches and peanuts and orange blossoms. Atlanta and Charleston and Savannah and Miami. The litany of warm and exotic places convinced Raymond to orient his escape in a new direction.

It was somewhere in the middle of Georgia, early evening under threatening skies. Raymond was losing track of time and geography, and he was tired. The small rest stop had fresh landscaping, a glossy parking area, and a row of metal portable toilets. Don't stop. Keep going, he commanded. Yet, he slowed down and glided onto the off ramp and cautiously examined the surroundings. The car came to a hesitant stop in the middle of the parking lot. A large trailer truck, humming loudly, and two cars, silent and dark, had staked out their stalls with adequate distances between them. I've got to take a leak and I need to stretch. There's nothing wrong here. Raymond pulled in directly beneath an overhead spotlight. He stood next to his car and stretched, pulling up his shoulder muscles and rotating his hips to free his body from the tightness of repetition and constraint. On a bluff, the rest area overlooked the last of Georgia's foothills. He was reminded of New Hampshire. The air was humid and tall pine trees swayed in the wind.

During the entire time on the road since leaving Packers Falls, he avoided all rest areas and welcome centers and truck stops, convinced they were full of cops setting another trap. Between motel stays he took only the busiest exits offering the basics: gas stations with a bathroom, hot coffee and snacks. And it was always fast, in and out, no loitering.

Raymond concluded this place was safe. He started walking towards the Port-O-Lets and noticed some shapes moving behind them. He changed his mind. This place was dangerous, as dangerous as his rest area in New Hampshire – and as tempting. He froze, his hand on the door handle of the makeshift bathroom, trying to determine exactly what was going on. Finally he stepped inside. He listened carefully and heard only the echo of his urine as it hit the bottom of the storage tank. When he was done, he scrambled to his car, his head down. He jumped in and locked the door. A corner of his eye spotted movement and he turned to stare at a man standing at the end of the portable toilets, his legs squarely set on the new grass, his arms folded over the soft belly peeking out from under the edge of his tee-shirt. Raymond scanned the parking lot and noted that one of the cars was gone. He glanced at the large truck which sat humming away. His hand reached for the ignition key while keeping his eyes glued on the lone figure near the toilets. He turned his car on and, as he pulled out of the parking space, he shifted to gain speed. Raymond watched the row of portable toilets turn into a wall, concrete and tall, barbed wire stretching and tying them together. A prison wall, his prison wall! His foot became heavy with anger. He accelerated and the Subaru climbed onto the new lawn and headed directly towards the toilets. "No prison. No prison," he yelled out. Inches away from the first unit, Raymond suddenly veered away. Slowing down, he glanced back. The portable toilets were back. The stranger was gone.

For the next several miles, Raymond argued with himself, sometimes pleadingly, sometimes plaintively. He mumbled and growled, then he screamed at the top of his lungs. He told himself he was being silly. He imagined it all. He yelled at his demon to stop tempting him. He told the State Police to leave him alone. He searched for the next exit. He wanted to turn and go back. He wanted to see what would happen. He knew what would happen. They'd arrest him again. His car was marked. He was a known pervert. Maybe that guy wasn't a cop. Just a lonely old guy, just like him. Eager to explore. You should go back.

"Oh. Please. Wake up. It's a trap," Raymond screamed.

Would he always be tempted and repulsed at the same time?

He slowed down. He was out of breath and his eyes were watery. He was pissed off and he was scared. He understood clearly that his demon wasn't about to give up without a fight.

The high school band ended its concert with *God Rest Ye Merry Gentlemen.* Claude was amused. All night, he barely paid attention to the music, but at the end of the evening, the familiar carol hit him as appropriate, and he thought it might have been meant for him. Especially the *God Rest* part. Like an epitaph. The *Merry Gentlemen* didn't refer to him at all and he knew it. He was not in a very merry mood. In fact, he was seriously depressed. And, he looked like shit. He was hungry; he was out of money; he had no place to sleep.

The band members packed their instruments and lined them up along River Street, creating a divider between the roadway and the vendors with their carts loaded with Christmas baubles. A clunky bus slowly rolled through the pedestrian traffic and came to a stop with a groan. Claude observed it all and turned the scene into a remembrance of the day when the driver stuffed his bag into the hold of the bus idling in front of Gallant's Pharmacy. It was no more than six or seven weeks since he left Connecticut, but it felt like years. Transfixed by the image playing itself in front of him, Claude walked up to the front of the bus, and, like a sleep walker, placed his right hand on the hood as if to calm the beast. "Hey. You. Get out a there," yelled the bus driver. "You crazy or somethin'? You'll get run over." Claude gave him a blank look, turned and started walking towards the river. He wanted to die and he could think of worse ways than being run over by an old bus filled with high school kids.

As the plaza fell silent, Claude Simard chose a bench facing the Savannah River. Hey old river, old friend. You know, if the bus driver won't oblige, there's always drowning. He was just a few feet from the murky waterway and he felt as old as the river itself. He imagined the bustle that would have surrounded him in past years. This waterfront had given up any pretense at genuine commerce. It had become a prettified remnant, a space devoid of real inhabitants, defined by a wide promenade, with bricks, blocks

124

of granite, and cobblestones scrubbed clean for the tourists.

"Chandler, come back here." The intruding voice came from behind Claude who turned to see a tall man walking swiftly in his direction. "Come back here, young man. That's close enough." Claude noticed a child stopping dead in his tracks a few feet from the water. The father caught up to him and grasped his hand. Claude observed the duo walk away towards the street and saw his own son Mikey. In the gloomiest moment of the evening, the homeless man inhaled the sulfur-laden air of Savannah and slumped over, gagging on a mixture of guilt and misery. "Mikey. Mikey. Mikey." He chanted the name like a recluse would pray to his desert spirits. "Mikey. Mikey. My boy Mikey."

It was his third night on the riverfront. He spent the evenings listening to the Christmas concerts; he watched the strollers and the gawkers and tried to stay out of their way. He remained there until everyone had gone home, killing time until the cops drove by and flashed their spotlights in his direction. He walked the streets near the river until he found a sheltered spot that hadn't already been claimed for the night, usually against the wall of an empty building. There, he waited for his hunger to subside and make way for a coma-like sleep. He assumed that this night would be the same. He forgot what day of the week it was. He couldn't remember how long he had been in this town.

Shoulda stayed in Philadelphia, asshole. Claude started referring to himself as asshole and shithead since his arrival in Savannah. This isn't a good place. At least you had a roof over your head in Philadelphia and you might have found some work. He harbored a deep hatred of Father Mondésir not only for the evil he knew the Haitian was capable of, but, even more so, for driving him away from Father Tony.

He spent his first days in Savannah making the rounds of the homeless shelters and soon discovered that the food and bed came with a price: buying into whatever they were preaching, plus living with some true lunatics. He returned to the least distasteful of the shelters once – out of desperation – for some food and a shower. Reviewing his recent existence, he tried to count the days. He concentrated and mumbled, but still, he was uncertain. Determining the date became important and he worked at it diligently as he sat on the riverbank. The night turned silent. Can't be a weekend. Too quiet.

An occasional cab would drop off passengers at one of the bars on the far side of River Street, and for a brief moment the spot would come alive. A large ship laden with containers piled as high as five or six stories would slide by noiselessly. Once in a while, a couple would meander down the esplanade amorously hand in hand. A lone dog scampered towards Claude and moved on quickly as if aware there was no handout to he had. A woman slowed down as she walked behind his bench. He smelled her perfume. He waited for her to pass by before looking her way. She was wearing a short skirt, and her hair was flowing freely the length of her back. A veil fell on Claude as he tried to remember the last time he smelled the perfume of a woman, the last time he touched a woman's hair, the last time he held her breasts. He closed his eyes and tried to remember a date and place and all that came to him was a vagueness caught in the cobwebs of his brain.

Claude wasn't sure what he was hearing when he first detected the sound. A man's voice, soft, hesitant. The tune was vaguely familiar, the words foreign. Claude scanned the area and spotted someone sitting on a bench just like his, also facing the river. The song slowly grew in clarity and intensity. He recognized the melody first, extricating the air from his childhood and attaching it to the voice of his father's aunt Yvette. As his recollection grew, he identified it as a Christmas song she would sing to him those evenings when she babysat while his mother and father went shopping for presents.

Claude glided to the end of his bench to be closer to the singer. He wanted to catch the words, to see if they were from his great-aunt's canticle. He grasped the first few words: *Il est né, le div...* The rest was lost, carried by a wind that changed its course. Claude forgot who he was and where he was and what he looked like and he approached the singer and stood a few feet away from him, listening, hoping. The man stopped his song. "Oh. Please don't stop singing. Please."

The songster gave Claude a perplexed glance. He nodded his head and, looking straight ahead, resumed singing tentatively.

Il est né, le divin enfant,
Jouez hautbois, résonnez musettes

He paused and looked directly at the stranger. He continued.

Il est né, le divin enfant,
Chantons tous son avènement.

"That's so beautiful," Claude said in a low voice, directing his words not only to the singer but beyond him, out of reverence to his great-aunt and to the happy moments she bestowed on his childhood.

"It's a very old Christmas song. It's French," explained the singer.

"Yes. I recognized it. My great-aunt used to sing it to me when I was a kid."

The singer examined the man speaking to him and saw in the dimness of the boardwalk an intriguing figure. He cautiously slid his body to the end of his bench. Claude interpreted the movement as an invitation to join him.

"My name is Claude Simard. My father's aunt would sing it. Her name is Yvette." Claude extended his hand.

"I'm Ray," Raymond said as he accepted the hand. He noticed an aggressive tug. Rugged, a man who works with his hands. Dirty. Smells of sweat. Maybe worked all day.

Claude felt uncharacteristically bold. He forgot his appearance. "How come you happen to be here on this bench singing my childhood Christmas carol?"

"Well, first of all, I don't think it's *your* carol. It's in the public domain." Ray knew he was sounding official and professorial and felt a bit foolish. "And, I happen to be here because I'm visiting Savannah for a few days, and this place – this esplanade – I find it matches my mood."

"So, where you from?"

Ray's body stiffened. In his head, he heard a reproach: beware of men in public places. He sent a suspicious look in Claude's direction and was startled. In his face, with its scrubby beard and deep set eyes, there was a melancholy that Ray had rarely seen. Ray felt a sudden kinship with this young man who insisted on listening to his song and was now drawing him into conversation.

"I'm from New Hampshire."

"I'm from Connecticut."

Both men nodded in silent acknowledgment.

"And, my full name is Raymond Champagne."

"So, Raymond, what you doing here in Savannah?"

"I'm running away from home."

"Me too."

A new wind greeted their confessions, bringing with it a fresh trace of sulfur from the paper mills upriver. The men were quiet, listening to the city behind them and the river at their feet, delving into the flashbacks that suddenly invaded each one's mind. The pause was neither awkward nor apprehensive. It was just there. After a while, Claude spoke – softly, almost as if there was a third person there who shouldn't hear. "Funny. Two grown men sitting on a bench late at night talking about running away from home."

"Yes. Odd, come to think of it." Ray realized this was his first real conversation in two weeks. He turned to stare at the stranger seated next to him and he wondered what it was about this guy that pulled at him, that tapped a dormant need for companionship.

"Why are you running away from home?" Ray asked.

"Had no choice. Got thrown out." Claude paused, inhaled deeply and continued as he expelled his stale breath. "Went sort of crazy this summer and my wife threw me out of the house. She got a restraining order and I can't even see my own kid. I was living in some rotting warehouse when they put me on a bus heading south so I wouldn't freeze to death this winter." He stopped speaking, thinking he had just capsulated so clearly and so effortlessly his situation.

"That's quite a story," Ray responded. "I mean, that's amazing." He wanted to go further. He was tempted to say the predicament was right out of a novel. Dozens of questions surfaced. "So, you're sort of homeless?" was the only one he voiced.

"Not even sort of. Definitely homeless. At least for the last few days here in Savannah." Claude grabbed a couple of deep breaths, his body erect. "Oh. By the way, what day is this? What's the date? I've lost track."

"Wednesday. December 19th."

"Thanks. Just wanted to know how close we are to Christmas. Wouldn't want to miss it."

"No. Can't miss Christmas," added Ray.

"Imagine if I showed up here some night, and there'd be no Christmas music. That would be my only clue. Now, that's depressing." Claude laughed.

"Well, there's no way I can miss it. I was born on Christmas day. Just like little Baby Jesus."

"No kidding. My son was born on Christmas Eve. That's why we called him Nick – short for Nicholas. Jolly Old Saint Nick."

"Well my middle name is Noël. Raymond Noël Champagne. That's Noël with an umlaut on the letter *e*. That makes it French."

"I see." Claude didn't want to show he was being put off by the detail.

Ray picked up on it anyways. "Sorry, didn't want to sound like a teacher. But, as they say, once a teacher always a teacher."

"Oh. You're a teacher?"

"Yes. But, now I'm a school principal."

Another weighty pause fell on the duo. Claude remembered his first-born and how Nick always felt foreign to him. He was Margie's kid. He just happened to be present at the conception. He wondered how he was doing, realizing that his son would soon be turning 20. Claude felt old.

"And, Raymond Champagne, the school principal who sings French carols, why are *you* running away from home?"

Taken by surprise, Ray searched for a response. Since his hasty departure, he had avoided putting into words, at least for someone else's ears, the reason for his flight. He wasn't sure how much he should share, but he felt he owed this guy something in response to his frankness. "Well. How do I put this? I guess the simplest answer is that I was caught doing something I shouldn't have been doing, and instead of facing the consequences, I just left everything behind."

Several small fires burst in Claude's mind, but he extinguished them. Gently, he said, "You're traveling? On the road?"

"That's it."

"How long?"

"Be two weeks this Saturday. This is the first time I've really stayed in one place." Ray was grateful that his friend didn't ask for details. "I really like Savannah."

"I don't. Thought I would. But, I guess I'm not in a mood to try the tourist thing."

"I suppose you're not in the best situation to enjoy the place," Ray replied. "To me, it's a fascinating city. Real old world atmosphere. Lots of history and great architecture, and so green.

Trees and parks everywhere, and the streets are shady and elegant."

"Cobwebs. That's what it reminds me of."

"I'm sorry. Didn't mean to sound like a tour guide."

"Don't be sorry. I wish I could just walk around and take in the sights and let myself be inspired," Claude admitted. "I've started writing poetry and I want to write about this place, but I can't get started. I'm so empty right now."

Ray was surprised by the abrupt change of subject and was further intrigued. This guy, whom Ray had assumed was a rough workman, had an artistic side. Teach you to judge, Mister Teacher Man. "You write poetry?" He needed confirmation.

"I try. Just discovered Ginsberg and Kerouac this summer. I'll never be that good. But I have my own shit to write about, and it seems to fall on the page naturally. So, maybe, someday, you can tell your students you met a great writer one night in Savannah."

Ray chuckled. "You never know." He wanted to ask him to recite some of his poetry but he decided not to. "What is it about Savannah that inspires you?"

"Not sure, really. The humidity. I've never seen so much humidity, not in December."

"It is damp all the time, isn't it?"

"Like the other night, I had this thing going. All the words were coming to me: humidity and humility, wet and sweat, and mold and old, and all kinds of images that didn't even rhyme and didn't make much sense but were really beautiful. But, when I went to write it down, I couldn't because I had lost them all."

Ray was fascinated. Inside, warmth seized the folds of his lungs, blowing newness into his limbs, replacing the ache he told himself resulted from the long ride but knowing it was really caused by the emptiness of his escape. "A lot of things get lost when you try to get them out of your head and onto a sheet of paper," he offered.

"Yeah. It didn't help either that my head was swimming in booze."

Surprised by the admission, Ray had to confront his naiveté. Of course, the guy drinks. Comes with being homeless. Probably does drugs too.

"Cheap whiskey. Shoulda known better."

"Where did you get it?"

"Couple of guys I bunked with. It's amazing, even among homeless men, there's a certain protocol. If someone offers you something you better accept it or they'll think you're too good for them, or worse, that you're a cop."

"And drugs?"

"No. Not me. I take the booze and I say I'm real drunk and I'll be sick if I add drugs to it. Usually works. No, sir. Been able to stay away from the drugs. They're mostly pills, prescriptions, and God knows what they are. Just too scary. Not judging anybody, you know. Whatever works, I suppose. But, not for me."

"I see," said Ray.

Claude grew quiet. He knew he had said too much.

Ray heard alarms ring. You don't know this guy from Adam. Maybe, he *is* a cop. But he's not coming on to me. He's not a cop, this isn't a trap. "It's really none of my business," Ray said, "about the booze and the drugs." He tossed the conversation around his mind and convinced himself that Claude was honest. He sensed he had glimpsed something forbidden. It felt like the sweet coating of his stomach when, as a teenager, he spotted his next door neighbor taking his clothes off and parading through the house in his boxer shorts, and many years later when he'd walk through his school's gym and smell the sweat of the boys after a basketball game. Without realizing it, Ray inched himself closer to his friend on the bench and allowed the humidity of the night to carry the smell of Claude's clothing to his nostrils. Slowly, he drew in deep breaths of the odor. "Where do you sleep?" Ray had lost control of his curiosity.

"Where I can." The answer had all the brevity and finality of a judge's sentence. Raymond realized he should respect it.

"You know, I saw some street musicians this afternoon in Franklin Square near City Market. There was this one fellow who was reciting poetry. His poetry was awful, but people would stop, and you'd be surprised how many of them dropped money in his hat. Maybe you should try that sometime." Claude didn't respond, and Ray didn't pursue the thought. The older man toyed with his curiosity again, wondering what it would be like to live on the streets, speculating that, despite the deprivation, the experience could be enlightening and freeing. He remembered his grade school religion classes and how the nuns spoke with such awe about the holy hermits and the ascetics who wandered in the

131

desert eating grasshoppers. Fasting was a virtue, solitude was a sacrament. What kind of person could give himself up to that life?

"Could you sing more of that Christmas carol?"

Wrenched from his reverie, Ray looked at Claude intently, and picked up the song where he had left it.

> *Depuis plus de quatre mille ans,*
> *Nous le promettaient les prophètes,*
> *Depuis plus de quatre mille ans,*
> *Nous attendions cet heureux temps.*

Ray continued with the chorus, and Claude started humming along.

"I don't know the words," Claude said meekly. "But I know it's beautiful." Ray stopped and listened to the younger man try to sing. He found Claude's voice vulnerable.

At that moment, the performance was abruptly interrupted by the invading flash of a spotlight and a deep baritone voice. "There's a curfew in effect. You have to leave the area, gentlemen," said the policeman through his bullhorn. The cruiser had stopped on River Street, and the spotlight was arcing back and forth over the plaza.

"That's my cue," said Claude as he went to pull his gym bag from under his original bench.

"Curfew? What are they talking about?" asked Ray.

"All I know is that the cops want me – us – out of here. And, I don't argue with these guys."

Ray gagged on his thoughts. Damn cops, everywhere. Drawing you in. Throwing you out.

Claude stood up and waved a hand over his head and nodded to the police officer as a signal that he was on his way. "I think you should go too. Although you don't look like a bum. Maybe this is a selective curfew."

Ray was about to invite Claude to join him for a coffee somewhere, but Claude was several steps away.

"Thanks for the Christmas carol. That was nice," he said, turning back towards the singer.

"Hey. Claude." Ray caught up with him. "You want to…" He couldn't finish his sentence, an equal dose of caution and pity having overcome him. "Here. Get yourself something to eat."

Ray stuffed the loose bills from his pocket into the hand of the homeless guy.

Looking at the dollars, Claude said, "I'm the one who's supposed to pay the guy who sings, you know."

"Next time. Ok?" Ray smiled.

The men took a few steps from each other and walked in opposite directions, leaving the empty esplanade to witness the rest of the night on the banks of the Savannah River.

"Huh! Thought they were faggots," said the cop to his partner as he drove the cruiser away, the tires making an odd squeal against the cobblestones.

Father Tony missed Claude. He regretted Claude's precipitous departure that left the childhood pals at a loss to say the right thing and give each other the farewell they deserved. And now, Father Tony could use Claude's help. There was no one else to turn to; everybody, it seemed, had abandoned him. It was already late – well into Advent – and he was rushing against time and was overwhelmed. The year before, the Nativity scene had gone up by itself, had appeared out of nowhere. He walked into church one afternoon and there it was: Mary and Joseph, shepherds, angels, sheep, even the mule and the ox. There was real straw waiting for Baby Jesus. A dozen pine trees decorated with tiny white lights formed a background. Father Tony had ooohed and aaahed, congratulated everyone for their work, and promised to keep them in his prayers at Midnight Mass.

This year the army of workers had vanished. Nicolette, who usually enlisted family and friends, was on the warpath. Father avoided the subject, knowing she'd turn him down. He recruited Father Mondésir to round up some Christmas trees. Three trips with the parish station wagon resulted in a harvest of five rather scrawny specimens. Father Tony didn't dare criticize. To make matters worse, the Haitian priest made himself scarce for the next several days. Two altar boys were hired to help out but they were young and not very strong. Father Tony was left by himself to do most of the work.

As he struggled to carry the nearly life-sized crèche figures from storage, Father Tony felt helpless. He mumbled Claude's name under his breath, and remembered how his pal – the longest-serving altar boy at St. Patrick's – had tried to enlist Tony to help him take down the crèche figures after Christmas. They were in the ninth grade and Tony had started to hang out with the college track students and declined to help with the manger scene. "Well, one good turn deserves another," Tony said to the shepherds.

On the second day of the undertaking, the priest decided to

134

leave the heaviest pieces, the mule and the ox, in their crates. He placed the statues of the magi in the sacristy, all in a line, waiting for their marching orders on Epiphany. He searched for the sets of white Christmas lights and couldn't find them. Father Tony, breathless and sore, examined his creation: the trees were naked; there was no straw to cradle Baby Jesus.

The priest sat in the front pew and thought of the heavy winter coat he gave Claude. He wondered where Claude had wound up. Did he sleep out of doors? Did he use his coat to stay warm? Alone in the empty nave of the church, Father Tony offered up a prayer for his childhood friend. Then he asked Jesus to forgive him for the cold marble floor of His crèche.

As he was leaving, he glanced back at the Christmas tableau and persuaded himself that simplicity had its advantages. Instead of taking the side door and the shorter route to the rectory, he walked slowly all the way down the nave and stood in the vestibule. A single stained glass window in the apse filled the wall above the altar. It depicted Saint Petronilla, the virgin patron saint of the parish, and the late sun plunged the sanctuary in the brilliant red of her dress.

Father Tony turned and faced the newly-painted doors and their glossy surface. The priest walked to the doors and placed his hand reverently on them. "Brother Claude, thank you. Forgive me for not giving you the solace you sought here."

The use of the word *brother* surprised him. He doubted ever having used it to describe his friend and was amazed that he hadn't. Claude had been present when he – the one boy in a family of females – most needed a male companion. Truly, he thought, standing in the growing darkness of his church, Claude was a brother; they did all of the brotherly things of adolescent boys. Father Tony smiled the smile of recognition, and, belatedly, he whispered as he walked out of the church, "Thank you, brother."

Margie Simard stopped her Kia next to the snow bank that Wally from the hardware store had cleared for access to her mail box. "There has to be some mail, some sign of life from Claude. Mister O'Regan promised," she muttered.

She turned to tell Mikey to stay put while she went to check on the mail, but her little boy had fallen asleep. She watched him breathe gently, droplets of perspiration forming on his brow. Afraid to wake him, she resisted reaching over to the back seat to remove his knitted hat. Instead, she allowed her eyes to fill with tears. Her little Mikey had just broken her heart.

The car still running, the radio tuned to her favorite Classic Rock station, the heater on medium, Margie descended into a watery vision of her morning at the mall. It was two weekends before Christmas and she had promised to take Mikey to see Santa. Surrounded by fitful children of all kinds and sizes, Margie held Mikey's hand as the line crept between plastic candy canes and gingerbread men toward the oversized throne that held Santa Claus. She suggested that Mikey be brief because Santa was probably very tired. He answered there was only one thing he really wanted. She asked what that was, and he said he wanted to see his daddy.

Margie was blown backwards as if someone had opened a door to the real North Pole. She resisted the temptation to yank her son out of line. She wanted to tell him that's not the kind of request you make of Santa, and, besides, what's Santa going to say, what can he say? Mikey stood firmly in line, unaware of the cold wind he had blasted at his mother's face.

The mall employee in her old-fashioned dress and white wig and phony granny glasses opened the gate to Santa's domain and told Mikey Simard he was next. Margie watched her son walk timidly to Santa and allow himself to be picked up and perched on the man's knee. Mikey was somber, unlike the other kids who squealed and gushed. She couldn't hear what was being said between her boy and Santa Claus, but she noticed the man's sudden glance in her direction. She felt Santa's accusation. How could a mother deprive her son of his father's presence at Christmas time? As mother and son meandered through the crowded mall towards an exit, Margie wondered what Santa had said to her son's request. She fought the urge to ask.

They drove back into town, both of them silent, listening to a radio announcer from far away promising all sorts of Christmas delights. Margie tried to focus on the music, but nothing could shake her mood. She decided she was as much a victim as her son. She did what she had to do: protect herself and her boy with a restraining order. Her father had encouraged her; the judge had agreed.

Distractedly, she ran her hands over the cushioned dashboard, and she remembered the day when her father drove up with the new red Kia. Just a present for his favorite daughter, he told her. She was positive it was a bribe. Her dad had never bought her a car before. Why now? Because he wanted to buy her silence about her crooked brother. Embezzlement was the ugly word her father refused to hear. A lot of things were missing and her older brother Frank was gone. But, the police were never called, and that's the way Stan Pelczar wanted it. The new car may have been a bribe, but it was also a down payment, a gentle reminder of which came in November, when Pelczar told his daughter he needed her. The new bookkeeper wasn't working out and he needed her at the store – at least for the Christmas season.

Margie accepted the job and the salary that came with it. But, each day at the hardware store, sitting in that office, she was reminded that Claude was right all along about her brother. She should have sided with him. If she had, none of this would have happened. And, she wouldn't have to face her little boy's sad eyes. Margie hoped that the memory of his father would fade quickly and easily, and that her little Mikey would accept his absence. She knew that was foolish.

The mail box was stuffed with sales flyers and nothing else.

It was Christmas morning when the bubble burst – the one Jane had spun in reaction to her husband's arrest and disappearance. She was supposed to go to church with her daughter and granddaughters. She was supposed to be in the kitchen, waiting to be picked up, wearing her Sunday best. Instead, she was cowering on the floor of the bedroom closet, half dressed and frozen with fear. It took two weeks for despair to set in, and now it was firmly in control. Surrounded by shoes, discarded and current, Jane Champagne saw the recent events collide around her. She reviewed the steps that led to this moment. She tried to slow her breathing, but she only fell into a fit of coughs.

The first night, when she came home to an empty house, she had a brief moment of panic, but she talked herself out of it. She turned on the TV while preparing the usual Saturday night supper of pasta. She thawed some shrimp to add to the sauce – one of Raymond's favorites. She waited a few hours and, when Raymond didn't come home, she called her daughter who had no idea where her dad was. Jane called her husband's cell phone. It rang once and then went dead. A part of Jane died at that moment as well.

The police were useless. One more husband out carousing on a Saturday night. Nothing to get excited about. They told Mrs. Champagne not to worry. They were sure things would be all right. Jane took their advice; she desperately wanted to. Three glasses of brandy later, she was able to fall asleep. She called the police the next morning. Again, the cops tried to reassure her. The worst scenario was that her husband ran out of gas somewhere. They said they'd patrol the outlying roads and keep an eye out. She didn't buy it. She knew her husband; he'd *never* run out of gas.

It wasn't until Sunday evening when the local constabulary contacted the State Police that pieces of the puzzle started falling into place. The police chief himself, an old friend of the senior Mr. Champagne, was pressed into service to break the news to the distraught wife. The words *sting operation* meant nothing to her. He had to explain. She didn't believe him. By midnight, an all-points bulletin was issued. Monday evening, the Packers Falls School Board – in emergency session – appointed a temporary principal at the junior high school and consulted with the town attorney, just in case. When the mid-week edition of the local newspaper hit the streets, a front page article carried the details. The next day, a TV crew from Manchester was in town interviewing people.

Confused and feeling betrayed, the daughter nevertheless tried to console her mother. Jane reacted by building a bubble of defiance. She went to work as usual at the drug store and gratefully accepted the Christmas-rush overtime. She buried herself in house cleaning and holiday shopping. She went on a diet, started running in the early morning hours, cut down on the brandy.

A week after the incident, there was a letter in her mail box. She wrinkled her nose at the return address, a hotel in Terre Haute, Indiana. She didn't know anyone in Terre Haute. She convinced herself it was a mistake. She buried her doubts and curiosity and stuffed the envelope back in the mail box.

The police paid her a visit the following week asking if she had heard from her husband, if their credit card statements showed any unusual activity. One of the officers said something about a ransom note. Jane found that preposterous. That helped her dismiss the entire interrogation.

Little by little, cracks began to appear in her defenses. She kept stumbling on the gazes full of pity: co-workers, Christmas shoppers, nosey neighbors, people at church. Christmas was supposed to be her refuge, supposed to keep her busy. As it neared, however, the warmth of the holiday, the closeness of family and loved ones, the happy memories, all battered the walls of the protective cocoon she had created. She began to fear its approach. She became terrified of the days that would come after Christmas, their emptiness, their finality.

The mailbox started overflowing, and Jane had no choice but to empty it. Early Christmas morning, she scattered the mail on the dining room table, quickly discarding ads and flyers. All that was left were Christmas cards, the usual bills and statements and the letter from the hotel in Indiana. She held the envelope in both hands and was about to tear it to shreds when a burst of sadness – from a place that hadn't hurt before – stopped her. She took the envelope to her husband's den – his perfect refuge. Jane sat in his chair and read the brief note on hotel stationery. She recognized the handwriting. She didn't understand the words. She read them again, out loud, deliberately, like she would have read to a child.

Sorry for the confusion. Rest easy. I am well. Have always loved you.

She read the name signed on the bottom. She repeated it many times. She threw the piece of paper on his desk. She stared at it. She picked up Raymond's Montblanc and stabbed the missive in long broad strokes, hoping to drown the message in expensive blue ink. Jane Tracy Champagne jabbed and poked at the paper until finally she recognized the letter for what it was: the epitaph to the life she had known for some 30 years.

Suddenly, she heard a car door outside. Jane knew her daughter had arrived to take her to Christmas Mass. She clutched the letter and crumpled it in her hand. She heard the car horn and ran upstairs. She threw herself into the dark comfort of its closet. She listened to the downstairs door open and her daughter's voice saying her name, looking for her from room to room.

Jane saw her life flash before her eyes and she decided that this closet, dark and familiar, was where she would remain until she became so numb that none of it would matter.

Ray was not about to do anything that remotely resembled a birthday celebration. That was his resolve, firm and heavy, adopted in the days before Christmas. Rising earlier than he had become used to, Ray looked out his third floor window. Fog was rolling in along the far side of the Savannah River, obscuring half of the bridge spanning the waterway. It looked chilly, but he couldn't be certain, since the Quality Inn folks didn't believe in windows that opened. He turned on The Weather Channel and watched a shapely blond meteorologist warn about a major blizzard in the Colorado Rockies. The local forecast called for clouds with possible showers, clearing in the afternoon, and a high of 65 degrees. Briefly, he wondered about Christmas Day weather in New Hampshire.

"Happy Birthday, Baby Jesus. Wherever you are," he declared in his best Jimmy Durante imitation. Ray was immediately cloaked by two very different recollections: his father repeating the line *Good Night, Mrs. Calabash, Wherever You Are* and laughing madly at his rendition; then Sister Rose staring disapprovingly when he, a nine-year old Raymond, had used the phrase in class one day. He never understood why his father found it so funny and he'd forgotten in what context he had used it to make Sister Rose wrinkle her nose. "Happy Birthday, Baby Jesus. Wherever you are," he repeated.

Ordinarily he would have been buoyed by the Jimmy Durante mantra, but not today. As much as he wanted to ignore his birthday, especially this one which saw him turn 60, the date made it impossible. Christmas had always intruded on his birthday. As a boy, he resented it. All the other kids had two days of gifts and special attention; his were packaged neatly into one, and he learned early on that he couldn't compete with Baby Jesus. As an adult, he welcomed the shifting of everyone's attention to the happy meal and gift giving that had nothing to do with him. He didn't mind that his birthday became a footnote.

Paul Paré

His days in Savannah, as lazy and unencumbered as they were, fortified the fixation on his age. He tried to play the tourist, but for most of his uncharted days he would fall into a haze of uncertainty. His cozy life, his predictable life back home, its sudden rupture and his flight, the ambiguity of his itinerary. Have you lasted 60 years for this, Raymond Champagne? Often he managed to walk it off, taking in the old-world charm and southern sophistication of Savannah. There were days when the discoveries – the college of art, the churches, the sidewalk cafés, the squares and parks – placed him in a certain state of grace. He lounged in book stores, he sampled the low country cuisine, he toured historic homes, he took in a play at the repertory theater. One day, he drove to the beaches south of the city. "I could live here," he said to himself on a number of occasions. Yet, each time, the demon of his escapade gnawed at him, and Ray descended into a bottomless questioning. How long are you going to run? Would you ever go back? Could you?

Ray decided he wouldn't spend the day in his room. He found the empty streets grayed by a nippy drizzle. The hollow sound of his footsteps on the cobblestones and the opaque light that obscured the landmarks reinforced his uncertainty. He walked swiftly to his usual breakfast spot at City Market. It was closed. Security shutters down; no one around. Back on West Bay Street, Ray sauntered into the lobby of a high-end hotel and took a linen-covered table in its fancy restaurant. Surrounded by genteel folk in their Christmas best, he ordered the cheapest item on the menu: peach pancakes with hazelnut topping and coffee. He was the only single person there: couples, most of them his age and older, and families with bored teenagers and agitated toddlers. Ray felt lonely. During all the Christmases of his life, he was never alone. He never thought of those people who had no family, no friends, no neighbors, and who spent the entire day by themselves. But he did now, and he didn't know if he should feel sorry for them. He wound up, instead, feeling sorry for himself.

The mountain of pots and pans overwhelmed Claude. It would take all day to wash them, so he turned to the supervisor, Jules, and said, "No way, I'm out of here."

Jules, a square-jawed former boxer and recovered alcoholic,

folded his arms and stared down his kitchen helper. "Listen, man, you keep your end of the bargain: a clean bed, a shower, Christmas dinner with all the fixings, for a few hours cleaning up after." He spoke slowly, without a trace of the southern Black accent. He didn't want this homeless white kid from up north missing any of his meanin'. The two were arguing in the kitchen on the lower level of Calvary Mission, a combination shelter, food pantry and church – all founded by Jules Aiken when he left the ring for good. Over 100 men, women and children had just finished their meal and had gone upstairs for services, praising and thanking the Lord. Christmas eve, Jules had made the rounds of the usual haunts and sweet-talked several of the men into spending Christmas at his church. He was upfront about the work detail, and Claude was leery, but in the end, the promise of a warm bed and a good meal had won out.

"Sorry, old man," was all that Claude offered as his getaway. He grabbed his belongings and walked out the back door into the alley.

"I knows where to find ya," Jules hollered. "And, I'm not too old to give ya a good lickin'."

Claude scurried away from the church shelter, his stomach full for the first time in several days, his back straight, his mind filled with new thoughts. As if to punctuate his mood, the clouds suddenly parted and allowed the sun to flood the street.

Claude wanted to check out his newest spot, Lafayette Square. Maybe there'd be strollers, maybe he'd recite some poetry, maybe folks would be in a generous mood and toss money his way. It was a long walk down Oglethorpe to Colonial Park Cemetery and Claude had to cross the cemetery to reach the square. That usually depressed him, but not today. He defied the ghosts, he scoffed at the doom. He took his time and found himself admiring the manicured expanse of lawn dotted with gothic monuments.

His conversation with Ray the week before had impelled him to become serious about his poetry. He pushed himself to write down his thoughts instead of dismissing them as the rants of an idiot or the hallucinations of a drunkard. In a few days, he collected a dozen poems which began to sound legitimate. He remembered Ray's comment about poets reading to the public and making a bit of money, and he started hanging out at City Market and mingling with the street entertainers. To his surprise, he

143

discovered that folks would quite easily toss a few coins – even dollars – in the containers at the feet of the performers. Eventually, on a very hungry and damp day, Claude Simard joined them, and wound up collecting nearly four dollars for his day's work. He was pleased with himself. City Market, however, was a narrow place, and the competition among the musicians and singers and jugglers and clowns and poets was fierce. Upon hearing about Lafayette Square, he investigated and soon migrated south to a new venue.

The afternoon turned out sunny and Lafayette Square quickly filled with a variety of citizenry. Folks strolled leisurely, joggers stopped to catch their breaths, families spread out for picnics, lovers found refuge in the shady spots, old-timers napped on benches. Two ladies in colorful dresses played a banjo and an accordion; a Black fellow sang a calypso tune and accompanied himself on an assortment of drums. Around each performer gathered a small crowd. There was applause and some of the folks dropped a token of their appreciation. The entertainers replied with a "thank you" or "God bless," and there were smiles all around.

He selected the base of a fountain to sit and recite his poetry. Claude wasn't doing as well as the others. He knew he was not a performer, and as much as he tried, he felt hampered by the intimacy of his poetry. These were not the lyrics written by someone else, this was not some stranger's poetry, these were his thoughts and fantasies and nightmares. He felt naked before the good folk of Savannah; they were dissecting him, and the amount of their offerings depended on their inspection. Claude kept his eyes lowered and his voice muffled. If anyone stopped to listen, it might have been as much out of pity as genuine interest. On this Christmas afternoon, the crowd at Lafayette Square seemed more demanding than usual. Locals, Claude figured. Not as free with their coins as the tourists and curiosity seekers at City Market. Claude became ornery and pulled out from his collection of memorized poems the more depressing. After one especially wretched night, he had penned some lines with a serious tone of suicide. He decided to share one of them with his sparse audience, and without introduction or title, he started reciting.

When I woke up this morning, I was put on backwards,
It took me a while to catch on;

144

I'm not too fast these days,
Backwards or forwards, can't tell 'em apart most times.
At least backwards I've seen before.

Backwards, I'm still hungry; backwards, I'm still dirty.
I wish the tears would flow backwards, maybe that way they'd
take the pain with them.
I wish my body would ache backwards, maybe that way it
would stand straight again.

When I woke up this morning, I couldn't turn around.
Nothing was working the way it should.
I opened when I closed,
I let go when I pulled,
I stopped when I started.

When I woke up this morning, I bled when I cried.
Breathing out, never in; falling, never rising.

When I woke up this morning, I didn't.

Silence greeted his last words. Claude had learned to expect it and to ignore it. No smile, no bow, no signal that it was over. He just waited. The crowd of a dozen or so shuffled, some clearing their throats, others throwing a puzzled glance about them, a few digging into their pockets to feel how much change might be stored there. Suddenly, a voice broke through. "Bravo. Bravo!" Loud and clear, to the point that everyone took notice and focused on the speaker. The man applauded and sent out another set of bravos as he came forward to drop – rather ceremoniously – a dollar bill in Claude's can.

"Thank you, sir," Claude said, eyeing the man suspiciously. "Oh! It's you. The guy with the French Christmas carol. Thanks again."

Ray placed a hand on Claude's shoulder. "Don't mention it. Glad to see you've got poems to read." A couple of people followed suit and left a few coins in the receptacle, and then everyone moved on.

"So, this is where you hang out," Ray said. "I've been going to the riverfront hoping to see you again."

"Sort of moved on. The cops were getting pushy. And, besides, no panhandling or performing allowed there. So I found this place. At least, I can make a few bucks here." Claude was glad to see a friendly face. "And, nights are getting chilly near the river."

"Yes. This morning was wet and cold," Ray added as he sat down on the edge of the fountain. "Mind if I join you?"

Claude moved over and brushed off the top of the bricks in an exaggerated motion. "Please, sir, rest thy weary self."

"Aha! Shakespeare."

"Doubt it. Skipped it in high school. Must be a piece of some movie that got stuck in my brain somehow."

"You really are into poetry," Ray said. "For me, it's always been the theater." He went on to expound on his interest in the stage. He talked about his college days and how he was heavily involved in productions, – always behind the scenes. Claude listened politely.

"By the way, would you mind – eh, what's your name again? I'm sorry I don't remember."

"Claude."

"That's right. So, Claude, would you mind if I gave you a few pointers about how to improve your performance? Might make more money, you know." Without waiting for an answer, Ray suggested that Claude move away from that spot since his voice was drowned out by the sound of the fountain, and that he should take one of the benches at a junction of two paths where there's more room for a crowd to gather. Ray told him to stand and look up over the heads of the people and to place his tin cup on the bench instead of on the ground, and to keep his bag and his stuff out of sight, and to smile and to nod his head to let the audience know when a poem is finished.

"And, what's *your* name? I forget."

Ray told him and laughed, apologizing for preaching to him about his performance.

"You did say you were a teacher, didn't you?

"Yes, always going for that teachable moment."

"Well, it all makes sense. What you said, about moving away from the fountain and everything else." Claude placed his tin can in his duffle bag and grabbed his coat. "Let's do it". Within a few minutes the duo had moved and people started gathering around his bench. Claude threw a surprised look at Ray.

"Do you know any funny poems?" Ray asked.

"What?"

"Something light and cheerful."

Claude was taken aback. He always assumed that poetry was supposed to be serious and weighty. "I don't have any. Everything that comes to me is depressing."

"Well, improvise. Come up with one. Just give it a try. Something quick and..." Ray paused. "Make it funny," he added with a laugh. "Think about something while I introduce you."

Ray turned to the growing crowd and, with his best voice, welcomed everyone. "Today, we are fortunate to have an impromptu performance by the famous poet from New England, Claude..." Ray hesitated. He couldn't remember the young man's last name. He decided he would have to improvise too. "Ladies and Gentlemen, Master Claude." He ended with a vocal flourish and, bowing slightly, waved a hand in Claude's direction.

The poet resented being forced into the spotlight, but not enough to warrant his silence, and he soon came up with an idea he had been juggling for some time. What the hell... This one deserved a title. "This poem is titled *Word Game*," he announced.

Why did we ever get into that stupid word game?
The road to our next honeymoon stop was long and barren
Let's play a word game, she said
In a perfect world, she said
Just complete the sentence:
In a perfect world, she waited
You go first, she said."

Claude stopped, unsure of what to say next. He scanned the audience, and, to his surprise, people appeared interested. They seemed to know he wasn't finished. He took a long breath, closed his eyes to draw deeper from his fantasy, and continued.

Why did I ever go first?
In a perfect world, I hesitated
Yes, go on, she said
In a perfect world,
In a perfect world,
The roll of toilet paper would never run out

147

Why did I ever say that?
Why was she so silent?
She wanted something romantic, I understood
Something like
In a perfect world,
I would always wake up to your smiling face. "

The poet knew that his imagining was nearly exhausted. He stopped again. He saw Ray's face in the middle of the crowd. He saw him wink and give him an encouraging thumbs-up. Still, Claude decided to bring his creation to a quick conclusion.

Why was the ride to the next place taking ever so long?
Why am I still so bad at word games?

Despite Claude's hesitations, the poem had flowed easily. In line with his mentor's instructions, he smiled and took a deep bow. The recitation was greeted with applause. Claude took another bow. One by one, members of the audience stepped forward and deposited their tokens. Claude wanted to look down at his tin can, but he caught Ray's disapproving eye, and said a simple thank you to each person. Ray beamed his approval from the other side of the cobblestoned walkway. When nearly everyone had moved on, he crossed over to Claude and, throwing a quick glance into the tin can, saw there were a few bills. "Great job. Where did that poem come from? It was perfect…" Claude was about to explain the origin of the poem when they were interrupted by a diminutive voice. They looked down at a little girl in a pretty dress.

"Do you know any Christmas poems?" she asked. Claude and Ray gave each other a look of uncertainty.

A woman came forward and placed a protective arm around the youngster. "Now, don't you bother the gentlemen," she said. A man stood behind her. Ray assumed he was the girl's father. The two men exchanged a glance that seemed to linger, as if each one was searching for a moment or a place, a shared experience.

"I don't have a Christmas poem, but this gentleman knows a

very unusual Christmas carol." Claude tugged on his companion's sleeve.

"What?" Ray was confused.

"The French carol you were singing the other night. You know the one. Sing it for the little girl." Claude enjoyed placing his friend in an unexpected spotlight.

"Only if you sing with me," Ray said.

"Don't know the words."

"Hum."

"We'll both sing it for you," Ray said to the little girl who clapped her joy as she and her parents returned to their viewing spot across the way.

Ray started on a false note, a note he suspected was too high. He gave Claude a knowing glance and started again. Ray didn't know the words for the entire song, so he made up the last couple of verses. To their mutual surprise, the two voices blended well, and by the time the carol was done, a large crowd had gathered. More applause, more bows, more money in the tin can. The girl's mother nudged her through the crowd. "Thank the gentlemen for that beautiful song," she said to her daughter.

"You're welcome," said Claude bending down.

"My pleasure," said Ray, still erect, his eyes glued on the dad who had remained across the way. Ray was fascinated by the handsome and rugged father, and he fought an urge to lunge through the crowd to reach him. Ray wanted to touch him, to say something, anything. The mother and daughter returned to the waiting dad who gave his daughter a long hug, all the while staring at Ray. Finally, the father gave Ray a smile and Ray responded in kind.

"There must be twenty dollars in here," Claude said as he sat down. "Look, Ray. Look at this money." Ray didn't hear him; he was intently watching the family walk away, admiring the father's well defined backside.

"Ray."

"Yes." Ray joined his friend. As Claude counted the money, Ray's mind returned to the encounter with the girl's dad, unsure how to interpret his feelings. Finally, he forced himself to pay attention. "Looks like we've got a promising career, the two of us."

They sat on their bench under a live oak, watching the shadows grow. Ray said he still wanted to know what had inspired the poem about the word game. Claude suddenly remembered sounds from another place. He smelled the wood stove, he listened to his best friend Tony and his sisters snoring – a gentle chorus that he envied – and, above it all, he heard Tony's parents talking sweet things to each other. The Diangelo tradition called for the family to spend a weekend each fall at the lake. Claude went along for the first time when he was 13. In his bunk, Claude listened as Tony's father and mother reminisced about their honeymoon and how they had their first argument over a stupid word game. Tony's dad suggested they play it again.

"In a perfect world..."

"Now, be careful," she said.

"In a perfect world...I'm always inside you," he said. She laughed and hushed.

That afternoon in Lafayette Square, Claude confessed to Ray that the memory of that night surfaced during his adult life, when he thought of weddings and lovers. He revealed he often wished his own parents had such interesting little secrets. Ray advised the fledgling poet to delve into his past for more inspiration. "Stories like that make good poems, they ring true".

They talked until the bells of the cathedral overlooking the park interrupted them. Ray said the bells could be pealing the six o'clock Angelus. Claude replied that as a kid the six o'clock bells from his church reminded him that it was time to go home for supper. The two listened as the sound of the bells enveloped the square. In the diminishing light, the strands of Spanish moss took on an otherworldly look. Claude said that the strings of moss were attached to the bells and the ghosts of monks were running around the park tugging at them.

To the bass vibrations of the final bell, Ray and Claude walked out of the square and headed north towards an undeclared destination. Claude slipped into a variety store. He returned and, smiling broadly, he wished the older man a happy birthday. He offered, with a grand gesture, a cellophane-wrapped chocolate Ring Ding. "Your birthday cake, sir."

"You remembered," Ray said.

On Bay Street, some of the cafes and bars had opened for the evening. The men ordered hamburgers and beers. They split the cupcake, and Ray said it was his best birthday feast. They ate and drank in silence and watched the strollers and the traffic. Music rolled down the street from a lounge; the night air was invading the place.

Someone was having sex in the next room. The queen size beds in rooms 322 and 324 would have been back to back – or more accurately, head to head – without the wall separating the two units, and Ray, lying awake in his, could feel the movements and hear the sounds of copulation. He lifted his head and recorded the time on the alarm clock: 2 a.m. "Thank God, another Christmas has come and gone," he mumbled, allowing the date and time to distract him briefly from the sex next door. Ray focused his eyes on the sliver of light trapped along the bottom of his door. He watched intently as something obscured it briefly. He heard voices from the corridor: laughter and shushing, male and female voices. "Busy night at the Bates Motel," Ray chuckled.

Totally awake, Ray lay in the darkness and let his mind wander back to his love-making. There was only one: Jane, the pretty teacher and his wife for the past 30 years. He wondered if she became bored with him as quickly as he tired of her. He wondered if it was his lack of interest in sex that killed the flame of those first few months of marriage. Often, he revisited the conversation with his father that summer just before his wedding. His father declared that women were dangerous. Dangerous – that was the word he used. Ray discovered that Jane was far from dangerous, just unexciting. His father also said women were around for the purpose of procreation, and he wished there were a better way, a less messy way of having babies. Ray sat up. "Well, Raymond and Jane Champagne did procreate and it was messy and it happened only once," Ray announced to no-one. He dropped back into bed and concluded that both he and Jane wanted the same thing out of their marriage: respectability. He buried his face in the pillow and smothered his next thought: until some handsome phony lumberjack entrapped you in a rest area.

The goings-on next door shifted, and Ray could feel the pounding. Louder and faster. Stronger. As if the beds in each room were one, connected by an invisible tension, the heavy breathing and the sweating spreading from one to the other, the smell of abandon filling the air on both sides. Finally, the yelps of the female voice, the grunts of the male voice. Then quiet. The tension eased. The two beds came apart.

Ray imagined the lovers descending into that special space that follows fierce lovemaking. He saw their limbs still tangled, he caught their smiles, he recognized their faces: his and the handsome daddy's – the father of the girl who asked for a Christmas poem in the park that afternoon. The image did not startle or upset Ray. He had imagined the scene before, countless times, always with an unknown man whose sudden gaze sparked a connection, a link to the impossible.

In the darkness of his motel room, Ray heard the words of the French carol he had sung for the little girl and, this time, the song was being carried by a boy choir and bell ringers. He was kneeling alone inside a vast Romanesque sanctuary somewhere in Provence, and the singers were perched high in a balcony and the scent of oranges and fruitwood filled the air.

Leaving this church he had never seen, Ray imagined himself as a guest at Christmas dinner with Claude as a child, with his mother and father, and the great-aunt who was offering the song in her feeble yet clear French-Canadian voice. *Il est né, le divin enfant...Chantons tous...* Ray ached to sing. Out loud. But, for the moment, all was quiet. The lovemaking in the other room had ceased; the boy choir and their bells had become but a wish that lulled him back to sleep.

When he woke up, the light had changed. The motel alarm clock revealed the time: 8:30. Nothing like sex, even in the next room, to guarantee a sound sleep, he mumbled. He turned on the TV set and found a weather report. The forecast was gloomy: the day after Christmas was ushering in a stretch of heavy rain and winds with chilly, below average temperatures. He went to the window and opened the draperies to reveal a steady rain falling over Savannah. Ray stared at the obscured streets below. Turning to face his room, he inventoried the unmade bed, the lamp that never cast enough light, the clothes thrown over the desk chair, the TV set with its self-important weatherman. Is it time to go, time to move on? But where to? Ray, where is next? Will there always be a next? He argued with himself, one wishing to escape the prison that his hotel room was turning into, the other, comforting, soothing, calming. He walked around the room, back and forth, circling the small space. Finally, a pronouncement: "Well, this inn has lost its quality. Time to move on."

First, the wetness, on the side of his hood, on his exposed cheek, then the warmth. Claude woke with a start. It took him a second to recognize the smell of urine. He protected his eyes, yet he saw the beam from a flashlight and recognized a pair of boots a few inches from his head. "Damn it, you're pissing all over me. Stop it; you crazy or something?" Claude sat up.

"Thought you'd be used to being pissed on."

"Ah, c'mon, Jules. Leave me alone."

"Leave ya alone?" Told ya I knew where to find ya. Teach ya to back down on a promise – specially to Jules Aiken"

"Ah c'mon Jules. Leave me alone."

"Ya know, on my way here, I was thinkin' I'd take ya back and keep ya workin' in the kitchen for a bit. But now that I sees you living like this, in this shithole, I wants nothin' to do with ya." Jules moved forward and kicked Claude on the side of his head.

Claude dissolved into the berth he had created for himself and pulled the hem of Tony's coat up for protection. Jules kicked him again, and one more time. Claude cringed.

"Now get yourself outa Savannah, you stinkin' piece of shit."

Under Tony's coat, Claude moaned as he massaged the swelling of his upper cheek. His right hand ached and the smell of urine on his skin and his clothes seemed to be gaining strength. Slowly, he pulled the coat off his head. He saw that everyone who had shared his hideaway had scattered. The cold and dampness of the rainy Savannah morning crept over him; he sat up, looked at his makeshift bed now in disarray, the littered and slimy remnants of the night scattered about, the isolation of the place, and he wept – like he hadn't for months.

It took very little time for Ray to pack. He returned to the TV set to check once again the weather forecast and heard no retraction: still wet, dismal, and cold. At checkout, he found the guest coffee urn already empty as was the lower level parking garage. Savannah had closed down. A few blocks later he stopped for gas at a 7-Eleven and realized that in his hasty departure from the hotel, he hadn't been to the bathroom. That realization strengthened as he walked to the back of the store towards the bathroom and his bladder decided it was about time.

The restroom was occupied. Ray knocked on the door: "Please, a near-emergency here," he said. Someone answered something that sounded like *be right out*. Ray thought he recognized the voice as he stepped from foot to foot.

"Claude!"

"Ray. What you doing here?"

"Trying to pee. Have to go badly. Oh, you look like hell. Claude, wait for me outside. Please?"

Claude nodded then quickly looked away.

Outside a few minutes later, Ray scanned the small parking lot. No Claude. The rain had slowed, but the sky seemed heavier. At his Subaru, Ray glanced around and found no one that even remotely looked like Claude. He drove out to clear the gas pumps and hesitated before pulling out of the 7Eleven lot. You can't leave him like this. Something's happened to him. He's the only friend you've made in Savannah; you can't turn your back on him.

A knock on his passenger window stirred Ray out of his soliloquy. He waved to Claude and leaned over to open the car door. "Get in; it's starting to rain again. Throw your bag in there," Ray said, pointing to the back of the vehicle. Ray headed for an empty parking lot across the street. He stared at his passenger who kept his head down and remained silent. "Listen, Claude. I'm leaving. Had enough, heading south. You can join me if you want."

"You sure? I need to get out of Savannah; someone's out to get me."

"No explanations necessary."

The car pulled out and headed for I-95. "You ever been to Florida?"

For several miles, undulating stretches of I-95 played with countless inlets of the Atlantic. The sky gradually lightened to dullness and clouds tinged with mauve reflected on grasslands bleached of their summer glow. Like a blessing on the decision to head south, the rain stayed in Savannah. This was new territory for both men and they took it in with anticipation.

Claude thought of Jack Kerouac's *On the Road*, a book he had struggled with and pledged to read again. Scanning the empty plain spreading ahead of him, Claude felt a kinship with the beat author and his quest to connect with the vastness of America. He knew that Kerouac's roads were western ones, yet he saw himself as a new Dean Moriarty coaxing the writer to explore the south. Ray ventured into his own reverie as he sped towards Florida. He could imagine the sails of galleys spiking the low skies and he wondered how many early explorers from the Old World had been lured into these inlets hoping to find the great waterway leading into the interior of the New World.

As they crossed into the Sunshine State, Ray asked Claude to find a good station on the radio. The choices were limited: Christian sermons or country music. They acknowledged with a nod that silence was better, and Claude turned off the radio.

"It's none of my business, but if you want to tell me what happened…," Ray said to break his self-imposed silence.

Claude stared at the roadway ahead. Several moments of quiet followed. "Just got into a fight, that's all," he ventured softly.

"A fight? Doesn't sound like you, the mild-mannered poet and troubadour."

Claude ignored the remark. "Didn't look for it; just came and found me where I was sleeping. Actually, I *did* look for it in a way; shouldn't have been surprised. Christmas eve I went to this crazy guy's homeless shelter. For a good bed and Christmas dinner, I promised to help clean up the next day, but there were a hundred people eating there, whole families with tons of children and they made a real mess, and this guy Jules who runs the place put me to work and I didn't feel like spending the day washing pots and pans and so I walked out on him. Jules said he'd find me and make me pay. You should see him; he's old, but he's a big fellow, used to be a boxer." The dam had been breached and Claude couldn't stop. "So this morning he found me and kicked me and…pissed on me."

"I see," said Ray.

"You see? I doubt it."

"I mean, I…" Ray went on.

"I'm sure you haven't seen it. I certainly haven't seen anything like that. You have no idea how humiliating it is."

Silence returned to the vehicle, heavier than before – the kind of silence that follows a confession that challenges the priest to find an appropriate penance.

Finally, Ray suggested they stop for a break. "I'm hungry. Had no breakfast. I'm sure you must be hungry too."

Claude mumbled, "Yeah, I am."

The next exit delivered the travelers to the outskirts of a place called Santona Beach. Ray was driving up to a Burger King, thinking that they should have fast food in the car, when his eye noticed a Walgreens across the street. "Why not. Let's go across the street and clean you up first, perhaps get you a new sweatshirt that smells…nice. Then we can go to a real restaurant."

"I don't have much money."

"Never mind, I'm sure you'll pay me back later. You stay in the car; I'll get what we need."

Ray returned with a bagful of antiseptics with Q-tips and bandages, and proudly displayed a new sweatshirt that sported the words *Sunshine State* in pink script.

Claude grimaced while Ray cleaned the bruises, silently acknowledging that it felt good to have someone care for him. The dirty sweatshirt went into a trash receptacle. Claude remembered Mrs. Washburn handing it to him months before while picketing at the Post Office and he smiled.

"Want to get rid of that heavy winter coat? It's quite dirty and doesn't smell too fresh."

"No. No, the coat stays."

They rode by the usual collection of chain motels and restaurants and after a couple of miles, they stopped at Sophie's Café. The place was empty. Both men paused at the door, hesitating. Ray yelled out and received an answer from what he assumed was the kitchen. "Come on in, take a seat, I'll be with you'all in a minute. Let me turn on the AC." A woman's voice, robust and friendly. Sophie emerged from the kitchen wiping her hands on an apron. "You'all have the whole place to yourselves. Nobody comes in for another hour. But the food's hot and mighty good. Hi, I'm Sophie. Come, come. Sit down."

Claude dropped himself into the closest booth, squeezing into the far end of the seat. He rolled up his sleeves like a worker about to undertake a task. Sophie slapped two menus down on the table. "Crab cakes' the special today. And minestrone's the soup. All homemade and mighty fine."

"Thanks," said Claude.

"Ice tea, fellas?"

The men nodded. "Unsweetened, for me," Ray said.

"You too, hon?"

Claude looked at her, smiled. "Yes, maam."

A minute later Sophie brought utensils wrapped in yellow napkins and a pair of paper place mats that welcomed travelers to *Beautiful Santona Beach, a Slice of Paradise*. Claude and Ray found themselves perusing the ads on the perimeter of the mats before scanning the menus. Another minute and Sophie returned with their ice teas. The men ordered and heard their choices echoed to an unseen person behind the kitchen door. The owner-waitress then busied herself by taking down the silver Christmas trim from the windows and the cash register counter.

"I guess that makes it official. Christmas must be over," stated Ray. "Thank God." He took a long sip of his ice tea.

Claude looked half-eyed at his companion, as if his gaze could head straight for him and then simply circle around him like a piece of debris in the road. It was a habit. A self-defense device picked up to avoid having to watch someone's face turn to evil. Especially people he didn't know well. "How was it?" Claude threw the question at someone who wasn't there, who would have been directly behind Ray.

"How was what?"

"I mean, how was Christmas for you this year?"

"Not so great. I turned 60."

"Well, 60 isn't that old."

"Maybe not for you. Wait until it's your turn."

"Suppose you're right. Anyway, you don't look old. No older than 59." Claude smiled. Ray laughed and studied his new friend. He wanted to tell Claude that he should smile more, that he had an endearing smile. His eyes followed the contours of Claude's shoulders and down his arms, stopping on the scars on the inside of his forearms. He wanted to ask him how he got the marks.

"Was it tough for you?" Ray asked. "I mean, being away from home for Christmas?"

"I tried not to think about it."

"You said you had a son..."

"Actually, I have two. Nick, my oldest, is with the Marines... in Iraq. My other boy turned five in October. His name's Mikey."

"I often wished I had a son. It's an old-fashioned way of thinking, I suppose, but you're not complete unless you have a son, a replica of sorts, someone to carry the name into history."

"Never thought of it that way,' Claude added.

"I have a daughter. She's grown and married and has two little girls."

"I see. And, your wife?"

The question belted Ray. His mouth dropped, and he stared at his companion.

"Ah..." Ray searched for an answer.

Sophie provided the perfect pause as she placed their food in front of them. "Here we go fellas. Eat up."

"Thanks," said Ray, grateful for both the food and the interruption.

Sophie looked at the two diners and their steaming plates. She puffed up with pride. "As I say to my Canadian snow birds, *Bone Happatee*." She giggled and walked back to her kitchen.

Claude dove in. Ray glanced outside and noticed a square of blue sky. "Rain's definitely over," he offered.

As the men ate, they wondered how they might continue the conversation.

Ray spoke first. "Yes, I have a wife."

"D'you talk to her and your daughter at Christmas."

"No. I didn't. Wouldn't know what to say."

"I didn't talk to my boy either," said Claude.

"Which one?"

"Well, the older one and I, we're not on speaking terms. I didn't talk to Mikey either.

159

"What about their mom?"

"Mikey's mom doesn't want to hear from me. As far as she's concerned, I might as well fall off a cliff. And, the restraining order prevents me from having any contact with my son."

Ray became aware that the moment was turning heavy, that Claude was struggling. He reached over and touched the younger man on his forearm. Claude let him. He coughed and covered both eyes with his hand. Neither man moved. Ray felt Claude stumbling all over his thoughts and he tightened his hold on Claude's arm.

"The only real hurt I have is when I think of Mikey," Claude said softly. He pulled his arm away. He pushed his empty plate away. He scanned the restaurant, his eyes flirting with an escape.

"Look. I'm sorry. I shouldn't have brought it up. We can change the subject." Ray felt a mixture of sympathy and relief. Apparently there was too much recent turmoil in both their lives. There was no reason to pick at the wounds. "You want some dessert?"

Claude declined. Ray waved at Sophie and asked for the check.

Without a word, they filed out of the eatery, Sophie's cheerful wishes for a fine day drifting behind them. The men walked slowly to the car, automatically heading to their respective sides.

They pulled off I-95 for gas. Ray went inside to pay. He had cleaned out his credit cards in Terre Haute to avoid being tracked. Cash purchases couldn't be handled at the pump. That irritated him, yet he accepted the inconvenience as a small price for anonymity. Back at the car, he suddenly felt an urge to use the bathroom – a need that was becoming more and more pressing and frequent. "Can you take this?" he asked Claude pointing to the gas hose. "Use regular. It's paid for." Ray rushed to the Quick-Mart. Claude took the hose and selected the grade, noticing the price and trying to remember how much it cost the last time he purchased gasoline. He had no idea.

Later, the Subaru back on the interstate rolling south, Claude watched the sun fall over the western horizon into a dense line of palm trees. He opened his window to feel the warm moist air, examining the lush landscape, watching the trees shimmer in the dusk. He thought he could actually see the warmth rising from the soil and recalled his nights in the cold warehouse back in Connecticut. He felt grateful for Mister O'Regan's intervention.

"By the way, thanks for the ride."

"My pleasure." Ray didn't feel like talking. He also noticed the landscape turn tropical as they proceeded south. He felt tired, yet elated: the palm trees and the humidity meant he was in Florida. He had found his destination after nearly 20 aimless days.

Claude felt like sharing. "Did I tell you that I spent most of the time alone? I was living in this abandoned warehouse next to the river, a huge space with skylights and a whitewashed brick wall over thirty feet tall. I painted most of the wall with all kinds of crazy designs." He paused a moment to see if Ray would respond. Claude continued. "Did you ever hear of Chagall? I found a book of his paintings at the library and I copied some of the drawings on my wall. I liked the pictures of people floating in air, high above the buildings." Ray nodded as Claude took a breath and continued. "Chagall has this special kind of blue. It's his favorite color. I tried to reproduce it, but I don't think I was able to. My mural was huge. I worked on it all summer and fall. In the end, I added words from Ginsberg and Kerouac." Claude was about to say that his handiwork included – as a postscript in a lower corner – the evil people with their scary masks that haunted him since he was a kid, but he decided to keep that to himself.

Ray turned on the AC. He wasn't paying attention to his passenger's tale. He was consumed by the uncertainty of his final destination. Was Florida the right place? The right place for what? What would he do here? What would he do anywhere?

"Funny, I never set foot in the Williams Public Library before," Claude continued. "But last summer I went three or four times a week. They didn't like it at first, but I stayed out of the way and finally nobody noticed me. The only other time I left the warehouse was for the anti-war protest every Saturday morning."

Ray didn't hear; he was revisiting his life in Packers Falls. Scenes raced through his mind: walking the hallways at the junior high – his junior high – the certificates and awards on the wall of his office: New Hampshire teacher of the year for 1997; his speech at the banquet when he celebrated thirty-five years as an educator; the squeals of his granddaughters when he tickled and teased them; the quiet evenings at home with his wife…

"Strange how I never thought about surviving the winter,"

Claude continued. "The place was cold even on the warmest days. A chilly moisture that made my bones ache. Most of the windows were smashed. It never dawned on me that it would snow inside. I could have frozen to death." Claude glanced at Ray. "Again, thanks for the ride. Thanks, Ray, for getting me to Florida."

"Yeah. Florida. The Sunshine State. Only good things happen in Florida." Ray was emerging from his flashback. He reached to the control panel and turned the AC on high. "It's getting stuffy in here."

"Sorry for all that, boring you with the gritty details of my life as a homeless bum."

Ray didn't respond.

Claude saw a sign for a rest area ahead and asked Ray to pull in there, explaining he needed to use the bathroom. Ray panicked. He had avoided highway rest stops since Georgia. Bad places, bad places, he repeated in his head. Yet, he moved towards the exit lane and fell in with several other vehicles heading to the crowded rest stop. Ray probed the place, trying to convince himself it was safe.

"Can you make it fast?" Ray said as he came to a stop. "I hate rest areas. They give me the creeps." Alone, Ray rested his arm on the door, his elbow outside the vehicle. He took in a deep breath of warm air and a section of his brain recognized it from another place and time, and he saw the brawny Paul Bunyan stretch in front of his vehicle, swagger over to Ray and engage him in conversation. He watched his hand reach over and unzip his fly, his eyes glued to the seducer's groin on the edge of the car window, then he felt the struggle with the lumberjack-turned-state trooper and he heard the warning about resisting arrest. The panic of that moment swamped him. He closed his eyes, tried to slow down his breathing.

"Sorry, took so long. There was a line."

Ray heard the voice and took a moment to process it. He looked out the car window and saw the faded jeans and the brand new sweatshirt. The state trooper was gone; Claude was back, opening the passenger door and taking his seat. Ray took a deep breath and headed southward again.

Claude was curious. He wanted to ask his companion why he hated rest areas, but decided against it, thinking Ray was entitled to his idiosyncrasies like everyone else.

The morning of December 29th, Nicolette stopped making coffee. It was an easy decision. She hadn't stayed up all night planning it; the thought hadn't even occurred to her it until it did. She was reaching into the kitchen cabinet for the can of Yuban when she heard the two priests shuffling behind her. Abruptly, Nicolette pushed herself away from the counter and, pointing to the can next to the coffeemaker, she said, "*Voilà!*" As an afterthought, she reached for the coffee can, lifted it and slammed it on the countertop. The sound bounced around the small kitchen, punctuating her one word phrase and cementing her resolve.

Nicolette faced the door and waited for the priests to back away and let her pass. She harvested her winter coat and her bags and walked in front of them without saying a word. As she tackled the stairs to her office, a delicate smile of defiance graced her lips. "*Voilà,*" she repeated once inside the parish office. She had made her point. She was certain that both priests had understood, but her use of the French word was meant especially for Father Julien. She knew he would get the message: she was not going to be his servant. She went to her desk, straightened out the paperwork, reviewed the week's calendar. The wind scolded outside, whipping the previous day's snow into sheets and waves. The final days of 2007 had turned bitterly cold, and Nicolette examined the lacy buildup of ice on the edges of the window panes. The old furnace at Saint Petronilla's was working overtime.

Her initial reaction to Father Mondésir's invasion – that's how she referred to his arrival – was one of fear, a palpable dread that found its anchor in both her gut and her memory. She quizzed her mother again and again for details, for confirmation: what exactly transpired back in Cap-Haïtien, why does the name Julien Mondésir carry so much terror? Was he truly the one responsible for the death of her father and her brother? Maman Saintolien said nothing. She refused to even utter the name, the name she banished from her family's history once they set foot in America. When her daughter pressed on, she placed both hands over her ears and wailed. "All I have to say to you, *ma p'tite*, is that you must watch this man. Be vigilant."

She went to Father Tony and apologized for her outburst on the day she and Claude confronted him about the new priest. She explained there were many horrors from her childhood in Haiti. "Those were terrible days and I was so young and fragile and the name Julien Mondésir will forever be associated with that terror." She also exhorted the priest to be vigilant.

Father Tony was unsympathetic. A day later, he announced in very dry terms that he had checked with the Chancery and that Father Julien's credentials were impeccable. "You must be confusing him with someone else. I am convinced he will bring new life to the parish. And, I welcome him with open arms."

"Just be careful he doesn't chop them off," she said.

"Please, this isn't a joke."

"I am not joking, Father."

"Well, I want you to keep your thoughts to yourself. I want you to treat him with respect," he said coldly.

Nicolette decided that respect was more than she could muster. Avoidance became her strategy.

Sitting in her tidy office, she congratulated herself. Her strategy was working. Each day, she felt calmer, more confident. It was easy to avoid Father Julien. When their paths crossed, she didn't look at him. If he spoke to her, she would reply drily and walk away, or, better still, make believe she didn't hear him. "He does not exist," she said to herself. Nicolette closed the door to her office. She wanted to shut out the cold air from the corridor and the male voices from the kitchen below. She couldn't understand why Father Tony was so much in awe of the Haitian priest. Father Tony seemed to enjoy his company, in stark contrast to his mood when Claude, his real friend, stayed at the rectory.

Nicolette often wondered how Claude might be faring. The day of his abrupt departure, Claude hardly spoke to her, except to announce late in the afternoon he was leaving Philadelphia.

"Where will you go?" she asked softly.

"Tony will drive me downtown, to the bus terminal."

"It will be a sad place again. You brought life and comfort, you know."

164

"I never intended to stay this long."

"Are you going to Florida?"

"That was my destination. But, I think I'll stop along the way. Who knows? This is my chance to see the country."

"You will be missed, Monsieur Claude."

"Thank you, Madame Nicolette. I'm glad I met you."

They gave each other a hug, arms wrapped protectively around shoulders. Claude held the embrace a bit longer than she did, remembering the softness, the power of closeness. In a single summoning, he felt the comfort of his mother's arms after a fall in the back yard, the playfulness of youthful tumblings with his friend Tony, the amorous nights in Margie's bed, the cradling of his young son. He pulled away from Nicolette and offered her a gallant but brief kiss on the hand. "Take care of yourself and your two little boys."

"Of course."

"And..." he hesitated. "Keep an eye on Father Tony for me.

That last request still haunted her. Almost a month after leaving, Claude's words followed Nicolette around the rectory. She could hear him; she could see the sadness in his eyes.

Back at her desk, Nicolette plunged into her bookkeeping and for a while dismissed her guilt. The phone rang. She automatically picked it up and started giving her usual response when she heard Father Mondésir's voice interrupt her. The call was for him. Silence followed. Both the secretary and the priest waited for the other to hang up. A male voice asked in Creole to speak to Father Julien. Nicolette placed the receiver down. Most phone calls were for Father Julien these days. New voices and new faces wandered around the church property. The Haitian priest's Masses attracted new people, most of them men. Father Tony was thrilled; she grew more suspicious.

Her eyes wandered to the framed photograph of her two little boys. They brought a timid smile to her face.

Nicolette turned to look out the window. A naked branch rapped against the glass. She closed her eyes and heard gunfire. She shivered, but not from the cold. Nicolette Saintolien had shrunken into the young girl crouched in the corner of her room in Cap-Haïtien listening to the sounds of gunfire and screams outside.

III

Thrill to Romance

Dushayne leaned over the highway railing and stared at the Tuesday night traffic as it crunched to a halt in the distance. In the southbound lanes, dozens of cars and trucks were collecting behind the collision like cattle waiting for a gate to open. *Shit, that's all I need, a fucking accident.* Dushayne draped himself over the side, his eyes sweeping the southbound lanes passing beneath Broward Boulevard. The roadway was eerily empty as was the ramp leading to his perch.

Tuesday nights can be good, but not this one. Too hot and humid; drivers don't lower their windows – not to give money to a homeless guy. Besides, that accident's gonna piss people off and when people are in a pissy mood they're not in a givin' mood.

The nineteen-year-old had started panhandling less than two months earlier. He was a fast learner, quickly figuring out what it takes to get the motorists to cough up their quarters and dollars. His tee-shirt for instance. *Guns and Roses* or *The Grateful Dead* were sure winners. Bob Marley was pretty safe. But rappers, never. Nobody opens up for rappers. Especially when the panhandler's a young Black dude. On this late October night, he wore his *Grateful Dead* tee-shirt. Without that accident, he'd get at least three or four guys who'd roll down their windows, give a thumbs up, and drop a couple of bucks in his cap. It's always that way with the *Grateful Dead*. And, if they're at the head of the ramp and

167

there's plenty of time before the light turns, they'd talk about the band and their favorite song. Never misses.

Dushayne looked down at I-95 flowing empty below him towards Miami. His eyes scanned the northern horizon and stopped on the blue glow of the cop cars and the red of the fire trucks. All six lanes blocked, not even room to squeeze by. Might as well go home.

It had taken him a long time to get a weeknight. At first, all he got were noontimes and a rare weekend. But when Sterling had to go to the hospital, Dushayne was the first to show up on the guy's Tuesday night and lay claim to it. After a couple of weeks, he was surprised to find motorists inquiring about Sterling. Some knew his name; others simply asked where the old army veteran was. So Dushayne played it up and said Sterling was real bad off, and a few of the people gave money for the guy, which of course Dushayne kept for himself.

Because of the accident and the bottleneck, there was no sense walking around like a cripple, so Dushayne bent down and took his sneaker off. He removed the crumpled paper stuffed in the toe of his shoe. Folks like their homeless to be hurtin'. Specially a young stud who otherwise would look too healthy. He was tall like a basketball player and that didn't work in his favor. He learned to bend his torso and twist it just a bit. He kept his head down, but he got the idea that people wanted to see his face. There was something reassuring about giving money to someone who looked at you straight in the eyes and showed gratitude. At first he smiled a lot, but after practicing in the mirror, he concluded that his teeth were too damn straight. And he had all of 'em. Homeless people don't have good teeth. He started to look at his benefactors straight in the eye and say, "God bless." No smile. He wouldn't look too long, either. Don't wanna make 'em uncomfortable. The last thing he wanted to be was threatening. Folks want their homeless to be meek.

Dushayne returned his gaze to the traffic pileup and watched a pair of ambulances race to the accident scene, followed by an armada of tow trucks. What the fuck, no sense hanging around. Nothing's gonna happen.

Dushayne decided to wait until the evening cooled off before heading home. He pulled his watch out. Seven-thirty, days already gettin' shorter. He put the watch back in his jeans.

Homeless people don't wear watches. You gotta think of everything. This is like a job, there's skills to learn. Like an acting job. Everything's an acting job. Selling cell phones at the mall, flipping burgers at McDonalds, making payday loans, it's all acting.

There was a lot of acting at his other job: weekend bar back at Hips. He licked the ass of all those bartenders and bouncers and drag queens and he had them all convinced he was not only the sweetest little nigger around, but that he enjoyed being their boy. Not that he hated the job. The money was ok and all cash. Plus, he enjoyed watching the drag queens. Now *that* was acting.

The ambulances wailed their way south, a fire truck extricated itself from the accident scene, and, a few minutes later, a lane opened up and a line of vehicles started making its way towards Dushayne's exit. He stuck the lump of cardboard back in his sneaker and put on his acting face.

The first car on the ramp turned out to be a good one. An older guy looked at the homeless lad, shook his head, and said, "Quite a mess. Somebody got killed for sure." He dropped a five dollar bill in Dushayne's cap.

"God bless. Makes me glad I don't drive," Dushayne said. Using his cap was another lesson he'd learned quickly. People didn't like dropping money in a bag of any kind. But a sports cap, held out like a small bowl – that worked wonders.

Another driver, the third one in line, tooted his horn, and Dushayne limped up to him. The driver dropped a dollar bill and a couple of quarters.

A young Black woman sitting in her late model sedan idling in the inside lane waved him to come closer.

"Can't you get a job?" she said as she gave him a bunch of coins. "Why you young bros always lookin' for a handout?"

"I tries, man, I tries. God bless." Dushayne walked away quickly, amused and pissed off at the same time.

The traffic grew steady but the donations dropped off. Several vehicles clambered up the ramp, stopped in the two lanes facing the red light, waited for it to change, the drivers trying to ignore the homeless lad with the limp. Dushayne went through the motions, waiting for at least three or four vehicles to be in line before stepping out onto the bird-shit-stained apron of the ramp, his home-made sign held at waist level pleading: "Homeless and

Hungry. Please Help." He was thirsty and tired and he wanted to go home. The false lameness of his foot became real; his acting skills were fading as fast as the Florida sun. Enough of this shit. I'm outta here. He returned to the top of the exit ramp, but when he reached the overpass, he changed his mind. Like an addict, he decided to wait for another surge of cars – just in case.

Dushayne Elwin Brown was homeless in many ways. Not as destitute as his highway beggar role would have people believe, but he still didn't have much. A good disposition, a quick mind, and the talent for adaptation were his strong points. He was a dropout – not even a high school dropout, the last day of his seventh grade having been his final day in school. Dushayne quit because he was the tallest kid in class and he thought he deserved some respect. Instead, they teased him with the name Douche or Douchebag. He hadn't honed his acting skills yet and he battled it out – turning tormentors and teasers into hard enemies. He quit school because the streets of Fort Lauderdale wound up being safer than the school yard. But there was little safety in the all-male household of his father and four older brothers, and, at the age of 15, he followed his mother's example and ran away. *She* had been the smart one. He admired his mother for having the guts to get out as much as he resented her for abandoning him.

After a year on his own, he wound up at Aunties where he still lived. Roberta wasn't his real aunt – she wasn't anybody's real aunt. But she deserved the name. A very large woman, Roberta Wellington always claimed she had more than her share of the maternal instinct. The Lord hadn't blessed her with children of her own, but he gave her a big heart, she would explain.

She and her husband Octavious owned a two-story half-assed motel on Sistrunk Boulevard. A do-goody project of the seventies, the building was among a slew of efforts to create an economic revival in Fort Lauderdale's ghetto. Without adequate funding, the complex was sold at auction before it was even finished. Roberta turned the first floor into an odd collection of mom-and-pop businesses: a pawn shop, a liquor store, a beauty parlor, a Laundromat, and, occupying the northern half, an auto repair shop that was as much graveyard as fix-it place. The second floor became a rooming house. Auntie and Octavious– no one ever thought of calling him uncle – lived in two of the motel units joined as one. She called it the master suite, and since it occupied a full wing at an angle to the rest of the building, her home gave Auntie a clear view of all the other rooms and their vague inhabitants. She didn't pry, but she had her rules, and in a voice large enough to resuscitate the old carcasses in the auto repair lot below, she spelled out their meaning: no drugs, no whoring around, no stealing and no visits by the cops. She was a good Christian woman and she expected everybody to respect that.

Roberta took an immediate shine to Dushayne. She saw his intellect. She also detected a kind soul, perhaps a fragile soul, one that would need her special brand of nurturing. Dushayne saw in her the first adult he could respect. He thought it the highest irony that a woman like Roberta couldn't bear children while his mother had five sons she didn't know what to do with. Mrs. Wellington took him in rent free for the first two years, and it was Dushayne who started paying the modest rent, without prompting. Auntie's only condition: the money had to be earned honestly. That was fine by Dushayne who was intent on staying out of trouble. Living at Aunties was crowded and noisy, but it was safe.

By eight-thirty, traffic had weakened to a trickle. The young beggar concluded he had pinched all there was to be pinched out of the evening. He counted the bills and coins he had stuffed in his pocket: nineteen dollars and seventy-five cents. A miserable sucky night. Shoulda stayed home. Just then, he noticed a vehicle slowly making its way up the ramp. The beat-up commercial van stopped although the light was green. A big guy with a shaved head rolled down his window, waved to Dushayne and yelled: "Hey. You. Come here."

Dushayne wondered what the guy was up to, but he donned his homeless look and hobbled over cautiously. "Yessir. Grateful for any help, sir."

"Here you go. I've been there." The Samaritan held up a fifty dollar bill to the light of the street lamp and slapped it hard into Dushayne's outstretched hand. The nineteen-year-old saw the denomination but didn't believe it. He instinctively put the bill up to the light himself, just to make sure.

"Sir. God. Bless. You." He gave each word as much weight as possible as he watched the truck spin out of the ramp and turn left onto the overpass. Dushayne still had doubts. Must be counterfeit. Too good to be true.

He was standing close to the travel lane when another vehicle crawled to a halt next to him. The light was still green, but the car stayed put. Inside, an older woman, a grandma probably, was smiling at him. She turned to speak to a child strapped in a car seat behind her. "This is a homeless man," the woman said to the child. Then, she reached into a grocery bag on the passenger seat, and pulled out a bunch of green bananas. "For you, young man, I'm sure you must be hungry." Caught off guard, Dushayne was speechless. "And, here's some cookies." She grabbed a package of store-bought cookies and handed it to the homeless lad. Before he had a chance to say anything, the woman looked at him and said, "God bless you and keep you safe."

"You too," was all that he could muster. The lady drove away, and Dushayne saw the bumper sticker: *Smile. Jesus loves you.*

Dushayne was halfway home when he realized he didn't have to limp anymore. He removed the lump of candy wrapper from his sneaker and, his mouth full of Toll House cookies, laughed out loud. He swore he would go to church with Auntie on Sunday.

Claude visualized himself from above, as if he were an actor in a movie. He was the school kid staring from the side of the road at an old woman brandishing a kitchen knife. She was cutting off the hands of young boys. She threw the hands at Claude – a salvo of still-warm body parts – in an attempt to shoo him away. Boys were lined up waiting patiently to have their hands chopped off. The sidewalk was littered with bloody hands. Claude screamed at the woman to stop, but she laughed and hacked faster. "Enough. Stop, Mrs. Sinclair. Stop," Claude said in his movie-actor voice.

He was waking up. Not easily, not clearly. His head moved first, then his legs, then everything in between, as he started the escape from the deep sleep of his night. With his sticky eyelids half open, he inspected his surroundings. He heard gentle snoring and remembered whose room he was sharing. Ray was deep into his sleep, his breathing measured and thin, the sheets pulled up to his chin. Claude could see daylight, still subtle as it framed the motel room window. He walked quietly to the bathroom. In the mirror, he examined the welts on his face and the cut on his lip. He stretched his bony torso and shook his head vigorously to untangle his crazy hair.

He reached behind the shower curtain and turned on the hot water and recalled his first dream of the night: a butterfly trying to free itself from a clear plastic paperweight. The beautiful wings fluttered weakly against the interior of the convex vessel; again and again the butterfly rose in a feeble attempt to crack open the paperweight. Claude decided he preferred this dream to the one with the hands and reminded himself that the butterfly inside the paperweight might make for a good poem.

The sound of the shower became a wake-up call for Ray. Gathering several small pillows, Ray propped himself up and glanced around the motel room. He knew that once again he had underestimated the distances in Florida and that, the night before, long after sunset, he had pulled over halfway down the peninsula at Ferry Landing. What's the rush? As if there's a destination.

That evening had been unnerving. Their beachfront motel turned out to be headquarters for a squad of local college kids home for the Holidays. They overran the cocktail lounge, the swimming pool and the beach in a rehearsal for Spring Break. A honky-tonk boardwalk not a block away was frequented by a colony of bikers who competed with the college kids in a marathon of noise and obnoxiousness.

Claude went for a walk. He told Ray he wanted to see what was going on. He hoped that somehow the revelry would reconnect him. To what was imprecise, he simply felt a need to be with happy carefree people. He walked along the boardwalk, dodging the crowds; he grabbed a bench and observed the goings-on, but quickly felt alienated, like a wanderer in the midst of a primitive ritual. He returned to his room and when Ray asked him to describe the scene he simply said he must be getting old.

"Good morning," Claude said as he emerged from the bathroom wrapped in a towel. "Sorry if I woke you."

"Not at all." Ray sat up and, checking the clock, announced it was already past 10 a.m. "Hope you slept as well as I did."

"Slept great. Best night in a long time."

Ray let his legs hang over the side of the bed. He told his companion he planned on doing laundry and that if Claude had anything to wash he could add it to the pile.

"Thanks," said Claude. As he reached for his gym bag, the bath towel around his waist fell to the floor. Ray's gaze lingered for a moment. He turned on the TV set, surfing for a weather report, and, finding it, sat on the edge of his bed in his pajamas, a naked Claude standing a few feet away. The forecast called for above-average temperatures. Ray kept his eyes glued to the television set, refusing to look at Claude's body. For a few seconds, just before a commercial, the screen darkened and reflected the younger man's figure. The seconds seemed like an eternity to Ray, a blessed eternity. He wanted the apparition to remain but it melted into an ad for a local ambulance chaser. Ray moved to the bathroom to get dressed. When he emerged, Claude had moved to his bed and, wrapped in its covers, was flipping through the channels.

"Mind if I watch some TV?"

"No. Go ahead. I'll go down to the laundry room." Ray picked up two plastic laundry bags and his wallet. "I can bring us some coffee and muffins or something from the lobby if you want."

"Great. Thanks."

Ray unlatched the security chain and looked back. A brief hesitation later, he was greeted by an air-conditioned blast of air and by a Spanish-accented good morning from the cleaning lady about to assault the mess in the room across the hall.

Finding nothing of interest on TV, Claude stared out the window. He fashioned a robe out of the quilted bed cover. He got his notepad from the gym bag and sat at the small desk and started writing. He struggled with the idea of a butterfly in a paperweight. The image offered nothing. He started to record his vision of the severed hands and the flashback to the crazy Mrs. Sinclair. He referred to it as a vision for lack of a more appropriate term. He felt he should really call these events hallucinations, but he feared the medical implications of that word. He preferred visions because of the spiritual dimension. He was beginning to see himself as a mystic. A mystic and poet like Ginsberg and Kerouac. And, abruptly the ideas forged into an embryonic poem. Claude grasped the moment and started to focus:

In the morning sun I walk in a field
where my footsteps are cradled by countless hands
At the edge of night I wade into a lake filled with hands,
beguiling and thirsting for my body.

His face twisting with effort, Claude threw himself into his work. He jabbed the words onto the page. Messy, shapeless, stains of ideas. He painted the words onto the paper, cautious, shapely flowers full of potential.

Soft cuddly hands of infants
Tight and thin-stretched skin over old bones
Hands barely touching, painted on the ceilings of
*   chapels, creator and created*
In dark cemeteries, hands carved on headstones
The lost hands of wooden statues, angels and saints
*   who can't touch*

Paul Paré

Hands caressing a breast in the warmth of the night.

Claude stopped writing as suddenly as he had started. It often happened this way. The ideas came to him in a torrent and they vanished just as easily. Some little devil in his brain turning a spigot on and off. The room felt warm and suffocating. Claude's eye wandered over to the air conditioning unit. If he turned it on, would his inspiration flow back? Was that the connection? He looked at his poetry and read it again. He decided there was nothing else to be done with it. Not today. Yet, the urge to write was strong. He turned to a new page and started writing about the events at Lafayette Square and the beating the next day when Jules found him and how he and Ray wound up leaving Savannah. Not elegant lengthy sentences but brief strokes, single words loosely linked – not unlike his life of the past several months.

He stopped his jottings and stared at the unkempt beds and speculated as to how he came to spend the night in the motel room with Ray. At that moment, it dawned on him that this man was truly a stranger, a kind stranger perhaps, but a stranger. What did he want with him? Was this just kindness? Friendship? Who *is* Raymond Champagne? What happened back home that was so terrible he had to run? He turned to a new page and put his questions to paper, filling the margin with large ornate question marks.

Two floors below under the stark fluorescent lights of the laundry room, Ray couldn't shake the image of Claude's nakedness: lean alabaster with swirls of dark hair. He leaned against the clothes washer and felt its vibrations massaging his lower back. He inhaled the moist air, listened to the rhythm of the machine and sank into a haze. He allowed his brain to absorb the nude portrait and gave his imagination permission to explore. Seeing Claude's nudity displayed so clearly and so casually forced him to ask himself how he should have reacted. What could he do? Nothing. Nothing at all. Even if he wanted to do something, he had no idea what. None of his fantasies had prepared him. And, what of Claude's intentions? Why did he remain naked like that? He had no clothes to wear, that's why. He's probably used to walking around naked. Lots of men probably do that. Ray bombarded himself with what-ifs and whys until he felt sick to his stomach. "I need some breakfast," he said to the rumbling washing machine, pleased that he had found a possible antidote if not an answer.

"How do you take your coffee?" Ray asked on returning to the room armed with coffee and creamers and sugar packets.

"A bit of cream, thanks."

"Got some of these tiny donuts. Don't know if they're any good."

"Thanks. I'm hungry."

"I can get some more. There's plenty down there. Looks like most everyone left early."

Ray and Claude shared their motel breakfast silently. Ray stared out the window, looked at his watch. "The laundry should be done. I'll go transfer it to the dryer."

Claude noticed the older man's hands. Long and smooth, delicate. Like his mother's. "I'll go back to my writing," he said with a wave.

He decided to write about his mother's hands on a new page. Annie Stover, the teenager rubbing sun lotion on her legs and arms on a beach in Maine; Annie Simard, the bride watching her groom slipping a wedding ring onto her finger; Annie, the old woman in the hospital wringing her hands in pain.

Back in the laundry area, Ray decided to wait out the drying cycle. He found it awkward going in and out of the motel room. He thumbed through a couple of the celebrity magazines left behind. He went to the lobby and picked up a copy of *USA Today*, glancing at the day's news for New Hampshire, then for Connecticut, then Georgia, then Florida. He ventured outdoors and stood under a canopy to catch the slanted rays of winter sun. He got himself another cup of coffee. He thought of striking up a conversation with Nassaj behind the desk, but he seemed busy with his computer. Ray returned to his newspaper and read about a tiger attack at the San Francisco Zoo. The clothes were finally dry, and Ray folded them in the laundry room. As he pulled a pair of faded Jockey shorts from the pile and realized they were Claude's, he stumbled on the intimacy. He quickly rolled all the clothes into a ball and rushed upstairs. When he entered the room, Claude was still at the desk, wrapped in a blanket.

"Some new poems?" he asked.

"Well, maybe not full-fledged poems, but bits and pieces, the

177

makings of new poems, hopefully."

Ray stood beside Claude, looking down. The handwriting was chaotic, all over the place. Once again, he spotted the scars on the inside of Claude's forearms. They looked like crosses. Ray wondered if they had anything to do with drugs. He wanted to ask, but didn't. "So, you write a lot?" Ray finally said. At least they could talk about his writing. He caressed the wish that the poet might share something.

"Whenever I can. Whenever I find the place and the time." He chuckled. "Time. I've got plenty of that now. More time that I ever thought I'd have. More time than I knew existed."

Ray found himself wordless. He heard insight in Claude's voice, much more than a man his age should have.

Without speaking, the men spread the clean clothing on the bed, separating what belonged to each one, folding the items and placing them into two neat piles.

When Dushayne heard the voice, he was reminded of the first time he stayed out late and violated curfew. The singer's voice carried Dushayne back to the thrill of being on his own and the nervous expectation that something might happen. He heard the rumbling from a distance, a low muffled hum that grew steadily, until the lights started flashing and the warning gate dropped before him. A baritoned whistle rose to ear-crashing force as the freight train crossed Sistrunk Boulevard. Dushayne jumped back. He had seen the train cross his neighborhood countless times during the day, but in the middle of the night, the speed and the noise created a whirlwind that nearly blew him off his feet. It was a storm meant for him, for him alone, and Dushayne had rarely felt so special. The singer's voice floated off the dimly-lit stage with the same contradiction: the words soft and soulful, coming from afar, until their impact shattered the routine of the bar and exacted total attention.

Dushayne set the tray of dirty glasses down and listened while standing in the doorway, swaying gently to the beat of the music, his eyes attached to the drag queen under the narrow spotlight.

> *C'est si bon,*
> *Lovers say that in France,*
> *When they thrill to romance,*
> *It means that it's so good.*

Miss Sashay had returned to the stage. The bar was empty except for Zany, the sound technician, and a couple of bartenders who were straightening up their respective stations. The night was over.

It had been an unusually large and upbeat crowd for a Friday night. The big nights at Hips were Saturday and Sunday, but as Zany explained, November always brought change. Maybe it was the cooling down Fort Lauderdale witnessed that time of year, but things were indeed different: new faces, crowds peaking earlier, patrons staying later and definitely drinking more. Customers seemed more interested in the show, yelling and applauding wildly, throwing dollar bills at the drag queens. It was the best time for management to try new things: drink specials, theme nights, new performers. This had been Miss Sashay's debut, and her performance had been far from stellar. The audience hadn't paid much attention to the new talent; the applause had been reticent.

Earlier, Dushayne had overheard the argument with Stevie Stevens, the owner, who wanted the new drag queen to put more pep into her act. "This isn't a lounge; it's a bar, a loud gay bar with an unruly bunch of guys out looking for a crazy time." Miss Sashay had retorted that a place like Hips needed variety. She said something about *dynamics,* and all that she needed was a proper intro and more familiarity with the *acoustics* of the room. "Well, as long as they keep on drinking and they don't run out the door when you take the stage, girl, I guess you can stay." Stevie had a way of summing up a discussion that left little room for response.

> *C'est si bon,*
> *So I say it to you,*
> *Like the French people do,*
> *Because it's oh…so good.*

By this time, the singer had claimed the lighting and the sound as her own and was in complete control of the stage. She gave the lyrics her full voice and put her entire body to work. Dushayne was captivated by the slender hips that swayed so slightly and provocatively under the satin and sequins, and by her elongated arms and hands that accented the high notes. Miss Sashay went through the song twice. After the second rendition, the few people left in the room applauded. Just plain applause, strong and sustained, no yells, no whoops, no whistles. Like people do at a real concert. And, like a real star of the stage, Miss Sashay cast a beguiling smile and took a slow, deep bow, an elegant expression of acceptance. The young bar back thought the movement stretched her glittery evening gown in just the right places.

Dushayne watched the drag queen retreat to the DJ booth to reclaim her background music. His gaze followed her to the dressing room. He found the courage to approach her. "Great job," he said.

"Why thank you, young man." By this time, the wig was off and the dress was hanging at the waist. "And, what's your name?"

"Dushayne," he said, staring at the drag queen's hairy chest. He extended his hand and the drag queen shook it vigorously. Dushayne noticed that her long white gloves had concealed a lean, sinewy arm. "Loved that song you just did."

"It's one of my favorites, but nobody can belt it out like Eartha Kitt did."

"Who?"

"Eartha Kitt. She's the one who made the song famous..."

"Missed it when you sang it tonight, earlier."

"I didn't try it. I wasn't sure about the sound system, this being my first time here..."

The bar owner stuck his head in the door and interrupted. "Hey, kid. You gonna finish tonight? Still lots to clean up."

"Yessir!" Dushayne saluted and marched into the bar. Looking back, he saw the drag queen give him a warm smile.

"Eartha Kitt, Eartha Kitt" the bar back repeated under his breath, wondering how the name was spelled.

A few days later, Dushayne was climbing to his room after a long and unproductive night at the I-95 exit, when he noticed Auntie's light shining in her master suite. He had been itching to ask her about Eartha Kitt for several days. "I know it's late, but can I ask you something?" the lad said timidly.

"Why, of course. What's bothering you, Dushayne?" Roberta looked up from a desk littered with correspondence and tons of receipts.

"Nothing's bothering me. I just don't like to bother *you*. I can see you're busy."

"Oh. Sweet child, you know I'm always here for you. What is it?"

Dushayne felt like a shy teenager and he didn't quite know why. He bent over and mumbled. "Have you ever heard of a singer named Martha Kitt?"

"Who? A singer?" There was a hint of irritation in her voice.

"Yes." He hesitated.

"Who'd you say? Eartha Kitt?"

"Yes. Eartha. Not Martha. Yeah, Eartha Kitt? You heard of her?"

"Of course I have, dear boy." Roberta invited him to sit next to her, and she proceeded to recite all she knew about Eartha Kitt. "A very, very famous singer." Dushayne detected a change in Auntie's mood. She had become softer, younger, almost vulnerable. "A pioneer. A beautiful Black woman, a sensuous singer. She came out of poverty and made it big – maybe not the most God-fearing – but still, everybody loved her." The descriptions cascaded out of Roberta. She spoke softly, lovingly, and closing her eyes, she started humming.

"That's it! That's the song." Dushayne proclaimed. He stood. "You know that song, Auntie?"

"Of course. Everyone knows *C'est Si Bon.*"

"Well maybe not everyone. Not now, but they will."

"All right, boy. Calm down. What's this about anyways?"

"Oh. Auntie. Thank you so much." He didn't pay attention to the question and started walking out of the room. "Oh. And, can you write her name down for me? Please."

Roberta searched the clutter on her desk and wrote the singer's name on a scrap of paper.

"Ah. Eartha Kitt," he muttered reverently. "Thanks again, Auntie."

Walking to his room at the other end of the boarding house, Dushayne felt a flush he would later identify as the birth of an obsession.

Banyan Cove was the kind of place that most people would discover quite by accident. Claude and Ray were not the exception. In their case, the accident involved a jackknifed trailer truck and a pileup on southbound I-95. Highway patrolmen diverted traffic off the throughway and everyone had to interrupt their itineraries and venture into the little city that not long before had been home to lush stands of Banyan trees and to the tropical birds they harbored – and very little else. It was late afternoon, two days after Christmas, and Ray was tired of driving. He welcomed the roadblock and the detour.

Ray's Subaru was channeled onto Florida Route 44 and soon he came upon a downtown with stuccoed two-story commercial buildings that were unanimously empty. Across the main street was hung a banner announcing the Fiftieth Anniversary of the City of Banyan Cove – 1958-2008. Several blocks later, after a series of drab apartment complexes, the usual South Florida commercial institutions marked the landscape. Ray and Claude chose the Denny's for lunch and ordered a hearty meal. There, they were treated to a generous serving of local gossip. The town's changing. Used to be northern retirees, most of them Jewish. Great location, just far enough from the beaches to be affordable. Lately the place had been overrun by Cubans and Jamaicans. Downtown's dying, but there's not just one but two Walmarts. The town used to be known for its track for dog races until folks started going to those Indian casinos. City Hall's still run by the old-timers, most of 'em crooked. The city's 50th anniversary's a big waste of money. Nobody cares, not really. There's a nice little motel, Tropical Gardens, owned by a local couple, real nice people. Quiet and respectable place, reasonable. Back on Route 44, head north through downtown and make a right at Capri Street. Can't miss it.

Tropical Gardens in bright pink neon welcomed at curbside. A hand painted sign in reserved script announced a friendly hostel owned by Esther and Chester Blake. As he turned into the parking lot, Ray thought of Bates Motel and wouldn't have been surprised to see Anthony Perkins peeking at them through the blinds. Six rooms, all in a row, cinder block exterior painted chocolate brown, garden variety ferns overflowing from beds between the parking lot and the motel rooms.

Claude had his doubts. He thought the place looked too quaint, too personal, like they'd be living with someone. "You sure about this?"

"It's quiet. Looks clean," replied Ray.

"Suppose we could stay a couple of nights," Claude said. They followed a sign and came to an office in a double-wide trailer planted between the motel and what appeared to be a canal.

"We only rent by the week," Esther said routinely. Her business tone changed when she saw the two men standing at the counter. "You look like nice people. You father and son?" she asked.

"No. Just friends," Claude stated.

Chester looked up from his desk and scrutinized the pair. "Plates from New Hampshire. Pretty far from home," he said.

"On a long vacation. Never been to Florida before," Ray explained.

"You army buddies?" asked Chester.

Ray answered brusquely. "Is there a questionnaire we have to fill out before we can get a room?"

"Of course not." Esther reached over and patted her husband's hand. "Of course not. I can tell you're respectable gentlemen."

"Let's get outa here," whispered Claude.

"We rent only by the week. Two-hundred-forty. And that's for the both of you. And that's with a kitchenette."

"A whole week?" Claude threw a worried glance at Ray.

"That sounds reasonable," Ray responded.

"With maid service, its' an extra 50 dollars."

"I guess we can make our own beds."

"Double beds?" asked Claude.

"Of course…well, two single beds, that is," Esther explained.

Ray agreed immediately and reached for his wallet. The younger man wrinkled his nose, acknowledging that he had no say in the matter.

The men unpacked and settled in without speaking. The room

was small. An ancient air conditioning unit stuck in the bottom of a window gave off more rattle than air. Tropical Gardens offered Spartan but polished furnishings. Faux bamboo and lots of plastic, a framed picture of palm trees probably from a calendar, pillows that had turned flat, the false fir scent of a commercial deodorizer clinging to everything.

For the next day or two, Ray would wake up early and leave quietly so as not to disturb Claude. He'd return with a couple of newspapers, a cup of coffee and a pastry, and lay siege to a patio chair that received a couple of hours of morning sun. At one point Ray announced he would be going to pick up a few groceries. He had started a list and invited Claude to jot down whatever he wanted.

Claude spent his first days walking around town, enjoying the feel of the ground with each step. He made believe he was on the road again; he wondered what discoveries he had missed by riding in a car on the interstate since leaving Savannah. His longing for the lonely road, the endless slow road, surprised him. Even the hardship of sleeping outside, with the uncertainties of the night, called to him. Claude wondered how long he could last in a tiny motel room, how long before the pull of the road would take over.

Observing the people and places around him, Claude found that Banyan Cove enjoyed a certain lethargy that went beyond tropical slow motion. The retirees and the newcomers from the Caribbean shared at least one thing: no need to hurry. As a New Englander, Claude was taken aback: in his world, people scurried about all the time.

"You sure you want to do this?"

"Yes, I'm sure."

Zany, the sound tech went on, "Look, it's none of my business, but you just got started. Stick with Eartha Kitt. That's a crowd pleaser. Besides, who you gonna be with this song? There's no drag side to Don Henley."

"Why can't Eartha Kitt sing Don Henley?" Miss Sashay asked. "Just have to tone down the sashay. I can make it work. A more introspective Eartha. It's the same range..."

"I tell ya, Mr. Stevens won't like it," Zany said. "He'll tell you to stick to the sexy *femme fatale* stuff. That's what these guys come here for. They don't want serious. They don't wanna cry. They wanna hoot and holler. With plenty of cheer..."

Miss Sashay interrupted. "Sad songs make for good bar sales."

Zany acquiesced with a nod. The singer asked him to dim the lights and give the intro lots of bass, pulling the volume down once she started singing. Miss Sashay allowed the steady piano and guitar beat to create the attention-getting mood she wanted. She dragged a stool into the spotlight and gently removed her bouffant wig and started to sing.

Remember the days were long
And rolled beneath a deep blue sky
Didn't have a care in the world
With mommy and daddy standing by

Not in the usual Eartha Kitt dark murkiness, but in his natural baritone, robust and edgy. His eyes glued to the area above everyone's heads that held only cigarette smoke. Gone were the sensual swaying and teasing and the winks and blown kisses, replaced by an intensity the tiny stage had rarely seen. The crowd hesitated, questioning glances thrown about, until the sense of uniqueness took hold. One of the older guys hushed the men in back, and everybody gradually became accomplices. Dushayne was pulled out of his cleaning routine and stepped into the bar. Stevie Stevens emerged from his office and stood next to Dushayne. The bar owner listened to a couple of verses and muttered, "Fucking diva!"

> But this is the end
> This is the end of the innocence

A couple of guys sitting at the bar joined in a sing-along, the words a whispered echo from their late hippie days. One of them ordered a round of drinks for himself and his buddy, and Stevie, watching them from his office door, smiled and nodded. The song ended as it had begun, the artist on the stage alone and motionless in the spotlight looking into space, into a moment that was generous enough to contain both past and future. Applause, steady and strong, followed, punctuated by whistles. Without a bow, the singer left the stage, fist held high.

Stevie greeted him. "One a night, no more, just one of those each night. At the end of the night. You hear?"

Dushayne ran to the singer and squealed with glee. "Beautiful. You're so beautiful, Miss Sash..." The bar back was about to gush on, when he hesitated. "Can't call you that. Not after that song."

"Well, call me by my real name, Derrick James."

"Oh..." Dushayne couldn't reply. What a fucking great name, he thought, so masculine, a Hollywood leading-man kinda name. "Ok. Derrick James. That was great. Never heard the song before. Who sang it?"

"Look, you finish your work and after closing we'll talk about it."

Thirty minutes later, Dushayne and Derrick were in deep conversation about the hit of the night. While changing into what he called his street clothes, Derrick produced the lyrics of the Don Henley song and ceremoniously presented the sheet to Dushayne.

"Wow, can I keep this?" Dushayne asked, reading the words under his breath.

"Sure. But what happened to C'est si bon and Eartha Kitt?"

"Ah...Eartha Kitt is still the queen, but I really like this one."

Derrick talked about the Don Henley song and how it was a wake-up call for him. "I heard it in 1990, I think. I was sick of my

187

life and these words really spoke to me. They gave me the courage to leave home." Dushayne leaned forward, his hands cupping his chin. He sensed that Derrick was going to reveal himself. The drag queen told his story. He was born on the Alabama-Georgia border, in a small town with scarce tolerance for a Black man who liked to dress and sing like a girl. He moved to Florida in his late teens, first to Orlando and more recently to Fort Lauderdale. He worked as a desk clerk at one of the fancy hotels on the beach. He said he was very religious and that he converted to Catholicism, an act that further alienated him from his family and neighbors back home. He knew he wasn't the most popular drag queen at Hips, but he could identify a handful of loyal fans. Derrick confided he didn't need the money. His day job took care of all the bills. "It's that dressing up in all that glitter and fancy dresses and crooning those sultry songs responds to a spiritual need, like going to Mass on Sundays."

In awe, Dushayne confessed that he hadn't yet identified *his* spiritual needs.

"But tonight you put away the drag queen for a while…"

"Yes, I know. Oh, don't you worry, your Miss Sashay isn't about to retire, not for a long, long time." They both laughed. Derrick explained, "There are times I want to be myself on stage and sing the songs that mean something to me…in my voice, not someone else's."

"Ok, girls. Party's over." Stevie stuck his bald head into the dressing room to tell them he was going home and was kicking them out.

Derrick and Dushayne gathered their stuff and headed for the back alley. The drag queen offered Dushayne a ride home.

"This is it?" Derrick stopped his car in front of Wellington Plaza.

Dushayne remained silent in the passenger seat. "Yeah. This is it. Thanks for the ride." He searched for words. He looked at the traces of makeup on Derrick's forehead and the specks of sparkle clinging to his neck visible under the glow of the street light. "Looked like rain for a while there, so I really appreciate the ride." The two, usually so talkative, measured the silence that followed.

"So this is where you live."

"It's where I have a room. But it's not my favorite place, not one bit."

"Where is your favorite place? Don't tell me its Hips."

"No, not Hips." Dushayne hesitated. "There is a place though..." He left his thought unfinished. He opened the car door and looked at the sky and noticed it was filled with stars. "Wanna see it?"

"What? Your room? Why, young man, are you inviting me up?"

"No. Well, yeah. But not here...somewhere else, to my favorite place."

"Why, young man, just you lead the way."

Derrick didn't hesitate. He shifted, and the car lurched. Dushayne closed his door and they drove downtown towards the New River.

This was the one place where Dushayne felt truly at home. A special plot of land where he could be completely alone, except for the lizards who didn't mind the intrusion. For him, being alone meant being at home. A vacant lot on the sunny side of the river, beneath an unfinished condo tower, miraculously unnoticed and unguarded, with an even more secure refuge, an alcove under the bridge that carried one of Fort Lauderdale's main arteries. Hidden in the tall reeds, Dushayne would spend hours listening to the city and its river, thinking about his job at Hips, about his panhandling, about his time spent on the balcony and in his room at Wellington Plaza. It was in the solitude of his riverside lot that Dushayne felt completely at ease and most protected. A child of the water, a brother to the quiet trusting lizards, an artist who would extract one day from the warmth of the soil his true vocation. A rooted self he would share only with the patient manatees that poked at water's edge. An aboriginal misplaced.

It hadn't always been a refuge. When he first chanced upon the spot on one of those nights he couldn't bear to go to his father's apartment, he was searching for an escape. He had just turned 16 and the April night was hot and sticky and he walked aimlessly until the early morning hours, finally stumbling onto the empty lot. He immediately felt the pull of the river and its outgoing tide and wondered what it would be like to live underwater and never have to hear the bluster of a drunken father and the bullying of older brothers. He fell asleep on top of a wooden pallet, and when the first rays of the sun awakened him, he decided to make his escape permanent. He went about making the place hospitable with whatever discarded cartons he could find. His third night he was terrified when a pair of old druggies stumbled into the lot searching for a party, and Dushayne retreated into the alcove under the bridge. The next day, he returned to his father's place and waited for everyone to leave before going inside and retrieving clothing and blankets and raiding the refrigerator, a booty he carried away in a stolen grocery store cart. At that moment, he realized he was making the commitment to living on the streets of Fort Lauderdale and on the banks of its river.

Riding with Derrick downtown, Dushayne suddenly had misgivings about sharing his "home." The lad knew the place and the spirit it fostered were fragile, and he doubted if anyone might embrace it as he had. He looked at Derrick, and his doubts vanished. Miss Sashay would understand. Dushayne directed Derrick to a parking spot and the duo walked silently towards the riverside refuge, Derrick entertaining thoughts of a sanctuary and Dushayne feeling giddy like a virgin. The grass was dewy and the breeze gentle. They sat on a wooden plank and talked about each other's dreams and needs. The nineteen-year-old bar back shared his story of abuse and abandonment. He admitted how deeply he yearned for a real family. Derrick assured him that family was overrated. An ambulance raced by on the roadway above them, and neither of the men paid attention to it. They wrapped their arms around each other. The drag queen and the bar back listened to the river with the outgoing tide pulling away from the city.

"This is a good place," Derrick said.

Dushayne looked at the slice of sky directly above and saw the moon breaking through a cluster of puffy clouds. He took Derrick's hand, cradled it, and kissed it, placing his lips around the tips of each finger, one by one. Dushayne took the hands and placed one on each side of his face.

"I'm the filling to your pastry," he said.

"My, where did that come from? It's quite poetic."

"My mom. When I was little, she'd take my face and squeeze my checks between her hands. She called me her 'little pastry fillin'' and she'd kiss me all over."

"Like this?" They kissed. For a long time. Dushayne gently

pulled Derrick up to his feet and led the way to the alcove under the bridge where the two spread themselves out on the cardboard boxes covering the soft earth. They resumed their kisses, deep and probing, and allowed no separation between them, their hands exploring the contours of their union.

Suddenly, Derrick pulled away. "I don't think we want to do this," he said.

"*I* want to do this, and more," Dushayne whispered in his friend's ear.

"It's too soon. We need to get to know each other first; we've only known each other a few days."

Dushayne listened to his river and took a long breath. "Been exactly two weeks tonight. And... never felt like this before."

Derrick stood. "Look, Dushayne, I like you. I like you a lot. And, I...It's just that I can't let myself take advantage of your feelings..."

"Ah...the end of the innocence – just like the song."

"Yes, something like that. You're just 19. I'm a lot older...I'd feel responsible."

"If it's my innocence you're worrying about, don't bother. You think a sixteen-year-old living on the streets hasn't had his innocence taken? Taken and used, let me tell you." Dushayne also stood and, flailing his long arms about, faced Derrick and spoke in defiant tones. "Right here, several times. You got no idea how many fancy white businessmen like to get down and dirty with a young Black stud."

"I'm sorry," Derrick said. He placed a hand on Dushayne's shoulder. "I'm sorry."

"I was hungry, I was cold. I was tired, and once or twice, I was real lonely."

Derrick pulled at the lad and the two hugged, Dushayne sobbing gently.

"Look, I understand. I understand."

A strong winter wind came up brusquely from the river, and the two felt a chill that had nothing to do with Dushayne's confession.

"Ah... let's get in the car," Derrick said. Dushayne allowed himself to be escorted to the vehicle. The two sat for several moments in silence, listening to the palm trees bend before the ocean breeze.

"Listen, Derrick. Sorry for slobbering all over, for being such a mess." There was no reply from Derrick. The lad had expected one. "What a way to end the night...I can be so fucking stupid," Dushayne blurted out.

"Not true. Listen, I want you to say what you feel. I want you to tell me everything. I really want to get to know you." Derrick hesitated. "You're so special...you have no idea..." He started to sing a few lines from *C'est Si Bon*, then stopped, acknowledging Dushayne's silence. Derrick looked at the pinkish hue in the empty sky and turned the key in the ignition. "Time for Sunday morning breakfast at the South Florida Café. I'm starved."

As they drove down the deserted streets of Fort Lauderdale, Dushayne felt his disappointment ebb. Nothing of this night had been planned, but he welcomed it. All of it. Even breakfast, anything to spend more time with Derrick, he thought.

"You know, the café is quite an institution, open 24 hours, popular with both gays and straights, the best breakfast in Broward County, and the craziest décor." Derrick was turning into a tour guide.

Dushayne was only half interested; his brain had left his riverside alcove and was now re-attaching itself to the familiar and soothing melody of Miss Eartha Kitt. As they were parking in front of the restaurant, Dushayne grabbed his friend's hand and slipped himself closer and whispered *C'est Si Bon*.

The two sashayed into the café, Derrick carrying his makeup case. They selected a table directly beneath a framed poster of the movie shot with Marilyn Monroe attempting to keep her skirt down. While waiting for their meal, they delved into a serious conversation about dressing in drag and performing on stage. Dushayne wanted to know about the mechanics. The mundane stuff. Like where do you find the outfits and the make-up? How long does it take to transform a man into a glamorous vixen?

"Not long at all, not for an expert like Miss Sashay," said Derrick. He opened his case and started applying makeup. With just a few well-placed strokes and an occasional glance in the mirror next to them, Derrick turned himself into a stage diva. The two talked about makeup and wigs and the accoutrements of dragdom. When their food arrived, they kept on hamming it up to the delight of their waiter, an older guy who identified himself as Rufus and said he recognized the duo from Hips.

Derrick asked Dushayne if he wanted to try some makeup. First came the rouge then the eye shadow. After playing for an hour with colors and highlights, the men had clearly been transformed. Derrick said he envied Dushayne's body: "Tall and willowy, perfect for drag." The young man replied that his drag name would be Miss Willowy and Derrick laughed. None of the patrons seemed to notice. They were all ensconced in their own slice of reality, flavored by the time of day and the aura of this special place that enshrined local eccentrics among posters of Hollywood greats. Slowly, tourists started coming in and the two makeup artists decided to leave. On the way out, Dushayne scanned the walls of the eatery hoping to see a photo of Eartha Kitt, but found none.

In the car, Derrick pulled out a large blond wig and adjusted it on Dushayne's head.

"There you are, Miss Willowy."

"Not without Miss Sashay. Where's her hairpiece?"

They drove in the direction of Sistrunk Boulevard, the rising sun at their backs, two Black men with wigs, singing at the top of their lungs the song of the eternal Miss Kitt. Only at the edge of Wellington Plaza did things become serious again with Derrick asking the lad if he felt better about their evening.

"Think so. Yes, I'm Ok," he replied. "Just that I'm 19 years old and I don't know what love is."

"Listen, Dushayne, most people, no matter what age, don't know what love is. I for one have never found it. I thought I had once, but it didn't work out. Which is why I want to go slow this time. I want to be certain it's real and I want it to last."

"I know." Dushayne said. The two leaned in and gave each other a long easy kiss, only to have the moment disturbed by rapping on the passenger window. Dushayne looked out and yelled, "Shit, holy shit. They're on their way to church." Dushayne yanked the wig off his head.

Roberta and Octavious Wellington were standing on the sidewalk, both in their Sunday best, both frowning. Auntie was doing the tapping on the window. She gestured that Dushayne should lower his window. "You can't park here. This is a no parking zone...Why, glory be, is that you Dushayne?"

The lad started to open the door, as Auntie bent over to get a better look inside the car. "And who is this with you?"

"Auntie. Just having some fun. No harm..." Dushayne had stepped out onto the sidewalk and was sandwiched by the two Wellingtons, Roberta in her yellow church dress and matching hat and Octavious in his best suit and fancy white shoes.

"Young man. Do you know what time it is? You been out all night?" She looked closer. "And is that makeup? Just you tell me, young man, that that is not makeup all over your face."

"Ok, Auntie, it's not makeup."

"Don't you get sassy with me. Dushayne Elwin Brown, this is unacceptable behavior. You know, Wellington Plaza has a code of conduct."

"Yes Auntie, I've read it and it doesn't say anything about makeup." Dushayne walked away.

Roberta and Octavious turned their attention to Derrick. "I said this is a no parking zone. Skedaddle before I call the police." Roberta slammed the door shut and turned just in time to see Dushayne blow kisses at the driver and scamper towards his motel room.

"Humph," Roberta said with a heave of her ample bosom. "After church, we'll have to have a talk with that lad." Octavious curbed a chuckle as he fell in line, and the two set out for the nine o'clock service.

Later that Sunday morning, Mrs. Blake left a note inviting the guests in Room 6 to the weekly barbeque. Ray looked forward to it all day and urged his companion to put on a cheerful face. Hot dogs from the grill and macaroni salad served on the screened porch attached to the Blake's trailer. Claude and Ray, Lourdes and her quiet teenage boy from Room 1, and Dexter, the businessman from Room 2, made up the guest list. Esther liked to create a family atmosphere at Tropical Gardens, she explained. Introductions and polite chitchat filled a couple of hours as the late afternoon turned into early evening.

By the time *Sixty Minutes* came on, everyone had left but Esther and Ray. The hostess welcomed the opportunity to get better acquainted with her new guest. The Blakes moved from Akron, Ohio, to Florida in 2005. They purchased Tropical Gardens in September of that year, six weeks before Hurricane Wilma ripped through and took several chunks of the roof with it. Eventually, they had half of the building torn down. "The worst half, of course," she said with a high chuckle. That's when they bought the double-wide to live in and gradually upgraded the small motel. They were both in their 70s – 76 to be precise, born four months apart. "Spirit of '76, we like to call ourselves," she said with an echo of her first chuckle. They were high school sweethearts, destined for each other. Maiden name was Lake. "Esther Lake and Chester Blake, would you believe? All I had to do was add a B to my last name." She had a career as a teacher, first as a high school math teacher and later as a third-grade teacher, moving down when "those high-schoolers just went out of control." Chester worked in the tire factories until they all closed, and then was lucky enough to get a job at the post office. "Still has strong legs; loves to walk and walk and walk."

Ray felt an immediate kinship. He confessed that he was an educator, affixing an explanation about scouting possible jobs in education in South Florida. The thought hadn't occurred to him until then, and he rolled the possibility around his mind for a while. He confided that he too had been put off of late by the lack of discipline and seriousness in American high schools. It was time perhaps for him to seek something on the college level. She encouraged him, adding that colleges of all sorts were sprouting up all over Florida. "Of course, it helps if you speak Spanish," she added with a sigh. Ray sensed that Esther wanted to know more. He simply offered that he was facing family issues back home, hence the trip south. After a pause, he explained that Claude was a young "adventurer," and that he was hitchhiking in Georgia when he picked him up. Esther nodded as if she understood perfectly what he meant.

Room 6 was dark when Ray returned. He checked his watch and was surprised that it was already 8:30. He wondered where Claude had gone. He was about to turn on the TV set when he decided there was nothing he wanted to watch. He sat in the lone recliner provided by the innkeepers and he wished he had something to read, promising himself that he would find a book store the next day.

"Oh. There you are."

"Hi." Claude gave his one-word greeting and sat down on the edge of his bed. He pulled an opened Bud from a paper bag and took a long draw.

"Where did that come from?"

"There's a Circle K down the street."

"That's where I get my paper."

"You want one? Got another beer here."

"How much money do you have left?" Ray didn't know where the question came from. It had been lurking in the back of his mind for a while, and he hadn't planned on voicing it. But there it was. He waited to see Claude's reaction.

Claude got up and walked into the small kitchen. "You sure you don't want one?"

"No thanks," Ray replied.

Claude deposited the second Budweiser in the refrigerator. As he sat again, he said, "Nearly broke. Gonna have to find a spot where I can recite some poetry. There must be someplace. Wonder if folks down here are generous? I was getting good at it in Savannah, thanks to your coaching." He took his shoes off, kicked them in a corner of the room, and spread himself on his bed. Ray wanted to tell him to pick up his shoes and place them in the closet. He said nothing and wondered why he was irritated.

"Bumped into Chester," Claude volunteered. "Walking back. Just came out of nowhere and fell into step with me. Man likes to walk. Says he walks at least five miles a day."

"Esther told me he worked for the post office."

"I know. He told me. So did my father."

"Really? I didn't know that."

"Well, he did. Got a postal route after the textile mill closed."

"Chester started at the post office after he lost his job too."

"I know. He told me." Claude placed the beer bottle to his lips and hesitated. "The old man's real nosy. Asks a lot of questions." He took a swig from his Bud.

"Like what?"

"Well, he wanted to know about the scars on my arms."

Ray became more interested. "What did you tell him?"

"Didn't know what to say. Told him they were war wounds. And he wanted to know where I served. Was I in the Army, in the Marines, in the Navy? And on and on and on. I told him there's all kinds of wars."

"This is true," Ray said in a low voice. The room grew silent. A neon stretching under the roof line the length of the motel turned itself on, and Ray pulled the drapes together. "Want to watch TV?"

"Sure."

The roommates knew their conversation had reached its conclusion. They would spend the next couple of hours like they had the last two nights, not watching or listening to whatever was on the screen but allowing the program to fill space and time. Each occupant of Room 6 would wait quietly for evening to turn into night. Each man would face a fitful night of questioning. Listening to the clumsy air conditioner, his eyes wide open, Claude stared at the ceiling, fighting off images of evil faces. When sleep finally came, it was never deep enough. Ray would wake up before dawn and question whether he would ever tire of running away, if this respite in Banyan Cove would amount to anything. For both men, the morning would be filled with lassitude and impatience. Already the routine, despite its relative comfort, had become burdensome.

"Look. It's my little Margie!" Eugene Simard made the announcement proudly, in a voice that anticipated approval from the handful of residents gathered for the Sunday afternoon visitors. He stretched his arms out to welcome his daughter-in-law, and he glowed. He was the center of attention, the envy of all these losers who never had anyone come to visit at Clover Nursing Home. "Come here," he said.

Margie pushed her son into Eugene's arms and stood back to watch. "Give Papa Simard a big hug." The old man closed his arms around the child. He threw a hesitant stare at the boy's mother. "You too, my little Margie, come and give an old man a thrill." Margie gave her father-in-law a peck on the cheek. She hated the *little Margie* reference. Eugene had explained it to her countless times, but she still thought it was stupid. She fastened her gaze on the old man in his slippers sitting in the middle of the activity room and recalled the scene on Prom Night when Claude had introduced her as his date. Claude's mother had smiled nicely, but his father had flown into a torrent of chatter about his favorite television program and how Margie looked like Gale Storm.

"How you doing, Eugene?" Margie asked.

"I'm Ok." He smiled at his grandson. "And, aren't you growing up fast!" Suddenly, he pushed himself forward in the wheelchair, his eyes scanning the room. "Where's Claude? Where's my son?"

Margie let out a sigh. She hated these Sunday visits. It was all for Mikey's sake. She felt obligated to make sure that he stayed connected to his family. "You know. I told you. He's on a trip. A buying trip for the hardware store. He's traveling."

Mikey looked up at his mother. She tapped him gently on the shoulder and pulled him to her side. "You got any games? C'mon Eugene, you know Mikey likes to play games." She scanned the room. "There. I see a checkers board. Over there." She pointed to an open game table. "Go over there, Mikey, and save that table for you and Papa Simard." She urged him forward.

"You remember, Margie, the night of your prom? The accident on Logging Road and that Rideout kid? I'll never forget that. And, the look on Claude's face when I showed up with the police. He looked so scared. I was so relieved he was Ok. I know Claude thought all I was worried about was my Buick, but that's not true. I was so glad he didn't get hurt. But that Rideout kid. He was all mangled up and…"

Margie stopped him. "I remember, Eugene. I remember." She pointed to her son across the room. "Look, Mikey's all set up over there. He's waiting for you." Eugene nodded and turned his chair. Margie placed a hand on his shoulder and said earnestly, "Don't say anything to him about Claude. He misses his father when he's away. Ok?" Eugene nodded and slowly rolled himself to the game area.

Margie stood abandoned in the center of the activity room. The Christmas tree occupied a corner next to the faux brick fireplace, with presents crowded at its foot, and a gallery of greeting cards taped to the fireplace mantel. Margie looked down at the false logs and their perennial burning. A heavy cloud cast its shadow on the nursing home and Margie noticed how the room darkened and she smiled as the artificial flames cast their rotary reflection on the ceiling. Fueled by her father-in-law's reminiscing, she saw herself under the glitter of the disco lights at her high school prom and how she whirled on the dance floor in her red formal dress in the arms of her new beau, Claude Simard. Her eyes closed, she swayed. Her feet shuffled lightly and her arms started to rise to the rhythm of the '80s dance music. Suddenly, Margie was assaulted by the cold realization that her memories were 20 years old and that they had been replaced by disillusion and bitterness. She was alone, working in her father's store, raising her little boy by herself, with another son in some unknown battlefield without a word at Christmas-time, and a husband chased away. She felt weak. She felt dizzy. She scanned the room for a safe place.

A frail-looking lady wrapped in a rainbow shawl inched herself to the end of her sofa and gave Margie a soft smile. She patted the vacant space as an invitation for the younger woman to sit down. "I see you're here visiting that dear Mr. Simard," she said. Margie nodded. "He's such a nice man. And, he's having such a hard time getting used to that wheelchair. Everybody here is so fond of him." The lady smacked her lips in satisfaction.

"He's my father-in-law." Margie was surprised by the weakness of her voice.

"Well, it's nice that you're here."

Both of them turned to check on Eugene and his grandson and their game. "Such a pretty picture," said the old woman.

Margie tried to remember the last time she saw her husband and she couldn't be sure. She thought it had to be at the courthouse with the judge. She couldn't recall what he looked like, what he was wearing, what he said. She was so angry. She was the one with the bruises. She was the one who was afraid. Then she remembered returning home after leaving Mikey with her mother. Margie wanted to make sure Claude didn't take anything but his stuff when he left. In the months that followed, she remembered hearing things about her husband: he wasn't working, he was living in the abandoned warehouse, he was hanging around with drunks and druggies, he was part of the rabble-rousers who marched in front of the post office Saturday mornings.

"Mommy, can we go home now?" Margie wrapped her arms around her boy. She needed to protect him; she needed the comfort of his little body. "Mommy, I'm hungry. Can we go home?" Margie turned her gaze to the game area and saw that Eugene had fallen asleep in his chair.

"Yes, Mikey. Let's go home."

"Macaroni and cheese, I want macaroni and cheese. And a hot dog."

"Ok. That's fine. Let's go." Margie pushed her son ahead of her, stopping near the exit to bundle him against the cold.

"It smells funny in here," Mikey said to his mother.

"What a stupid idea. Who ever heard of dressing up in costumes for Christmas? It's fucking Christmas, not Halloween. Maybe a Santa – of course a Santa – but costumes on Christmas, that's real fucked up." Dushayne was screaming his disapproval as he paced back and forth on the sidewalk in front of Wellington Plaza while waiting for Derrick to pick him up. His arms flapping in the mild suppertime air, he took quick syncopated steps in one direction then abruptly turned and walked back to where he started. He freely vented his condemnation: "Fine, Stevie, have your Christmas party, get a Santa, have people bring gifts; you can even have a fucking Yule log, but don't force me to dress up like Santa's helper." A passing motorist beeped his horn and Dushayne, too upset to discern if the driver meant approval or ridicule, turned to give him the finger. "Fuck you, asshole." He looked at his watch. "And, Derrick's gotta be late."

He heard a vehicle brake and turned around to see the van from the Baptist Church come to a halt and discharge Roberta and Octavious in their Sunday best. Mrs. Wellington focused on her thankyous and Godblesses and blew kisses to the occupants while Mr. Wellington stared at Dushayne with a half grin on his face. "Oh! Dear Jesus, oh my," Roberta said when she got a glimpse of her tenant. "What kind of outfit is that? Just what *are* you up to this time?"

"It's a Christmas costume," Dushayne replied drily. "Supposed to be one of Santa's elves, Auntie."

Octavious snickered. Roberta inspected the lad, her eyes like weapons. Dushayne followed her gaze to his leggings, striped red and green, up to his slightly too tight shorts, to his suspenders of fake leather, and finally to his wig of carrot-red yarn. He felt himself burn with rage. "Despicable display," was Roberta's assessment. Dushayne wanted to tell her that her Sunday outfit, a floor-length flowered print with matching bow balanced on top of her head, was the real despicable display. But, he kept quiet, withdrawing into the realization that Roberta already had plenty of ammunition and didn't need any more. He was about to say that the costume wasn't his idea, that it was required by his boss, but that could have turned into a discussion about his place of employment, an area he had managed to keep vague. He stood silently, facing the Wellingtons, shifting his weight from one uncomfortable foot to the other. Without realizing it, he was barring their way into the plaza. Octavious took a first step to walk around the costumed lad. Roberta grabbed his arm and pulled him back.

The faceoff ended suddenly when a car pulled to the curb. "Sorry I'm late," the driver said as he emerged from his vehicle. Derrick was in full costume: a buxom matron in white nightgown with an old-fashioned night cap. "Dear God in Heaven," exclaimed Roberta who, despite her dismay, craned her neck forward to take in the spectacle: exaggerated rouge on his cheeks, oversized spectacles hanging over a scabby and bulbous nose, unkempt wiry hair topping it all off.

"Well, howdy-do. I'm Mrs. Ebenezer Scrooge. Happy to make your acquaintance," Derrick said in his deep baritone.

Dushayne jumped into the car. "Let's go. Let's go," he commanded. The two drove off hurriedly, leaving the Wellingtons staring.

"That's one very ugly woman," Octavious said.

"That's no woman. That's the fellow Dushayne was with last time, with the wigs and the makeup. Something is going on there," Roberta said as she pulled her confused husband into the parking lot of their plaza. "And, I definitely do not like it."

The party turned into quite the success, promising to enter the archives of Hips as the best ever. Even Dushayne had a good time, managing to forget the curbside incident with Auntie. He was busy all night and well after closing. As he and Stevie locked up, they shared the best moments of the evening. They agreed that Miss Sashay as Mrs. Scrooge was the biggest hit, especially with her sultry rendition of *The Christmas Song*. Dushayne remembered the first few lines and in the empty alley did his best to recreate the moment.

His nuts roasting on an open fire
Jack Daniels…dripping from his nose
Ebenezer Scrooge hung like a sire…
And… and folks dressed up like frisky hos

Stevie applauded. "You know you'd make a good drag queen, boy."

Dushayne took a deep bow and said, "Don't think so, boss."

"Well, whatever. It was a great night. A full house, lots of fun and a good bar. Who woulda thought…Leave it up to a bunch of faggots to come up with so many outrageous costumes," Stevie said.

Dushayne congratulated him and walked away, wondering how Roberta would have reacted to all the Marys with doll Jesuses attached to their hips and the leather-clad Josephs and the bearish shepherds and the swishy angels.

Dushayne had turned down Derrick's offer of a ride. The bar back had scrounged some clothing from his locker and had decided to walk the two miles home. He had told Derrick he wanted to be alone, to plan a strategy, to find a way to face Auntie. Dushayne tried to wipe out the night's foolish revelry, but that damn song wouldn't let go. The tune percolated in his mind, forced its way out, and filled the empty street. Dushayne hummed, then sang at the top of his lungs.

Chestnuts roasting on an open fire…
His nuts roasting on an open fire.

Dushayne couldn't shake the tune. It followed him into the night. A few blocks later, he stopped dead in his tracks and out of frustration recited the *Pledge of Allegiance*, giving the words all the respect and formality they deserved. He repeated it three times, took a deep breath and started jogging down the street. The night was windless and cool, the streets of Fort Lauderdale surprisingly quiet. Finally, the silly song was expelled, replaced by patriotism and duty.

In the emptiness, he heard the chugging of a freight train punctuated by its whistle, once, twice, not especially insistent, but dependable, predictable. He listened intently, and even though the warning whistle seemed to be smothered by distance, he felt the kinship. He slowed his pace, stopped again, and stood quietly in the middle of the grimy sidewalk. He felt a new breeze and, not unlike Ebenezer, was visited by a shiver. Dushayne knew better: he dismissed the ghost of one of his past Christmases.

Yet, the phantom sounds were clear and persistent. He heard himself stifling his cries while his father was bawling in the next room. His father's wailings were the sounds of Christmas in the Brown household. Always depressed, the elder Brown would deal with the Holidays by going even deeper, wallowing for weeks in a liquored self-pity. He would barricade himself in one of the two rooms of their efficiency, the one that everybody would normally use as a bedroom, forcing his sons to fight for sleeping space in the other room. As the youngest of the five boys, Dushayne would invariably wind up sleeping on the kitchen floor. There was no room for – or any interest in – what other folks called Christmas decorations.

Dushayne and his brothers would come and go – only one of them had a job, part-time, at Winn-Dixie – but they would spend their nights together listening to their father cursing and weeping in the other room. The Brown boys would attempt to deal with the situation with some kind of bonding, but by the third week, they would aim their frustration and anger at Dushayne, the youngest and the weakest. Finally, Christmas Day would come, and the phone would ring and Dushayne's mom would be calling from her mother's house in Jacksonville. She'd ask to talk to each of her boys, keeping Dushayne for last. She'd tell him how much she missed him, and both mother and son would plunge into a chorus of sobs.

Traffic increased as Dushayne turned onto Sistrunk Boulevard. The noise jolted him into the reality of the current Christmas season. No more cries, not his, not his father's, not his mother's. Just some stupid costumes, a bunch of drunken gay men and drag queens singing parodies of real Christmas carols, and a lonely young Black man walking home at three o'clock in the morning.

Nobody paid much attention to the old guy who would hang around the back alley surrounded by the stench of the dumpster. Wrinkled and mangled, the man sat on the stack of old roofing tiles nobody had bothered to collect after Hurricane Wilma, often with a bottle of cheap liquor peeking out of the pocket of his oversized coat. He scavenged for cigarette butts left in the alley by the employees of Hips, at times humming tunes that made sense to no one and moments later yelling at invisible hecklers.

Stevie, the bar owner, would chase him away, but the stinky old man would return after a few days. Stevie toyed with the idea of calling the cops and have them take the guy to a shelter. The bar owner, however, didn't like attracting the attention of the police. The employees knew the man would squatter out back most nights; they didn't know what to do about him either, and they figured he wasn't their problem.

Derrick often talked to the vagrant between acts. Sometimes, he practiced lines from a new song. The homeless guy would calm down and listen. He told Derrick his song was beautiful. The two chatted. The old guy had no clue that Derrick wasn't female.

During breaks from his bar back duties, Dushayne would step outside. He felt sorry for the old guy, wanted to help him, but didn't know how. On those nights when he was depressed, he looked at the old man and saw himself in his later years. He'd give the man a buck and tell him to get something to eat and Dushayne would feel a bit better.

The bar patrons had no idea the man was there on the night that bridged the years 2007 and 2008. It was a late crowd, almost everyone having partied elsewhere first, and they all seemed to arrive at the same time. Stevie was ready; he had all hands on deck. He was going to take full advantage of the midnight festivities: champagne chilled, plenty of servers, party favors and the best drag show in South Florida. The crowd was large, boisterous and ready to party.

Paul Paré

The old guy out back was also in a partying mood. A buddy of his had brought a couple of jugs of cheap wine and the two were toasting the New Year when they started arguing. Soon they were screaming and pulling at each other. One of the men threw an empty bottle at the other. It landed on the sidewalk, smashing into pieces that spread into the street like confetti.

JC was fueled by a mix of anger and a need for distraction. It was New Year's and he had been grounded by his father for being kicked off the football team after drugs were found in his locker. The grounding order didn't bother JC: he had a spare set of keys to his Ford truck. But, being kicked off the team left a scar that he still nursed. He sought out two of his buddies who, armed with a six-pack, didn't hesitate to jump into JC's truck and head out on a joy ride. The school buddies were looking for thrills; JC was looking for vengeance. They rode their supersized wheels for half an hour, looking for trouble and finding none – until the empty wine bottle was thrown over the dumpster enclosure and shattered in their path.

JC brought his pickup to a halt, and the boys spilled out armed with baseball bats and chains. JC walked around the dumpster and into the alley, his buddies following him. Facing the homeless men, the trio formed a blocking wedge with JC at the center, swinging his chain over his head. "Well, what have we here?" he said. The homeless men held their arms up in a defensive position, protesting they weren't looking for trouble. "Trouble? You don't know trouble, but you'll soon find out, you fucking lowlifes," JC yelled out at them. The other two boys nodded and grinned. The vagrants realized what was about to happen. They scattered, the visitor running down the street, and the resident scurrying under his dumpster. JC jerked his head as a signal to his henchmen and they started clawing at the homeless guy. One of them succeeded in pulling a leg out and started striking it with his baseball bat.

At that point, the back door opened and Derrick in full drag walked out. Everything stopped. The boys stared at Derrick, their weapons dangling at their sides. Derrick looked back, his mind attempting to decode the moment. The old man remained frozen in a fetal position. The place was soundless; not even the grackles in the trees, the traffic on the street, or the partying inside the bar disturbed the suspended moment.

The old man was first to move. He dragged himself back under the dumpster and clenched his eyes shut. That was the trigger. JC threw a sharp glance at his buddies and said in a throaty voice, "Well, well, well, what a pretty little faggot we've got here." He moved towards Derrick who took a step back. Not quickly enough, since JC was able to grab Derrick and drag him down with a snap of his chain. JC drew on the strength of an angry linebacker and tied the chain around Derrick's neck. Tightening his hold, he yelled out, "How's that for your necklace, faggot? Don't you look real pretty now?" JC nodded at his buddies and they moved in, striking Derrick's legs with their bats. Derrick attempted to free himself from the strangling chain. One of the attackers placed his boot on Derrick's arm, plowing his foot into the flesh like he would to put out a cigarette. Derrick let out a scream and JC kicked him in the face. More blows with the bats, more kicks, to the groin, the ribcage, the head, each blow punctuated with mockery: faggot, perve, homocunt, asshole.

Derrick's desperate cries became internal, finding hardly any will or wind. "Jesus, Jesus," he mumbled. His brain was trying to understand and all he could ask was, "Jesus?" The answer came mercifully in the form of darkness.

The boys stared at their victim. One of them pulled Derrick's wig off his head, the other tore his stage dress off. JC tore the underwear, grabbed a baseball bat and pushed the handle end up Derrick's ass. "Hope you liked that," he said, slowly, almost reverently, like an epitaph. The teenagers examined the bloody mess at their feet and, as if on cue, raced to their truck and vanished into the new year.

The silence that returned to the alley behind Hips was total except for the occasional whimper from a terrified old man hiding beneath his dumpster. It took no more than ten minutes for someone to notice that Miss Sashay was missing. Stevie told Dushayne to find him. Another ten minutes and the alley was drowning in the glare of police cruisers, the wail of sirens, the crackle of radios, and the screams of an inconsolable young bar back.

IV

The Grateful Dead

On a cloudy morning a few days after New Year's Day, Ray announced they should explore downtown Fort Lauderdale. Esther had informed him he would find a college campus and a brand new library as well as an art museum. Claude was unable to camouflage his lack of interest yet accepted the invitation. The Subaru Outback blended into the morning commute heading south on I-95 into Fort Lauderdale and Miami beyond it. "Esther told me to get off at Broward Boulevard," Ray said.

"The two of you seemed to have bonded."

"She was a teacher. We have that in common. Would you believe her maiden name is Lake? Esther Lake marries Chester Blake."

"That *is* weird. They're a weird couple, but nice. In some ways, it feels like I've known them all my life. He reminds me of my father," Claude said. The car left the traffic stream and climbed onto the ramp leading to Broward Boulevard. At the traffic light, both men spotted the panhandler. "Look at the beggar."

"That's a terrible word," Ray retorted.

"Sorry, but that's all I can come up with. Never saw any back home. Savannah was full of beggars. And, they're here too."

"We all beg – in our own way."

"At least, I perform for my money. I share my poetry, a part of me, and those who appreciate it throw some money my way."

"I'm sorry. I didn't mean to imply that you're a beggar."

Claude shrugged. Ray examined the panhandler who limped along the side of the roadway, largely ignored by the motorists. Tall and graceful, the young Black man held a sign that announced he was homeless and hungry. Ray felt a surge of sympathy. "Come on, let's give him something." He opened his window and waved to the boy who approached hurriedly. Ray took out a crumpled dollar and poked his passenger to make a contribution. Claude reached into his jeans and found a quarter.

"God bless, gentlemen," Dushayne said, nodding his head.

Ray replied: "Wish I could do more." The two stared at each other for a moment before the traffic light changed and the cars started to move.

"He has a beautiful voice," Ray said as he drove away.

As much as the cavernous library seemed to swallow him up, Ray felt he was not the fodder, but instead it was he that was being nourished. The first moment he set foot in the atrium of the Broward County Library, he fell back into his teenaged body when, on a senior class trip to New York City, he had wandered into Grand Central Station and was numbed by the vastness of the place. There was power in these great spaces. He saw it then and tasted it again, realizing that in both places the possibilities were endless.

"I'll see you later. Got to get some air. I'll be in the park in front."

"Ok. Let's say we leave at six o'clock," Ray said.

"Fine. I'll look out for you. I'll be near the entrance." Claude had taken a strong and immediate dislike to this library. He was used to the more intimate spaces of his library back home with corners and small alcoves. He thought this Florida library was more like a bus station or an airport terminal.

Ray watched his companion walk into the sunshine and understood that the pattern of their afternoons in Fort Lauderdale was being established. Ray scoped out the entire library and quickly made peace with the vastness and the wealth of its offerings. He felt a need to connect with national and world news. He started by focusing on what might be happening back home. He became curious about the aftermath of the sting operation that had launched his escape. He consulted on-line newspapers, perused law enforcement and court system websites, even the sex offender hotline. He found the article from the hometown newspaper that outlined the incident and a second article about the School Board appointing a new principal. He swore when he read the name of the appointee. "That idiot! Should have fired him years ago." A fellow patron gave Ray an unkind look. Ray found nothing else in his research and admitted he was disappointed. "Well, it's been almost a month. Maybe they've found other perverts to ensnare," he muttered.

Claude chose a shady slope facing the main entrance and spread out on the grass to watch the downtown traffic that slowed before him at the corner red light. They all stop to see who's the stranger in town. Well that's a two-way street: I'll stare at them while they stare at me and I'll wonder who these locals are and what they're up to. He wondered if any of the motorists noticed he was talking to himself. Absentmindedly, he rubbed the remnant of his swelling from his fight with Jules, and, as much as he said he was grateful to be away from Savannah, he recognized that his life at Tropical Gardens was confining.

"Stop the war. Now! Time to get out. Now! Stop the war. Now!" The chant's cadence filled the plaza, crossed the street and invaded the park, ricocheting off the expansive live oak a few feet away from Claude. The snappy words worked their way through Claude's stubborn reverie where they met resistance and became muddled. Eventually, they gained substance and made their way to his lips which started to move in mimicry. "Stop the war. Stop the war. Now...Now...NOW!" Claude Simard sat up and scoured the green space around him, looking for his compatriots from the protests in Williams. He realized he wasn't in Connecticut and, although the refrain was familiar, the place wasn't. He stood and, brushing dry twigs off his shirt, he anchored himself to the dark soil that he now recognized as belonging to the new place. "Stop the war. Stop the war." He allowed the rhythm to pull him to the edge of the park. Across the street a group of 20 or so protesters marched before the entrance to what appeared to be an official building.

Suddenly the protest was drowned out by sharp engine noise. Claude looked up at a small airplane buzzing the downtown and towing a banner that announced two-for-one nights at the

Beachcomber. He didn't know if he should be irritated or if he should welcome the interruption. "I'm done protesting. It's useless." He turned and walked deeper into his park.

The park with no name – that's what Claude called it, since he had found no plaque or sign – was filling up with what he assumed to be the typical weekday late afternoon crowd. A few young mothers with unruly kids, several older men, kids fresh out of school on bikes and skateboards, workers escaping from office buildings. An occasional loner would wander around or sit quietly, simply taking in whatever the first few days of 2008 had to offer. Claude read their faces. He grew bold and he felt safe looking at people straight on: plenty of sadness, a bit of craziness, a hint of happiness, plenty of anxiety, but no evil.

Only one performer – a Caribbean fellow with an avalanche of dreadlocks – was in the spot that seemed reserved for entertainers. Strollers slowed down as they passed by. Mothers pointed him out to their children. Some old timers sat on benches a safe distance from the musician. A few passersby dropped coins in his open guitar case.

Claude walked to an empty bench within sight of the performer and wondered how this crowd would react to his poetry. The thought depressed him. His inspiration seemed to have stayed behind. Perhaps too comfortable here. Poetry needs misery. He read the dedication on the back of the bench: "In memory of Sophie Steinberg – her loving husband and children." He hesitated. He had seen inscriptions on most of the benches, and he felt that in a way the seats belonged to those individuals listed on the plaques. He sensed that he was desecrating a sacred space by sitting on them. Well, maybe Sophie wants some company. He reverently set himself down. He scouted his surroundings, listened to the half-toned guitar picking carried to him by a gentle tropical breeze, and thought that perhaps this place could inspire some writings. He pulled his backpack onto Sophie's bench and took out his writing pad. He paused. At the top of the page he jotted down his own inscription:

Thursday, January 3rd, 2008, in an unnamed park
on a Jewish lady's bench.

Eyes closed, he waited for inspiration, as if the date and the place should urge him on. They didn't. His page remained blank.

The sun seemed to set earlier than usual, although Claude wasn't sure about the time the sun should be setting. He still didn't have a watch, and most often, that was not an issue. Time was immaterial, and it was not what dictated when he should be doing anything anymore. Nothing seemed to. Claude was drifting and he knew it. It wasn't a coasting like that which accompanied his homelessness back in Connecticut. As he sat on his bench with his empty notepad on his knee, Claude compared the two: the frightful downhill nihilism that filled his daytime roamings and bizarre nights right after losing his job, his marriage and his son; the languid blandness of empty ease that now escorted him day after day in South Florida. Claude's brain split in two and he saw both scenarios side by side playing themselves out. One was accompanied by crashing cymbals and full percussion, the other by a repetitive and gentle guitar sound. He started to write:

> *I was running away from a train*
> *that was catching up to me*
> *and now I'm sitting*
> *in the station waiting*
> *for a train that never comes.*
>
> *Always downhill, boulders at my back,*
> *gnarled branches around my heels,*
> *old voices always insisting:*
> *reasons, duties, destinations.*
>
> *These days, smooth and flat,*
> *warm winds gently flowing*
> *around me like a delta,*
> *never shoving, never pulling.*

Claude managed to transfer his thoughts onto his notepad. He read them aloud. There was no one to hear them except the guitar player who seemed to be in his own world of nonsense. Claude was unhappy with the result and he didn't know if the failure was with the ideas themselves or their transcription. He brusquely stuffed his pad away and stood. He walked to the corner of the park where he had promised to wait for Ray.

While heading toward his pre-arranged meeting spot, Claude noticed a group in another section of the park and went to investigate. In a peninsula of greenery between the library and what looked like a college building were some musicians and a small crowd of listeners. That's where he first saw Aurora. She was the drummer. She was beautiful. She had presence. She gave the musical group its sound, its rootedness. Claude listened and watched. A musical set concluded to not very enthusiastic applause, and Claude began to approach the girl when someone yelled out her name and she responded with a wave. That's how Claude learned her name, and he thought it was enigmatic and enticing. He observed the girl as she pranced over to a tall Black man and he watched them hug and walk away hand in hand.

"There you are," Ray said, approaching Claude from behind. "Is that a concert?"

"Think so. But, it seems to be over." The group of spectators started to disperse, many of them walking down the broad aisle in the direction of the two men from New England.

"Was it good? The music, I mean."

"Not sure. Only heard the last song."

They started walking to their car. "Here, I found this book for you." Ray handed over a thin booklet to Claude, explaining that he found it on the dollar rack at the library. Claude accepted the volume and read the title out loud: *Satori in Paris.* He wasn't sure how to pronounce the first word; he gave Ray a questioning look.

"Jack Kerouac. It's by Jack Kerouac," Ray said. "You told me you like his writings."

"Oh," stated Claude in a tone of voice loaded with surprise and recognition. "I do. Thanks. That's nice."

"It's one of his last books. He goes to France to find his roots."

Claude examined the thin book and thought how Kerouac had kept him both sane and crazy during his summer in the abandoned textile mill. He re-read the title. "Maybe Kerouac and I can go to Paris together...as stowaways," he mumbled.

"New year, new roommate." That's how Roberta brought up the subject: pointblank, final, official. She didn't even knock; she just walked in and made her announcement. Dushayne was already in a bad mood and the last thing he wanted was a new roommate. But Dushayne didn't say a word. He looked at Roberta blankly. Dushayne's thoughts raced through his murky Sunday afternoon mind and he tried to shut out both the intruder and the slice of sunshine that followed her into his room. The slanted sun cast its light on dirty clothes, magazines, empty pizza boxes.

As she bullied her way into the room, Roberta nearly tripped on sneakers littering the entryway. From behind her she yanked a small person and said his name was Ezekiel and that he was moving in. Dushayne wanted to yell. Auntie, not now, and thanks for the fuckin' warning. All he did was shrug and send an annoyed look her way. Roberta Wellington was on a mission and Dushayne had learned that when she was on a mission, nothing would stand in her way. The landlady explained that Ezekiel was 15 and that his mama was in the church choir and there was trouble at home and that it was their Christian duty – hers and Dushayne's – to take him in. She pushed the lad further into the room and told him in her sweet churchy voice that Octavious would be up later with his belongings. She told the boy to make himself comfortable. Roberta re-arranged herself, pulling and patting the folds of her dress. She adjusted her hat and, before leaving, gave Dushayne a glare that defied protest.

Dushayne knew Auntie was trying to punish him. Since she spotted the makeup, Roberta had been on a crusade, accusing him of harboring what she called vile inclinations. She made it clear that she had her eye on him. He made it clear he had a right to privacy. Auntie would wait up and accost him as he came home from work. She would inspect him. She would preach to him. At first, Dushayne tried to ignore her, but gradually she made him all the more combative. He started wearing eye makeup on a regular basis, he played loud disco music, he swished about.

Dushayne's last roommate had left in October. Harold was an easy roommate: out most of the time. One day, he and his disability checks moved back to Virginia. Dushayne enjoyed the solitude; being alone made it easier for him to become more and more like his muse Eartha Kitt. His angel mother and sister and lover and soul keeper, Miss Kitt reigned from her poster enshrined over Dushayne's bed from where her aura filled the air, turning the dingy motel room into a fabulous cabaret.

Attempting to ignore his new roommate, Dushayne looked up at Miss Kitt as he straightened out the mess on the empty bed. He contemplated removing the poster. Would she feel discarded and would she abandon him? Would she prefer to stay in her place of honor and have this new kid learn of her beauty and brilliance? Dushayne swayed between the privacy of his adoration and the urge to proclaim it. The kid with the name of a prophet asked who the lady in the funny costume was, and Dushayne decided to leave the poster up. The kid made a feeble attempt to be friendly, saying his name was Zeke although his crazy mother insisted that he was Ezekiel, like some scary old guy in the Bible. He liked rap and listened to it all the time. His mother and Roberta were against it. They were against everything. Zeke's jeans were hanging in puddles around his sneakers and his oversized tee shirt looked like a choir gown. The kid was sickly-looking and the chain he was wearing around his neck seemed to weigh him down. With his baseball cap perched off center, Zeke stood in the middle of the room, his eyes closed, mouthing some lyrics known only to him.

Stevie Stevens had informed Dushayne that in January business always dried up and that his services would no longer be needed. Dushayne wasn't surprised; he wasn't even disappointed. He was sick of bar backing. He was tired of cleaning up after everybody.

Panhandling had been lucrative just before Christmas, but had dropped to zero after the holiday. He still offered his shy smile, but all he got were nickels and dimes. Everybody's all Christmassed-out, the veteran panhandlers explained. People had no money. Dushayne was seriously considering taking the old timers' advice and moving to another spot, a couple of exits north perhaps. He understood that if commuters see the same face at the same place all the time, they don't see it anymore. January for Dushayne loomed bleak. His rent was due and he knew he would be late. He needed to find a job and a new spot to panhandle. He needed to avoid a showdown with Auntie. What he didn't need was a fifteen-year-old roomy.

The hospital elevator stopped on the fourth floor. Two nurses faced the open door. "You getting off here?" one asked. The passenger looked up, found the number four etched on the corridor wall and moved forward. The nurses stepped back and watched the young man shuffle down the corridor, clinging to the wall, looking down at the floor. "Poor kid. Comes every day," said the nurse.

Since the attack, Dushayne spent most afternoons staring at Derrick in his bed. The hospital staff treated him with deference if not sympathy. No one, however, would tell him anything about Derrick's condition – something about not being next of kin. But, Dushayne had eyes and ears. He could plainly see the bandages covering his head, the tubes and wires attached to his body, monitors registering. He overheard the doctors and nurses discuss the prognosis: severe brain damage, vital organs not functioning, a matter of days.

The cops had interviewed him twice: one time at Wellington Plaza, which had proven embarrassing, and another time at the hospital. He told them everything he knew, which was practically nothing. The police had also interviewed the homeless man they found under the dumpster, but he was no help. The beating couldn't be classified as a hate crime without corroborating evidence. Dushayne didn't care; wouldn't make any difference.

"Afternoon, Mr. Brown."

"Afternoon, Mrs. Alvarez."

She picked up her clipboard and made some notations. He took his usual seat, cupped his chin in his hand and stared at his friend. A new, rasping sound came from Derrick's partially open mouth. Derrick's head leaned to the side in an unnatural way, reminding Dushayne of a manatee he had found floating upside down, its head nearly severed by a gash from a boat propeller. He had felt helpless then as he did now. Mrs. Alvarez placed a hand gently on Dushayne's shoulder. "He's breathing with great difficulty. There's not much we can do."

"I can see that."

"You know Mr. James' family will be arriving later this afternoon and they've made it clear they don't want anyone but family here, if you understand. You can stay for now. I'll come in and warn you just before they get here."

Dushayne crumbled as he whispered, "I understand."

"I'll leave you alone now."

Dushayne leaned over the bed and placed one hand on Derrick's knee. He closed his eyes and concentrated on how strong his friend had been, how gracefully he had sashayed around the stage, how confidently he had carried himself, in and out of costume. His vision blurred and his throat tightened, Dushayne muttered the words to his song – their song.

> *C'est si bon,*
> *So I say it to you,*
> *Like the French people do,*
> *Because it's oh…so good.*

He sang the words over and over, swaying his tall frame imperceptibly, gently massaging Derrick's knee, his bandaged forearm and his neck. There was so little of Derrick's body that wasn't bruised or broken. He leaned over and placed a kiss on the layers of dressings covering his friend's forehead. "Goodbye, Miss Sashay," he whispered.

He stopped at the nurses' station to thank you to Mrs. Alvarez.

"You don't have to leave now. They're not here yet," she said.

"Don't want to be chased away. I won't wait for you to come and warn me that his folks are here. Won't let those people force me away…" Distressed, Dushayne glanced at Derrick's room. "This is how I want to leave him, peacefully, lovingly. It's all I can give him."

"Mr. Brown, I'm so sorry."

"I know. Thanks," he replied.

In the elevator, alone, he reprised the song – Miss Sashay's song, clearly, defiantly.

It was just too pretty. The plastic of Tropical Gardens in perfect color combinations, the neatly trimmed bushes tidily corralled behind false picket fences, and at night all of it bathed in pink neon. Claude felt homesick for the chaotic clutter of his dirty warehouse. The daily drive into Fort Lauderdale with Ray to spend time in the manicured park next to the library only made things worse. Claude started to hear the song of the vagabond and the call of the whiskey.

One morning, he told Ray he wasn't feeling well and wanted to stay in his room. Earlier, Chester had talked about a mangrove swamp a couple of miles west that had miraculously escaped South Florida's bulldozing frenzy. As soon as Ray left for the library, Claude sought out the motel owner and got directions to the swamp. The day was brilliant with a low winter sun and dry air. It felt like one of those perfect days in May in New England when the detritus of winter had faded and the promise of summer was tangible. He stopped at the Circle K for his usual coffee and Krispy Kreme. He hesitated in front of the cooler filled with rows of cold beers; he decided this was not a beer kind of day. He carried with him his plastic grocery bag overflowing with legal-sized tablets, along with a couple of dollar store ball points. The most essential and probably most precious part of his cargo, however, was what he hoarded in his head. For the past few days, his nights filled up with crazy ideas and wild escapades and, as much as he felt on the edge of instability, he welcomed them along with the urgent need to record them.

He found the swamp easily and quickly allowed himself to be absorbed by the mature stillness of the place. He followed a path into the undergrowth and came upon a small body of water. Claude dismissed the thought of snakes and lizards and alligators. Balanced atop a couple of logs at water's edge was a scavenged car seat used by fishermen and dreamers. Claude identified with the latter and didn't hesitate to make himself at home. He sat facing north, the sun on his neck, his writing tablet on his lap. Claude started writing. A cascade of words, half sentences, brief images, in the precise order they came to him. He made no distinctions. The demarcation between idle half-sleep thoughts and fierce nightmares eluded him. He wrote it all down, swiftly filling half a page with his left-slanted script.

A clan of white egrets performed their morning ballet a few yards from him, and some unknown insects skimmed across the surface of the pond. Claude didn't notice. He was struggling with an image, attempting to capture its fullness and its resonance. From mind to hand was not always an easy or direct route. Claude's fascination with words and phrases was a recent acquisition.

Forests thick with trees, various northern trees, unlike those on the banks of his murky swamp: pines and spruces and maples and tall thin birches. He had spent what seemed an endless part of his night running around and between them. He would fall at their feet; he would lie on the sweet grass and look up into a gray windy sky and watch the treetops sway. He would hug the trunks; he would run his hands over the leathery bark of some and the silky casings of others. Laughing loudly, he would scoop up fallen pine needles and shower himself with them, letting them cover his head like confetti, spitting out the ones that made their way into his mouth and brushing away those that filled his eyes. He would pluck leaves from the overhanging branches and compare their texture, their veining, their color. He would spin himself around and around until his dizziness threw him onto the bed of dry leaves that cushioned the ground.

All of this, he hurriedly jotted down, attempting with a good measure of desperation to get it all on paper without trying to make any sense of it. The recording was the priority; the interpreting would come later, sometimes much later. If any emotions or reactions came to him, he would scribble them down in the margins. Often, upon re-reading his manuscript, these annotations would be meaningless, or worse, mysterious and distracting. But he noted them anyways, just in case.

After writing furiously for several minutes, he put the pad down. He rested his head on the worn leather of the thrown-away car seat. He closed his eyes and his nocturnal frolic returned, thrusting him into a mix of confusing feelings. Claude felt childlike in the discovery, refreshed by the landscape of his dream, yet embarrassed by the foolish abandon. You're a grown man with a young boy of your own. A grown man doesn't sprint through the forest, hugging trees. He looked down and examined his words. Slowly, he began to understand how deeply he missed his son, how absolute was his homesickness. He sank deeply into his seat and inhaled the humid air of this new place. Everything surrounding him was alien: the flat and monotonous landscape, the extravagant foliage, the exotic flowers, the people. Everyone he met came from somewhere else. Everyone had something to hide. Their bodies were peculiar, sun-worn and twisted or bloated.

The sky filled with a bevy of blackbirds with wide wing spans. Gliding in and out of the air space above him, the large birds formed circles and funnels, then quickly flew off, only to return moments later to continue their loud tour of inspection. "Fucking vultures," Claude yelled, shielding his eyes from the sun. He hated the birds. He knew they weren't vultures. Ray had told him they were hawks. But, still he hated them. He didn't trust the screeching animals; they were out scavenging and they were after the likes of him.

Claude remembered another episode of his nighttime meanderings and he returned to his notepad. Claude and his best friend Tony were sunning themselves in their favorite spot: a moss covered ledge overlooking the Quinnipiac River. They were teenagers, yet it could have been the day before. Tony was napping, and Claude was staring down at the rushing waters when he noticed a ribbon of red flowing into the river. He traced it to his friend who was dressed in full vestments – the robes, chasuble and all – that a Catholic priest wears to celebrate Mass. The hem of his alb was soaked with blood and the stream of red was widening.

"Wake up, wake up, Tony. You're bleeding." Claude said, shaking his pal.

"What? What do you mean? I'm not bleeding."

"Look!" Claude pointed to the blood-soaked vestment. "Look, it's flowing into the river. The river's turning red. There's a lot of blood here."

"I don't feel a thing."

"I tell you, Tony. You're bleeding. Take off these clothes so we can see where you're bleeding. It must be a terrible wound."

Pulling away, Tony replied with alarm: "No. No. I will not remove my vestments. I am not bleeding. And, anyways, if I were, it would be a holy blood."

"Holy shit. Holy fucking shit," Claude heard himself say to the grouping of egrets. His outburst sent the birds scattering. The bloody image of his dream vanished. He tried to bring it back, to remember more, to complete the episode, only to acquiesce to the abrupt ending. The nearby birds returned to their spot and resumed their graceful pecking.

Claude had become accustomed to puzzling stories, to incomplete portraits. Although he knew better than to attempt to make sense of these scraps, he couldn't help himself about this particular dream. Claude illustrated it with a very fancy asterisk, gradually elongating some of the spokes and turning it into a crucifix. Eating away at Claude was the certainty that when, at some point in the future, he would review his scribbling, he would discover the meaning of this one. The vision of his bleeding friend in priestly garb would then make sense.

For the moment, he had enough. Should his memory regurgitate anything else from his most recent nights, it would have to go unrecorded. Claude stood and stared into the dark waters of his mangrove swamp. Such a sad piece of water, he thought. So unlike the wide and vigorous lakes and streams of New England, his New England. He tucked his tablet away and started walking out of the swamp, a pair of Muscovy ducks with their unsightly red scars blocking his path briefly in a vain attempt to keep him there.

When Claude saw the musicians again, he searched for the girl with the odd name. His memory of that event had already taken on the glaze of mystery and chivalry and he had grown determined to meet the girl. The sun kept plunging behind fluffy fantasy clouds, throwing the downtown park into an ever-changing patchwork of dark and light. Claude thought it set the mood perfectly. But, the girl was nowhere to be seen. He inspected the small gathering, recognizing the two guitarists as well as the older man with the concertina. They played a couple of standard tunes that were greeted with half-hearted applause. Moments later, office workers on lunch break joined the crowd. A group of students strolling by between classes also stopped, and at that moment, as if on cue, the girl sauntered in and took her seat. A few in the assembly applauded. The girl laughed heartily and offered a quick curtsy and proceeded to play her drums, blending easily with the other performers. She seemed joined to her instrument, a pair of small drums brightly decorated with beads and leather strands. She kept her eyes closed, and folded her small body over the drums like a breast-feeding mother.

During a break, Claude approached the group. "Great," he said as he dropped a couple of quarters in the open guitar case. Turning to the girl, he said, "Like your drums."

"Wow. That's quite the line," she replied, giving him a smile tinged with mischief.

"I mean those." Claude pointed to the drums anchored on her lap. He felt foolish.

"Of course. What else could you mean?"

"Ah. Nothing...I don't know."

Aurora stood, and the two discovered they were of equal height. She brushed her hands back and forth against her long and ample skirt in response to some inner rhythm, and Claude thought the movement made her look like an Olympic swimmer about to plunge. She said, "It's just that no one's ever used my drums to start a conversation. Never."

"Well they're quite beautiful. Never seen anything like them."

"My grandfather made them. He lived in Africa for a while and he learned all kinds of crafts."

"Really. And he gave them to you."

"Sort of. I just took them. He died and there was so much stuff and no one else wanted them."

"I see." Claude was reminded of the many awkward moments of his high school years. He wanted to say how talented she was, how graceful she looked. He wanted to talk to her all afternoon.

"Excuse me," she said as she took a few steps back to accept a soft drink from one of the guitar players. Turning to face Claude, she said, "Aurora. That's my name. And yours?"

"Ah, that's it," he said under his breath as he recalled how she had responded when the Black guy had called out to her. He remembered thinking that the name was sensuously exotic. The crumb of jealousy he felt then suddenly returned, and he coughed. "That's such an unusual name. It's beautiful," he said.

"It means the dawn. We all have odd names in my family. My grandparents were hippies."

"I see."

"And yours..."

"Oh. My name. Yes, my name is Claude," he offered, avoiding the English pronunciation. "It's French."

"Pleased to make your acquaintance." She curtsied again. The older guy with the concertina called to her, and Aurora faced her fellow musicians. "Back to work," she said over her shoulder. "Lunch hour's short. Gotta make the most of it."

Claude watched her walk away and he saw the Olympic swimmer turn into a ballerina. Under her flowing skirt and halter top, there was an athletic body in constant motion. Claude tried to guess her age and couldn't. One moment, she had the spontaneity of a teenager, the next, the poise of a mature woman.

Dushayne thought he had lived through lots of shit, but he had seen nothing compared to the power of his grief in the days following Derrick's death. The shapelessness of his life was thorough and relentless. Dushayne knew what was happening, he saw the hole, the emptiness that pulled at him, and he didn't care.

He would tell his young roommate to get lost. The drapes drawn, Dushayne stared at his poster of Eartha Kitt and listened to her music, plaintive and throaty like the sounds of Arab women wailing in the movies about war. All day, this was his ritual: sitting at the foot of his bed, facing Miss Kitt, rocking his lean body from side to side, imagining that the voice was Miss Sashay's. The light was reddish and the air was stale and he found a minor measure of comfort in that. Late in the afternoons, he would enclose himself in the bathroom and talk to his reflection in the mirror, asking himself what he had done wrong, what terrible things he had committed, why he was being so harshly punished. Then, he'd remember that Derrick was the one who was assaulted, whose body was broken and violated, and who lay in a coma for days. He'd feel guilty and he would cry for Derrick. The nights became intolerable. Often, Dushayne could sense Derrick's presence. He would feel his breath and his touch and Dushayne would spend sleepless hours caressing his own arms and face and torso, rubbing his lost friend's essence into his own pores, kneading the remembrance, hoping to make it tangible like a new skin.

Roommate Zeke would wander in and out and complain, throwing his *you gotta shake it, man* and *stop givin' me the creeps* as he rummaged around the place. Evenings, Dushayne would move to the balcony and chase Zeke and his friends away. He'd sit on a wooden bench and blankly observe the sky grow dark.

Auntie would glance up at her tenant and worry. She knew the narrative. She understood that his friend had been killed. Roberta prayed for Dushayne. She didn't say what she wanted to say: that his friend was being punished for dressing like a woman and that he – Dushayne – was being tested by the Lord. She kept silent and allowed her frustration to grow into fear.

One day, a fierce thunderstorm disturbed the routine. The motel room grew dark and the sounds of wind-driven rain and rolling thunder obscured Miss Kitts' *C'est si bons*. Dushayne thought of the end of days and became possessed with the need to describe it, to give this end of the world a proper name. He couldn't find the word. Shit, shit, what is it? That movie with the helicopter and the crazy opera music. In Vietnam. What's the word? Shit. Derrick would know. Dushayne begged his brain to recall, but there was no response. He opened his door and advanced into the fury. He walked to the edge of his balcony and whipped himself to the railing and observed the lightning split the sky. The end of the world still had no name when Dushayne launched his torso out into the torrent and kept it there defiantly until the need to name the final catastrophe had vanished. He witnessed the entire wrath of the storm, and in the end was left alone on his balcony, thoroughly soaked and out of breath, yet happy to conclude this was a conquest – his conquest. He watched with half a smile as the sky turned light and the clouds separated to allow a January sun to bathe Wellington Plaza with its *I'm sorry but it felt good*. Dushayne looked at his bare feet straddling puddles of cold water and, standing erect, he saluted the sun with his own *I feel pretty good too*.

Later that same day he felt the need for food, then the need to conduct an inventory. He realized he had nothing to eat and just a handful of crumpled one dollar bills. The job at Hips had dried up as expected. His panhandling spot was still reserved for him two days a week but he hadn't shown up and might have jeopardized it. His rent was due.

He decided to go to Hips and ask Stevie for a loan, maybe an advance. The bar owner said all he could spare was fifty dollars and that it was definitely a loan, and that he'd expect repayment in two installments, maybe five, but sixty days was the time limit. He asked the lad how he was dealing with Derrick's death and told him to keep on truckin'. "Don't forget to pay me back or I'll be lookin' for you."

Walking back to his room, Dushayne stopped in front of the tattoo parlor he had passed a hundred times before and spotted a design in the window. He went in and asked Harold, the old hippie owner of the place, how much the tattoo would cost.

"Depends where you want it?"

"Want it where it'll show. People gotta see it. That's the idea."

"Your upper arm or shoulder's cheaper."

"Inside my arm above the wrist?" Dushayne turned his arm to show what he meant.

"Same price." Harold said impatiently.

"So, how much?"

Harold grabbed Dushhayne's arm and inspected it. "You're thin, boy. Not much meat there. But that's a good place. Skin's lighter there. Tattoo'll show up better."

"Well, can you do it? And, how much?"

"What design you pick out?" the man asked him.

Dushayne pointed to a rose on a stem with one thorn and a large tear falling from the flower as if it were crying.

"For you, eighty dollars." Harold quoted him half price. He felt sorry for the kid. Everyone in the neighborhood of bars and smoke shops and tattoo parlors knew about the attack on Derrick. "But, that's not a good one for you. The red color won't show up on your skin. African-Americans should stay away from colors. Strong black shapes and patterns work best. Like letters, you know: words."

"Really? Words…like a love song?"

"Here. Right it down, kid. I'll tell you if it'll work."

Dushayne studied the tattoo artist with his thin braid of yellow-gray hair falling nearly to his waist. Carefully, Dushayne wrote the words from the song, the love song from a Black woman that had become Miss Sashay's epitaph: *C'est si bon*. He read them slowly to himself. Confidently, he showed the pad to the old guy who read the words out loud. "Sure. That's short enough. With a good heavy script, along the length of your arm, from your wrist to inside your elbow, that'll look good."

"Ok, how much for that, then?"

The man hesitated. "That was your friend's song. The drag queen. Heard him sing it at Hips. An old Eartha Kitt piece. Sweet."

"That's right"

"Tell you what. A special price. You know, in his memory. Just fifty dollars."

227

Dushayne hesitated. "All I got is twenty."

"Hey kid. Twenty can't get you shit. You know that."

"I'm sorry, sir." He put on his panhandling face.

"Tell you what. I'll take the twenty and you can pay me the rest with a good blow job."

The idea surprised and repulsed Dushayne. He took a step back. The man looked older and uglier than before. "I...dunno. I'm not..."

"Listen kid. I'm partial to young thick black lips around my dick. Boy or girl...makes no difference. Don't even need dope no more. But I don't beg for it. Never have."

"When? Where?"

"Right now. In back. Got no other customers in here."

A few hours later, as he walked on Sistrunk Boulevard, Dushayne felt both sullied and cleansed. The taste of the man's penis stayed with him. The smell, too. He spit nothing on the sidewalk, but he kept on doing it. He carried his left arm folded at the elbow, perpendicular to his torso, the bandage upwards, as if carrying a tray or an offering. He cleared his throat and looked at his arm. He felt the fusion of pride and shame. He had his tribute to Derrick; in time he'd forget the price.

Claude had found a reason to join Ray on his treks downtown: a group of musicians and the beautiful drummer with an exotic name. Ray would leave his friend at the main entrance to the Broward Library and Claude would head to the shady park.

On the afternoon of January 12th, Claude listened and watched as the crowd ebbed and the cast of musicians changed every few hours. Claude posted himself on a bench that offered a full view of Aurora. The music was eclectic and not especially good, but Aurora's bravura caught everyone's attention. Very few of the strollers could resist stopping. They'd smile at her, and she'd smile back. She knew to throw herself into the conclusion of each song with a flurry of drumming that rarely failed to extract some form of donation. Claude would give her a thumbs-up and she'd respond with a knowing nod.

During a break late in the afternoon, Aurora announced that the group was moving to the beach. She walked over to Claude and explained that the evening crowd in the downtown park wasn't very interesting, so she and the musicians usually headed to the Pompano Beach pier which was much more profitable. She invited him to come along.

"I'll be right back. I've got to see my friend and tell him I won't need a ride," he said. For the moment, getting back to his motel had lost all importance. When he returned to the park, the tall Black guy had showed up. Aurora introduced him as Gary and explained that he was "bitchin' good" on the keyboards and that he'd often join them at the pier and make the group sound professional. Claude smiled drily as he watched the two leave hand in hand, Aurora swinging her arms like a teenager. "You comin', Claude?" she yelled out. He hustled to catch up.

Aurora was right: the music had a fuller sound with a keyboard, and the beach crowd was generous. After three full hours of playing, Aurora thanked the crowd and said they'd be back Friday and Saturday. The musicians packed up and counted the money. Aurora announced they should celebrate with pizza. "You too," she said to Claude.

"Thanks, but I've got to head home."

"Where do you live?" asked Gary.

"A small motel on Route 44 called Tropical Gardens."

"In Banyan Cove?"

"Yup...lovely Banyan Cove."

Aurora and Gary looked at each other and let out a deep laugh. "I live in a trailer park further down Route 44," Aurora said. "Don't worry, we'll take you home."

In the back seat of Gary's Jeep, Claude wondered about the pair. Aurora and Gary seemed close, but not like lovers. Gary displayed genuine interest in Claude. Stopped at a traffic light on Atlantic Boulevard, he asked Claude if he played any instrument. Claude volunteered that he wrote poetry. Gary suggested that he should read his poems. "Aurora could accompany you on the drums; it would be great between songs."

As they approached Tropical Gardens, Claude announced he'd be getting off. Aurora turned to face him and said the plan was for him to meet her grandmother and to see where they lived. "It's just up the street," she said.

"I don't know if I should," was his weak offer of resistance.

"Ah, c'mon. Grandma don't bite, at least not lately." Aurora laughed, and Claude melted into the warmth of her invitation.

They parked in the back lot of a warehouse, a large structure sheathed in rusting metal corrugation. Most of the building's lights were broken and brush-like weeds had found strong footholds here and there in the cracked asphalt. For a second, Claude suspected he had been abducted and his musician friends had something perverse in mind.

"I'll leave you guys here," Gary said.

"Will I see you Friday?" Aurora asked.

Gary said he'd be there, and they agreed to meet at the park at the usual time. He shook Claude's hand. "Happy to meet you."

Claude didn't have a chance to reply. Aurora took him by the elbow and edged him away from the Jeep. Gary turned on the car's high beams and sent a spray of light against a wall of tall bamboo and rushes in the distance.

"C'mon, follow me," she said.

"Where you taking me?" Claude didn't try to camouflage the

confusion in his voice.

"This is where we live. This is the back way, there's a bridge here over the canal. Just follow me and watch your step." Claude wasn't convinced; he wanted to protest. He tried to see where Aurora was taking him and all he could see were tall reeds swaying in the wind. Suddenly, the lights from the Jeep moved away. Aurora reached into a metal box on the ground and extracted a flashlight. She took the lead, lighting the way. "The bridge is narrow. Just follow and stay close."

On the other side, the pair climbed onto a flat stretch of asphalt. To Claude, it looked like a street, but there were no street lights. Aurora offered an explanation: "The trailer park was destroyed by Hurricane Wilma. There's hardly anyone living here now." She waved her flashlight ahead of them sweeping both sides of the roadway to prove her point. "And we're all squatters now, anyway," she added as an afterthought. "Officially, this was Royal Palms Trailer Court."

"Royal Palms?" Claude asked.

"Yes, the trees. Maybe I shouldn't tell you this but when I was in junior high school, the boys who lived here were always teased by the other boys. They called them the palms." Aurora giggled. "I didn't get the joke for a long time."

"What joke?"

"The palms. The outsiders said the boys who lived here couldn't get girlfriends so they had to use their palms."

She waited for Claude to react. "You don't get it?"

"No. Sorry.'

"They had to use their palms, you know…to jerk off."

"Oh." He chuckled, thankful for the darkness that obscured his embarrassment.

As they walked further, Claude was surprised by the scope of the emptiness. The place was practically treeless; there were mounds of debris here and there, and in the far distance – perhaps two or three miles away – was the glow of Banyan Cove. He heard the barking of a dog and expected Aurora to comment. She remained silent.

"Is this Gary your boyfriend?"

Aurora laughed. "No. He's sort of my guardian. When we first met though, there could have been something there. But that would have been unprofessional. And, he's older than me. Quite a bit older."

For Claude, that was just enough information to warrant his renewed fascination. He wanted to know more. "Your guardian, you say?"

Aurora laughed. "Well, that's what I call him. He doesn't like it though. He used to be my counselor, and I was one of his cases, but now we're just friends."

"I see," said Claude.

Gradually, the landscape revealed signs of life. Groupings of lights flickered at odd intervals, always far from the pathway. Claude smelled food cooking and he thought he heard voices. But, everything was muted, unsure. Claude remembered that Aurora had used the word "squatters." Rounding a pile of debris, he saw what was clearly a mobile home surrounded by sheds and abandoned cars. Aurora stopped walking and grabbed her companion by the hand. "Listen, Claude, here's the story. I'm gonna tell you now because I don't want to talk about it in front of my grandmother."

"Ok," Claude said expectantly.

Aurora explained in short breathless sentences that a few years back she had a problem with drugs. She had a job, a good job as a bus driver for Broward Schools, but one day, she forgot this kid on the bus, a kid with disabilities, and he had to spend several hours alone. She was stoned that day and she got fired and it was in all the papers and on the news and that's when her grandma put her in rehab and that's how she met Gary who worked there. "But that was then; I've been clean for a long time, and I've learned to use music to keep clean and to make a bit of money. "Now, don't say a word about any of this to Grandma."

They approached the trailer cautiously. "You stay here," she said to Claude. "Don't want to spook her. I'll tell her I have a friend with me and then I'll call you over. Ok?"

"Ok." Claude was still absorbing all the information.

"Where you been, kitten?" An old woman opened the trailer door and let a slice of kitchen light out onto the deck. "It's so late. Where you been?"

"You know, Grandma. I went to the pier to play music with Gary and the others. We did real good tonight."

Claude listened to the women speak in muffled tones and he thought of the residents of his father's nursing home. He watched as Aurora hugged the older woman and escorted her back into the trailer. He wondered if he should stay there. He listened for voices, but he only heard the hum of machinery coming from somewhere in the back and assumed it was a generator. He saw shapes moving about on the deck and recognized two large cats. Then, he noticed Aurora in the doorway waving at him to join her. "She's making tea. Means she's in a good mood," Aurora whispered.

The introductions were direct and brief. The three of them sat around a kitchen table and sipped their chamomile tea. Grandma's hair, mostly gray with streaks of pure white, was very long and luxuriant and held together by a band of indigo-colored fabric. She was in her nightclothes. Claude noticed that her feet were bare and leathery and bore several scratches. He was never told her name. She had been introduced as Grandma and that seemed to be enough. Grandma inspected Claude in a manner that she probably thought was discreet but was blatant and direct. Claude felt uncomfortable at first, but he was drawn into her broad and deep smile, and he was fascinated by the nests of wrinkles about her eyes. He thought she looked like a stuffed doll, a harmless stuffed doll. They talked for a long time, Claude and Grandma, Aurora doing the listening or adding emphasis here and there. Grandma was curious about this young man that her kitten had brought home. Claude was amused by the nickname; Aurora didn't look like a kitten to him. He laughed whenever the woman used the name. Claude said he was staying at Tropical Gardens with a friend. They were both between jobs and had come to Florida to see what they could find. His friend was a retired school principal from New Hampshire. In Connecticut, where Claude was from, he worked at a hardware store.

Grandma jumped on the word "Connecticut" and grabbed Aurora's wrist, nearly forcing her to spill her cup of tea. "That's where your mother vanished: Connecticut." The granddaughter showed little interest. Grandma went on, "She went to find your father. She tracked him down at a submarine base someplace in Connecticut."

"That would be New London, I bet," Claude volunteered.

"Young man, you're one hundred percent correct. I remember it now, from the postcard she sent me. That was in 1979, fall of 1979. That's right. New London, Connecticut." Grandma nearly jumped out of her chair. "Where did I put that postcard? Let me show you."

"Grandma, you don't have to. Just sit down. I'm sure Claude doesn't want to see the postcard."

"But I know it's got to be here. I had it out just a few days ago."

Aurora gave Claude a concerned look and shook her head. "Grandma, sit down. Relax. Just finish your tea while it's still warm."

Claude chimed in. "You can show me the postcard some other time." He leaned towards the old woman and covered her hand with his. The hand was cold, so cold that Claude wanted to pull back.

Grandma was sobbing and, through gasps and whistles, she recited the tale of her poor daughter who got knocked up when she was only 17 by a Navy boy off a boat in Miami who left her high and dry. "Her name was Constance. How ironic," she declared. The old woman pulled her scarf off, and her hair cascaded over her face and covered her shoulders like a shroud. She took a deep breath punctuated by several gaps and went on with the story, adding that her kitten, little Aurora, the dawn, was the only good thing to come out of it all, that Constance left town as soon as the baby was born and she never came back. The postcard was the last sign of life.

Aurora's face took on the appearance of total boredom. Claude looked at Grandma as she sniveled. He watched as his hand reached to her hair-covered shoulder in a gesture filled with sympathy. Pulling back suddenly, he announced, "I have to go home."

"Well, young man, it was very nice having you visit," Grandma said. No more sobs. It was like nothing had happened. She stood, brushed her hair back, and started clearing the kitchen table. Aurora gave Claude an intense look and forced a smile.

Claude opened the door and the two cats strolled in. Aurora followed Claude outside and assured him her grandmother would be fine, that she could turn off the spells and be perfectly normal. "I'm sorry you caught her in such a mood. This was stronger than most and it lasted longer. But she's Ok."

Claude told her not to worry and that he found her grandmother charming.

"Will you be all right?

"Me? Why do you ask?"

"I mean, walking home. You know the way?"

"I think so. I have a good sense of direction."

Aurora thanked him for participating in her musical soiree at the beach and said she hoped to see him again.

Suddenly, they heard Grandma's voice. "Aurora, Aurora, ask the nice gentleman from Connecticut if he knows your mama, will you?"

"Oh, oh. Gotta go." Aurora rushed inside.

Claude started walking and, a few yards into the emptiness, he turned and was surprised to see the old woman on her deck looking at him. He waved to her and was disappointed when she didn't wave back. He found a pair of discarded tires and sat down and he and Grandma stared at each other, or at least in each other's direction. She was far from him, and he couldn't tell exactly what she was looking at.

The old woman raised her arms to the sky and started swaying and her voice carried some kind of wailings that reached Claude. He saw her weave her hands together then release them quickly. She repeated the movement again as part of a little dance. She bowed in all directions as if accepting the adulations of an invisible audience. Finally, she stepped inside.

Claude laughed the laugh of a free man. He allowed himself to be absorbed by the tranquility of the empty trailer park. It was unlike all else in South Florida where the drone of traffic never ceased, even in those middle-of-the-night hours when he would search in vain for stillness. Unlike his Tropical Gardens, the abandoned trailer park whispered in natural ripples. Claude recognized the sound as one related to the bubbling of his river and the crooning of his swallows, and he felt a longing for the shelter of the old textile mill in Williams.

He kept his eye on Aurora's trailer and he saw the door open again and he heard clearly the voice of an old woman talking gently to her cats. "Now, ladies, you know that your bedroom is outside, under the stars. I will see you in the morning for breakfast. Shoo, shoo, ladies."

Claude watched as the lights went out, first in the kitchen and then in another room and he assumed grandma had gone to bed. He wondered what her nights were like, what kind of crazy dreams she might have, whether she had any dreams at all. He thought of Aurora and he tried to imagine her lying in bed. Did she sing? Did she hear the beat of African drums? Did she still yearn for whatever drugs had possessed her? Did she ever wonder what happened to her mother?

Claude was pleased with himself. He felt peaceful. He felt young again, as young as the school boy who spent his time watching and wondering outside people's houses and imagining what these strangers' lives were like. He thought of his summers with his pal Tony. He thought of his Sundays serving Mass and coming home to the smell of old-fashioned and simple early dinners. He remembered the excitement of the World Series each fall and he remembered the Christmases with his great-aunt who sang the old French carols.

He finally decided to go home, and for the entire walk back to Tropical Gardens, Claude talked to himself, feeding the remembrances.

"What should I do about Dushayne?"

"You're asking *me*?" Octavious gave his wife a charged look. He wasn't used to being consulted. Roberta always knew what she wanted and how to get it.

"Yes, I'm asking you. I really don't know how to handle him."

"What's to handle? He lost his job. His friend got killed. So, he mopes around. What you expect the boy to do, Roberta? Join the choir at church and sing Halleluiah?"

"There's more to it than just being melancholy. There's something else. There's some bad stuff brewing there. I can see it, I can *feel* it. I tell you, Octavious. I don't like it."

The Wellingtons were installed in their plastic chairs between the Laundromat and the liquor store, a strategically-chosen perch from where Roberta could keep an eye on the evening's activity in her plaza. She had learned that if there was going to be trouble it would come from either place – or both. The Laundromat had the potential for catfights while the liquor store attracted cockfights, she liked to say. Things were quiet on this Thursday evening late in January. The breeze carried with it a gentle reminder of the traffic from the interstate to the west and from downtown Fort Lauderdale to the east. Closer to home were the sounds of children protesting their bedtime rules, the hum of washing machines and dryers, the coughing of older cars dropping off customers at the pawn shop and the liquor store. Usually, it was Roberta's best time of day. Her mind, however, was wrapped around her problem tenant. "You know, Octavious, I've always had a soft spot for that boy. He calls to my mother's instinct."

"Yes, I know," replied her husband.

"It really hurts me, this turn he's taken."

"I know."

Roberta unwrapped her theory about Dushayne. She'd seen it coming; it was all that friend's fault. That's when something very sinister had been released. Now, his room was untidy and he didn't take care of himself and he was late with the rent. His sulking and foul language were bad enough, but things had escalated in the past week. "It's that outlandish makeup," she said to her silent husband. "And he walks around in that gaudy bathrobe. And, did you see that bandage on his arm?"

Octavious said he hadn't noticed.

"Well, I've noticed. And, it's the bandage that worries me. The rest, I think most of it is just to irritate me, but that bandage, it scares me, I tell you, Octavious. Really, it does."

"So, he hurt himself. And he's got a bandage. I don't see the problem."

Roberta paid no attention. "What if he's violent? What if he inflicted some violence on himself? It looks to me very much like he tried to cut his wrist...or something like that. I tell you the devil's at work there. I'm afraid he could turn against someone." Octavious cleared his throat and was about to say something when he decided it would make no difference. His good wife was on the warpath. "And, when you think that poor little Ezekiel has to live with him!"

Octavious waved at two of his buddies as they drove into the plaza. He asked the driver how his car was holding up, offering to fix it anytime. He watched as the passenger went into the liquor store.

Two women, both regulars, stumbled out of the Laundromat and approached Roberta. They said they needed to lodge a complaint. They spoke of thievery. They said they weren't the only victims, that for the past few weeks, lots of customers had been losing clothes. Someone was stealing from the dryers when they went to look after the children or to the variety store across the street. The two customers added in a whisper that the missing items were always underwear – women's delicates.

At first Roberta wasn't concerned. Clothing was always going missing. But, the last bit of information penetrated her indifference and rang an alarm. She knew instantly that Dushayne was the culprit. She became furious. "Thank you, ladies," she said. "I am very sorry this had to happen. I will see to it that it stops. Immediately." The Laundromat ladies seemed satisfied. One of them thanked Miss Roberta for listening. They returned to their folding.

"Did you hear that, Octavious?"

"Hear what?"

"Dushayne's been stealing clothing from the Laundromat. Women's clothes. Undergarments." She punctuated each phrase with a nod of self-assurance.

"Roberta," Octavious stood up. "That's stupid. Doesn't make sense."

"Makes sense to me."

"Well, sweetheart, don't you go make a spectacle of yourself," he said to Roberta. Calling her *sweetheart* was his way of being sarcastic, a tactic he used so rarely that Roberta didn't notice.

Dushayne quickly became impatient with having to care for his tattoo. He followed the written instructions the old hippie had given him but it seemed that the tattoo wasn't healing. His skin became dry and blotched and reddish; the tattoo itself was hard to read. He wanted the world to see how he had branded himself, how he carried Derrick's words on his skin. An entire week after being tattooed, Dushayne still had to keep his arm bandaged. Frustration sent him into a new area of his depression, a dark place screaming for recognition. The eye makeup became dramatic, the rouge darker. He swished even more. He rarely got dressed, strutting around in an open bathrobe over his dirty boxer shorts. The days and the nights blended, barely distinguishable, repeated landmarks on the landscape of his grief, one after the other, one just like the other.

Roberta stomped up the stairs with the certainty of a missionary and confronted Dushayne as he sat half asleep on his balcony. "Time for an inspection," she announced as she walked past him. "And, for God's sake, get dressed."

Dushayne followed her into his room. "What's this all about? You've never done this before, Auntie."

"Is Ezekiel here?"

"No."

"Good. I don't want him to see this." Roberta stopped in the center of the room. Her eyes swept the space, squinting. "It smells terrible in here." She took several resolute steps toward the closet, opened the door and with a wide arm, swept everything from the top shelf. She used her foot to search through the items that had fallen to the floor.

Paul Paré

Dushayne thought she was desperate. "Auntie, are you all right? What *are* you looking for?" She ignored him, walking past him to his bureau, pulling out the drawers one by one, dumping their contents onto the floor. Dushayne yelled at her to stop. Roberta hadn't found what she was looking for and it was making her angry. She was sweating heavily, her eyes darting here and there, searching out a prey.

Pointing suddenly to the bandaged arm, she said, "And, what's that for? What did you do to yourself?"

Dushayne stood erect, extending his thin body, towering over the invader. "Got nothing to hide. But, Auntie, some things are private." His voice was strong. "When I'm ready, I'll tell you." He pulled his bandaged arm away, hiding it behind his back.

Roberta had already focused on her next maneuver. She knelt next to his bed and, panting and wiping her brow, she thrust a fleshy arm into the darkness under it. A brightness lit her face, and the woman pulled out a plastic grocery store bag. "Ah! What's this?" She spilled the contents onto the floor. "So, Dushayne, how do you explain this?"

The lad looked down at the pile of panties and bras and shook his head. "I don't know. Never seen any of it. Please, Auntie, you gotta believe me."

Roberta Wellington approached her tenant, her chest pushed forward, her head high and with a voice reserved for Sunday services, announced that she was hereby evicting Dushayne and that she was affording him no more than 15 minutes to gather his belongings and vacate the premises. "May the good Lord forgive you, Dushayne Elwin Brown," she proclaimed. "And, for God's sake, put some clothes on."

For several minutes, Dushayne was motionless. Then, his body started to twitch and his legs weakened. He dropped to his knees and cried until anger took over. Within the prescribed 15 minutes, he got dressed and stuffed his belongings in two oversized gym bags. Roberta was at the foot of the stairs waiting for him. Outside, Dushayne stopped on his balcony and cast one last look at Wellington Plaza. After a few steps down the stairs, his body changed, and he became Miss Sashay, swinging his hips provocatively, holding his head high, and, through pursed lips whispered *C'est si bon* just as he passed inches in front of Roberta.

The idea of returning to the exit and actually talking to the lad came out of the blue. Ray, however, recognized it immediately as a good one. He was seated at a desk daydreaming, in a corner of the Broward Library that he had made his, slightly out of the way in the reference section. He had convinced himself that it was his office, his work station, even if there was no real work. Ray's routine consisted of going online to follow the primary campaigns, catching up on the latest movies and Broadway shows, scanning the Boston and New Hampshire papers. He made a list of magazines he never had time for back home and he scoured them methodically.

While reading the latest issue of *The Atlantic Monthly*, he spotted an article on homelessness in America. His mind snapped and he saw the scribbled cardboardy words *homeless & hungry* and the tall svelte Black boy as he scuttled from car to car. The kid had been absent for some time and Ray wondered if the boy had found another spot, a more lucrative one. That morning, however, the boy was back at his usual place.

Ray pushed himself away from the library desk. He took a moment to assimilate the idea. Go ahead, get to know the kid. Better than sitting here day after day acting like a retiree. Go ahead. That's what you really want to do, isn't it?

Heading to his car in the county parking garage, Ray noticed storm clouds in the west and feared that the homeless lad might have left his spot. He knew that to connect with the kid he'd have to drive to the exit north of the Broward exit and retrace his steps. Ray had climbed up that exit ramp enough times to absorb the timing of the place. He knew how long the light would be in his favor and he knew which lane to take. Like the script for a familiar play, his approach was flawless.

He saw the boy and was relieved. There were plenty of cars ahead of him, and Ray had time to observe and to think. He smiled the smile of the huntsman. Ray guessed the lad was in his

241

early twenties. He watched him walk to a couple of vehicles, collecting an offering at each one. Ray noticed he had a pronounced limp to his gait. It surprised him how sad that made him feel. A wounded gazelle was the picture that came to mind. He wanted to reach out and sooth it and heal it.

"Hey, young man. Over here." Ray was extending his arm. Dushayne wasted no time and headed for the Subaru. Ray held out a five dollar bill, waving it at the boy.

Dushayne thought of the older guys at the bar and how they'd egg on the young dancers by waving money at them. "Morning, sir," he said, accompanying his greeting with the sweetest smile he could conjure up.

"Here you go. Spend it well."

"Will do, sir. That's very generous. God bless."

The boy stood near the open car window and Ray smiled up to him. Neither spoke. The boy placed his hand on the door. Ray looked down and held his gaze on the thin elongated hands, ignoring the overlong and dirty fingernails. "Thanks again, have a nice day, sir," the lad said as he pulled away and shuffled to the next vehicle.

The traffic light changed, and Ray was forced to move on. Driving away, he stole a glance in his rear view mirror and saw that the panhandler was watching him. One of Sister Rose's demons, he thought. Probably not even homeless or hungry or destitute. Might be an act. A devilish trick. He had to find out. Ray repeated his circle, heading north and coming back to the exit. The sky was darkening quickly and it occurred to him that the brewing thunderstorm could become his accomplice.

"Oh! You again," the lad said.

"Yes. It's going to rain, so I thought you might need some shelter." As if on cue, the downpour reached the exit ramp. "Get in." The panhandler folded his sign and headed for the passenger door. He hesitated. "Get in, you can't stay here," Ray said, just as a sheet of wind-driven rain bleached the roadway. The boy jumped into the car, and Ray was overwhelmed by the strong odor of perspiration. He found it intoxicating.

The heavy rain slowed the traffic to a crawl, yet an impatient motorist started pumping his horn. "Fuck off, asshole," said the boy. He brushed the water off his face and hair and looked back at the motorist, and then peeked at Ray. "Sorry about that. I just

242

don't have no patience with people with no patience."

Ray was amused. He thought the comment was witty and right on target. "Listen, this rain's here to stay. You can't go back out there, so let me buy you lunch. Ok?" Ray was as surprised by the invitation as was his passenger.

"Oh," the lad said.

"Look. You don't have to accept." Ray felt embarrassed.

"You're not some pervert, are you?"

"Of course I am," Ray replied with a nervous laugh.

"Well, Ok then."

A bit later, halfway between the interstate and downtown, at a Miami Sub Shop, the two sat across from each other and observed an awkward silence.

"Haven't seen you at the highway for the last few days." Ray said.

"Couldn't make it until today."

Ray picked up the menu, and the banter at the interstate exit came back like a thunderclap and all he saw was the word *pervert* in various scripts and sizes all over the glossy menu. Pervert – pervert – pervert – you're a pervert. The menu selections were all the same, and Ray felt nauseous. What are you doing, you old fool? You *are* a pervert. This is a mistake. An awful mistake. He decided to abort the undertaking, to confess.

"Listen, I just want to say that…"

"You have no idea how much I appreciate this, sir," the lad interrupted him. "I really need a good meal. Thank you so much, sir."

"Don't call me sir. Please…"

"What should I call you?"

"Pervert."

They both laughed, and Ray recognized the absurdity of the moment.

"Seriously, name's Dushayne."

"Call me Ray."

"Well, thanks, Ray. For the food – and for your generosity. Not many people drop money like that in my cap."

Ray felt relieved and ashamed. He gazed at the menu. What exactly are you doing with this kid? You should come clean. Tell him you think he's the most beautiful person you've ever seen. You want to take him in, take care of him. You *are* a pervert. He's young enough to be your grandson. What are you thinking, Raymond Champagne?

Dushayne knew exactly what was going on. He had never been picked up before, but he knew the game. And, he wasn't opposed to the idea. He could use a kind old friend. He certainly could use a good meal. The two ordered their lunch and while waiting they waded cautiously into conversation.

"How do you spell it? Your name. Dooosh something is it?"

Dushayne laughed, repeated his name and spelled it out. "Douche or douche bag is what the other kids used to tease me with."

Ray had no reply. He took a sip of water and looked around for their server whose eye he caught and to whom he gestured, pointing to his glass. In silence, the two watched him replenish the drinks. Ray leaned back and rested his head against the coolness of the booth. He thought his young companion looked majestic. Despite his unwashed and unruly hair – or perhaps because of it, – the lad's face was radiant. Ray saw no flaws on the skin, and he found its dark coffee color inviting. A few days' worth of sparse young beard formed a perfect frame. The lips were generous and seemed to be always on the verge of a pout. Charmingly teasing, Ray thought. He resisted the urge to touch them, dropping his gaze and attention, instead, to Dushayne's neck and shoulders. "That tee-shirt. That's very poetic and appropriate."

Dushayne looked down at his shirt. "Grateful dead?"

"Yes. The folktale. It's perfect," stated Ray.

"All I know is a lot of older guys comment on the shirt. More likely to throw in an extra dollar or two. Guess they like the music."

Ray didn't hear. He was caught in the poetry of a panhandler wearing a shirt that referenced the old story. "It's about a traveler who encounters a ghost who wanders about because he had an outstanding debt and never received a proper burial. The traveler agrees to pay the debt. You see, both you and your generous donors are the grateful dead. You give each other the chance to right the wrong, and the poor ghost can finally find rest." Ray finished his tale and was pleased. He smiled at the young man, seeking some form of acknowledgment.

Dushayne smiled back.

Without thinking, Ray placed his hand on the lad's left arm

and realized he hadn't noticed the worn bandage. Dushayne pulled away. "What happened to your arm?" Ray thought it perfectly natural that he should inquire. "Let me see," he said, pointing to the arm and waving his hand in a *let me see, bring it here* sort of gesture. "We should change that bandage, son." Ray sensed no problem with his insistence. He thought it appropriate that he should care, that he should touch the arm, and that he should call Dushayne *son*.

Dushayne extended the arm. "It's a tattoo," he murmured. "Not healing well."

"You have another bandage? You really need to change it."

"No. This is the last one."

"Well, we can get you some new ones. And, some antiseptic lotion or something. I've never cared for a tattoo before, but I imagine you have to keep it clean. What does it represent? The tattoo, I mean." Ray was talking in a rush.

Dushayne gave him a probing look. His eyes, like a frantic moth, went from his arm to Ray's face and back again. He brought both hands up and covered his eyes. He was silent for several minutes.

Ray waited, distracted by the dirty finger nails, yet sensing that the young man was searching for something. He started to regret his curiosity about the tattoo.

"So. You want a blow job? That what you're after?" Dushayne saw the man's face drop, his mouth turning into a void of surprise, his eyes filling with confusion. "Sorry, sir. I mean, I don't know what you want from me."

"Ah. That's not..." Ray searched for an answer. The words were absent. He looked down at his food. "That's...completely inappropriate," he said slowly in a voice he hardly recognized.

Dushayne wished he could melt into his vinyl-covered seat. He realized he had never been so wrong. "Can we forget I said that?"

Ray remained quiet. He played with his food. He looked at the empty tables around him. He searched for the waiter. His brain processed his loneliness. In a burst of remembrance, he saw himself fighting arrest at the picnic area in New Hampshire, speeding in his Subaru over state line after state line, sitting on a bench in Savannah talking to a young stranger late at night. He examined his hands and he saw the early signs of age spots. Ray closed his eyes. He knew they sagged into fleshy pouches. He tried to imagine what he looked like to this lad facing him. He was sure he embodied exactly what a lecherous old coot looks like. He felt repulsion at the thought. He blamed his disorientation since darting off in the middle of the night and leaving everything behind, everything… his pride and respectability and security and the love of the few who loved him.

"I've given you the wrong impression. Listen, young man, I'm not interested in…I really don't know what I'm doing. This is so humiliating." Ray spoke in broken gasps. "I'm sorry. Sorry. Really."

"Look, eh, Ray. I'm the one who's sorry." Dushayne felt dirty. "Got to use the bathroom." He stood and darted away.

Restroom number 148 had been inspected last by Miami Subs employee number D-11 at 12:15 that afternoon. Dushayne absorbed the information as he closed the door behind him and he took comfort in knowing that someone was doing what he was supposed to and doing it well. There were still places where things were working right. "What the fuck *you* doing, Douche?" Twice he asked himself, using the name his tormentors had used. He waited for an answer and when none came he cleaned himself up as best he could. Gone were all traces of makeup. They had been replaced, he thought, by the signs of grime and fatigue and fear. He remembered to remove the piece of crumbled cardboard from his sneaker and place it in his pocket for later use. As he was walking out of the restroom, he wondered if Ray was still there. He approached his table from an angle, stealthily. He was surprised – and not unpleasantly – to find Ray at his seat. He walked slowly and studied him, deciding that his host was no more than an old guy, a kind and lonely old guy. Harmless.

"What the hell?" he mumbled.

"What was that?" Ray asked.

"Ah…Deserts look good in that case over there. Mind if I order one?"

"Not at all. Whatever you want."

Moments later, with brownie crumbs on two plates and coffee cups waiting for refills, the two Miami Sub patrons plunged into a flurry of give and take. Without divulging what had precipitated his trip to Florida, Ray narrated the details of the drive, listing each state he had driven through, describing the towns he had stopped in. Dushayne said he had never been outside Fort

Lauderdale, his two square miles of city around Sistrunk and Broward being the only place he ever knew. "Not even The Everglades," he added. "Was going to in the seventh grade, on a field trip, but this bunch of guys beat me up just before I got on the bus and I spent the afternoon in the nurse's office."

Ray was taken aback. "Amazing! That would never happen in my school," he blurted out. He felt obliged to explain his life's work, reciting a brief chronicle of his teaching career. "I've been lucky, all the schools have been rather easy, the kids mostly well off and well behaved."

"Some schools like that here, but I never went to 'em."

"That's too bad. Every child deserves the best possible education. I bet you were a bright kid."

"Not sure, wasn't in school long enough. Dropped out after the seventh grade."

"Oh! What a shame. And you seem so confident and...articulate."

"Don't know what that means, but if it's a compliment, I'll take it."

"It is."

Dushayne felt a chill through his body. It was brief – quickly replaced by an airiness he found soothing. He felt like a feather falling before a gentle breeze until it landed softly on fresh grass. He remembered the image from a television commercial for some soap and he giggled as he thanked Ray. "Don't get too many compliments." He sighed the breath of a person who locates his comfort zone. "What's it mean?"

"Articulate?"

"Yeah."

"It means you have a good command of the language, you can express yourself well." Ray enjoyed the teachable moment.

"Ok. Well, thanks again." Dushayne beamed. He felt emboldened, enough to share with the old guy the rough side of his childhood. Ray listened to the story of abuse and abandonment and grew solemn. He searched through all his years as an educator, but couldn't find any parallels.

Dushayne read his mind. "You musta had some kids who were fucked up like that, didn't you?"

For a spark of a moment, Ray thought of his wife and daughter and granddaughters and wondered if they viewed his disappearance as an act of abandonment. "You mean, in school. Of course, I'm sure there were."

"How they turn out? As adults, I mean."

"I don't know," Ray blurted. "I should, I suppose. But, I truly don't." The teacher took over suddenly and he said to the young man, "How are *you* turning out?"

"Thought I was doin' good. Had it under control... that is, until a few weeks ago."

"What happened?"

Dushayne hesitated, grabbed a paper napkin and blew his nose. He stared at the vacant space behind his tablemate.

"You don't have to tell me. Sorry, I don't mean to pry."

"No problem. No one else to tell it to."

Ray wondered suddenly if the kid was being honest, if this wasn't an act, part of his panhandling shtick, a ploy, a tactic for sympathy.

Dushayne listed the recent events: how he met Derrick and how he was killed, how he was thrown out of his room. He left very little out. As the events unfolded, his voice grew louder, his hands started flying all over the place. He paused only to swallow deep gulps of water. Finally, he removed the bandage from his arm and proudly displayed his tattoo. How's that for a final act? he seemed to be saying.

Ray looked at the script etched into the flesh of his companion and he read the words out loud. "*C'est si bon.*"

"It's in French."

"I know," said Ray.

"It's a song by Eartha Kitt."

"It is? Oh yes, you're right."

"I know I'm right," Dushayne said, a touch of impatience in his voice. He then explained how he learned the words and how special their meaning had become and how the tattoo was a tribute to his dear friend and how it's all he could do to show his love for Derrick and he wished he could do so much more.

At that point, the story crashed through the wall of naiveté and delusion in Ray's brain. He cried out, "That means you're gay." It wasn't a question; Ray's voice was triumphant.

"Thought you already figured that out." Dushayne was confused. "Haven't you been listenin', man?"

"Yes, yes. But, sometimes things don't sink in."

"Of course, I'm gay. Always been gay, that's why I couldn't fit in as a kid. Real swishy, always loved girly things. It took me forever to understand, to accept it. Derrick's the one who made it easy for me."

"Well, I'm gay too." Ray said the words with more aplomb, enthusiasm even, than he would have ever expected.

"No kidding. Surprise, surprise."

"You knew?" Ray asked. Once again, he wondered if Dushayne was leading him on. Playing him. "Seriously, you could tell." He spoke slowly and soothingly, as much to himself as to his companion. The wall he had carefully and steadfastly built over so many years crumbled at that moment. Through the dust, Ray saw himself, his true self. He didn't take time to evaluate the new person. He stumbled forward into the acknowledgment, into the acceptance, and started discharging the story of his life. The bulk of his confession focused on his more recent fascination with the rest area atmosphere and the potential for mischief and adventure, contrasting that with the boredom of family and job. He placed the incident with the state trooper where it belonged in the narrative, and gave context to his road trip.

"Caught by an undercover cop in a park…hey, happens all the time down here," Dushayne said.

"Well, not where I come from, and certainly not to me."

Dushayne didn't hear. He went on, his voice high with drama, "Wow, and you just ran away. Rolled over and played dead. Can't believe it. Those fucking cops. We shouldn't let them get away with it."

Ray stopped him, placed his hand on Dushayne's forearm. "Listen, there's no *we* here. I'm the one who got caught; it's *my* life that was shattered."

"Sorry. I know. It sucks. But down here some guys are fighting. Going to court, suing the cops for harassment, making a big stink…"

Ray had stopped listening. He swirled his near-empty cup, gently mixing the beige cream back into the cold coffee. With his spoon, he pushed the brownie crumbs into a neat line on the edge of his plate. In his head, it was after the booking and he was riding back to the rest area with his friend the lawyer. That's the voice he heard: "You can't roll over and play dead…You can't roll over and play dead." Ray pushed the plate away and it sailed off the table, landing on the floor with enough clatter to rouse everyone's attention. Dushayne leaned over to pick it up and their server rushed over to rescue it. Ray took no notice of the accident. *You can fight this you know… You can fight this you know…* The voice was Jimmy's, the Lone Ranger turned lawyer.

"I don't know how," Ray heard himself reply. His eyes hidden behind his hands, he felt the sun setting over the mountains and on his life as he knew it. The Lone Ranger wants me to fight. Well, this isn't Halloween. I'm not the Crusader King. What am I supposed to do? I'm not in the sixth grade making believe I'm somebody else. My dad isn't around the corner waiting to take me home. There's only me. The real me.

Dushayne could see him struggling. He didn't know what to do or what to say. He rested his hand on Ray's elbow. Dushayne still wrestled with the narrative. For so many years, you have a life, then all of a sudden everything changes? This man just walked away…from his wife and daughter, from his job, from his town. "So you left everything…just like that. Wow. That takes something…courage, I guess."

"I'm not sure what it takes. Courage or lunacy." Ray stopped for a moment and thought that his demon's name was really lunacy. "I'm still processing it. It just happened, you know. Time will tell, but right now, I feel like I've closed a chapter and started a new one. It's all new, all fresh…There are times I feel brave, adventurous."

"Nothing pulling you back? You must have terrible nightmares."

Ray reflected for a moment. "Not yet."

"Wow! What a trip," Dushayne said.

"Exactly," Ray replied. He smiled warmly at his new friend, this youngster, this Black kid he hardly knew, this person who now knew him better than anyone else.

"A new chapter, huh? Maybe that's what *I* should do. I mean, being homeless now, for real."

"I'm not sure I understand." Ray said.

"You know, having no place to live."

Ray refreshed the story in his mind. "Oh, that's right. You did say something about being thrown out of where you lived. I'm sorry, I forgot." He realized he had been focused on himself.

"So what's on your cardboard sign about being homeless is

250

true."

"Now, it is."

"But, what do you mean, a new chapter?"

Dushayne gave him a wink. "Guess I'm not that, eh...articulate."

"Just be patient with this old fart."

"What I mean is I should do like you did. You left it all and that's a new chapter. I should see my situation like a new chapter too. A fresh life."

"I see." Ray felt a prick of guilt. "So, you are really homeless," he said meditatively. "Tell me about it."

Dushayne repeated how he was behind on his rent and how his roommate framed him with the stolen ladies' underwear. He explained that for the past three nights he had been sleeping on the banks of the river, that he stashed his few belongings under a bridge, hoping each day that they hadn't been stolen, that he washed in the restrooms at the mall and in parks. Ray was astounded. He kept interrupting Dushayne, asking for details, clarification, his curiosity tinged with large doses of empathy. He felt he should do something to help. Give him money, take him in. He wondered if there had been any homeless people in Packers Falls. There were poor people, especially on the outskirts of town; large families, no education, low expectations. Junk collectors, woodsmen, trappers. Unemployed and in poor health. He never helped any of them. Homeless folks, if there were any, were invisible.

Again, Ray examined his new friend, and he wondered. A nagging thought: this kid's just too smart to be homeless.

The two men observed a long silence. There seemed nothing else to be said. Ray had paid the check a long time before and the dirty plates had been cleared. Ray looked out the window and wondered how long the sun had been out.

"Storm's over," Dushayne said. "Should get back to the highway. Afternoon rush, you know."

"Certainly."

The two filed out of the sub shop and crossed the parking lot towards the Subaru. Ray observed his young friend from behind. He figured he was close to a foot taller than him. He saw how lean and athletic he was and how gracefully he carried himself. Again, he thought of the gazelle, this time rested and well-fed.

"Hey, what happened to your foot? You're not limping."

"Oh. That's not real. An old trick I learned. People are more generous that way."

"I see. So what else is fake?" Ray was visibly irritated. He wondered again if this kid was posing all this time, if he was a con artist.

"Believe me, Ray. The bad leg's all that's phony."

"You sure?"

"Yes, sir. Eh, except the part of my sign that says I'm hungry. Not anymore."

Ray caught the reference. Articulate and witty. Smart.

"And thanks again," Dushayne said.

Fifteen minutes later, Ray dropped his friend off near his spot on the exit ramp. "Will you be here tomorrow?" he asked.

"Yup. Got nothin' else going on. You?"

"I'll see you then," Ray said. As he drove off, he caught the reflection of the panhandler in his rear view mirror. The lad was waving to him.

Claude had slept late and was taking longer than usual to assimilate his surroundings. Sitting on his bed, his head down, he examined the cracks in the linoleum, looking for a pattern, some definition. He dragged himself to the bathroom. Moments later, he sauntered out and plopped himself down on his patio chair. He shielded his eyes from the mid-morning sun.

"Good morning," Ray said.

Claude massaged his temples and avoided looking up. "Morning," he said in a voice still gummed up from his night. Claude passed his hands through the locks of his hair and thought he should get a haircut. He shuffled his bare feet against the rough surface of the patio stones in a vain attempt to relieve an itch. He stretched backwards and, with his hands clenched behind his neck, let out several low *aaahs*, allowing them to expand and grow louder, finally morphing into a yawn.

"Rough night?" Ray asked. He rose from his plastic chair. "I'm getting myself more coffee. Want some?"

"Yup. And, throw something in it – like Drano or bleach – to clear my head."

"Ok. I get it. You got drunk last night or did drugs with that new gang of yours and you're disoriented and your head feels groggy." Ray stood in the doorway to Room 6 and waited for a reply.

"Not true, Doctor Champagne." He hoped Ray caught the sarcasm in his tone. "A couple of beers, that's all. Aurora's grandmother's acid days are long gone." Claude thought it better not to mention Aurora's more recent drug problem. "My head feels so full, heavy, overloaded."

"Hold that thought, let me get the coffee," Ray said.

Claude tried to focus on the reds and pinks of the hibiscus bushes planted by Esther and Chester in an obvious effort to make Tropical Gardens worthy of the name. The colors clashed with the somber images that crammed his brain. Claude looked away and stared at the dwarf pines. They reminded him of porcupines back home.

"So your head feels full...full of what? Ray said as he returned with two mugs.

"I don't know...it's just that I spend my nights with all kinds of dreams, very intense and visual stuff, scary shit."

"Like what?"

"You really want to know?" Claude asked.

"Yes. Of course."

Claude took a gulp of coffee and started cautiously.

"I'm always walking somewhere – looking for something or trying to get away from something. The last couple nights, there are skeletons following me. Not gaining on me, just always there. But last night, all of a sudden one of them turns out to be Jules, the guy from Savannah who beat me up. He was the tallest and had a loud voice, one I recognized immediately. He was telling the others to speed it up, to catch me and to bring me down and piss on me." Claude shrugged. "Scared the shit out of me. Couldn't shake it."

Ray had nothing to say.

"What, no diagnosis?"

"No. The doctor isn't in."

Claude smiled and added that just as daylight was breaking, he fell back to sleep and had another dream. "This one was easier, it was about my father."

Ray thought about his own father, and a scene at a barbecue in his parents' backyard a long time ago floated before him. He shook his head and dismissed the episode; he felt he owed this moment to Claude's nightmares, not his. "So when you dream about your dad, what comes to mind?"

"Most of the time, I see him when I was a kid. In my dreams, I worship him. Really, I kneel before him and I pray to him like a statue of Saint Joseph. A few nights ago, the statue actually cried. But, it didn't say anything; it simply cried. In one dream last week, my dad found me on the side of the road. I had been hit by a car and he picked me up in his arms and carried me to the cemetery and threw me in an open grave."

"Wow. Did that really happen? I mean, in real life?"

"Of course not. But he found me once in a car crash, the night of the prom."

"You survived that crash. Obviously. You're here to talk about it."

"Survived it physically. But that night still haunts me."

"In what way?"

"That's another story." Claude wasn't about to rehash the night when Kevin Rideout tried to kill him. He moved on to a more gentle vision. "Many times, I dream of my dad when I was real young and he worked in the mills. He was a loom fixer and very proud of it. I didn't know what that meant; I only understood much later what kind of work he actually did. Strange how that part of his life keeps coming back to me since we're here."

"It must be important to you."

"Maybe. I don't know. But, those are the easy dreams," Claude said in a wistful voice. A circle of blackbirds funneled its way over the motel, heading east towards the ocean. The two men raised their heads to watch. Claude wondered if the birds had been listening to their conversation.

"I might write a poem about my father. Maybe, I'll read it tomorrow night at the Pompano Pier." Claude had already briefed Ray on his latest exploits: joining up with Aurora and her musician friends and going around performing for the crowds. He was making a bit of money and had started paying for the groceries. Ray welcomed the change, recognizing the two men needed their own space.

"Had lunch with that kid, the one you called a beggar," Ray said out of the blue.

"What kid?"

"We saw him at the exit on Broward Boulevard. He had a sign that said he was homeless."

"Oh. That kid."

"Yes, took him to lunch yesterday," Ray confessed. "He's a good kid, very smart. Name's Dushayne."

"Say that again…"

"Dushayne." Ray repeated the name slowly.

"I don't mean his name, I mean…you *took* him to lunch, you bought him lunch?" Claude sported a knowing smile.

"Yes, I did. He looked hungry and, you know, he is truly homeless."

"That's what the sign says."

Ray fidgeted. He was becoming irritated by the inquiry. "Yes

255

that's what the sign says," he said drily. "And the sign is accurate. Dushayne is an honest young man who's had a very difficult life. I enjoy his company."

"Well, I think you'd prefer someone your own age. Some retired person, a teacher or something like that. I'm sure Mrs. Blake could introduce you to someone."

"I am not retired. Just taking some time off, that's all."

"Just be careful. Sometimes you can be too trusting, you know."

"Don't worry. I am a very good judge of character. I picked you up off the streets didn't I? And, you haven't murdered me."

"Not yet." Claude left his chair and, halfway back into the room, said, "Not even in my dreams."

Ray chuckled. He checked his watch. "I have to shower and get ready for my trek to Fort Lauderdale."

"Another day at the library? Haven't you read everything yet," Claude asked.

Ray threw him a killer glance and went inside.

Claude was spending more and more time walking around Banyan Cove, developing familiarity with the space and the people. The clerk at the Circle K would display a flicker of recognition which Claude would acknowledge. A couple of old codgers occupied the same park bench, the bus always let out the same people at the corner.

During one outing Claude came upon a large pawn shop. There were no pawn shops in Williams, and he ventured into the establishment like an explorer in search of a long-lost kingdom and its hidden treasures. He walked up and down the aisles, he bent over the glass cases, he peered into the locked cabinets, his eyes scanning and recording. He wondered what story lived in each item, he speculated about the lives of their owners, about the circumstances that had forced them to abandon their possessions: jewelry, watches, gadgets, silver, all precious and meaningful to someone at some time. He entered a room at the back of the shop filled with knives and guns, weapons of all size and manufacture. Rusty ones and new shiny ones, for the hunters, the collectors, the paranoid. A large display of war implements labeled sloppily as German Nazi, Japanese, Korean. A wall decorated with taxidermy, from the smallest rodents to mountain cats and cougars, birds of various velvety plumages, dried lizards.

Turning around, he spotted a deer head above the door: a young buck, a beautiful animal with willowy muscles still intact beneath the dry skin of his neck. Graceful. Eyes sad and questioning. Antlers regal.

Claude remembered the doe he stumbled upon many years before on a quiet stretch of Rhode Island roadway. That animal, freshly killed, dwelled in a special place in his memory. He felt ashamed. He remembered how he reacted to the sight of the road kill: feeling sorry for himself, not the animal. His mind, still fragile from the Prom Night accident a few weeks before, had transferred his own limp body into that of the twisted and bloodied deer. For a few agonizing moments, Kevin Rideout had been successful in crushing him and his father's Buick. Then, reality won out, but he felt no sympathy for the dead animal, just relief that it wasn't him. Now in a creepy pawn shop in South Florida, Claude Simard found time to grieve for the doe. Did it have a soul? Did it cry in its last moments, struggling in the roadside dirt for its final breath? What would have been its prayer? Claude stood rigid in the center of the small room, surrounded by stuffed animals and weapons of war, his head aimed high at the taxidermied buck who, like a god, surveyed the domain.

He searched for a prayer, a set of words, or a song, that would tell that doe of long ago that he was sorry. Nothing came to him. His youth as an altar boy hadn't taught him a prayer for dead animals. He pushed harder into the memory of a boy who went to church every Sunday and suddenly the words appeared to him.

He stretched his hand upwards; he stroked the buck's strong neck, caressed its wispy whiskers. "Peace be with you," Claude whispered. He repeated the phrase and its response. "And with your spirit."

Claude felt that his words would probably be viewed as sacrilegious. They weren't meant for animal heads in pawn shops or, worse, roadkill. But, he felt a tremendous amount of satisfaction. Like the few times as a teenager he went to confession and dumped an especially bothersome sin on the priest. He repeated the words from the Mass and felt a weight lifted.

On the way out of the pawn shop, he toyed with the idea of asking the clerk what the price of the deer might be, just in case he

Paul Paré

came upon some winnings. He decided not to, and some of his
sadness returned.

There were mornings when the motorists seemed to have entered into an accord obliging them to ignore the panhandler. Many of these drivers used the Broward exit every day, nearly always at the same time, and on certain days they would roll down their windows and toss something in his cap, a dollar or two, some coins, or – more often than one might think – a piece of half-eaten donut. Yet, these same drivers on another day would be unanimous in their cold-hearted stinginess. Dushayne wished he could pinpoint exactly what made it go one way or the other.

Had he been able to predict the mood of his motorists, he would have stayed in bed on the bad days. Dushayne examined the line of cars, pulled his watch out, registered the time: 10:20. He glanced at his empty cap. Shoulda definitely stayed in bed. He knew that Ray would not have let him sleep in. He would have lectured him mildly, would have said that begging was an age-old profession, very common in many countries.

He had known Ray over a week and had yet to figure him out. It seemed that all Ray wanted was to have Dushayne around, and, in a way, take care of him. The lad had a hard time believing things could be that simple. Often, he'd catch Ray staring at him with a worried expression and he'd send him the widest smile he could muster and Ray's face would crackle.

Dushayne stood at the end of the exit ramp waiting for the traffic light to turn and release the dozen cars stacked behind it. He half-heartedly hobbled down the length of the traffic line, aiming his sign in the general direction of the motorists. He didn't feel like putting on his sad face, but he forced himself to act the role of the hapless young man, and he gave each driver his look of need and appreciation – to no avail.

A few traffic light changes later, he heard a car horn at the very bottom of the line and moved quickly, his hopes remotely in gear. He recognized Stevie Stevens, his former boss. Dushayne followed the man's instruction and got in the car. Stevie spoke rapidly. He told the kid he wanted him back at work the next week. Business always picked up in February with all the tourists and his bartenders were screaming for a bar back. No hesitation on Dushayne's part who yes-sirred him several times.

"And, don't forget: the first fifty's mine. You never paid me back."

"Yes, sir!"

The cars moved on. Dushayne checked his watch again and decided to quit his stint at the exit and walk to the Miami Subs Shop and wait there for Ray. He folded his cardboard sign and removed the paper from his sneaker. The sidewalk was dusty and the street smelled of fumes and teemed with the grunting of trucks and buses, but Dushayne failed to notice.

In his mind he was standing in the shadows listening to Miss Sashay belt out her signature song and he heard the crowd yell its approval and throw dollar bills at her. He remembered when he and Derrick had their first conversation in the dressing room and the times the two of them had watched the sun rise from his private spot on the river. He avoided thinking of the night his best friend was beaten to a pulp in the alley and shrank from the vision of Derrick in a coma at the hospital, but those pictures were engraved on his brain. There was no way to obscure them. Going back to work at the bar would have both good and bad points.

At the diner, he headed to his usual table and waited for Ray. He stuck his hand into his pocket and found it empty, and he accepted both the assurance that Ray would pick up the tab and the prospect of going back to work at Hips – at least for the money.

The restaurant got busy with the usual noontime crowd. Dushayne watched customers come and go and finally spotted Ray heading straight for their table. Dushayne gave him his warmest smile and noticed a layer of years melt from his friend's face.

The three of them wound up having a very civilized discussion. In the end they agreed that Claude would move out of the motel room and leave Ray and Dushayne to themselves. The decision was made over lunch at the Miami Sub Shop where Ray and Dushayne had become regulars. They even knew their waiter Felipe by name, and he knew theirs along with their drinks and their favorite deserts. Ray was extremely relieved and he said so, repeatedly. He thanked Claude for being so understanding. Dushayne felt guilty, as if he was breaking up something. He wasn't sure what, but the kid understood that he had intruded, that an arrangement had been upended.

Claude held no strong feelings about the three-way accommodations, except that the motel room was too small for three people, even if no one had much baggage and even if one of them slept on the floor. Finding other quarters was no big deal. He couldn't remember the last time he had grown attached to one given place. He had already concluded that it didn't matter where he slept – or tried to sleep. His nightmares and crazy visions would certainly follow him.

"You're the one who's paid all along; it should be your decision," Claude said matter-of-factly to Ray.

"That has nothing to do with it. This isn't about money."

"I know. I'm sorry," Claude added quickly.

At first, Claude resented Dushayne's presence. It was one of those nights when he had stayed at Aurora's very late, and, as he walked into the motel room, he stumbled over someone sleeping on the floor. His initial reaction was to utter an *excuse me* since he thought he might have entered the wrong room. He turned the light on to examine his room key and spotted a person wrapped in a sleeping bag. He wondered about Ray, unsure if he was safe.

Ray introduced Dushayne and explained that he needed a safe place to stay.

"You just don't take strangers in like that" Claude said.

Ray replied that he knew Dushayne and he trusted him. Dushayne kept quiet and listened to the two men. He got up and went into the bathroom only to emerge a couple of minutes later and announce that they needn't worry, he'd be gone in the morning.

Claude had the last word. "Don't have to. We'll manage," he said out of a combination of guilt and sudden kindness.

The trio did manage. They stayed out of each other's way, picked up after themselves, rotated the use of the bathroom, adopted a routine that attempted to respect each person's privacy. Claude kept stealing glances at the new roommate, trying to catch whatever evil might be lurking there waiting to pounce. It dawned on him that there might be something else between his two roommates. After a few days, Claude was quite sure that Dushayne was gay. He watched the two interact and wondered if Ray was also gay.

They often drove into Fort Lauderdale together. Once, the two older guys had a heated argument after Ray left Dushayne at his interstate exit. Claude saw the kid place a piece of cardboard in his sneaker before grabbing his homemade sign. He watched him wave to Ray and then limp up to the head of the ramp and turn to face the traffic. "I promised I'd keep my mouth shut. But, look Ray. You know what the kid's doing. He's faking it. The limp, the homeless thing...It's a rip-off."

"You promised to keep your mouth shut?"

"Well, to myself. But I can't sit still and let him take advantage of you. You don't know what you're getting into."

"And you know, and, of course, you're going to tell me." Ray was trying to find a tone of voice that wouldn't betray his irritation. Claude decided to shut up, and the two men made their way downtown in an awkward silence.

Walking out of the parking garage next to the library, Ray finally spoke. "You don't know what you're talking about. You just don't know." His words came out slowly, and Claude heard the suppressed anger. "At first, I had my doubts. But I believe him. He's a good person."

Claude wasn't convinced. "This kid's trouble. Just watch yourself, Ray. I mean it." The two men parted, one headed into the library and the other to the park.

Eventually, Esther Blake was the one who forced the issue.

One morning, the three occupants of Room Six opened their door on the way to the car, and there she was, arms folded, with a determined expression on her face not unlike the one she would have used with unruly children in her third grade class back in Akron. "Gentlemen, the room is for two people." She placed all the emphasis she could on the word *two*. "You're paying for two, not three. There's room for two, not three." Ray stepped forward and attempted to say something.

She didn't let him. "I expect this to be corrected today."

Claude made arrangements to move in with Aurora that afternoon. He apologized for the inconvenience and insisted it would be for just a short while. She brushed it off, stating that his timing was good since this was one of the first times in a long time she and her grandmother didn't have anyone staying with them. One of those sheds was really a little guest room, she informed him. He could move in that very night.

"Wow," was the only word Claude could come up with. "Wow, wow," he said, shaking his head. His wonderment failed to subside and that evening at the Pompano Pier, his poetry sailed through the crowd. His words were graceful, his voice was strong. He even composed a little ditty on the spot which he thought was brilliant. The artistry became contagious, and all the musicians seemed to play at a new level.

As usual, Gary drove them to the trailer park, stopping on the way at Tropical Gardens to pick up Claude's few belongings. As he let them out in the back of the warehouse, Gary smiled at Claude and said to him: "Don't do anything I wouldn't do."

The words hit Claude with the force of tree limbs cracking after an ice storm in New England. He felt a chill and thought that the move might be a mistake. He looked at Aurora for some clue.

"Gary, you're such a clown," she yelled out as the Jeep backed away. She took Claude by the hand and the two crossed the crude bridge into the defunct mobile home park. They spoke about the evening's performance, agreeing that everyone had been in top form.

Grandma greeted him warmly and showed him the shed. "It's not the penthouse suite, but it's dry and safe." She fluffed up the pillows and smoothed the afghan. "Made this myself. Years ago, was probably smoking something at the time. Might explain the weird colors." She laughed a wicked little snicker, then became somber. "My husband spent his last few months here. He said it was peaceful." Claude thanked her profusely. She patted his cheek and he recoiled imperceptibly. "You're welcome to stay, but just watch yourself. My Aurora's a good girl. Be nice."

He wasn't sure what she meant, but he accepted it as a warning. He remembered how he felt the electricity of Aurora's touch and how he relished the way she walked and the way she laughed. "Oh, well..." he muttered, not knowing exactly what he meant. He shoved his bags under the bed and sat down to inspect his new abode. The shed was solid, built out of plywood sheets with a metallic roof, probably intended to house bicycles, a lawnmower and tools. Claude bounced lightly on the bed, testing it and finding it firm. "Not bad," he said, adding "anyways, beggars can't be choosers."

Immediately, the face of Dushayne came into his head, and Claude began to wonder about what was really going on between his former roommates. He began to worry about Ray, and, as he turned off the light and lay down on his new bed, he knew his sleep would be fitful like all the others.

Dushayne managed better than he expected his first night back at Hips. It was an adventure: seeing old friends and co-workers, listening to the new crop of entertainers, diving in and out of the mad hustle of Friday night regulars and vacationers. Dushayne thought he would be haunted by Derrick, but the ghost of Miss Sashay failed to appear.

Ray showed up early. He found the bar to be surprisingly understated. Ray assumed a gay bar that featured drag shows would be showered in bright lights and fancy signage. Hips announced itself with one simple painted sign over the door lit by a row of old-fashioned crooked neck fixtures that could have come from a '50s drug store. A small neon sign alerted those close enough to read it that shows started at 10 o'clock. Music spilled out into the parking lot whenever the door was opened by a giant of a man wearing a reflective safety vest. Everybody seemed to know him by name. At that hour, more people were exiting than entering, but Ray could tell that the place was still busy. He parked his vehicle next to a pair of taxis. He listened to the drivers as they chatted, their behinds resting on the hoods of their cabs. They spoke in a language other than English. Ray thought he heard Creole and assumed the drivers were Haitian. He wondered what these men thought of their assignment. Did Hips and its drunken patrons remind them of voodoo ceremonies and dances back in Haiti? He acknowledged never having seen a voodoo ceremony outside of film and television and he doubted their accuracy, yet he enjoyed the juxtaposition he had just created.

A group of men emerged from the bar and created a circle not far from Ray's car to chat and smoke. There was plenty of laughter and playfulness. Ray watched some of the men as they kept their arms around each other. One fellow made a joke and stroked another guy's ass while the others whooped it up.

Ray was tempted to go inside. He knew the bar would soon be closing, and that made it seem safer. In his 60 years, he had never seen anything like a strip show, male or female, and certainly not a drag show. He thought about it and decided he would wait for another night. There would be many, he told himself. For some reason, his decision not to enter the bar depressed him. He scolded himself: life is short, especially when your 60, grab hold of it, make your own space, jump into the unknown. Finally, he told himself he was being overly dramatic.

The beefy doorman approached Ray. "You Ray?" he said.

"Yes."

"Dushayne sent me. Told me to look for an older guy in a Subaru Outback. Told me to tell you he'll be done in a while."

"Thanks." Ray felt small and intimidated.

The big guy lumbered back to his post and propped the door open. The music had stopped and the place was flooded in bright lights. Ray watched the string of patrons stumble out of the bar in twos and threes, guys of all ages and sizes. The taxi drivers jumped into their cabs, and the exodus proceeded in an orderly fashion. The last to leave were the single guys, and Ray observed them carefully as they lingered, some of them walking in front of his car as if inspecting it. These guys seemed to be in no hurry; no one waiting for them, no special place to go. Some looked at each other only to be ignored. They looked older, overdressed or underdressed, rumpled and tired. Ray imagined they had spent a long evening working, not having much fun, hoping, being rejected, giving up, yet lingering for a better ending. He caught himself: what do you know, Raymond Champagne, about single men in a gay bar? Be serious.

Dushayne appeared suddenly, emerging not from the main door, but from an alley alongside the building. He spotted Ray and gave him a huge smile. Ray returned the smile and leaned over to open the passenger door.

"So, how was your return engagement?"

"Went Ok. A bit rusty at first."

"I bet everybody was glad to see you."

"Seemed like it."

On the way home, they stopped at an all-night Dairy Queen. They slugged down their frappes and watched the flow of bar refugees – as Ray called them – coming and going. Dushayne made a joke about dairy queens which Ray didn't grasp. Half a dozen bikers filled the space, all looking heavy and worn. They were joined by a group of teenagers piled into the back of pickup trucks. At the edge of the parking lot, away from the glare of the lights, Ray noticed a pair of persons wrapped in blankets despite the warm night air. As the parking lot emptied, the couple slithered toward the dumpster. Ray nudged Dushayne and they observed the shorter of the two jump into the dumpster, the other keeping watch. Dushayne noticed that the one on the ground was a female. She stood there until her partner tossed a few things out of the dumpster, then scrambled to pick up the bottles and leftovers on the asphalt. As they retreated, Dushayne said, "Scum."

"What do you mean?" asked Ray.

"Look at 'em. Raiding dumpsters. Don't care how hungry I got, I never climbed into a dumpster. That's disgusting."

"They're desperate, that's all." Ray felt genuine compassion for the two. "I feel sorry for them."

"That what you feel for me? That why you took me to lunch the first time?"

"No. I admired you. Your gumption, your determination."

"You have no idea how desperate I was."

Ray felt there was nothing to add. The two were silent for most of the ride to Tropical Gardens.

Emerging from the shower, Dushayne said he couldn't shake the image of that guy jumping into the dumpster. "That's dangerous. God knows what shit's inside those things."

"Listen, Dushayne, we all do dangerous things at some point, some of us more often than others."

"Doesn't sound like you, Ray. Why you so down?"

"Not down, just realistic. Listen, don't mind me. I'm not usually up at this time of night."

Dushayne turned off the light and climbed into his bed. "Sorry to make you stay up," he said in the darkness. He waited a moment and then asked, "You be there tomorrow night? You should come early and see what's going on. Saturday nights can be lots of fun."

His words were lost; Ray had already fallen asleep.

On the first day of March, a Saturday, Ray and Claude had agreed to touch bases. It was Ray's idea; to his surprise, he found he missed his traveling companion. He tracked Claude down in the downtown park and suggested they do something together, perhaps take in a movie.

They drove to a Cineplex that catered to senior citizens with not-so-recent releases at discounted ticket prices. The two stood in the lobby staring at the movie posters, each one waiting for the other to decide which film to see. None of the titles meant anything to Claude who estimated he hadn't been to a movie in a couple of years. He read the titles out loud: *Atonement, Charley Wilson's War, Sweeney Todd, There Will Be Blood* and looked at Ray.

"None of these sound very uplifting," Claude offered.

"Let's see *Sweeney Todd*. It was a Broadway show once."

"Ok with me."

"Let me buy the tickets," Ray said.

"I can pay my way. I've got some money."

As they left the theater two hours later, Ray began a dissertation about the Sweeney Todd character, tracing the origins to Victorian England and how he's been adapted throughout history. He opined that Burton's film adaptation was much too gory, but that Sondheim's absolutely inspired musical score redeemed the film. Claude listened patiently. Ray expounded on the quality of the light and the costumes and the makeup, yes, the incredible makeup.

"Hard to understand how that movie can make you feel good. All that blood..." Claude replied.

Reaching their parking space, Claude decided to change the subject: "So how's Dushayne doing?"

"He hasn't slit my throat yet."

Claude retorted, "You know that's not what I meant."

"Sorry. Couldn't resist that one. He's doing fine. You'll be happy to know he's cut back on his panhandling. He's down to just two days." Ray and Claude sat waiting for the parking lot to clear. Neither was in any hurry.

"Where is he tonight?"

"Who?"

"Dushayne."

"Oh...he's back at his old job on weekends."

"I didn't know he had a job."

"He's a bar back at a club in Fort Lauderdale."

Explosions racked Claude's brain and brought back a series of lingering doubts. "It's a gay bar?"

Ray felt the flush of guilt. "Yes, a gay bar." He looked into the emptying parking lot and saw his reflection in the windshield. "With drag shows."

"I'm not sure what that is. Oh, yeah. Drag shows: guys in dresses and makeup doing comedy and singing."

"That's the gist of it," Ray responded drily.

"Do you join in?"

"I've never set foot in the place."

"Maybe you should, being gay and all." Claude was surprised by his honesty.

"I never said I was gay," Ray offered in a low voice.

Claude regretted his words. "It's not an accusation, Ray. Anyways it's none of my business." Claude rapidly reviewed the times the two shared a room, the time he stood naked watching TV, all the conversations about their lives back home. "Do you think I'm gay," he asked.

"No. Maybe when we first met. But not now," Ray said turning to face his friend. "Listen, I've always been gay and I never did anything about it. Until last December when I found myself in a sting operation."

"That's when you ran away?"

"What do you think?" Ray's voice turned bitter. At that moment, he hated this homeless man he had been so generous to, he hated the turn his life had taken, he hated the admission, he hated himself. Ray used the back of his hand to wipe the sweat from his face. He wanted to get even.

"And, how's Aurora and her grandmother?" Ray asked abruptly.

"Just fine. We get along Ok." Claude was pleased with the change of subject.

"Anything going on between you and the girl?"

Claude stared at his companion. "Anything going on between you and Dushayne?"

The questions invaded the cab. It was as if the vehicle was in a collision and the air bag inflated and turned into a sex doll and sucked all the air out of the cab. The sex doll squeezed a leering *gotcha* through its ruby red lips. The two men stared away from each other and held their thoughts. Ray digested Claude's question and recognized it as one he had asked himself. Claude, on the other hand, was insulted. He thought Ray's question was vicious.

They started at the same time, Claude saying just a couple of words like "It's none of your..." and Ray starting with "I've asked myself..."

Both men stopped and hesitated. "You go first," Claude said.

"Ok." Ray drew a deep breath and covered his eyes with his hands. "Believe me, I've asked myself what I want from Dushayne. There are times I feel like a pervert, a lecherous old man; at other times I feel peaceful and fulfilled."

"What the hell does that mean?"

"Well, for the first time in my life, there's another person who needs me, who truly needs me. And that makes me feel wanted, necessary. It's fulfilling."

"Aren't you the guy with the wife and a daughter back home and how many grandkids?"

"Yes. Guilty as charged. But I told you I always wanted a son."

"And, your family back home, they aren't homeless ..."

"Don't be sarcastic, please." Ray interrupted. "This isn't easy for me. I'm trying to think this out."

"Sorry. I'll leave the sarcasm for you."

Ray paid no attention. "You know, there haven't been many men in my life. My father tolerated me, my brother hated me. Damn it, my biggest role model growing up was a nun. It feels good to be with a man all the time, even a nineteen-year-old."

The other cars in the Cineplex parking lot had left, and Ray felt the two of them had become an island in an ocean of asphalt and painted lines.

"We can go now," said Claude.

"No. Let me finish." Ray opened his window. He recounted how both his wife and daughter never asked for anything. It was all assumed he would provide, and they took him for granted. "In life, you have to have people who need, and people who respond. Then people appreciate each other and people can love each other. I've never believed that everyone should be equal in a relationship. Perhaps, that creates respect, but not love."

"Frankly, Ray I don't know what you're talking about."

"Dushayne is the generous one, sharing all there is to share about him, and giving back in many ways. You know that he likes to shave me, my beard, my face. And, he trims my hair. He says it makes him feel like he's creating something."

Claude wanted to scream out *like Sweeney Todd*.

Ray couldn't be stopped. He talked about Dushayne having had such a terrible childhood, how he has "this natural intelligence and creativity." Ray explained that he'd started tutoring him for his GED.

"You know what it sounds like. You and Dushayne have this father-son relationship."

"It *is* that. But it's more. I feel like his mentor, his guardian; I'm there to show him the way, and in return he makes me feel so rich, much richer than I've ever felt."

"You know that's not going to last. Your little boy is gonna grow up and go on his own and leave you high and dry, a lonely old pervert, to use your own words."

"You don't understand. And, what you just said, that's downright mean."

"Sorry, but it's true. He's gonna dump you."

"Shut up, Claude. Just shut up."

Each one fell silent, searching for the words that could salvage their friendship. Ray toyed with the realization that Claude was probably right, but he held his disappointment and his anger.

"Can we go now?" Claude said.

Florida Route 44 was stagnant with both northbound lanes towards Banyan Cove clogged with vehicles of all kinds. "Must be an accident up ahead," Ray volunteered. The Subaru crawled past the strip malls and the bowling alleys and the empty department store converted into a flea market, and finally the Denny's Restaurant which had served to introduce them to the local citizenry. The sidewalks were filled with people and everyone was headed in the same direction.

"It's the fireworks," Ray declared. "Tonight's the 50th anniversary of Banyan Cove. I've driven by the banner in front of city hall a hundred times."

"You want to go?" Claude asked, grasping at an opportunity to change the mood.

"Not really. Not in a celebratory frame of mind."

As they came to a stop before the entrance to an athletic field, the sounds of a marching band reached them. Ray recognized a Sousa march. Once again, Claude suggested they should participate.

"You can go if you want. I'll let you out and you can walk home after the birthday party."

Claude was reminded of the Fourth of July band concerts back home. There was always an old-timers' brass band and their music was awful, but everybody gathered around the gazebo and had a grand time. The Rotary Club had games for the kids and there were hot dog vendors and the ladies of some church always sold brownies. "We didn't have fireworks in my town," he said under his breath. Turning to Ray, he added "Always had to go to Putnam for the fireworks."

"We had to go to Rochester at the fairgrounds," Ray added.

"Do you think you'll ever go back?" Claude asked.

"You mean back home?"

"Yes."

"They say you never go back."

"Some people do."

"Well, I really can't." Ray was becoming irritated again. "I can't go back. That's final."

"Ok. It's really none of my business. I just think that someone with your education and background, well, you could do something more than wandering around a library day after day and living in a rundown motel with a gay panhandler young enough to be your grandson."

"You said it was none of your business. And it isn't." Ray didn't attempt to hide his anger.

Just then, the police officer signaled and traffic started moving again. A few yards up from the athletic field, Claude told Ray to stop the car. "I will go to the fireworks. See ya. And, thanks for the bloody movie."

Ray didn't attempt to stop his passenger. "Have fun," he yelled to him.

Ray picked up speed as the traffic thinned and was about to enter the parking lot at Tropical Gardens when he stopped at roadside and stared at the motel. Claude's words rushed at him. "Lonely old pervert, lonely old pervert," he repeated while rocking back and forth in the cab. Instead of turning into the motel lot, he revved the engine and speeded onto Route 44, in the path of a pickup truck. In his rear-view mirror, he spotted the driver, leaning out his window. "Fuck you, old man," the driver yelled. "You wanna get both of us killed?"

He scrunched the sections of his face, forcing himself to keep his eyes shut tightly. He didn't want to see the concrete abutment swell as he raced towards it. He wondered for a split second what the impact might look like, but he dismissed the thought. That wasn't the last sight he wanted to record. He didn't have to see any of it. He'd hear the metal scream and crunch, he'd feel the slivers of shattered glass, he would sense his body – his tired old body – collapse, and he would retreat from the dead-end life that had become his. That was the scenario that flashed through Raymond Champagne's mind moments before he slammed his vehicle into the side of an overpass.

It was just before 2 a.m. on a quiet stretch of Interstate 95 near the Pompano Beach exit ramp. Ray knew the spot well from travels to and from Fort Lauderdale and had noticed how the northbound lane sloped so naturally towards the abutment. A collision just begging to happen. It would be fast. It would be efficient.

But it didn't quite work that way. Ray sat there with his legs crushed under the dashboard, the steering wheel locked against his cracked sternum, his left shoulder twisted out of its socket, and blood flowing from his left ear. Ray couldn't believe he wasn't dead. He had tried. He had tried. He had unbuckled his seatbelt; he'd revved the engine, aimed the car at top speed, at the corner of the abutment– not the middle – so it would cut deeper into the front of the vehicle. He had tried. But it wasn't good enough. Stupid old fool. He wanted to yell, but he had no voice. Anger was all he could feel. There was no sensation in any part of his body; none of it worked. Just his brain. Was he in a coma? Would he live out the rest of his years as a broken vegetable in some nursing home? The questions fed his anger. Damn old fool. Can't even kill yourself. Suddenly he understood he'd probably bleed to death. He had, after all, chosen his spot well. The roadway was badly lit, and at that time of morning there was little traffic. If anyone came upon the crash, it would take a good amount of time for the police and the ambulance to show up, long enough for the life to flow out of him. He couldn't open his eyes nor could he hear anything. He had no way of discerning if anyone was coming to his rescue. His last prayer was that nobody would. No rescue, please.

The piece of his brain that was still working gave Ray a chance to review his night and his final conclusion. He only remembered the negative: Claude's accusation that Dushayne would tire of him, the realization that he could never go back to New Hampshire, that his life in Florida was totally empty.

Upon leaving the Tropical Gardens parking lot, Ray drove around aimlessly for over an hour, finally heading to Hips. He parked facing the bar entrance and debated what he should do. The crowd looked like a carbon copy of the patrons, in groups and singles, he observed several times before. A pair of guys stood nearby both smoking. One was young – in his mid-twenties – and the other was a much older man, late 60s, perhaps early 70s. The older guy had his arm around his friend's shoulders and kept whispering in his ear, nibbling on the ear lobe. Suddenly, the bar door opened and a young guy emerged. The two younger patrons hugged and kissed, one threw his cigarette butt on the ground, and together, they went back into Hips, leaving the old guy by himself. Ray watched the smoker as he scoured the lot, walked to a few of the cars, found them empty and finally returned to the bar.

That's me, Raymond Champagne, a commodity, soon to be useless, soon left to shrivel up, alone, desolate, perhaps hunting for new prey. But you love Dushayne. How do I know if I love him? How do I know if I ever loved anyone? He's a kid, an exotic and beautiful young man. Does he even know what love is? What can you offer him? You're not that guy outside the bar who probably has a fortune and a big house on the beach. All you've got is a dingy little motel room, and just a few bucks to pay for it for a few more weeks. Bye, bye, old man...

He broke away from his monologue and took several deep breaths. Sitting in his getaway car, Raymond smelled the left-over tobacco, heard the tired music, and found no room. He started his car and moved away. From his spot across the street, he stared at the run-down drag bar. Just go home, back to New Hampshire. Are *you* kidding? There goes Raymond Champagne, the closet faggot school principal. You want to live with that? You want your wife and daughter and granddaughters to hear people say that? *You can't just roll over and play dead.* The words of the lone ranger turned lawyer. You didn't listen to him and you ran away. Good for you! Three months nowhere, three months absent; you've been playing dead for three months. You just didn't know it.

Ray couldn't stay there; he drove to the Interstate and pointed his car northward. On the controlled stretch of roadway, the car drove itself, leaving his mind to delve into his monologue: useless old pervert, useless, no one wants you, no one needs you, useless, useless. He screamed, "You win, demons." Then he headed for the highway overpass.

The next morning, long before Aurora and her grandmother were awake, Claude walked to Tropical Gardens. He had hardly slept, reliving his argument with Ray, witnessing the anger and despair his words had caused. He had given up the notion that the episode was another of his mad dreams or wild visions, yet he hoped that some intervention would have delivered the Subaru and its driver safely to his motel room during the night. He approached the motel cautiously and stood motionless on the sidewalk under the pink neon sign, his head bowed, trying vainly to pull from the dark Catholic corners of his heart a prayer, the prayer for miracles. Finally, he lifted his head and opened his gaze to the widest and emptiest parking lot he had ever seen. There was no car; there was no Ray.

Claude walked to Room 6. The drapes were open; nothing seemed disturbed. It was as if the previous evening had never happened. He wished he still had his room key to make sure nothing was missing.

It occurred to him that the Blakes might know something and he rushed to their mobile home. He stepped onto the veranda and saw that Esther and Chester were having breakfast. He smelled fresh coffee and toasted bread. They invited him in. Esther said she was glad to see him. "Sit down, have some coffee."

Claude walked in and noticed that the TV set in the living room was turned to the morning news. "Is that the local channel?" he asked.

Chester answered flatly: "I like to get the weather."

Just then, a local reporter with her Hispanic name scripted at the bottom of the screen said, "Here's the latest about the accident on I-95 last night." The Blakes and Claude moved to the living room and stood in a half-circle around the TV set. Briefly, Claude imagined the three of them standing in the same formation in front of a casket at a wake, possibly Ray's. Angry with himself, he discharged the thought. The reporter placed the mike in the face

277

of a man in a police uniform. "Can you tell us what happened, Chief Hammond?" Claude didn't listen to the answer. He looked at Esther and Chester and asked them if they had heard from Ray. They signaled no with their heads and then looked at each other quizzically. Esther said Ray was probably in his room. Chester added that Ray was probably already on the road with the kid, noting that the two had a habit of leaving early for God knows where. Esther threw a reproachful look at her husband.

Chief Hammond recited in a rehearsed tone, "There was only one car involved. A Subaru Outback with a New Hampshire license plate. We found no identification in the vehicle. A single individual was involved – a male. Of course, there will be an autopsy.

The reporter thanked the police chief and closed her segment by urging anyone with information to contact the Pompano Beach Police Department, as an 800 number scrolled at the bottom of the screen.

"Why are you asking about Raymond? Were you with him last night?" Esther had begun to comprehend that something wasn't right. "Oh, no," she said, her face sandwiched between her hands. "That's Raymond's car, isn't it?" She signaled her husband to come over and join her on the sofa. She adopted the calming voice of the veteran school teacher. "Now, Claude. Talk to me. Tell me what happened."

He summarized the events of the night, emphasizing that he wasn't sure about anything, except that Ray seemed upset and angry and had dropped him off on Route 44 just south of the motel. "I don't know where he went from there. I assumed he came here. Now, what am I supposed to think? What am I supposed to do?" Claude started to feel his fear turn into tears. He wiped his eyes with the sleeve of his shirt and hurried out of the living room. On the veranda, he thanked the Blakes for their hospitality and promised to keep them informed.

A few steps down the path, Claude heard Esther walking to catch up with him. "Here. Take the key to Room 6. See what you can find out. Ok?"

In the motel room, Claude was amazed to find everything the way he left it several days before, except that his belongings were replaced by Dushayne's. Everything was neat and organized, kept that way undoubtedly by Ray. Claude pulled a jacket out of the closet; it had Ray's scent: Old Spice. Anger and betrayal filled the room, and Claude started blaming himself, asking why he couldn't have foreseen the accident. He saw death lurking in the shadows his entire life, coming after strangers or himself. Why didn't he see it this time? He sat on Ray's bed and reviewed all his faces of evil, from Mrs. Sinclair onward. Suddenly, he understood that this time, death was an accident. There was no one; there was no face of evil. It just happened. Claude felt even more powerless. For the first time in a very long time, he craved the numbing power of whiskey. He knew there was no liquor in the room and for that he was grateful.

What might he take from this room? Scanning the simple furnishings and dingy blinds, he settled on the jacket and folded it reverently. He also knew that Ray kept a suitcase beneath his bed. He opened it and discovered that all it contained was an envelope with some papers and twenty dollars bills. Without thinking, he slid the envelope in the pocket of his jeans and put the suitcase back.

In their trailer, the Blakes were quarrelling about whether or not they should call the police. Chester kept saying that they really knew nothing about the guys in Room 6, that they could be thieves or murderers or terrorists. Esther argued that she had good feelings about Raymond, that he was an honorable man. Then, as an afterthought she said that if he indeed was killed in that accident, there was nothing they could do about it. It wasn't their responsibility to notify next of kin.

"But the kid has to go," Esther said. "The rent for March is due next week. Assuming that Ray is... no more, and assuming that the boy can't pay for the room, then I'll have to evict him. I have no choice." She went into her office, opened a file cabinet, and pulled out the folder for Room 6.

"But you gave a key to Claude, just now."

"Let him keep it...for a couple of days. If his friend has passed, he might need a bit of time. To wind things up, you know. To pay his respects..."

The husband wasn't convinced. "You sure, Esther? Is that wise?"

"Yes, I am and yes it is." Her voice made it clear that the decision was irrevocable. Back in the kitchen, she started clearing breakfast dishes. She glanced at the clock. "Get dressed, Chester.

We're going to church. This is Sunday and we're going to church."

"What?" her husband replied. "We haven't been to church for months. We even skipped Christmas."

"But we have a reason to today," she replied. Her voice was grave, and Chester knew not to argue.

He had slept in more uncomfortable circumstances – more often than he wanted to remember – but Dushayne's night in the storage room at Hips proved to be one of the worst. It was the noise mostly, from an ancient walk-in refrigerator that might have been necessary to keep beer cold in the Florida heat, but entirely unnecessary if one was trying to sleep next to it. Every ten minutes the motor seemed to die down only to erupt a while later angrier than before. Dushayne swore the thing was alive. And then there were the smells: stale, musty, sour. He couldn't blame Stevie; the storage area was all he had to offer. The bar owner had thrown a pile of old stage curtains on the floor and tossed Dushayne a couple of blankets. "At least you'll be safe," Stevie said.

In the early morning hours, Dushayne gave up trying to sleep and went outside. The air was still, the smell of humid trash filling the alley. What happened to Ray? He said he'd pick me up at 2:30. Where was he? He promised. At daybreak Sunday morning, he viewed the trash and the broken fence and the bird shit and became angry at Ray for abandoning him.

Claude was just about to leave when the phone rang. The sound, dry and strident, pulled him back into the motel room. He stared at the clunky black plastic and realized that all those days he lived in that room the telephone had never rung. He picked up the receiver cautiously. "Hello," he said in a faint interrogation.

"Hello." The voice was also questioning. "Who's this?"

"Claude. Who's calling?"

"Dushayne."

"Oh. Where are you?"

"Where's Ray? He was supposed to pick me up."

"Oh. You're at the bar?"

"Yes. Outside. Been here all night. Where's Ray? Is he there? Let me talk to him."

Claude sat down on Ray's bed. He struggled with what he

should say; he identified with the burden of the survivor. "Dushayne..." Saying the kid's name didn't help. He swallowed and became rigid. "Listen to me. Something's happened. It's about Ray."

"What happened? He all right?" Dushayne's voice rang high through the old telephone receiver. "He can't come get me?"

"No."

"The buses must be running now; I'll catch one. Take me a while, but I'll be there. Wait for me. Stay put and wait for me. You hear me, Claude?"

"Yes. I'll be here."

V

Lawn Ornaments

Grandma had been searching the compound and was out of breath when she came upon Claude sitting next to the canal. She squatted before him and waited for him to say something. Claude looked at her and smiled. She made herself comfortable, her thin legs wrapped beneath her, her head arched forward. Claude was reminded of one of her cats. Grandma extended a hand and placed it on Claude's knee. "Death is funny," she said. Claude gave her a look of mild shock. "I don't mean funny ha ha, more like funny crazy. You know. It can carry a punch and cut your legs off if you don't know how to deal with it." Claude waited for more. He thought her explanation was lacking. There must be more to it than that. He waited. She remained quiet and the two listened to the subtle licks of the dank canal. Claude examined the shape of the shadow they cast jointly over the water. The sun was already hugging the horizon at their back and he could feel the coolness of the night spreading in their direction.

"How did you deal? When your husband died."

"I collected things."

Again, Claude expected more. "Like what?"

"Just things that he had, things he had touched, things that had been part of his life."

"I see. Well, I don't have any of those. I hardly knew the man."

"I'm sure there's something. He had to leave something."

283

"There's his clothes, that's all. And a book he gave me a few weeks ago. And one thin envelope with some pictures." He held back about the money.

"Claude. Come with me. I have to show you something." They walked to the trailer, hand in hand, in the same way her granddaughter had guided him into the vacant park the first night. "Let me tell you the story of this place." There was a combination of pride and mischief in her voice. Claude fell into step and the two wandered into a new area of the compound. She was taller than him, and she favored long skirts and shawls and brightly colored ribbons to highlight her hair. Claude felt like the son to her mother as they nearly skipped along the roadways. Once they reached the extreme western edge, Claude could hear traffic the from Route 44.

"Never came this way before," he said.

"This used to be the main entrance. This is how everybody went in and out of Royal Palms." Now, that's all that's left."

"What do you mean, all that's left?"

"That," Grandma said. She pointed upwards to a billboard that was catching the last rays of the sun. Claude read the faded and peeling letters: "Royal Palms Court Luxury Condominiums." And, in smaller lettering: "starting in the $350s – spring of 2007."

"Condominiums? Luxury ones? What happened?" he asked Grandma.

"Not sure. Ran out of money is what I heard. Which is fine with me." She pointed to two palm trees that framed the sign. "See those? Those are royal palms. Among the tallest in the world. The smoothest bark you'd ever see, like a baby's behind. So majestic. I love these trees. The trailer park used to be full of them. Had one right in back of our trailer. That's why it's called Royal Palms Trailer Park." A series of shivers, delicate little spasms, interrupted her speech.

"Shall we head back, Grandma?"

On the way back to her trailer, she explained there were more than a thousand mobile homes with nice people: families, retirees, good neighbors, helpful but not nosy, plain simple average people. "It was our own little town, nice and peaceful. You know, all the streets had female names. It was nice. This was Nanette Street." She went on to say that Hurricane Wilma in 2005 was the end of it all. Claude tried to remember the girl names of the streets in his development in Williams, the streets that he and Tony roamed all those summers. Grandma continued, "Most of the trailers were destroyed; people didn't have insurance, so they just left, went to live somewhere else. The few who stayed were bought out by the park owners, an outfit from Texas somewhere. By the summer of 2006, the place was all but empty. What remained was bulldozed into those mounds you see here and there; you know, all that twisted metal and chunks of concrete. They started hauling it away in giant trucks that made the most god-awful noise. Day and night, those trucks came and went, chewing up the streets. Sometimes, I can't get that noise out of my head." Grandma was walking sprightly on what had become barren paths, pointing in the creeping darkness to different areas: where the swimming pool and activities center were located, where a stand of Royal Palms formed a little park, the spot where her best friend Sylvia lived. "One of those cats I take care of was hers," she confided. "Then one day the trucks stopped and they fixed the fence around the place and we were alone, apparently forgotten by everyone – which was fine with me. Believe me."

"How did *you* survive?" Claude was intrigued.

"A miracle. Wilma blew off the roof on the porch and one of the palm trees crushed our car, but that was all," she answered.

"I mean, since the hurricane."

"Oh. Well, Elliot – that's my husband – was dying. We had set up sort of a hospital room in the shed where you sleep now. Someone started a rumor that he was dying from a horrible disease he got in Africa and that it was terrible and very, very contagious. I think it was the Jamaicans – they were clearing brush and fallen trees – who started the rumor. I didn't mind and I didn't try to hush it up or anything." Claude and his guide had reached her trailer and they stood facing each other. "Now, a few people, not many, mind you, have found this place, and they camp out here and there. I think they're mostly homeless. I mean, in the sense they don't have real homes. I feel sorry for them," Grandma said.

"As long as you feel safe."

"Safe? Nobody's safe, not anywhere, not anymore."

"I guess…"

Grandma interrupted him. "All you can expect these days is to be left alone. This place has fallen off the map, slipped off the radar, ignored by the authorities. And, that's fine with me. And you're not about to change that are you?"

"Of course not. I like being invisible."

"Good." She grabbed him by the hand. "One more thing. This is what I really wanted to show you." She steered him towards the smaller of the two sheds located to the rear of what had become Claude's bedroom. It was a tiny building, made of metal, surrounded by garden tools strewn about wantonly. Grandma opened the door and reached in to find a flashlight. She handed it to Claude. "Take a look." The beam of light revealed a jumble of items crowded together, hanging from the ceiling, in piles on the floor, all over an industrial shelving unit. Claude thought of his visit to the pawn shop. An ornate carpet, a pair of matching vases, tall and in a brilliant shade of blue, a tribal mask, baskets of all sizes, bolts of fabric. Claude aimed his flashlight at each item like an inspector looking for health or safety violations. "What did your husband do in Africa?" Claude asked.

"He was a spy."

"What? A spy? Who did he spy for?"

"Can't say. I was sworn to secrecy."

Claude smiled. He vacillated between sympathy for Grandma and feeling like he was being played. He aimed the light at the rear of the shed and stopped it on a group of shapes, all nearly identical, all painted a vivid pink. He looked at Grandma. She chuckled and volunteered, "Flamingoes. You know those plastic pink flamingoes. Lawn ornaments. Elliot loved them."

"Really? Wow, there's a lot of 'em here."

"Around 30 or so. Forgot the exact count. Elliot had these things all over the place. It was hideous, but endearing."

"And, you've kept them all."

"That's what I meant by collecting things." Grandma dropped into a somber place. "Just think of what you can pull together, things that remind you of your friend. You can have your own memorial chapel, like I do for Elliott here." She retrieved the flashlight and put it back inside the shed and closed the metal door. "Good night, young man."

Claude watched her saunter away and he knew he wouldn't have a good night. Inside his shed, he sat on the bed and searched his brain and heart for what might constitute a tribute to his friend Ray.

The next morning, as he embarked on his usual walk, he saw the trailer park in a new light. He sprinted down the ashen paths and conjured up pretty girl names for the streets. He imagined the place with neat trailers on their manicured lots and people sitting on their screened porches, children on bicycles and retirees playing shuffleboard. "Wilma-Land. I baptize thee Wilma-Land," he said to his empty surroundings. He gave his christening all the solemnity he could muster, blessing each corner with an exaggerated sign of the cross. "You may be wasteland, Wilma-Land, but your desolation has become a haven for us humble squatters." Claude laughed, pleased with his pronouncement.

Back in his shed, Claude spotted the thin Kerouac book that Ray gave him. He had placed it on the shelf next to his bed and promised himself and Ray's ghost that he would read it. He read the title: *Satori in Paris*. He said it out loud, still unsure of the pronunciation of the first word. Ray explained that the word had a spiritual meaning for Buddhists. "What does that have to do with Kerouac who was a Catholic French kid from New England just like you and me?" he asked Ray.

"Read the book, just read it," Ray replied.

Claude had not opened it. He felt guilty and one kind of guilt brought on many others. He felt he owed Ray something and he started thinking about a poem for Ray. He felt a decent level of inspiration; he sat with his notepad and words came rapidly. When he was finished, he gave the results their first airing:

Christmas baby
What have you left us?

Two Halloween photographs
Two young girls as pirate and fairy
One young man as crusader
Twenty-dollar bills, neat and folded
Nineteen of them, practically new

A song of Noël, ancient and lasting
A rendezvous on a park bench
An escapade to Tropical lands
A book by Kerouac still unread

Paul Paré

> *Christmas baby*
> *What have you become*
> *If nobody knows you're dead?*

He read it again and was pleased with it. Perhaps, he thought, it might release all the other poems that were trying to emerge from his dreams and visions that lately fell upon the page in shapeless disarray.

The urge was strong. Dushayne needed the peace and consolation of his favorite place. He needed it desperately and on the Wednesday night after Ray died, he made his way to the empty lot at river's edge. The March evening defied the calendar and carried with it the steaminess of summer. Dushayne welcomed it. The bus ride into downtown Fort Lauderdale took him past Wellington Plaza and Dushayne changed his seat to the other side of the bus, the side away from the plaza. There was no reason to look back on his days there. Nor was there a reason to disconnect the few segments of his life that he cherished. Living with Ray the past weeks and all the times spent enjoying his riverside haven with Derrick, those were the pieces that belonged together. These were the happy moments in his short life; Wellington Plaza had forfeited its place among them.

He approached the empty lot cautiously. He walked on the edge, scouting for any activity. He told himself he had good reason to be careful. The lot was littered with dozens of empty beer bottles and jugs of cheap wine and all sorts of trash. Under the abutment where he had made his bed, there was soot everywhere and evidence of a fire. Dushayne went back to the alley for one last inspection. He looked in both directions and saw no one. There was the sound of traffic in the distance but the dead-end along his sanctuary was deserted.

He walked down to the edge of the river and, in the light of a full moon, watched a piece of debris, a log of some kind, float by, being carried by the outgoing tide. He heard the sound of a motor and assumed that a boatman was somewhere in the distance. His ears attached themselves to the hum and followed it upriver until the noise faded. Dushayne walked to the jetty and spread himself on its dew-covered stones, allowing an arm to drop to the river. His hand entered the water and he was surprised by its thickness and warmth. He pulled himself upright and sat on the edge of the concrete wall. He bared his feet and dunked them into the river.

He thought of Roberta who once told him he should attend church with her because on that Sunday they were observing the ritual of the washing of the feet and that if anyone needed to have their sins washed away it was him. "Well, here's to you, Roberta," he said.

Dushayne touched his tattoo and thought of Derrick. He looked away from the river and saw two figures sitting on a packing crate talking quietly to each other and he was glad he had shared this place, his favorite place, his only home, with Derrick. The bar back smiled the smile of sad acceptance and, his eyes closed, he summoned the face of his dead friend and sang the words of Miss Kitt's divine song, all the while caressing the same words engraved on the skin of his forearm.

His thoughts turned to Ray and he felt his entire body drop – a physical as well as an emotional plunge into some depth he had never visited before. He heard Ray's voice late at night saying things he often didn't understand. He heard his responses and wondered then and now where they came from. Dushayne suddenly hoped that this night, this visit to his favorite place, would in some way enshrine those secret conversations. The ones he remembered clearly were brief, always after the two of them had gone to bed. They would lie in the darkness, each in his bed, and talk in whispers.

Once, Ray asked Dushayne exactly how old he was.

"Twenty my next birthday."

"When is that?"

"Why you want to know?"

"I want to know everything about you. And, besides, birthdays are important, especially when you're young."

"When's yours?" Dushayne asked.

"My birthday?"

"Yeah. You tell me yours and I'll tell you mine."

"Ok. December 25th I'm a Christmas baby."

"Really! That's so cool."

"Well, I hated it. As a kid, I felt cheated. I had to share my birthday with Jesus and I felt I only got half the gifts."

"At least you got some."

"Ok. I told you mine…"

"April First. You're Christmas, I'm April Fool."

"You're kidding!"

"No sir, April Fool's Day. My dad always said I was a joke."

"That's so sad."

"Never got a party, never got gifts."

"I'm sorry."

"Best part was when I got older and everybody just ignored me, including my birthday."

"Well. Tell you what, this year, I'll give you a big birthday party."

"Don't have to."

"I want to," Ray said.

Ray was the one who initiated the conversations most of the time. Dushayne remembered lying there waiting, expecting, wondering what topic he'd bring up. It was like part of a game. Once, Ray asked, "Did you ever wish you were a girl?"

"That's a strange question. Did you?"

"I asked first."

"Why you ask?"

"You're fascinated by drag shows, you're interested in costumes and makeup, and sometimes you can be – what's the word – swishy."

"I get it. Really, never wished I was a girl," Dushayne said.

"I'm surprised."

"You know, my brother Durell, he asked me the same question once."

"What did you tell him?"

"Same I just told you. And, you know what he said to me?"

"No."

"Said I was lucky. If I was a girl, I'd have to worry about my father liking me too much."

"Wow. Was your father like that?"

"Don't know. I was young. Didn't really understand what Durell was talking about."

There were often long pauses between statements and questions. Dushayne could hear Ray's breathing and, maybe, his thinking. But even with the gaps, the kid felt nothing was being held back by either one. Even now, on the banks of his lonely river, Dushayne was confident those nighttime conversations were the truest of his life.

"What's love?" Dushayne had been the one to instigate the conversation that night.

"Wow. That's a tough one. Do you want an answer from

literature, from psychiatry?"

"Want *your* answer."

"I have to think about that one," Ray said.

"Never mind. Stupid question."

"No. No. It's a good question. A great one. Everybody's been asking it since the dawn of time."

"I think you're stalling."

"No. I'm not. But the answer I would have given you years ago is not necessarily the one I can give you tonight."

"And, that is…"

"Being with someone, emphasis on *with*. Having someone *with* you as well. Being in sync with someone on all those things that matter. Being able to share with someone even after all there is to share has been shared…There's a lot more, but that's the basics."

"Was just a simple question."

"It's not a simple answer."

"Never is with you," Dushayne said.

Dushayne remembered that they laughed themselves to sleep.

But there was no laughter, not any more. Dushayne was convinced there would never be any laughter in his life. Nor would there be any love. He had loved Derrick and he had loved Ray and both were gone. Dushayne listened to the night around his Fort Lauderdale refuge and found it unbearably silent. Not even the strain of a sad song, not even whispers of intimate conversations. High up, a set of small lights twinkled slowly and silently across the sky. Dushayne strained to hear the sound of the jet, but it was too far.

He felt there should be tears. With his feet, he stirred the river waters, hoping to conjure up some tears. His heart was dry and it scared him. Why wasn't he allowed to cry? What was left if he couldn't cry? Dushayne peered into the swirls of water that gathered around his bare feet. Perhaps they could ease his dry heart. He became fascinated by the power of the river and he removed his body from the anchor that had been the cement wall and he let himself drop into the water, slowly at first, and then with a determination that comforted him.

He was surprised by the depth and the panic that followed. His body wanted to rebel, to follow its natural urge to resist. He would not let it. Dushayne weighed himself down, pushing away the resistance. He knew that his fears and loneliness would soon vanish and that all else – the good things – would vanish with them, forever, and he thought the bargain was a fair one.

Claude woke with a start. He darted out of bed and stood in his tin cell and opened the door wide to let the night in. A humid wind filled his bedroom space. Claude's body was cold and shaky and tense and didn't fit in the warmth of the Florida night. Gradually, he started reconciling the flashes of fear that awakened him with the gentleness of the pre-dawn. He let himself fall back onto his cot and managed to tame his breathing. The dream had been strong and deep, deeper than most. He looked at his hands and expected to see blood. He moved closer to the door and in the growing light he opened his clenched fists and examined his palms and found them clean.

He had wrestled with Tony and there should have been blood, large quantities of it. He should have been drenched. Claude touched himself, his arms and shoulders and legs and his bright white jockeys. All perfectly dry. Only then did anger sift through his confusion. "Fucking shit, Jesus fucking shit. That dream again," he yelled to the empty trailer park. He dunked his head in his arms to muffle the sounds of his anger.

Of late, Claude dreamed almost every night of his best friend Tony. This time Claude was in Saint Petronilla's Church, at the baptismal font which had grown to the size of a bathtub. Father Tony was lying inside the font; it was filled with blood. Father Tony's throat was slit and blood was spurting and soaking his white alb with the brilliant red color. Claude tried to pull him out and nearly fell into the font. He leaned close to his friend's mouth. Tony was saying something but Claude couldn't make it out.

As he sat on the edge of his cot, Claude sobbed. He remembered that Father Tony had been speaking Creole.

The waves – a mere sampling of the millions over time – were ferocious and intent on destruction. Claude was mesmerized. He stood at the very end of the Pompano Pier and draped his body over the railing and watched the waves come and go in their eternal assault, and he thought there was nothing like them in his corner of New England where a tame little river was all that flowed by. Perhaps a flood, every few years, but never this relentless pounding. He wondered if that made the people who lived on these ocean shores sturdier, more steadfast. Claude promised to turn his observations into a poem.

"Come on back. The crowd's building now," Aurora called from behind. Claude felt trapped between the waves lapping at the underpinnings of the pier and the urgency in her voice. He turned to face her. He wanted to refuse her, to say he couldn't add to the soiree, he wasn't in the mood to throw words at the crowd. "You know, it doesn't matter what you recite. If you're not happy with the poetry, just make believe you're in a trance or something. They like the idea of a poet more than the poetry itself. It's the same with my drumming. Sometimes, I'm convinced the spectators don't care what it sounds like, all they want is to see a girl and her drums." Claude was amazed that she could read his mind so well and he was amused by the reference to her drums.

He nodded to her and, hand in hand, they walked to the performance area close to the street. The dozen bystanders quickly grew to a Saturday night audience of 40 or so. Claude let the musicians carry the show, joining them when Aurora gave him an unmistakable *get off your ass* look. He read his old poems in a bland distanced delivery and, to his surprise, very few in the audience walked away. He wouldn't have admitted it, but he knew Aurora was correct. She knew her stagecraft. Claude threw into the mix a bastard version of Ginsberg's *Howl* and the crowd applauded. He thought that if he recited the Greek alphabet the audience would love that too.

Competition gradually invaded the space and performers and listeners alike became distracted by a deep thumping rhythmic noise. Some of the folks at the edge of the crowd, those closest to the street, turned to watch as a large pickup atop oversized wheels amble by, slow down, and double park, its radio discharging a loud bass. The sound blanketed the area and despite pleas by members of the crowd, the driver refused to turn down the volume. The musicians stopped. Aurora looked at Gary who left his keyboard and started walking towards the intruders. Three punks emerged from their truck. They stood facing the crowd defiantly and started to sway to the beat of their music. Gary approached them and was about to speak, when one of the kids sent him a dance move, waving his hands in front of his torso, the middle finger of each hand poking up boldly.

"Please, guys, we're performing here," Gary said to them.

"Hey, boy, you think you own this place?" said the kid who appeared to be the leader. "Far as I know, it's a public place." He pulled a chain out of the back of the truck and started walking towards Gary.

Claude stared at the scene before him and what he saw took him back to the worst moments of his life. The kid with the chain had turned into a monster. Claude closed his eyes and told himself to walk away. He couldn't move and was forced to gaze upon the face of the devil – the same ugliness and evil he had seen on Mrs. Sinclair and Kevin Rideout and Julien Mondésir. The three trouble makers sensed something in Claude's reaction and, in unison, moved their eyes from Gary to Claude.

"Who's that? Your boyfriend?" asked the leader, pointing at Claude.

Gary whispered: "Just walk away. Just walk back to the pier." Aurora and a couple of the street musicians came forward and formed a circle around Claude and Gary, and headed them back to their instruments and the few remaining spectators.

"Go ahead, go play with each other and your pretty little songs," the leader yelled. His buddies nudged him back to the truck and moments later they vanished in a roar of dust and screeching tires.

Claude, with visions of demons in his head, broke away from his protective group and started running down the street in the opposite direction. He was very soon out of breath and his

295

stomach ached and his head pounded, but he was propelled by the memory of Mrs. Sinclair hacking away at her son. He kept seeing the hate and venom that spit out of his brother-in-law Frank that night in back of Pelczar's Hardware. He kept on, running by families and kids on dates and seniors taking a stroll on a lovely Saturday evening by the ocean. Finally, Claude slowed his escape to a walk and, moments later, he heard the sound of a motor vehicle behind him. His thoughts immediately went into panic mode. He heard Aurora's voice and stopped. He sighed.

"You think we were those kids coming after you?"

"I did. For a minute."

"Boy, did you split..." Gary said.

"Didn't want any trouble, that's all." Claude stood at the edge of the street and looked down. He felt ashamed for running.

"I got the license number, by the way," Gary added. "JC 101. Ford truck. In case we want to report it."

Gary and Aurora invited Claude into the Jeep and everyone agreed the night was over and they should all be heading home. They had traveled a block or two when Aurora let out a shriek. "I forgot my drums at the pier," she said, throwing a helpless glance at Gary who turned the vehicle around. Claude, in an attempt to dispel his flashbacks, said something about her drums being very valuable, the single objects she could not live without. Aurora scolded him and said she didn't appreciate his brand of humor. He apologized with a snicker that clearly meant he didn't mean it. Gary gave both of them an eyeful of reproach like a dad having to deal with unruly teens.

Back at the Pompano Pier, the two men were alone for the time it took Aurora to fetch her drums.

"How you two getting along?" Gary asked out of the blue.

"Me and Aurora?"

"Yes."

"Fine."

"I mean, you're being low-key with her."

"Not sure what that means, Gary. But, everything's fine, mellow, no drama."

"Good. Just remember she's delicate, fragile."

"I know, you told me more or less, the other day..."

"She says you're acting funny since your friend..."

"Yeah. There's a lot of shit in my head right now. Ray didn't go gently into the night, you know."

"I know."

"And I'm working through it."

"Listen, Claude, there's something else I've been meaning to ask you."

"Oh…" Claude was cautious. "Shoot."

"It's about those identical little scars inside your lower arms, they look like incisions. What's that about?"

Claude let out a strong laugh filled with relief.

"What's so funny?"

"Nothing. Nothing's funny. This, this is nothing," he said, pointing with a free hand to the inside of his arm. "Just one of those crazy dark nights when I was first homeless and I spent the night with Ginsberg and I thought we were both mystics and saints and I used some broken glass to give myself something like the stigmata."

"Ginsberg who?"

"The poet. Allen Ginsberg."

"What's Ginsberg got to do with those scars?"

"Nothing really. He was sort of an inspiration. My guru. And, I thought he'd approve of my stigmata, even if he was a Jew."

"Ok. And, what stig…stigma…what?"

Claude laughed. "That's right, you're not Catholic are you."

"No. What's that got to do with it?"

"Listen. If you look closely at these, you'll see they're in the shape of a cross." Claude lifted his arm and presented it to Gary for his inspection. "Stigmata are what Catholic saints get. If they're lucky." Claude thought that was very funny and laughed deeply. "I have a great-aunt who goes every year with a church group to a cemetery in Rhode Island and they pray at the grave of this woman who had the stigmata. They believe she's a saint."

"Does that mean you're a saint?"

"Oh yeah. I have apparitions, like those crazy kids at Fatima. Saint Claude Simard. Saint Claude of Connecticut. Why not?"

Just then Aurora jumped into the vehicle. "Here they are. Thanks guys…for coming back. I don't know what I'd do without these."

"No problem," the two men said in unison.

Gary drove in silence for the entire distance back to the trailer park. He let his passengers off at the usual spot behind the warehouse. Claude and Aurora thanked him for the ride and headed for the bridge. Claude looked back once they crossed over the canal and noticed that Gary was still there, standing next to his Jeep, staring at them. Claude waved. Gary didn't wave back.

Just before reaching their little corner of Royal Palms, Claude started talking about Aurora's grandfather. He felt there was more to Grandma's story about her husband. "Your grandmother showed me the shed with your grandfather's stuff," he said.

"The memorial."

"That's right. Quite a collection. All those flamingoes and that stuff from Africa. Amazing. I asked Grandma why her husband went to Africa…"

"What she tell you? The spy story or the Foreign Legion?"

"She said he was a spy."

"Sometimes she says he was in Morocco in the French Foreign Legion."

"None of it is true, is it?"

"Of course not. Nothing that glamorous. Grandpa told me he worked for something like the Peace Corps, building irrigation systems."

"How long was he in Africa?"

"Don't know. Most of my life. He'd come and go. He'd be home and he and Grandma were all lovey-dovey and then he'd be gone. Didn't take me long to learn to stay out of her way whenever he left."

"He came home to die."

"Right. He had some cancer and it shriveled him up. But his mind was fine, all the way to the end. That's when I really got to know him. That's when I decided to clean myself up…you know, get off the drugs."

"Why did he stay in the shed? Sounds pretty weird to me."

"Grandma's idea. She said he smelled. Couldn't stand it. But I think it was her way of getting even."

"Sounds like she loved him. She seems to miss him."

"Probably. She took good care of him, all the way to the end."

"She says I should create a memorial to my friend Ray who died a couple of weeks ago."

"Well, not here. One mausoleum's enough."

"Don't worry. I wouldn't have anything to put in it. Ray had nothing. The man had a past, but he hardly shared it. He lived a simple life. He told me he ran away from home. He was 60, and he ran away. Took nothing with him." Claude spoke reverently and slowed his gait.

They stopped in front of Claude's shed. They listened and heard a dog bark. "Hope Grandma didn't hear that. She'd easily go on the warpath after that dog. Would want to hunt him down. Nothing's more precious than her mangy cats."

For Claude, the sound of a barking dog in the distance made him melancholy. He looked at Aurora and wondered if a night in her arms would be a good antidote – against his loneliness and his visions of evil.

"Aurora. Aurora." The voice, high and desperate grew stronger. "Aurora. Talk to him. Don't let him go." Grandma emerged from the trailer and a pair of cats scattered.

Aurora lowered her head and let it perform a ballet of negatives. "No, no. Grandma. Not again. No. Please."

"What's she saying?" Claude asked in a whisper.

"Grandpa. She's thinking he's going to leave again, go back to Africa."

"Aurora, darling. Do you hear me?"

"Yes, Grandma. I'm here." She moved towards the trailer, looking back at Claude in front of his shed. "Don't worry, Grandma. Everything's ok." She waved Claude away, into his shed and out of sight. "Give me a minute. I'm tucking him in for you. You can talk to Grandpa tomorrow." Standing in the doorway of his makeshift lodging, Claude watched the young girl climb the few steps to the veranda and gather her grandmother in her arms and nudge her into her trailer.

Lying in bed, Claude struggled with the encounter with the trouble makers in their truck and their aggressiveness that fed his nightmares of evil. He replayed the conversations of the evening: back at the pier, with Gary in the Jeep, and with Aurora just before they parted. He heard a voice emerge from the darkness, a thin wail, like a chorus of old feral cats. It came from the trailer.

"Aurora…Oh-roar-ahh! I can hear them. They're coming. The trucks and the bulldozers are back.

For days, Grandma kept insisting that Claude was Grandpa and he was about to dump her for another adventure in Africa.

She kept watching him; she kept crying. Her delusions sent Claude into a series of nightmarish nights. It got to a point where Claude hated to go to bed. He stayed up late, reading *Satori in Paris* and not finding much enlightenment in it. He grew restless and took long walks through the labyrinth of Royal Palms, returning to his shed after the voices from Grandma's trailer had subsided.

One of Claude's recurring dreams had a man sitting on the steps of the post office back in Connecticut talking as if he were on television. The man identified himself for the camera. "Hello, I'm Jack Kerouac, and this message is for Claude Simard." Claude had no idea what Kerouac looked like, but the same face kept appearing to him night after night. In one dream the man was with a little boy. "Claude, your little Mikey is waiting for you." The boy didn't look like Mikey at all.

Finally, Claude decided to leave. Ironically, on that day Grandma was in a chipper mood, wearing a fancy dress and a wide-brimmed hat. She had established herself on the veranda and was dipping eggs in colored water. She invited Claude to join her, explaining that they were Easter eggs that she would lay out all the way to Route 44 as a trail for her daughter Constance to follow, to help her find her way home in case she didn't remember which trailer they lived in. She asked Claude to help her paint the half dozen eggs she had before her and when he declined, her mood changed and she started yelling at him, calling him Elliot and accusing him of never having loved their daughter.

Claude toyed with different scenarios: leave Royal Palms and explore Florida; maybe Key West for a few months; perhaps back to Savannah for a while. Claude understood he'd probably wind up homeless again, and if that were the case, why not head back to New England? He knew his way around in Williams; he could talk to the judge and get his restraining order revoked; he could see Mikey again.

As he contemplated his return trip, he wondered if he should take Tony's heavy overcoat. Warm spring days had returned to Florida, and he doubted he would need it. If it turned cold, he'd take the bus, or get himself a cheap motel room. He had a bit of money: his meager earnings reciting poetry and the twenties Ray left in his suitcase. Claude convinced himself that he probably wouldn't need the coat.

His decision to leave Florida having been made and espoused,

Claude walked his final tour of Royal Palms and stopped on the edge of the slow canal to say goodbye. He searched among his recent writings for an appropriate verse to recite, but found none. He thought a bit, and slowly gave life to a poem that seemed to fit the moment:

Patient channel, if I may address you this way,
Are your shores always hospitable
Where do your waters flow from
And, your destination, where might it be
And, your countless insects, what are their names
Do they, like you, ever tire of the same motion?

And, you birds of white elegance
How long do you fly before getting tired
Is there a north to your range
What exactly is the color of your eyes
Are there lost relatives somewhere
Who might know?

Nothing in the canal or on either of its banks responded to the ode; not even a protesting caw from one of the noisy birds. Claude accepted the obvious: there was nothing else to say. He stood tall and spread his arms like a priest and, in a tone he once practiced as an altar boy at St. Patrick's, he chanted: "Oh, Wilma-Land, to you, my thanks and my farewell."

Returning to his room, he got Ray's jacket from Tropical Gardens. He didn't know what to do with it. It still had Ray's scent and held an array of memories. Claude suddenly decided to take it to the canal. He wanted it to sink, so he found a thick flat rock that looked like a stoop and wrapped the jacket around it, using the sleeves to make a knot. Throwing it into the darkness of the water, Claude heard the bundle hit the surface with a smacking sound and he hoped that Ray might have found some rest.

In his corrugated cell, Claude immediately fell into a peaceful sleep but woke with a jolt while it was still dark. As usual, he had no way of telling time, yet he felt he had slept soundly. He examined his memory to make sure his night had indeed been free of nightmares and finally accepted it as an omen of good things. He washed in the tiny sink in the corner of his room and shaved his dark beard. He was pleased that he had let Aurora cut his hair when they first met. She had argued that poets don't look like beatniks or derelicts any more. He now agreed that hitchhikers don't either. As he packed the little he had to pack, he glanced at his pads and the pages of poetry and thought he owed something to Aurora for having taken him in. A poem perhaps, but, there was none in him. He decided on a note. He wrote quickly, addressing it to *The Dawn*:

Thank you for the shelter from the storm, a storm with an intensity you never witnessed. You see, all my life I have seen evil in people's faces. I've known by looking at certain people that they were to commit evil things, to me and to others. You need to know, Aurora, that while here, while resting on your shore, I've not seen any evil. Thank you for that and for all else.

He wondered how he should sign it, but he remembered how his friend Tony reacted to his confession about seeing evil and he crumpled the note in his hand and shoved it in his pocket. He looked around the tiny room that had been his, and at the last moment, Claude decided to take Tony's coat, tying it like a bed roll. He figured it would give him a reason to stop in Philadelphia, to return the coat, to check on his old friend.

Outside, he found a sliver of pale light in the eastern sky. The air was tinged with the scent of pine. A great day to start a quest. Claude was pleased with his decision to hitchhike north. He walked past the trailer where he assumed Aurora and her grandmother were asleep and he found himself wondering what sort of nightmares were eating away at Grandma. He wished for a moment that he had said a proper goodbye to Aurora. As he neared the faded billboard announcing the new Royal Palms, he wondered what Dushayne had been doing the last few weeks, hoping that the boy had weathered the death of his friend. Claude told himself that Dushayne was a survivor and that he would soon find himself a new benefactor.

Claude remembered Chester saying that Route 44 headed north much of the length of Florida, at least as far as Orlando, and he thought that would be his best route. Plenty of local traffic, hopefully kind and generous people who didn't mind picking up strangers, maybe some trucker looking for company. First thing: coffee and a Krispy Kreme from the usually jovial clerk at the Circle K – except that she wasn't jovial. Too early for the smile, Claude thought. He had hoped for some recognition from the teenage girl with studs through her nose, a sort of final parting from one who's morning *have a nice day* recitation he had started counting on. "Well, you have yourself a very nice day," Claude said to her, as he dropped a quarter in the muscular dystrophy donation jar on the counter. He wanted to start his march north on a generous note.

Outside, a drizzle surprised him. The sliver of light outside his room had been swallowed up, and the sky offered no hope for the nice day he expected. Claude stood at the edge of the Circle K under a canopy and gulped down his donut. Hitchhiking was no longer an option. At least not for his first day. He watched commuters come and go and he wondered why there were no Krispy Kremes back home. Just then, a bus stopped at the corner to pick up passengers. Claude ran to the bus.

"How far do you go?" he asked the driver through the open door.

"To the county line, about twenty miles up 44."

"How much?"

"Four dollars. Exact change."

Claude found four one dollar bills and handed them to the driver. He pointed to his stuff.

"You gotta use only one seat. You can stash that under, or pile it on you. This ain't no Greyhound, you know." Claude nodded. He selected a seat next to the skinniest passenger, a teenager totally immersed in the music from his headset.

Claude was the last passenger to be dropped off. It was cloudy, but the rain had stopped. When Broward County ended, so did the sidewalk. Route 44 was still a major highway with heavy traffic, and Claude found himself in a land with no tolerance for pedestrians. He walked as close to the edge of the roadway as possible, but constantly felt the hot air of trucks and heavy vehicles as they whizzed by. He jumped a guardrail and walked on the swale, a slice of marshy grass sloping towards a canal flowing northward parallel to the road. Wild flowers carved their space on the edge of the waterway, and Claude thought of Williams and the hundreds of tulips in the town square tended by the local garden club. He wondered if his refuge – the closed warehouse – was surviving the spring floods that often carried away a piece of textile mill.

The sky started to clear and the warmth of late March settled over the area. Claude hoped for another bus, but he suspected there would be none, so he accepted the rhythm and mood of the route he had chosen. Walking slowly but steadily, he began to leave the malls and outlets behind. He soon found himself among a series of landscape contractors with their greenhouses and yards filled with young palm trees and a great variety of flowering shrubs. Claude took in the smells: lush vegetation, young loam, steamy compost. He was grateful for the escape from the sterile landscape of Royal Palms where everything was used up. He had water and every hour or so, he'd sit in a shady spot for a drink. Thus began his first day back on the road and he was glad for it.

Several miles later, Claude hitched his first ride. Someone was pulling out of a parking lot of one of the landscapers and stopped.

"Heading north or south?"

Claude studied the speaker: a dry, wrinkly, sunburned man with more teeth missing than present, his bony arm leaning out the window of an ancient pick-up truck. "Going north," Claude said.

The driver removed a sweat-stained baseball cap and wiped his brow. "Gonna be too hot to walk, with all that stuff you're carrying. Hop on. If you want to, that is."

"Thanks. I will," Claude said, holding back a chuckle. The driver said he wasn't going too far, about 20 miles, but that would be 20 less than he'd have to walk. Claude agreed and said he was grateful. The older guy turned out to be quite loquacious, asking question after question. Claude was amused.

"Name's Gene, yours?"

"Claude. My father's name is Gene. Eugene, but everybody calls him Gene."

"I was named after Gene Autry. Really, I was. My dad worked in the film industry in Hollywood back in the day, and he took care of Mr. Autry's horses."

"Really?" Claude was tempted not to believe him.

"Yup. Gene Autry. Saw every one of his movies."

By the time Gene reached his destination and dropped off his passenger, the story of Gene Autry had grown by leaps and bounds. Claude was grateful for the ride and especially thankful for the tip on a place to spend the night. "I know this guy, an old geezer like me, who runs a campground with his sons. It's not that legit. I mean, I don't think the state inspectors know about it, but there's toilets and showers and lean-tos and it's pretty safe," Gene said. "Right up the road about ten miles, go half a mile on the left, Atchalaya Road. Can't miss it."

There was no sign announcing the camping area, just a hand-painted panel with the word *IN* and a pointing arrow beneath it. Another sign over the doorway of a barn-like building at the end of a long driveway announced there was an office inside. Everything about the place reminded Claude of a hillbilly movie he had seen as a kid. Two men in their early twenties ran the place. They looked alike, grossly overweight, blond beards, oversized yellowed athletic shirts, sockless. They said they were brothers. Claude thought the twenty-five dollar asking price for one night was steep. He hesitated; he reviewed his options. "Can I see the showers and the bathroom first?" They were in the rear of the office and to Claude's surprise they were quite clean. Not that you should be so fussy, Claude thought. It also dawned on him that this was tropical Florida with waterways everywhere teeming with crawly things and that he didn't want to sleep on the ground.

About half of the lean-tos were unoccupied and Claude selected the most isolated. He didn't feel like company or partying, which he suspected was the norm. In exchange for his twenty-five dollars, he received from one of the hillbilly boys a brand new printed sign that said *occupied*. "Got 'em at the

Paul Paré

Walmart," the boy said proudly. "Hang it on your cabin; people'll leave you be."

The sky remained cloudless and a new moon spread its glow on the land that sloped towards what looked like an orchard. Claude envisioned a plantation in the Deep South and saw himself as a slave who would have to get up at daybreak to work the fields. He played with that image as well as the hillbilly movie that was still in his mind and delighted in the fact that he was indeed free – free to roam the countryside and free to return home. There was nothing to enslave him, except his nightmares which, for one night, he prayed would stay away.

In the morning, Claude took to his notes again and jotted his impressions of his first day on the road. He estimated he had travelled about 50 miles.

Claude's second day on the road was far from successful. Only one person gave him a ride for about twenty minutes. The guy explained that Route 44 had only local traffic, no long distance drivers who took the Florida Turnpike or Interstate 95. "You can't hitchhike on either one of those, so you have to catch a ride off the road, near an exit, which makes the competition fierce," the driver said. He recommended getting as close as possible to the interstate or the turnpike and hanging out at coffee shops and gas stations and trying to find a snow bird heading north and dreading the lonely ride home. Maybe an older couple who had spent the whole winter in Florida and couldn't stand each other and were eager to have someone else to talk to. People in an RV might be his best bet. Claude thanked the man and, at the next gas station, asked for directions and was informed that in Frenchman's Cove up ahead there was an east-west road that headed straight for the Florida Turnpike.

That night, his feet sore, sweaty and dusty, Claude settled for a spot underneath a railroad trestle that crossed over a wide river. On a broad wooden platform that might have served as a dock in other days, he tried to sleep, thankful for the mattress that Father Tony's thick overcoat afforded him and mindful of the advice from the old coot in North Carolina who warned him never to sleep on the ground.

He was annoyed and he didn't quite know why. Having decided to hitchhike, Claude had expected lonely roads with quiet places. That was part of the mystique. Always alone, or, at least, among strangers who would remain strangers unless invited to become something else. He didn't know why, but he found that anonymity very appealing. In this crowded Florida country restaurant he was surrounded on both sides by gregariousness: loud and talkative folks – friendly is how they would describe themselves, nosey would have been Claude's choice. "Nice day, aint it? Where you headin? Try the lunch special today?" Claude mumbled his responses as if his mouth was full.

Claude finished his sandwich and sipped his coffee. He had walked all morning and was surprised by the change of scenery. Gradually, commercial development had given way to rangeland with hints of knolls and park-like groupings of low pines and herds of cattle seeking shelter among them. It looked like ranching country, and he thought of cowboys and Indians and his son Mikey and the cowboy hat Claude had bought him several months before.

Claude questioned how he might make things right in Williams so that he could see Mikey again. What could he say to the judge? He wondered about everything he'd have to do once he got home. He'd have to come up with something; he didn't want to spend the summer in the old mill. He thought of his father in the nursing home and he vowed to visit him often. "You visit your father if you want your son to visit you someday," his great-aunt Yvette used to say. Claude thought about Margie and hesitated to think that life would ever go back to normal with her. He admitted he had no idea what *normal* was.

An older couple selected the table next to Claude's and started arguing in hushed tones. Forgetting his want of anonymity, he allowed himself to be drawn into the conversation with words that sounded at once strange and familiar. He realized they were speaking French. Words like those his father would use when he got angry or bits of sentences that his great-aunt Yvette would whisper when it came time for birthdays and Christmas. Not sharp, but with an edge, an obstinacy. The music of crickets and other night creatures. The wife was agitated, the husband patient; she commanded, he complied. He patted her hand and used the words *mon chou*.

Suddenly, the wife stood and walked towards the rest room.

"Ah, women. What do you do?" the man said to Claude.

Nodding, Claude agreed. "Right…"

"Exact. They are always right."

"Well, that's not what I meant. But, you do have a point," Claude replied.

The man sent him a look of confusion.

"So… are you from Canada?" Claude asked almost bashfully.

"Ah. Ha, you listen when we talk. Yes. We come from Canada. We are going back to Canada, at this moment." He paused. "Alcide. My name is Alcide Cousineau, and my wife, she is Jeannette Cousineau."

"My name is Claude Simard." He pronounced his name as "clowed", the French way, and dropped the "d" on the last name. "Pleased to meet you."

"I am happy to make your *connaissance*," Alcide said. "You must be from Canada too."

Claude explained that his great-grandparents on his father's side came from Canada, but that he's lived in Connecticut all his life. Alcide revealed that he and his wife live in Coaticook, a small town near the Vermont border. "Where the people grow Christmas trees," he added.

"Quati…quati-what?" asked Claude.

"Ah. Yes, Coaticook. Co-a-ti-cook." Alcide started his explanation just as his wife returned to the table. "It is an Indian word. In Québec, all we have are Indians and Saints. For the names of the towns, I mean."

Alcide focused on his new acquaintance, peppering Claude with questions. Had he ever been to Canada? Did he know any relatives there? Had he done his genealogy? What village was his family from? Alcide offered that his wife had completed the Cousineau genealogy and discovered that the first Cousineau came from LaRochelle in France in 1682. "Now there are

Cousineau cousins, thousands of them, all over North America," Alcide proclaimed. Jeannette smiled and nodded. Alcide welcomed the thaw in his wife's attitude and went on to introduce his new friend, this young man named Claude Simard from Connecticut.

Claude was amused. He got up to refresh his coffee and when he returned he searched in his bag for his copy of *Satori in Paris*. Proudly showing it to his new acquaintances, he explained that it was a book by Jack Kerouac of Lowell, Massachusetts, and that it was about someone like him whose family came from Canada and who wanted to find his roots in France. Alcide repeated the name Kerouac a few times and finally announced that in Coaticook there had been a priest by that name a few years back and that undoubtedly the priest and this fellow from Lowell had been cousins.

"So, you, *monsieur* Simard, do you live here in Florida?" Jeannette asked. It was her first question.

"No. I came here for a little while this winter. I'm heading back home now."

"Is that your baggage?" she said, pointing to the duffle bag at Claude's feet and the heavy winter coat.

"Yes. This is all I have. I'm hitchhiking north." He spoke the words clearly, almost defiantly.

"Hitch...what is...?" She asked, confused.

Alcide made a sign with his thumb. "*Faire du pouce.*"

"Aha! A *vagabond*," she said to Alcide, pronouncing the word in French and clapping her hands once very sharply like she had just won the lottery. Alcide hushed her and looked apologetically at Claude.

Claude understood, and said, "I suppose I am, but an honorable one."

"What does this mean?" she looked at Alcide for an explanation.

"It means he is ok. A good *vagabond*."

Jeannette was not pleased but she found some mild amusement in the reply.

To change the subject, Alcide clarified that he and his wife were retired and that for the past five years had come to Florida in December – to Pompano Beach – and had sold Christmas trees from Canada. He further explained that his wife's three brothers owned a Christmas tree farm – one of the largest in Québec – and that after the big trucks delivered the trees to the Catholic Church in Pompano Beach, he and his wife set up their RV in the parking lot and handled the sale for the Christmas season. "Three thousand trees this year. Not bad."

"And, for the last time," Jeannette said firmly. "My Alcide is too old for this work. He is almost 80 years old, not a lumberjack any more. This is the last year." She was back on the war path and Alcide hushed her again. Jeannette turned the discussion to French and the two argued for some time. Alcide kept rubbing his hands and cupping one with the other, as if he were seeking warmth. Both were eating a full meal, the meatloaf for him and fried chicken for her. Alcide never stopped talking, even with a mouthful of mashed potatoes. Turning back to Claude, he explained that he and his wife spent the winter in a trailer park in Lauderdale Lakes after the Christmas tree sale.

"Ha! Lakes…nothing but ponds, little square ponds filled with dirty water," Jeannette said, placing a hand on her husband's forearm. "These people do not know how God makes a lake. They have to go to Québec to see a real lake." Alcide went on to explain that in prior years they had headed for Sarasota for the winter, but they decided on Lauderdale Lakes because many friends from Coaticook also stayed there.

"Big mistake. They never leave us alone," Jeannette interrupted.

Alcide chimed in, "It was always barbecues and playing cards. They even tried to get me to play golf. In Sarasota, the Canadians were all from Ontario, a bunch of snobs, but they leave you alone."

Jeannette wiped some food from Alcide's chin and told him to stop bothering the young man. They started bickering again in French. Jeannette removed a pair of prescription bottles from her purse and counted some pills onto the table, making sure that Alcide took each one with plenty of water.

Claude felt out of place. He looked at his empty coffee cup. He was about to get up when Alcide asked what were his plans for the rest of the day. Surprised by the question, Claude answered that he was heading towards the Florida Turnpike where he hoped to get a ride.

"But, where do you sleep?" Jeannette asked.

"Where I can. Outside, sometimes in rest areas. I enjoy the peace and quiet and the open spaces."

"What do you do when it rains?" She seemed suddenly solicitous.

"Oh, I have a bit of money. In bad weather I look for a motel."

"So you have some money," she said.

"*Assez*. Enough, Jeannette. Leave the young man alone." Alcide turned to Claude. "Forgive my wife; she is very suspicious and very nosy. With her, no finesse." Jeannette humphed her displeasure and rattled on in French.

Claude stood and announced he had to leave. He said there were still several good hours on the road. He wished them a safe journey.

"*Bonne chance*," Alcide said.

The road heading for Frenchman's Cove and the Turnpike was grimy with construction projects, and several times the traffic was stopped by flagmen who looked tired and bored. Claude maneuvered around the ditches and trucks and backhoes and some type of machine that was sucking a dark muck out of the soil. He covered his mouth with a bandana against the engine fumes and concluded that nobody would be picking up hitchhikers. Later, the construction project halted for no apparent reason and the road stretched unencumbered ahead of him. For a couple of miles, thick swampy forestland bordered the roadway on both sides and Claude was reminded of the North Carolina country road he had tramped on his way south. He searched for roadkill, scanning from side to side, and was surprised to find none. Claude concluded that either the cleanup crews were more efficient in Florida or nothing could live in these woods, let alone crawl onto the pavement.

At a barn-like structure that sold firecrackers and grapefruit, Claude stopped and bought a Coke to wash down the dust of the road. Traffic had thinned, and the sun had fallen behind some fluffy purple clouds. Claude thought his luck might be changing when a recreational vehicle drove into the parking lot and stopped next to him.

"Ah, *monsieur* Simard, *surprise, surprise*." Alcide rolled down his window. Claude stared in disbelief at the RV and its occupants, both sporting wide grins. Claude read the shiny *Alouette* logo on the side of the vehicle.

"Well, fancy meeting you here," he said. The idiom didn't seem to register and the Canadians looked at each other quizzically.

Alcide gestured for Claude to approach. "Ah! You do not have a ride yet?" he asked. Not waiting for a reply, he said "Come with me" and moved the vehicle to a spot where both Alcide and Jeannette stepped out into the crushed rock of the parking lot.

Jeannette said something in French and Alcide used the words *mon chou* again and nodded in agreement. "We are happy to find you because we have an arrangement to propose." It was the wife speaking. Her tone was official and serious.

Alcide interrupted: "What Jeannette is saying is: you want a ride, we want a driver."

Jeannette took over again. "*Monsieur* Simard, you understand. My husband has *arthrite* – arthritis, I think it is in English. His hands are all crooked. He is in pain. See. He cannot hold the wheel." She mimicked a driver with his hands on a steering wheel. "His leg, the one you use on the gas, also has pain. He should not be driving more than two or three hours at one time."

Alcide interrupted. "I have medication but it is not strong enough anymore. And, my Jeannette does not know how to drive. She has no license."

"The arrangement is that you drive and we give you food and place to sleep," she said.

"You have a license to drive?" Alcide asked.

"Yes. Of course, I do." Claude couldn't believe what he was hearing. He thought the offer absurd but attractive. "But you don't know anything about me. I could be dangerous, I could be a murderer."

"Ooh," Jeannette said, bringing a hand to her mouth. The Cousineaus resorted to a series of French back-and-forth jousting.

"Claude, are you a murderer?" Alcide asked with the hint of a smile.

The hitchhiker said he wasn't, and that he was an honest man and would bring them no harm.

"I know. I am a good judge of *caractère*," Alcide said.

The trio quickly came to an agreement. Claude would drive

their RV, they would leave immediately, they would take the Interstate to avoid paying tolls, and Claude would drive as late into the night as he could because they hoped to get to Canada for Easter in five days.

It did not occur to Claude at the time that he might want to stop in Philadelphia, nor did he ask himself if his new friends really intended him to go all the way to Coaticook.

Once on the road, Claude managed to stay alert until around three in the morning and well over the Georgia state line. He found the *Alouette* handled well, the midweek traffic light, his host and hostess increasingly trusting. He had never driven anything as large as an RV and was amazed to feel its weight beneath him; he felt both removed from and utterly connected to the road and that pleased him. The name of the recreational vehicle intrigued him and he asked early on what the word meant

"*Alouette*, that is the bird of the song." Alcide explained, leaping into the children's song: "*Aloutte, gentille Alouette, Alouette, je te plumerai.*" Claude said he had never heard the song and both Alcide and Jeannette were incredulous. "Everybody knows the song," they said.

"Maybe I know it, but your singing is so bad, I don't recognize it," Claude said.

An easy camaraderie had established itself with that exchange and a pattern defined: Jeannette would sit in the passenger seat while Alcide rested on a bench just behind the driver's seat. A few hours later, they would switch positions. Each one had his or her preferred music and the CDs changed with them. Jeannette's favorites included Charles Aznavour, Ginette Reno, and Celine Dion; Alcide was a fan of country music, especially Patsy Cline and Tex Lecor. Late into the night, music blasted at high volume inside the *Alouette* as it rolled through the marshy Southern lowlands.

Claude saw the signs for Savannah and remembered how barely three months before he had been at the lowest point of the trip until one night he heard someone sing a French Christmas carol on the waterfront.

After a night at a truck stop in the middle of North Carolina and the heartiest of breakfasts, they were back on the road with Alcide at the wheel. Mornings were best for him, and he wanted to do his share. While Jeannette made the beds and cleaned up, Alcide went into a lengthy pontification about the various types of Christmas trees and how the Québec variety was by far the best.

By mid-morning, Alcide was ready to turn over the driving to Claude. The routine of the trip had established itself. Alcide would drive for a few hours; Jeannette would sit in the small kitchen area and crochet when she wasn't dispensing her husband's medication. Alcide would talk about anything and everything almost constantly. Evenings, the music would be back on. Gigantic truck stops gave them a chance to get some sleep, Claude stretched out on a bench in the eating area, Alcide and Jeannette cozy in their little bedroom at the rear of the vehicle.

One afternoon, Alcide, who was smallish and very thin with the exception of a round belly that Jeannette liked to pat teasingly, started describing his life in the woods as a youngster. He joined his father and an older brother one winter working in a lumber camp near the New Hampshire border, although on which side of the border was often not clear. For close to 20 years he spent his winters away from the farm lumberjacking in the back woods, working in the cold, cutting trees and preparing them for their wild ride down the rivers as soon as the ice melted. Alcide talked about the friendship not the hardship, the hearty meals and hot coffee in the steamy camps, the songs the men sang. All of which came to an abrupt end when he married Jeannette who, much younger and a modern woman, wouldn't stand to have her husband leave her every winter to go "play in the woods." That was when he became a prisoner of the Christmas tree farms.

"*Qui marie, prends pays,*" Jeannette volunteered.

Alcide translated the phrase for Claude quite elegantly: "he who marries takes the country." Claude said he didn't understand, and Alcide explained that when a person takes a spouse, he or she takes the country that comes with the marriage. "It is an old French expression. And, when I marry Jeannette I get all that comes with her, you know, her brothers and the tree farm." He added that it could have been worse, like his best friend in the lumber camps, Henri, who married a pretty young thing and joined her family working in the mills in Biddeford. "At least, I still had the woods."

Claude found himself wishing that he knew more about his father's family. Were they lumberjacks or farmers or fishermen and when did they move to Williams? He had never asked, and no one had ever volunteered the information, not even his great-aunt Yvette who was the most connected to the past.

Before retiring one night, Alcide whispered to Claude that he could have a drink of gin if he wanted. "To relax, some Dekuyper," he said, hinting that Jeannette would not approve. Claude joined him and grimaced at the strength of the alcohol, having gotten the taste out of his throat and his mind over the past several weeks. Briefly, the image of a vagabond with his name and his foul odor lying on the floor of a cotton warehouse singing the praise of Kerouac and Ginsberg came to him and he put the drink down.

Jeannette didn't give up much information, and Claude had to be the one inquiring about the items she was constantly crocheting.

"What are those?" he said, pointing to the finished items neatly folded on a shelf.

"*Des foulards*," she replied. She saw the lack of comprehension in Claude's eyes and made a circling gesture around her neck.

"Oh, scarves. They're beautiful. For your grandchildren?"

"For the nieces and the nephews. Heaven did not give Alcide and me any children." And that was the end of the conversation.

Later that afternoon, Alcide decided to teach Claude the song *Alouette*, and after several laborious refrains going through all the body parts of the bird they would have to pluck, Alcide pointing to the head, the neck, the wings, the tail, he finally gave up with a sigh.

Long after he had gone to bed, Claude still had the song on the brain. He kept playing with the idea of children plucking an *Alouette*, pulling feathers one by one from various body parts and he thought of the vehicle named *Alouette* by some unknown manufacturer. Had the maker intended to have the vehicle plucked at some time off the highway or had he found a metaphor for a bird in flight? Claude pictured the skeleton of a poem in his ruminations and he turned on the small lamp above his makeshift bed and pulled out his notepad. He threw down words and ideas in a haphazard manner and concluded this poem would need more work at a later time.

He was about to turn in when Alcide emerged from the back bedroom. "What is wrong?" he asked.

"Can't fall asleep. Thinking about the song *Alouette* and was going to write a poem about it."

Alcide was genuinely interested. He had all kinds of questions. He told of a fellow who worked in the woods with him years before who would write poems in the middle of the night and sing them to himself. He remembered how everyone in the lumber camp thought this fellow was crazy. He, Alcide, was envious. How could anyone take the everyday things in life and turn them into poems and songs? He thought that was wonderful.

"Maybe, writing a poem is like making a baby," Alcide said in a low voice. "Do you, *monsieur* Simard, have any children? We have talked all this time with you and have never asked."

"Yes. Two boys, one is nineteen and the other is five."

"Ah. Boys, the best, you know for the *progéniture*, you know, to carry the family name forward into the future. You are a lucky man."

Taken by surprise, Claude suffered through a brief encounter with the shame of an absent father. "Believe me, I haven't been the best of fathers."

"We all do the best." Finally, Alcide said he needed to go to bed.

Claude waved him back to his tiny bedroom and for the longest time fought the most riveting sadness. He acknowledged that he had robbed his sons, both of them, of the father they deserved.

The next morning Claude firmed up his decision to stop in Philadelphia. He would set things right with Tony as a first step to becoming a better person. Tony first, Mikey second, and, yes, Nick also. Claude wrestled with different ways to broach the subject. He would have to leave his hosts eventually, he argued; he couldn't drive them all the way to Coaticook and hitchhike back to Connecticut. That was absurd, he thought, but deep in his head he suspected that was exactly what Jeannette had in mind when she acquiesced to having him drive their RV.

Aurora was begging him to take her with him; she was pleading, crying, walking back and forth the four steps it took to cross the width of his cell, saying he owed it to her to take her away from Royal Palms. "And what of Grandma?" he yelled at her, trying to match her cries. Aurora lurched towards him, throwing him backwards onto the door and the two fell to the ground outside. She pounded his head with her fists and he could feel Grandma's cats scratching and digging into his bare feet.

Claude woke up and was sure he had been screaming in his dream. He looked at the door to the sleeping area in the Cousineau's RV. It was closed. He listened. Nothing. Relieved, he got up and dressed and walked outside.

A chill wind marched against him, emerging from the mist shrouding Chesapeake Bay in the distance. Dark clouds, charged with rain for later, reminded Claude that it was March and that he wasn't in Florida anymore. A resonant bass sound filled the parking lot, emerging from the engines of dozens of semi-trailers. Claude scanned the vast expanse of dewy asphalt, speculating about the destinations and cargoes of the trucks. He hurried to the restaurant and ordered himself a dark coffee which he nursed while watching his fellow travelers. Mostly men, middle-aged, overweight, many of them bearded and long-haired, sitting by themselves staring through the smoke and humidity at their lives, their destinations, their rigs and goods, the people left behind or were heading to see. Claude felt both a kinship and an estrangement.

As he was leaving, he stopped in front of a wall map and traced the route that forked just before crossing into New Jersey, one way heading to Philadelphia, the other towards New York and New England.

Walking against the wind, Claude crossed the path of a couple coming from a recreational vehicle with a New York license plate.

Adequately bundled against the cold with an equally dressed poodle at the end of a leash, the elderly couple smiled.

"Good morning," the man said. "You can feel that cold, can't you?"

Claude nodded and smiled.

"Where you headed?" The stranger screamed his question over the din of so many trucks.

Claude wanted to ask who exactly gave permission to old folks to be so nosy, but instead told him he was heading to Connecticut.

"Up into more cold, eh, eh. Better bundle up."

The wife moved closer to Claude. "You have yourself a nice Easter, young man."

"Thanks, you too."

Back at the RV, the Cousineaus were stirring. Claude could hear them moving around in the constricted space of the bedroom and the bathroom: a routine that required no conversation. Claude sat at the kitchen table and opened the cookie jar. *Have a nice Easter*, he heard the old lady say to him. Back in Royal Palms, Grandma's constant ramblings about Easter eggs hadn't connected him to Easter as much as the simple wish from this nice old lady. *Have a nice Easter, young man.* He asked himself what precisely was a nice Easter and he drew from his childhood the picture of a seven-year old boy sitting in the pews of St. Patrick's church in his brand new suit from LeBlanc's Clothing Store that his great-aunt Yvette had bought him and he watched her lips mumble the rosary while the choir sang their happy songs. And, he remembered the photo session on the steps of the church with all the school kids in their finery and he remembered looking forward to the chocolate bunny he knew was waiting for him at home.

Claude Simard questioned if there would be a nice Easter waiting for him in 2008 in Williams, Connecticut.

"Good morning," said Jeannette. "I see you already have some coffee." she said.

"*Bonjour tout l'monde*," was Alcide's standard greeting.

Claude was surprised to find himself replying *bonjour*.

"Ah! You see, you are learning French, just like that. *Naturel.* I tell you, Jeannette."

"Listen. I have to tell you something, it's very important."

318

Claude asked his hosts to sit down. He coughed and looked at the two with all the seriousness he could muster. They listened, looked at each other several times, and at the end, Alcide broke the silence. "We can drive that way and drop you off in Philadelphia."

"What? But you promised to drive all the way to Coaticook," Jeannette said. Claude responded by saying he had not promised and asked how he would get back to Connecticut or did they have the intention of kidnapping him? She called him a vagabond and withdrew into a sulk. Alcide tried to calm her down with soft words in French laced with plenty of *mon chous*, but nothing worked.

"Leave now, *tout-de-suite*. Right now. The arrangement is over," Jeannette said.

Claude argued that he could still drive a few more miles. They could drop him off before crossing into New Jersey. Alcide repeated his offer to take him to Philadelphia which his wife pooh-poohed, saying he'd get lost.

Seeing a way out, Claude said he would leave right away and started to gather his things. Alcide threw up his hands and retreated into the bedroom. His wife busied herself, wiping the counter, preparing the breakfast dishes. Claude was ready within minutes and standing at the doorway with his belongings, he hesitated. Looking at his feet, he thanked Jeannette and wished her a safe trip. "*Bon voyage*," he said to Alcide still in the next room.

Outside, he stopped. He felt like a school boy, an ungrateful school boy. He heard the door open behind him and Alcide stepped out in his slippers and open shirt. The old man gave Claude a tight hug. Claude responded. No words were exchanged.

Seated at the counter inside the trucker's restaurant, Claude read from the menu. "The lumberjack special," he told the waitress with a broad smile. As much as he regretted the abruptness of his departure, he accepted that it had to be done. The terms, however, could have been friendlier, he argued, *should* have been friendlier.

Claude ate the various courses of his breakfast slowly, savoring them, not only for the taste but for the leisure. For the first time since leaving Royal Palms, he felt unrushed, eschewing any semblance of a schedule. He knew his destination: Father Tony's parish where he would spend just enough time to make amends, and then his home town, at his own rate of speed, no one expecting him, no one needing him.

"Morning," said a stranger as he took the seat next to Claude's.

"Morning," replied Claude through a mouthful of sausage patties sticky with maple syrup.

"Why that's a lot of food! What they call that?"

"Lumberjack special."

"Good."

Claude had assumed that truckers weren't much for conversation, which pleased his yen for anonymity. This one, however, certainly felt like talking. While waiting for his order, Barry introduced himself and proceeded to talk about the weather, sports, and the elections, sharing his views on every single candidate.

Barry wanted to know who Claude worked for, which trucking company. Claude confessed he had been hitchhiking since Florida, that his last ride had dumped him at the rest stop and that he would be looking for a ride to Philadelphia.

"Gotta talk to Slim over there," Barry said. "He's headin' for Philly."

Claude looked at a young blonde fellow sitting at a booth with two other guys. "Him? Doesn't look old enough to have a license."

"Looks are deceiving. Been a driver for two years. A real good one. Short runs, though, Virginia, Maryland, Pennsylvania, once in a while, the Carolinas."

Claude grasped suddenly that his next ride could very well be eating at the neighboring table. "You think he'd give me a ride?"

"Wouldn't be surprised. Likes to talk a lot, and not to himself. Let me introduce you."

Claude walked away from the warehouse district where Slim ended his journey.

With a handshake and a *good luck*, Slim sent him on his way, apologizing for not going into Philadelphia. "Got lots of paperwork, and I got a girlfriend waiting at home, if you know what I mean."

Claude managed to orient himself as he headed north, past downtown, into the old neighborhoods. The sun had shaken off the morning cloud cover and the streets were now filled with steam. In a neighborhood he thought looked like it should be the right one, he turned a corner and spotted the steeple of Saint Petronilla's above the tenements. "This is it," he said out loud, happy with the discovery. He walked down the street towards the church and thought of the people of the parish: the Haitians, most of them poor, but good people, simple people, working hard and happy to be free from the terror and poverty of their native land. He saw Nicolette and he heard her laughter as she talked about her two little boys. He saw the face of Julien Mondésir and he accelerated his gait.

He approached the rectory and stopped; he knew something was terribly wrong. The place looked abandoned, drained of the life he had briefly been a part of a few months before. The first-floor windows of the brick house were boarded up and a chain link fence ringed the property. *No Trespassing* signs everywhere. Claude turned back and scanned the streetscape, looking for some informant.

"Tony, Tony. It's Simmy. I've come back for you," he yelled out only to hear the last word echo down the street.

He ran a few yards to the church. The thick granite foundation created a buffer several feet long, running parallel to the street. The building was high and protected; no need for a cyclone fence here. The *No Trespassing* signs were just as ubiquitous. Claude searched the high windows for signs of life. He hurried to the façade and saw something posted on the front doors – his front doors. In English and Creole was a weathered notice announcing that Saint Petronilla's Church was closed as of January 30th. Also stapled to the red doors was a more recent message urging the faithful to attend Holy Week and Easter services at Sacred Heart of Jesus Church on 72nd Avenue.

Claude allowed himself to slip down onto the church steps. He buried his face in his arms and he saw clearly the evil in Father Mondésir's face and the terror in Nicolette's. In the darkest crevices of his mind where the most repugnant of his thoughts found shelter, Claude saw the bloody body of his friend. His recent dream came back to him in vivid detail and he gazed helplessly upon the gash across Tony's throat and the blood gushing out of it and filling the baptismal font.

He knew what happened; he needed no official confirmation. Softly, he repeated Tony's name, again and again. He felt a strong need to pray, for both his friend Tony and for himself for having allowed Tony to remain behind these doors where the devil dwelled. The words of the prayer, however, eluded him, and he searched for the appropriate verse or incantation –some approved formula – and none was to be found. Quickly, without thinking it strange or sacrilegious, the cadence of a poem by a beatnik Jew came to him and some of the lines he had memorized from Ginsberg flowed effortlessly.

In a voice full of reverence and bitterness, Claude recited the words, not loud, not for anyone to hear but for himself and hopefully for Father Tony.

who fell on their knees in hopeless
cathedrals praying for each other's
salvation…

Someone across the street opened a second-story window and looked down on the lone man clinging to the church doors. "It's closed," an old woman yelled.

Claude jumped to his feet and stepped into the street. "What happened? Where's the priest?" he screamed out.

"One's dead…the white one. The Haitian's gone. God knows where," she said. The woman pushed down her window and

322

withdrew into her tenement.

The portico with its shiny red doors pulled at Claude. These were the doors he painted only a few months before, where he carved his initials on the inside, out of the way, protected from the elements. Claude pounded his fists on the cold blood-red doors. He wanted them to open, to give him shelter, to chase the evil away from this church, from his mind, from the world. The doors resisted the assault as they were meant to. Claude threw himself at them in frustration. "Tony, Tony, Tony," he moaned in an angry litany.

He thought of breaking into the church, or maybe the rectory, of establishing himself here, of building a shrine. He abandoned the idea and pulled himself away from the portico. Claude remembered Tony's coat and calmly untied it, allowing it to unfurl at his feet. He saw traces of guilt in Tony's face as he handed him the coat as they said good bye to each other at the bus station a few months before; he heard him say that he'd need it to keep warm, to sleep on. Claude walked back to the doors and ceremoniously draped the garment over the first step like a priestly vestment, gently tucking it in at the bottom of the door panels.

He returned to the rectory and inspected the fortress that it had become. Through the fence, he gazed upon the small park where he and Tony met for conversation in the morning. He looked up at the window where he knew the kitchen was located and he heard Nicolette's accented banter and wondered if she had also been killed.

He ran back to the front of the church. He stared at the portal one more time. He grabbed the coat and tucked it under his arm. "It's mine now, dear Tony." Claude picked up his gym bag and walked down the used-up and empty street without looking back.

A number of blocks away, Claude sat on a bench facing a large billboard for Mike Huckabee. He had some thinking to do. He decided he could easily locate the bus station and take the bus to Connecticut. "That's how I got here. That's how I'm going back," he said to the candidate on the sign above his head. "Good luck to you, bud, and good luck to me.

He couldn't escape the feeling he was a tourist. It had been barely five months since he'd left, but as he ventured into a more familiar landscape, Claude examined the scenery, shifting his attention from one side of the bus to the other, like a first-time visitor, an explorer, a prospector.

Since leaving Philadelphia, he had envisioned how he would negotiate his return to Williams, Connecticut, what he would do first, who he'd go see.

While waiting to change buses in New York City, he even thought of stopping. You ain't been a bum until you've lived on the streets of New York. If you can make it here, you'll make it anywhere. Something like that. He thought of Ray and all his talk about the shows on Broadway. He entertained the thought of going to a show, of spending much too much of his meager funds to see a musical, to pay tribute to his friend.

"Have a nice vacation?" asked the ticket seller. Claude looked at the older man quizzically. "Got a nice tan." Claude thanked the man and smiled. He hadn't viewed his time in Florida as a vacation. He rolled up his sleeve and examined his lower arm and admired the brownish tint it had acquired.

While wandering through the massive Port Authority Terminal, his mind returned to the drivers who got him there from Florida, dwelling on the Cousineaus – especially Alcide who seemed to adopt him. Claude mumbled some of the children's' song: *Alouette, gentille alouette, je te plumerai…* and he wished them both a happy Easter.

He also had time to think about Father Tony and wondered what was done with his body. Had there been a funeral for him back in Williams? He still felt guilty for not having the proper prayer for his friend, having dismissed Ginsberg's lyricism as inappropriate. Claude thought of the familiar hymn, the only one that he knew. "Sorry, Tony, but this is all I've got," he mumbled.

Then he started: *Ave, Ave, Ave Maria*...Looking about him in all directions, he concluded that no one in the vast bus terminal cared if his canticle was correct or not, or if it fit the violent death of a life-long friend, and he threw himself into his song, bellowing the words loudly and proudly, *Ave, Ave, Ave Maria,* listening to the echo they made, ignoring the few who stared at him.

The departure call for his bus interrupted Claude's elegy. Feeling some kind of closure, he walked briskly towards his gate. He was surprised to find the bus near empty. The driver, a petite woman with the dark skin of the Caribbean, walked down the aisle inspecting everyone's tickets. "Ah. Williams, Connecticut. Driven there before. Nice place," she said.

"My home town," Claude replied.

"Nice place to be from."

"Not sure how nice to go back to," he mumbled. The driver smiled and went on to her next passenger.

The bus squealed itself out of its tight space and groaned as it returned to the life of the street, as if uncertain about its destination. Claude smiled inwardly and coached the vehicle on. "C'mon old chum, not the time to give up on me," he mumbled. "It's been a long ride."

The transfer to a Peter Pan Bus in New London went smoothly. So quick and seamless that Claude was slightly disappointed. The bus was already on its way north to Williams, and Claude was still pondering what would happen if he had stayed in New London. Take your cash and go to the casinos and win the jackpot and get drunk and... Claude knew that was his last chance; he also knew he was a lousy gambler.

In Williams, they were waiting for him. His father in the nursing home, his little boy Mikey, his wife, his father-in-law at the hardware store, his great-aunt Yvette, Mister O'Regan, that asshole. They were all on his list and he'd deal with them all, one at a time.

The Peter Pan Bus purred gently on I-395, as it climbed towards Williams and Worcester. The 17 passengers – Claude counted them – were in various stages of consciousness. He discreetly inspected each traveler and conjured up all sorts of scenarios and reasons for their trips. None of them, he was sure, had so much to face as he did. Claude Simard was scared to death. You're going to be 40 and you don't have anything. You just wasted the last year of your life. What have you become? Has anybody missed you?

He decided not to answer the questions; he decided not to ask them. He knew those were the questions that would lead him back to the streets, sleeping in his empty warehouse, drinking with his buddies Ginsberg and Kerouac. Claude patted the scars on the inside of each forearm and, in an effort to calm himself, sang in a low voice the *Ave Maria* that had become his.

When the bus pulled into its designated space in front of Gallant's Pharmacy it was late afternoon. One other passenger stepped down and was greeted by an older woman. Claude claimed a corner of the sidewalk and decided to play the tourist. The panorama hadn't changed except for a banner on the park gazebo announcing the annual Rotary Easter Egg Hunt. He wondered if Margie would let him take Mikey to the egg hunt. He gazed up the street and assumed the same peace protestors would be marching Saturday morning in front of the Post Office. They would probably have lunch at The Puritan. A strong but not unpleasant breeze swept into downtown from the Naugatuck hills.

Claude had seen enough and walked away slowly but determined. He decided in the final minutes of his ride that what needed to be done was to pay homage to his boyhood pal Tony. That had to be first on his agenda. Everything else would have to wait.

With his baggage strapped about him, he walked towards the houses where the boys had been neighbors. Like they did so many afternoons, Claude wanted to sit on the sidewalk. He would talk to Tony. He would say he was sorry. He would write a poem about his friend. When it got dark and cold, he would find the place where the Sinclair house had stood. He was sure the empty lot was still there. He would make a bed for himself in the overgrowth and cover himself with Tony's winter coat. He would sleep a simple night without visions because he was home.

About the Author

Paul Paré has had a lengthy career as a newspaper reporter, radio and television host and producer. He won an Emmy in 1980. He's also worked in public relations for a variety of non-profits. His articles have been published in Canadian journals, the *FORUM* of the University of Maine, and in *Wolf Moon Journal*. He took part in the 2011 Stonecoast Writers' Conference. His autobiographical novel *Singing the Vernacular* was published in 2008 by iUniverse. He lives in Ogunquit, Maine, and Pompano Beach, Florida, and is available in both areas (and anywhere in between) to promote his work. *Road Kill* is his first major work of fiction.